W9-CGV-480

**Praise for *USA TODAY* bestselling author
Rita Herron**

"Herron understands the bonds between mother
and child and presents a touching and terrifying
tale of evil and redemption."
—*RT Book Reviews* on *Unbreakable Bond*

"Rita Herron is a gifted writer with the ability to
draw her readers into the story and the minds of
not only her hero and heroine but also the mind
of the criminal. A real page turner, *Up in Flames*
will not disappoint the readers."
—*CataRomance.com*

"A slick plot combined with riveting characters
and unyielding suspense make Herron's latest
a star attraction for fans."
—*RT Book Reviews* on *The Missing Twin*

"This story will totally captivate the reader. A
tale packed solid with suspense and excitement
with a new surprise at the turn of every page…
An absolutely fascinating read that is definitely
recommended. Rita Herron is an extremely
gifted writer."
—*Fresh Fiction* on *Forbidden Passion*

RITA HERRON

USA TODAY bestselling author Rita Herron wrote her first book when she was twelve, but didn't think real people grew up to be writers. Now she writes so she doesn't have to get a real job. A former kindergarten teacher and workshop leader, she traded storytelling to kids for writing romance, and now she writes romantic comedies and romantic suspense. Rita lives in Georgia with her family. She loves to hear from readers, so please write her at PO Box 921225, Norcross, GA 30092-1225, or visit her website, ritaherron.com.

Books by Rita Herron

Harlequin Intrigue

Guardian Angel Investigations

His Secret Christmas Baby
Unbreakable Bond
The Missing Twin
Her Stolen Son

Bucking Bronc Lodge

Cowboy To The Max
Cowboy Cop
Native Cowboy
Ultimate Cowboy

Other Titles

Cold Case At Camden Crossing
Cold Case At Carlton's Canyon
Cold Case At Cobra Creek
Cold Case In Cherokee Crossing

Visit the Author Profile page at Harlequin.com for more titles.

Rita Herron

UNBREAKABLE BOND
AND
THE MISSING TWIN

HARLEQUIN® INTRIGUE CLASSICS

Recycling programs
for this product may
not exist in your area.

ISBN-13: 978-0-373-60140-0

Unbreakable Bond & The Missing Twin

Copyright © 2015 by Harlequin Books S.A.

The publisher acknowledges the copyright holder of the individual works as follows:

Unbreakable Bond
Copyright © 2010 by Rita B. Herron

The Missing Twin
Copyright © 2011 by Rita B. Herron

This edition published by arrangement with Harlequin Books S.A.

For questions and comments about the quality of this book, please contact us at CustomerService@Harlequin.com.

® and TM are trademarks of the publisher. Trademarks indicated with ® are registered in the United States Patent and Trademark Office, the Canadian Intellectual Property Office and in other countries.

www.Harlequin.com

Printed in U.S.A.

CONTENTS

UNBREAKABLE BOND

To my beautiful daughter Emily
and her new son, Bradford.

And to the real Rebecca.
Thanks for inspiring us all!

PROLOGUE

A THUNDEROUS BOOM rocked the hospital walls and floor, jarring Nina Nash awake. What had happened? Had she been dreaming, or had there been an explosion?

Screams and shouts suddenly echoed in the halls, and footsteps of people rushing around outside her room pounded. Somewhere a food cart crashed and glass shattered.

Then the smell of smoke wafted to her.

Panic seized her. Dear God, there *had* been an explosion. The hospital was on fire.

She threw off the covers, not bothering to grab her robe or slip on her bedroom shoes, but the stitches from her C-section pulled as she shuffled to the door and shoved it open. Smoke flooded the hallway in a cloud so thick that she immediately coughed, her eyes watering.

She had to get to her baby. Little Peyton had been a preemie, less than five pounds, and was in the neonatal intensive care unit.

What if the fire was near the babies?

God, no...

Stumbling forward as fast as she could with her sore abdomen, she heard the sound of voices shouting again, another person crying. The fire alarm trilled, adding to the chaos. Through the gray fog, she spotted patients stumbling outside their rooms, everyone searching for an escape, confused and frightened.

"The east wing is on fire," someone yelled.

"Find the stairwell and get out!" someone else shouted.

"Help me!" a woman screamed.

Someone bumped Nina as they raced down the hall toward the stairwell.

Heat flooded the hall and an orderly grabbed her arm to push her toward the staircase. "This way, miss."

"No, I have to get to my baby," Nina cried.

"No time, the nurses and firefighters are getting the infants out! And that corridor is engulfed in flames."

"Then I'll find another way," she said and tore away from him.

Another woman darted into the fog of smoke, coughing as she collapsed onto the floor, and the rescue worker rushed to help her.

Determined to save Peyton, Nina hurried down the hall. But just as she reached the end, the ceiling crashed down, and flames shot all along the wall and floor, blocking the turn into the corridor.

She pivoted and headed in the opposite direction, feeling along the wall until she reached the next corner, but the smoke was so thick she could barely see, and flames rushed toward her. No... There was no way to get through....

Tears mingled with the sweat on her face as the heat scalded her. She had to try another direction.

Coughing, she dashed back the way she'd come, but suddenly another explosion rocked the building, the floor shook, and the ceiling crashed down.

Nina covered her head to dodge the debris, but plaster rained down on her, and a piece of metal slammed into her head. Another pummeled her leg and foot, and ceiling tiles smashed into her stomach, ripping open stitches. Pain rocked through her, and she screamed as she collapsed onto the floor. The scalding flames crawled toward her.

Through the haze, more footsteps rumbled, then a firefighter appeared and scooped her up. "My baby," she cried. "I have to get her."

"We'll find her," he said. "Just let me take you outside before the whole wing is engulfed in flames."

Tears trickled down her cheeks as he carried her through the blazing hallway, dodging flames and more falling debris. She gulped in the fresh air as he burst out the front door and raced down the steps to the lawn. Blinking her stinging eyes to clear her vision, she searched the haze and chaos.

Firefighters were scrambling to help victims and extinguish the flames, but at least half the hospital was ablaze. Patients, hospital employees, doctors, nurses and visitors ran, crawled and helped each other from the burning building.

She spotted one of the neonatal nurses unconscious on a gurney, and two nurses holding infants, and hope shot through her. The firefighter carried her toward an ambulance, but she pushed against his chest. "Let me down."

"Ma'am, you need to see a medic. You've been injured."

She didn't care if her head was bleeding, that her stitches had popped or her leg was throbbing. She had to make sure her daughter was safe. "No, not until I find my baby."

She managed to get on her feet, then stumbled toward the nurses. But her heart sank when she realized neither of the babies was Peyton.

"Where's my little girl?" she cried. "She was in the neonatal unit."

One of the nurses frowned, and the other one shook

her head with worry. "I'm not sure. Maybe one of the other nurses got her."

Another baby's cry rent the air, and she turned and raced toward the sound. A medic was holding the infant, but when she neared him, she realized the baby was a boy.

Panic clawed at her, and she ran from medic to medic, from nurse to doctor to orderly. Screams and cries flowed freely as people were carried from the hospital and the body count began to rise. More sirens and cries reverberated as police, friends and relatives of the hospital employees and patients arrived, each searching for loved ones.

Finally she found one of the nurses who'd cared for Peyton lying on another stretcher, and she hobbled toward her. "Where's my baby?"

Sorrow filled the nurse's eyes as she looked at Nina. "I don't know. I thought someone else rescued her."

The sound of the NICU exploding rent the air, and Nina's legs gave way, a sob of terror ripping from her.

Dear God...

Where was her baby?

CHAPTER ONE

Eight years later

FINDING MISSING CHILDREN was the only thing that kept Slade Blackburn going. The only thing that kept him from giving into the booze that promised sweet relief and numbness from the pain of his failures.

That was, when he found the children alive.

The other times…well, he locked those away in some distant part of his mind to deal with later. *Much,* much later when he was alone at night, and the loneliness consumed him and reminded him that he didn't have a soul in the world who gave a damn if he lived or died.

Voices echoed through the downstairs as the agents at Guardian Angel Investigations entered the old house Gage McDermont had converted into a business and began to climb the stairs.

Slade's instincts kicked in. He'd arrived early, situated himself to face the doorway in the conference room so he could study each man as he entered.

Not that he hadn't done his research.

Gage had started the agency in Sanctuary and recruited an impressive team of agents.

The moment Slade had read about GAI in the paper, he'd phoned Gage and asked to sign on. Leaving his stint in the military had left him wired and honed for action, yet the confines of the FBI or a police department had grated on his newfound freedom.

Too long he'd taken orders, followed commands. Now he was his own man and wanted no one to watch over, not as he'd had to do with his combat unit.

But he needed a case.

Bad.

Being alone, listening to the deafening quiet of the mountains, remembering the horrific events he'd seen, was wreaking havoc on his sanity.

He refused to be one of those soldiers who returned from war damaged and suffering from post-traumatic stress syndrome.

He would not fall apart and become needy, dammit.

And he *would* keep the nightmares at bay.

By God, he'd survived his childhood and Iraq, and he wouldn't go down now.

Still, returning to the small town of Sanctuary, North Carolina, held its own kind of haunts, and when he'd passed by Magnolia Manor, the orphanage where his mother had dropped him off without looking back, he'd questioned his decision to settle in the town.

Gage McDermont strode in and took the head seat behind the long conference table while the others filed in. Slade maintained his stoic expression, honing his self-control.

Gage gestured toward Slade. "This is Slade Blackburn," he said. "He just finished his first case and returned Carmel Foster's runaway daughter to her."

The men surrounding the table nodded, then Gage gestured to each of them as he made the introductions. Slade analyzed each one in turn.

Benjamin Camp, a dirty-blond-haired computer expert with green eyes. Brilliant techy, he'd heard. Slade would bet he had a shady past. Maybe a former criminal with skills that could come in handy in a pinch.

Levi Stallings, former FBI profiler, black hair, military-style haircut, dark brown eyes. Intense, a man who studied behaviors and got into a killer's mind. He cut his gaze toward Slade as if dissecting him under his microscope, and Slade forced himself not to react, to meet him with an equally hard stare.

First rule of engaging with the enemy: *Never let on that you're afraid or intimidated.*

Not that he was, but he didn't like *anyone* messing with his mind or getting too close.

Adopting his poker face, he angled his head to study the man, seated next to him, whom Gage introduced as Brock Running Deer.

"Running Deer is an expert tracker," Gage said in acknowledgment.

A skill that would be needed in the dense mountains. He was also big, slightly taller than Slade's own six feet, had shoulder-length brown hair, auburn eyes and was part Cherokee. He scowled at Slade as if he were permanently angry, but Slade shrugged it off. He hadn't come here to make friends.

"And this is Derrick McKinney."

Slade nodded toward him.

Next Gage introduced Caleb Walker, who also looked mixed heritage. He had thick black hair, black eyes, and wore a guarded expression. Gage didn't elaborate on his particular skill, which made Slade even more curious about the man.

Gage gestured to the last man seated around the table. "This is Colt Mason, a guns and weapon expert." Slade sized him up. Short, spiked black hair, crystal-blue eyes, sullen and quiet. He had that military look about him, as well, as if he'd stared down death and it hadn't fazed him. Probably former Special Ops.

The door squeaked open and a petite brunette with hair dangling to her waist and large brown eyes slipped in.

Gage's face broke into a smile. "This is Amanda Peterson, our newest recruit. Amanda is a forensics specialist, and we're glad to have her on board.

"Now that we've all been introduced, I want to get you up to speed on the latest case and the arrests made in Sanctuary. Brianna Honeycutt, now the wife of Derrick, adopted an infant son when the baby's mother, Natalie Cummings, was murdered. Our investigation revealed that Natalie learned about a meth lab in town that was connected to the creators of a lab eight years ago, the one that caused the hospital fire and explosion that took dozens and dozens of lives."

Gage paused and twisted his mouth into a frown. "The police have made several arrests, but locals are up in arms now that they know who was responsible. There's also been speculation that there might have been more locals involved in the lab. Lawsuits are cropping up each day, and people who lost loved ones are asking questions. Due to the fire and contamination of evidence, there are questions regarding some of those who were presumed dead."

Slade frowned. "Presumed?"

"Ones whose bodies were never found or identified," Gage clarified. "Among those were women and children. I expect that we might have some work ahead of us."

Slade's blood began to boil. Women and children... who'd died because of some stupid drug lab. Women and children whose bodies had never been identified.

Families with no answers just as his own hadn't had

answers when his older sister had disappeared. Not until Slade had found her in the morgue.

Maybe it was right that he'd come back to Sanctuary. If he had the opportunity to find closure for even one of the families involved, it was worth it.

Then maybe he could finally find peace and forgive himself for his sister's death.

NINA'S BABY'S CRY haunted her every day.

Peyton would have been eight years old had she survived, the same age as the children Nina taught at Sanctuary Elementary.

She tried to envision what her daughter would look like now as she watched her students rush to the school bus, squealing and laughing, excited to be out for summer break. Most of the teachers were jumping for joy, as well.

"Freedom at last," one third-grade teacher said with a laugh.

"Vacation," another one boasted.

But instead of dreaming about long, lazy days at home or a vacation road trip, tears filled Nina's eyes.

To her, summer break meant weeks of being without the kids. Long, lonely days and nights of silence. Of no tiny hands reaching out for help, no sweet voices calling her name, no little patter of feet or giggles, no little arms wrapping around her for a big bear hug.

Tortured nights of an empty house and more nightmares of what her life would have been like if her little girl were alive.

For a moment, she allowed herself to dream of taking her daughter to the beach. They'd build sand castles, collect shells, ride bikes. She could almost hear her daughter's laughter in the wind roaring off the ocean....

The bus driver gave a big honk of its horn, jerking her back to reality. Kids waved and screamed out the window, and the bus roared away. Teachers cheered and waved, laughing and talking about their plans as they dispersed back to their rooms to tidy up for the day.

Nina wrapped her arms around her waist and watched until the last bus disappeared from the school drive, then turned and walked back inside, her chest tight.

She should be over the loss of her daughter, people had told her. "Move on with your life," her father had insisted. "Let it go," the ob-gyn had said.

But sometimes at night, she heard her baby's cries, and she sensed that Peyton was still alive. That she hadn't died in that fire. That she was out there somewhere, and that she needed her.

Moving on autopilot, she went to her classroom, packed up boxes, wiped down the chalkboard, stripped the bulletin boards and cleaned out her desk.

Finally she couldn't procrastinate any longer. The empty room was almost as sad and overwhelming as her house. Here she could still see the kids' cherub faces, hear their chatter and smell their sweet, little bodies.

She stuffed her worn plan book in her favorite tote, one emblazoned with a strawberry on the front and sporting the logo Teachers Are Berry Special, then added a copy of the language arts guide for the new language arts program the county had adopted, threw the tote over her shoulder, flipped off the lights and headed outside.

The late-afternoon sunshine beat down on her as she walked to the parking lot. The sound of engines starting up filled the air, and she noticed a group of teachers gathering for an end-of-the-year celebration.

Celia, her friend from the classroom across the hall from her, looked up and waved as she climbed in her minivan. Celia had invited her to join them, but she'd declined. Celebrating was the last thing on her mind.

Instead she drove to the little bungalow she'd bought in town, picked up the newspaper on the front stoop, then dragged herself inside and poured a glass of sweet iced tea. Hating the silence that engulfed her, she flipped on the television, then glanced at the front page of the paper.

The headlines immediately caught her eye.

Murder of Natalie Cummings and Kidnapping of Her Son Ryan Leads to Answers about the Hospital Explosion and Fire Eight Years Ago.

Nina skimmed the article, her own memories of the explosion taunting her. For years now the town had mourned the lives lost back then. Now they finally had answers.

Police have learned that a meth lab built by local teenagers at the time was the cause of the explosion that killed dozens. Recently Natalie Cummings had overheard students at Sanctuary High discussing a new meth lab nearby, and she was apparently murdered when she connected the current lab to the one eight years ago.

Derrick McKinney, an agent from Guardian Angel Investigations, was instrumental in uncovering the truth about the explosion, the kidnapping and murder connection.

Nina frowned, her heart racing. That night had been horrible. The explosion, the fire, the terrible confusion. The burning bodies.

Her frantic rush to find Peyton...

Her stomach knotted. She'd wondered if her baby

might have been confused with another that night, or if she could have been kidnapped in the chaos.

But the investigation had been a mess, and the sheriff had assured her her fears had been unfounded. Even worse, the P.I. she'd hired had been convinced she was just a hysterical mother and had done nothing but take her money.

Still, one question nagged at her. They had never found Peyton's body.

She glanced at the article again. *Guardian Angel Investigations*. They specialized in finding missing children.

Her hand shook as she went to the mantel and picked up the photo of her newborn. Peyton had been so tiny Nina had been able to hold her in one hand.

If someone had kidnapped her, how would she have survived?

Still, every night when she crawled into bed, she heard her cries. And every time she closed her eyes, a little angel's voice sang to her in the night.

Determination and a new wave of hope washed over her as she grabbed her purse. "I'm going to find you, baby."

If GAI had dug deeply enough to find out who'd caused that fire, maybe they could dig even deeper and find out what had happened to her daughter.

JUST AS THE MEETING was about to disperse, the bell on the downstairs door jangled. Gage gestured for the group to wait while he descended the stairs. A minute later, he returned, escorting a young woman with him.

A beautiful blonde with long wavy hair, enormous blue eyes the color of the sky on a clear North Carolina day, and a slim body with plump breasts that strained against her soft, white blouse.

But nothing about the woman indicated she was aware of her beauty.

Instead, those blue eyes looked wary and were filled with the kind of grief and sadness that indicated she'd lived through a hell of her own.

"This is Nina Nash," Gage said. "She's interested in our services."

Gage gestured for her to sit down, and Slade noticed her body trembling slightly as she slid into a leather chair. Why was she on edge?

Was she intimidated by the agents, or in some kind of trouble?

"How can we help you, Miss Nash?" Gage asked.

She bit down on her lower lip and twisted her hands together, glancing at each of them as if to decide whether to continue.

"Just relax and tell us your story," Gage said in a soothing tone.

She nodded, then jutted up her little chin, took a deep breath and spoke. "I read about your agency in the paper and saw that you found the people responsible for the hospital fire and explosion eight years ago."

"Yes," Gage said. "The police made some arrests."

"I…lost my baby that night," Nina said in a pained tone. "At least she went missing."

A hushed silence fell across the room as everyone contemplated her statement. Finally Gage assumed the lead and spoke. "Why don't you start from the beginning and tell us what happened."

She rolled her tiny hands into fists as if to hold herself together. "My baby girl was early, a preemie, and I had to have a C-section," she said as if she'd repeated this story a thousand times already. Then she rushed on as if she had to spit it out or she'd completely crumble. "I was asleep when the sound of the explosion woke me. Everyone started shouting and screaming, and I smelled smoke so I got out of bed and tried to get to the nursery, to Peyton…" Her voice cracked in the deafening silence stretching across the room.

But no one spoke. Her anguish was like a palpable force in the room.

"It was chaos," she said on a choked breath. "Everyone was screaming, desperate to escape. Patients were struggling and needing help, and an orderly told me to go to the stairwell, but I couldn't leave my baby so I pushed him away."

She hesitated and drew a shaky breath. "Smoke filled the halls, but I ran toward the corridor leading to the neonatal intensive care unit, but it was on fire, and I couldn't get past, so I tried the other way, then the ceiling crashed and debris was falling and I was hit…"

She swiped at a tear that trickled down her cheek, and Slade sucked in a sharp breath. Others shifted restlessly.

"I fell and was bleeding and a fireman carried me outside, but I wouldn't let them treat me. I ran through the crowd searching for my baby. I found two nurses holding infants, but none of them was Peyton…" A shudder ripped through her body. "Then the building crashed down in flames."

Slade knew the answer, but he asked the question anyway. "Did they find your baby's body?"

She shook her head no. "The scene was a mess. It took hours for the firefighters to control the blaze. Later the police said my baby must have died when the building crashed, that it would probably take months for the medical examiner to sort through the bodies." Her mouth tightened, then she looked up with steely determination in her eyes. "They never found her. And I know she didn't die that night." She pressed her hand to her chest. "I know it in my heart, and I want you to look for her."

"Nina," Gage said quietly. "I understand your grief, but if Peyton had lived, don't you think the hospital would have informed you?"

"I don't know," she said in a quivering voice. "It was so chaotic that night, someone could have kidnapped her, or she could have gotten switched with another baby."

Caleb Walker cleared his throat. "You had a breakdown afterward, didn't you, Nina?" His tone was low, not accusatory but understanding. "And you saw a woman who claimed to be a medium. You tried to communicate with your little girl, but it didn't work."

She clenched her jaw. "Yes," she admitted. "But I'm *not* crazy. I'm not. I can hear her cries sometimes at night. I'm her mother, I have instincts. We bonded." Another tear escaped but she didn't bother to wipe it away this time.

Slade gripped the arm of the chair to keep himself from going to her and wiping it away.

"Peyton would be eight years old now," she said, her voice growing stronger with conviction. "I know she's out there and she needs me."

Skeptical looks passed quietly around the room. Nina obviously noticed because she stood, anger sizzling in her eyes.

For some reason he didn't understand, Slade couldn't let her leave. Not yet. "You hired a P.I. before?"

She nodded and hissed in frustration—or rage. "But he didn't believe me. He just took my money, then told

me I was stupid to keep searching." Her voice rose another decibel. "But how can I not look for my little girl
when I think she might be alive? It would be as if I abandoned her."

Slade gritted his teeth. Plenty of mothers did just that.

She jammed her hands on her hips. "Everyone thought
that fire was an accident, and GAI proved it wasn't. Why
can't you believe that my baby might be alive, that someone might have taken her that night? Why can't you at
least just look into it?"

Because they all knew the infant had probably died
in the fire, Slade thought. But he refrained from saying
it, and so did the others.

"With all the revelations you've uncovered about that
fire, about people in the town covering up the reason for
the explosion," Nina continued, pressing, "maybe someone knows something about my baby."

Slade considered the possibility. The town had kept
its secrets and people had suffered for it.

He'd also seen and heard bizarre stories before, knew
that people could be devious. Gage had indicated that
there might be more locals who'd known the truth about
that night but hadn't come forward. That there might
have been more people involved.

Nina's theory that someone could have kidnapped
her baby in the chaos actually sounded feasible. If there
was a chance that she was right and her child was alive,
how could they not investigate?

CHAPTER TWO

NINA RECOGNIZED THE skepticism in the room, and frustration welled inside her. She'd been a fool to come here, to hope that someone would finally listen to her.

That they would open a case that had been closed for nearly a decade—actually a case that had never been opened.

Even her own father thought she'd lost her mind and that she should let it go.

It was the reason she hadn't spoken to him in months.

She glanced at the only female in the room, hoping she'd at least piqued her interest enough to take on the investigation, but pity darkened her eyes and she made no offer.

Irritated at them all, and with herself for thinking she might have found an ally in this group, she gritted her teeth. "Fine, if you won't help me, I'll ask around again myself." Although she knew that would lead her nowhere. Most of the people she'd talked to knew her story and thought she should get psychological help, not a detective.

She had just reached the doorway when one of the men said, "I'll take the case."

Uncertain that she'd heard him correctly, she froze and slowly turned around. The intense man who'd sat next to Gage McDermont stood. "My name is Slade

Blackburn, Miss Nash. I'll look into your child's disappearance."

Nina blinked in stunned shock. Of all the men at the
table, he'd acted the coldest, looked the hardest. He was
tall and big, his broad shoulders stretching the confines
of his black button-up shirt. Jeans hugged his thighs,
thighs that looked like tree trunks compared to her own.

Her gaze fell to the scar down the left side of his
cheek, a knife wound that had to have been done fairly
recently. Tousled brownish-black hair fell across one eye,
and he swept it back with his hand. A hand also scarred
with a jagged cut.

This man looked intimidating, impressive, like a
fighter.

"Slade," Gage began, but the man cut him off with
a dismissive gesture that seemed to surprise his boss.

"You don't have another case you need me on right
now, do you, boss?"

"No," Gage said. "But you just returned from one. I
figured you might want some time off."

"No," Slade said in a deep take-charge tone. "I came
here to work. I like to stay busy."

The woman spoke up next. "We'll help any way you
need us."

A chorus of agreements and nods followed, and Nina
finally released the breath she'd been holding. "Thank
you."

Slade didn't acknowledge her thanks. Instead, he gestured toward the door. "I'd like to talk to you in private,
ask you some more questions."

Nina's chest tightened. Searching for Peyton would
mean opening old wounds, but she had to suck up her
pride.

She'd do anything to find her daughter.

SLADE ESCORTED NINA to his office and gestured for her to sit. "Would you like coffee or some water?"

Her delicate body collapsed into the chair as if she were too weary to stand any longer, and the temptation to comfort her hit him.

But that would be a mistake.

"Water, please," she said in a low voice.

He disappeared for a moment, went to the kitchen then returned with coffee for himself and a bottle of water for her. By the time he walked in, she'd straightened her shoulders as if regaining control and bracing for an interrogation.

His suspicions mounted. What was she hiding?

"All right," she said. "What did you want to ask me?"

He offered a small smile as he settled at his desk, hoping to relax her, but she clenched the water bottle in a death grip.

"I need some background information," he said, then reached for a legal pad and pen. "Tell me the date of your daughter's birth. And her name."

"I named her Peyton," she said, then gave him the date and time of her birth. The realization that she'd counted the birthdays since made compassion twitch at his veneer.

"You said she was in the NICU?"

"Yes, she was premature," Nina said. "A seven-month baby. She had trouble breathing at first, and weighed a little over four pounds."

His gaze shot to hers. "Any other problems?"

"She was only a day old. The doctors planned to run more tests… They thought she might have had vision problems…"

Slade swallowed. If someone had kidnapped this pree-mie, and she had had health issues, she might not have survived afterward. He needed to check old police reports to see if any premature infants had been abandoned around that time.

Or if any infants' bodies had been found.

Damn. The thought made his own stomach roil. He couldn't imagine the torture this woman had suffered. The fear, the horror stories of other abandoned babies she'd heard about on the news, the not knowing or thinking that each time an infant's body had been discovered that it might be hers…

Forcing his mind back to his job, he glanced at her ring finger, but it was bare. No tan line where a wedding ring might have been either.

"Who was the baby's father, and is he still in the picture?"

She glanced down at her hands. "His name was William Hood. He was nineteen, and I was eighteen at the time. And no, he's not in the picture."

"Tell me what happened between you."

Her gaze flew to his, anxiety lining her face. "Is it really necessary for me to go into this?"

Slade leaned forward, his arms on the desk, his expression neutral. "I know this is difficult, but you came to me for help, Nina. If you want me to investigate, I need to know everything about that time in your life." He swallowed. "And I mean *everything*. So don't hold back or lie to me or I'm off the case."

Anger glittered in her eyes, but she gave a nod. "All right."

"How did William react to the pregnancy?"

"Not well. He had a scholarship to Duke, and didn't want his life interrupted."

"But your life was," he said calmly.

A tiny smile slowly softened her eyes. "Yes. Even

though I was young and the pregnancy was a surprise, I really wanted the baby. I felt connected to her immediately." Her hand automatically went to her stomach, and an image of a young, naive girl flashed in his head.

One who would have made a wonderful mother.

Slade tried to ignore the feelings that realization stirred.

"So, what did William do? Did he refuse to accept responsibility?"

Nina's mouth thinned again. "Pretty much. He and his parents tried to convince me to have an abortion." A shudder rippled through her. "His mother even offered me a bribe to leave town and get rid of the baby."

Slade studied her for a moment. "Did any of them threaten you?"

Nina frowned as if thinking back. "Not in so many words, although Mrs. Hood warned me that I'd be sorry if I ruined her son's life. William's father had died the year before, and she wanted William to follow in his footsteps and become a lawyer."

Slade tamped back his anger. "What did you say to her?"

"I let them all off the hook," Nina said calmly. "I told them I didn't want their money, that I didn't need or want William and that they could all go to hell."

Admiration stirred in Slade's chest. "Have you heard from him lately?" Slade asked.

"No. I did hear that he got married to a former girlfriend, a debutante named Mitzi. I'm sure his mother was thrilled."

"What about your family?"

Anguish flickered in her eyes momentarily before she blinked away the emotion. "I lost my mother when I was little. My father was upset with me about the pregnancy.

He also tried to convince me to abort the baby, then insisted if I kept her, that I should give her up for adoption." She uncapped the water bottle and took a long sip, then set it down and looked at him again. "He thought I was too young and irresponsible to raise a child. And when the doctors declared that Peyton died in that hospital fire, he assured me it was for the best."

Slade gritted his teeth. Was her father simply protective, or a bastard with an insensitive heart?

"He didn't believe that your daughter might still be alive?"

She made a sound of disgust. "No, he actually seemed relieved. He thought I was crazy and insisted I go into therapy."

"Because he loved you," Slade said.

Another sound of disgust. "That's what he said. That I was better off that my little girl died." She turned an anguished look his way. "How could anybody say that? That it was God's way of giving me a second chance at a normal life?" Her voice quivered again. "All I wanted was my baby back."

"Maybe he was trying to help," Slade suggested.

She shook her head. "No, he was embarrassed that I had an illegitimate child, worried about what it would do to his precious reputation." She looked down at her hands where she'd twined them in her lap. "He didn't give a damn about Peyton."

He let her words sink in. So her father was relieved to have the child out of the way. He already disliked the man. "And you did go to college?"

She nodded. "Not at first, but eventually I pulled myself together and earned a teaching degree. Now I teach second grade at Sanctuary Elementary." Her eyes softened again as if being around the children helped alleviate her suffering.

Slade considered her mental condition and hated the doubts assailing him. Needing to know the truth was one thing. Obsession to the point of stalking, another animal instead. "You stayed in Sanctuary because you thought your daughter might be here, didn't you?" Slade asked. "You looked for her in every child in school and in town."

But she didn't hide her motives or defend herself. She nodded instead, tears blurring her eyes. "I know that sounds pathetic, but I just felt close to her here."

Just as his mother had refused to move from their home after his sister had disappeared. She'd claimed that she had to be at the house in case his sister returned. Eventually, though, her obsession had driven her over the edge....

"No," Slade said evenly. "I understand."

Her eyes narrowed, and her voice dropped to a whisper. "You do?"

Unable to resist, he reached out and covered her hands with his own. "My sister disappeared from our house when I was fifteen. For days and months afterward, I looked for her in every teenager I spotted."

"You found her?" Nina asked.

God, he didn't want to answer that. Didn't want to shatter any ounce of hope she had. But the truth could be brutal sometimes.

"Yes," he finally answered. "But we didn't have a happy ending, Nina. She was in the morgue."

Nina inhaled a sharp breath. "I'm sorry," she said, then squeezed his fingers. "What happened?"

Hell, he'd already said too much. And she was looking at him with such compassion that emotions he'd long thought buried pummeled him.

No. He couldn't, *wouldn't* blurt out the rest.

"You don't want to know." He cleared his throat. "But think long and hard about this, Nina," he said gruffly. "What will you do if we investigate and find out that your baby did die in that fire? Are you prepared for that reality?"

NINA'S CHEST ACHED from trying to maintain control. Slade's question threatened to shatter that control.

Was she prepared? How would she respond if he discovered that Peyton really had died? All these years she'd lived on the belief that her little girl was out there needing and wanting her.

"How can I not find out the truth?" she finally said. "I need closure, Mr. Blackburn."

"Slade," he said automatically. "And are you sure it's closure you want? She might be gone forever."

Pain rocked through her, but she cloaked herself in the coat of armor she'd donned years ago. She would survive no matter what. "I realize that, but not knowing is no way to live."

He studied her with such an intensity that she was tempted to squirm. But she refused to show weakness or he might decide she was the nutcase her father and Dr. Emery thought.

He gave a brisk nod. "All right. But what if someone did kidnap your baby, and she's been adopted and is now happy? What will you do then?"

She had considered that theory, but somehow in her heart she knew that wasn't the case. "She needs me," she said simply. "I'm her mother. I feel it."

A muscle ticked in his jaw. "You have to consider

every scenario, Nina. What if she has loving parents
and doesn't know anything about you? What if she has
a family that she loves?"

"I don't know," she said softly, honestly. "I guess I'll
cross that bridge when, or if, we come to it. But I am her
mother and I deserve to know where she is."

"Fair enough." Slade nodded, then released her hand.

Odd how she hadn't leaned on anyone in years, but
for a moment, she'd felt as if she had someone on her
side now.

Someone she trusted. And after her father's and William's betrayals, she'd never trust anyone again.

SLADE HAD HIS WORK cut out for him. Even though Nina
insisted she could handle the truth, no matter what he
discovered, he understood the emotional roller-coaster
ride involved in looking for a missing child. The toll it
took could be dangerous.

His mother certainly hadn't survived the ride.

And judging from Nina's fragile looks, she'd been
surviving on hope for years. If he stripped that hope, she
might crash and burn just as his mother had.

Then again, beneath that tenderness, she was stubborn. Determined. And he also understood the torture
not knowing caused.

She licked her lips, drawing his attention to her
mouth, and a foreign feeling bled through him, one he
didn't want. He itched to draw her tiny hand back into
his, kiss it and promise her that he would make things
right.

His body reacted, hardened, betraying his better sense
and reminding him that his libido wasn't dead after all.
Geesh, a fine time for it to burst back to life.

Fortunately she didn't seem to notice.

"Where do we start?" she asked.

Reining in his sudden bout of lust, he forced his mind back to the case. "I'll put out some feelers across the States, search the National Center for Missing and Exploited Children website, check into adoptions that occurred around the time of the fire. I'll question nurses, hospital staff and other locals at the scene that night." He hesitated. "I'll also have to question your father, and William Hood and his family."

"They won't be happy that I've opened this up again," Nina said.

Slade shrugged. He already didn't like her father or the Hoods. "I don't give a damn who I piss off, Nina. I'm on the case now, and I will find out exactly what happened to your baby girl."

He just hoped to hell she could handle the truth when he did.

CHAPTER THREE

FATIGUE FROM DREDGING up the past pulled at Nina, but hope fluttered wildly in her chest. Slade would be opening up old wounds between her and her father, and her and the Hoods, but she'd survived their disdain before and she would again.

At least someone was finally going to ask questions.

"Does your father live in town?" Slade asked.

"No, he's in Raleigh." She gave him her father's contact information, including his work number at the bank. "I'm out of school for the summer and want to accompany you when you talk to him."

He arched a brow. "Are you sure that's a good idea?"

No, but she wanted to see her father's reaction. "I can handle it."

He gave a clipped nod. "What about William and his family?"

"They're in Winston-Salem. William took over his father's law practice there."

Slade jotted down the name of the firm, then ran his hand through his hair. "What was the name of the doctor who delivered your baby?"

Fresh pain burned her stomach at the mere mention of his name. The delivery had been harrowing enough, but he had been a strong proponent of adoption. "Dr. Don Emery."

"Does he still live and practice in Sanctuary?"

"Yes, I think so, although I haven't seen him in months. I tried to talk to him several times, but like everyone else, he encouraged me to move on."

Slade's mouth tightened slightly. "I know this is difficult, but think back to the night of the delivery and the day after. Did you notice anything strange, anyone suspicious at the hospital?"

"God, I was so scared that night and was in such a panic, that I don't remember much. Just that I knew my baby was coming too early, and that I was afraid for her."

"You were in labor?"

She nodded. "I'd developed complications. They rushed me to the operating room and took her immediately." Her heart quickened at the memory. "She wasn't breathing at first, and they had to give her oxygen. She was so tiny and weak that I didn't know if she'd make it…"

His eyes held compassion as she paused to pull herself together.

"What about the next day? Did you notice someone watching the nursery, looking at the babies?"

Nina massaged her temple as she struggled to force the details of the hospital stay to the surface. "Not that I recall."

"Did anyone make an odd comment to you about keeping the baby?"

Nina grimaced. "Dr. Emery agreed with my father and encouraged me to give Peyton up for adoption. They both thought that she needed two parents. A couple of nurses also mentioned that adoption might be a good idea."

"Do you remember those nurses' names?"

Nina rubbed her temple again. "I don't know last names, but one nurse was Jane and the other Carrie. I saw both of them outside the hospital after the fire, but they claimed they didn't know where Peyton was."

Slade frowned. Was it possible someone had taken the baby from the nursery before it caught on fire?

SLADE BIT BACK his thoughts. He hated offering Nina false optimism.

"So where do we start?" she asked.

Slade checked his watch. "It's already getting late. I'll start putting out contacts on the Internet tonight, call a couple of friends who might be able to help look into the adoption angle, and drop by the hospital and see if the administrator and Dr. Emery are there." He paused. "Tomorrow I'd like to talk to your father and meet the Hood family."

Nina gripped the armrest. "Let's get started."

Slade sighed. "Nina, why don't you go home tonight and rest."

"No," she said in a pleading tone. "I know this is difficult for you to understand, but I feel…lost in that house alone right now."

Hell, the trouble was he *did* understand. He knew how the silence could eat at you, how a person's absence could feel like part of you had been ripped out. How the walls could scream at you with recriminations.

"All right," he said gruffly. "But remember, we may not find anything."

She took another sip of water, then wiped her mouth. "Thanks. I appreciate your candor."

"Let me talk to Derrick, then we'll head to the hospital." He stood, then strode down the hall to McKinney's office.

Derrick was on the phone when he knocked, but ended the call and gestured for him to enter.

"I need to ask you a favor," Slade said bluntly.

Derrick pointed to the chair beside his desk. "You're taking on the case for Nina Nash?"

Slade took the chair. "Yes."

Derrick frowned. "You know that baby may not have survived."

Slade's gut knotted. "I know. But after hearing Nina's story, it's possible that someone could have kidnapped the baby in the chaos."

Derrick folded his arms. "What can I do to help?"

"Talk to your wife, Brianna, for me."

Derrick arched a brow. "How do you know Bri?"

"I lived at Magnolia Manor when I was a teenager for a while. We met there. I heard she's a social worker now with an adoption agency."

The realization of where he was headed dawned in Derrick's eyes. "She was," Derrick said. "But she's taken a leave of absence to stay home with the baby."

"But Brianna has contacts, right?" Slade asked.

"Probably." Derrick narrowed his eyes. "You know that adoption records are sealed?"

"Yes, but Brianna must have a friend who can look back through files quietly. Nina's baby was premature, and had trouble breathing. Handling an adoption for a preemie with medical problems would be tricky—and memorable."

"That's true," Derrick said. "I'll talk to her and see if she can help."

"Let me know if she finds a lead and I'll look into it."

Derrick agreed, and Slade thanked him and headed back to his office.

Nina was waiting when he returned, and she sat quietly as they drove to the hospital. That quiet strength roused his protective instincts.

Worse, her scent, some sweet fruity fragrance, stirred his desires.

But he tamped them down. Nina Nash was a case, nothing more. Slade would never give his heart to a woman. Loving and losing was too damn hard.

First his mother and sister. Then his men...all the people he'd cared about and failed.

He veered into the hospital parking lot and parked, and they walked silently inside. He introduced himself to the receptionist. "Is your hospital administrator in?"

She frowned and checked the schedule. "Dr. Lake has gone home for the day. He'll be in tomorrow at nine."

"How about Dr. Emery?"

She punched in a number, spoke into the phone then turned to them. "He's with a patient, but you can go to his office on the second floor and wait there."

"Thanks." Slade coaxed Nina to the elevator, noting the tense way she held her shoulders. When they passed the nursery, grief and a wistfulness settled in her blue eyes. Newborns filled the bassinets; pink and blue blankets indicating the gender, while a young couple stood goo-goo-eyed, waving at their son through the window.

The intensive-care part of the unit was housed in a separate room beside the regular nursery, and one tiny infant plugged with tubes and wires lay inside an incubator, kicking wildly.

"He's a fighter," Nina said softly as she paused for a moment to watch. "Just like Peyton."

He pressed a hand to her back in comfort, and she stiffened slightly, then inhaled and moved on down the hall to Dr. Emery's office.

Slade surveyed the room as they stepped inside. Medical journals and books overflowed a wall-to-wall bookshelf behind a massive cherry desk that was neat and orderly.

Nina slid into a chair, but Slade stood with his arms folded and studied the man's credentials on the wall between the windows. UNC. Duke. A third wall held a bulletin board decorated with photos of children he'd delivered.

"Is your baby's photo here?" he asked.

Nina's shoulders stiffened as she shook her head. He gritted his teeth, regretting the question. Some people reacted to a person's death as if they'd never existed at all.

A minute later a bushy-haired, freckled man around five-eleven strode in. The moment he saw Nina, a frown swept across his craggy face. "Nina?"

"Yes, Dr. Emery, I'm back." She gestured toward Slade. "This is Slade Blackburn. He's with Guardian Angel Investigations."

Dr. Emery's eyes narrowed, his thick, graying eyebrows crinkling.

"I need to ask you some questions about the night of the hospital fire," Slade said without preamble. "I want to know exactly what happened to Peyton Nash."

NINA TRIED TO STUDY the doctor with an objective eye. But too many times he'd encouraged her to stop asking questions, so many that his dismissal of her had roused her suspicions.

"Honestly, Nina, you've hired another private investigator?" Dr. Emery asked, his tone reeking of exasperation.

"Yes, she has," Slade said. "And I'd like to hear your version of what happened to Peyton."

The doctor fiddled with the stethoscope around his neck, then sank into his office chair as if weary of her.

"Nina knows exactly what happened, Mr. Blackburn, but she refuses to accept the truth, that her baby was lost in that fire." His frown accentuated the deep grooves carved by age bracketing his mouth. "It was sad, horrific, tragic," he continued. "But it happened."

Slade simply stared at the man. "According to Nina, nurses rescued three other infants. Why not her baby?"

"That I don't know," the doctor said. "I spoke with the nurses later, and they all agreed that the baby wasn't in the nursery when the fire broke out, that they thought she had been taken to another area for tests."

"They told me they didn't know where she was," Nina said, contradicting him.

A spark of temper darkened Dr. Emery's eyes. He shuffled a stack of papers on his desk, restacking them in an attempt at stalling. "I didn't want to add to your distress at the time, Nina, but I had ordered heart tests for your infant. I suspected your baby had a hole in her heart as well as underdeveloped lungs, and that she wasn't going to make it."

Nina's breath caught in her throat. "So she might have been somewhere else in the hospital, not in the unit when it burned down."

"We've been over this," Dr. Emery said as if talking to a child. "She did not survive."

"How can you be so sure?" Slade asked. "Did forensics ever prove the infant was in the fire?"

Dr. Emery glared at Slade. "No, but the place, the ashes…it was impossible to identify all the bodies."

"How about security tapes?" Slade asked.

"The explosion knocked them all out." He sighed. "Mr. Blackburn, you're doing Miss Nash an injustice by dredging up the past and raising her hopes. She needs to let her daughter's death go so she can heal."

Slade's jaw clenched. "You tried to persuade Nina to give up her baby for adoption, didn't you?"

The man curled his hand around a stress ball on his desk and squeezed it. "Yes. She was young, unemployed and single."

"But she wanted to keep the baby," Slade said.

"She was immature. And her father didn't intend to support her or the child. I was trying to think of the baby. *If* she made it," he continued, "there would be medical bills, therapy." He shot a condescending look at Nina. "Miss Nash was not equipped to handle those expenses, much less raise a handicapped child."

"That was my problem, not yours," Nina said bitterly.

Dr. Emery pushed away from his desk. "I was, as always, looking out for my patients."

Slade slapped a fist on the desk. "Well, someone didn't look out for Peyton Nash that night, did they?"

Dr. Emery paced to the window, agitated. "You have no idea how traumatic it was. The hospital staff did everything possible to save the patients."

Slade folded his arms. "And maybe you saw that chaos as an opportunity to take Peyton, to give her to someone else you deemed as a more appropriate parent. Or hell, maybe you sold her for the money."

Hot fury heated the doctor's cheeks. "How dare you imply such slander. I have an impeccable reputation. And I've lived and worked here in Sanctuary all my life."

Slade stood, towering over him. "I don't like the fact that you've stonewalled my client and dismissed her questions without adequately responding."

"I have answered them, but Nina is obsessive and delusional," Emery argued.

Nina flinched, but Slade continued, his voice cold and harsh, "I don't think so. And I don't intend to accept anything you say at face value or leave this case alone, not until all of our questions are answered to my satisfaction." He gestured to Nina. "And if I find out that you withheld information or that you've been lying, I'll be back, and I will hold you responsible."

Fear flashed in the doctor's eyes for the first time since Nina had known him. Was he afraid because Slade was right—did he know something that he wasn't telling them?

SLADE GROUND HIS TEETH as he and Nina left Dr. Emery's office. "Let's see if any of the nurses you mentioned are here."

Nina nodded, and they walked to the nurses' station. "Excuse me," Slade said. "Do you have a nurse named Carrie or Jane working here?"

A middle-aged dirty blonde with green eyes glanced up from the desk. "Yes, Carrie Poole, but she won't be in until tomorrow. And Jane is on vacation and won't be back until next week."

"All right," Slade said. "We'll be back tomorrow."

"What do you think?" Nina asked as they exited the building and walked to his car.

"I don't know yet, Nina," Slade said. "I don't like Emery, but that doesn't necessarily mean he's lying."

Nina's shoulders sagged, and he pressed a hand to her waist to help her in the car.

"But I meant what I said. I will find the answers." He offered her a sad smile. "I just hope the answers are what you want to hear. But I won't lie to you or B.S. you either."

"Thank you," Nina said, her eyes sincere. "I know some people think I'm unstable, but I'm not. I just have to know the truth."

He stared at her for a long moment, grateful to hear the strength beneath the fragile-looking exterior. He had a feeling Nina Nash was a lot tougher than anyone had given her credit for.

Moonlight flickered off her creamy skin and highlighted her golden hair, and a surge of sexual attraction shot through him.

Damn. Not good.

Determined to avoid personal involvement, he jerked his eyes away from her, started the engine and drove back to GAI headquarters.

He parked and told Nina he'd call her in the morning. A storm cloud rumbled, threatening rain, and she thanked him again and climbed from the car.

"Get some sleep," he called just before she turned away.

But her distressed look indicated that she didn't expect to rest, that dreams of her daughter haunted her nights.

Slade had his own share of nightmares, and as much as he'd like to comfort her, he wasn't a hero. The men he'd lost were.

But he would investigate.

Tomorrow he'd ask Gage and Amanda to pull all the police and medical reports from the hospital. Maybe Amanda could use her expertise to determine if Peyton Nash's body had been among those in the fire.

NINA'S PHONE WAS RINGING as she let herself into her house. Thinking it might be Slade, she hurried to answer it.

But the voice on the other end of the line startled her. William.

"Nina, what the hell are you doing hiring a private investigator?"

Nina tensed at the rage in his tone. "How do you know I hired a P.I.?"

"Dr. Emery called. He's worried that you're having another breakdown."

Nina gripped the phone tighter. "Well, I'm not. And what I do is none of your business, William. You gave up that right the day you walked out on me and our baby."

"Listen to me, Nina. I don't need some nosy P.I. in my business, especially asking questions about something that happened years ago."

"*Something* that happened?" Nina said, her own fury mounting. "What happened was that your daughter went missing. That I was told she died, but that no one ever proved it or even bothered to look for her."

"For God's sake, you need psychiatric help," William bellowed. "My mother tried to warn me, but I thought eventually you'd come to your senses."

"Maybe you don't want me asking questions because you have something to hide," Nina said between clenched teeth.

William's breath wheezed with anger. "If you make trouble for me, Nina, I'll make sure everyone at the school where you teach knows just what a basket case you are. Do you think the people of Sanctuary will want an obsessive nutcase teaching their precious children?"

Adrenaline sizzled through Nina's blood. "Are you threatening me, William?"

"Take it however you want, Nina, just leave me alone and tell that P.I. to do the same."

Nina started to shout at him, but he slammed down the phone, cutting her off.

She stared at the dead phone in her hand, then dropped it into its cradle, paced to the mantel and picked up Peyton's photo. "I won't give up," she whispered. "Not even if William did threaten me."

In spite of her resolve not to do it, she walked into the bedroom, dragged on her nightshirt then slipped open the drawer where she'd stowed the tiny pink dress with the butterflies on it that she'd bought years ago. The outfit she'd planned for Peyton to wear home. She knew it was crazy to have kept it. Pathetic.

But she crawled in bed, pressed it to her chest and inhaled the sweet scent of fabric softener.

Then she closed her eyes and imagined her daughter coming home.

EIGHT-YEAR-OLD REBECCA DAVIS fumbled for her glasses, sweeping her hand across the desk in the bedroom at her foster parents' house. Without the glasses, she was nearly blind. But at least the social worker had gotten her a computer with big print.

She hated the clunky glasses though. They were too big for her face, and some of the kids teased her and called her *Four Eyes*.

Other kids looked at her with pity just because she was handicapped, and she didn't have a mommy.

She didn't want them to feel sorry for her. She did want a mommy though.

She clicked on the keyboard, brought up her journal and began to type.

Mommy, I know you're out there somewhere. I prayed that you would find me on Mother's Day but that's passed, so maybe you will on my birthday.

I don't like it here. The house is dark and dusty. And Mama Reese says her knees hurt too much to play with me outside. Papa Reese's cigarettes make my eyes itchy and watery and then I cough, and then he tells me to shut up. They don't like my singing either.

I have to sing though. I dream sometimes that you're looking for me. That you didn't just leave me. That we just got losted from each other, and that you can hear me. That one day you'll follow my voice and come and get me.

SHE SWIPED AT a tear running down her cheek. Crying was for babies but sometimes she couldn't help it. Sniffling and swallowing to hold back more tears, she finished the journal entry.

I know I look kind of dorky, and I'm little for my age, and I can't run like the other kids. And one of my eyes looks funny because I can't see out of it, but I take my medicine every day so I don't have the seizures anymore.

I'm getting better in school, too. I'm only a year behind. I've been practicing my writing, and I can almost make the letters right now. I can pour my own cereal and make my own peanut butter and jelly sandwiches. And I don't mind wearing hand-me-downs if you don't have much money.

Please come and get me, Mommy. I promise not to be any trouble.

SHE SAVED HER entry, then pulled on her pj's and crawled in bed. Then she closed her eyes and prayed her mommy would hear her this time and come to get her as she began to sing....

CHAPTER FOUR

SLADE LET HIMSELF into the fixer-upper house he'd purchased on the side of the mountain. The wooden two-story needed painting, a new roof, the wood floors needed to be stripped and restained and boards needed replacing on the wraparound porch.

He'd thought doing the work himself would be cathartic, but he'd yet to change a thing. Still, the place had character and at one time was probably a cozy home for some family.

He scoffed. As a kid, he'd dreamed about having a home like this. Now it didn't seem to matter.

But the place was isolated and offered him privacy, as well as an abundance of wide-open mountain air. Something he'd desperately needed after Iraq and the place he'd been kept when he'd been taken prisoner. Cramped, dark, filthy, bug-infested, the stench, the human wastes…

And the blood from the soldiers who'd died trying to save him.

He inhaled a deep, calming breath, the summer air filling his nostrils with the scent of honeysuckle and wildflowers, chasing away the demons from his past. He had a job to do now, and he'd focus on that. Get through the day.

One hour at a time.

He spotted the bottle of whiskey on the counter, and

the temptation to reach for it, to pour himself a mind-numbing shot seized him. Just one drink to erase the images in his head.

No… He was done burying his pain. He'd have to learn to live with it or it would destroy him. Then he couldn't atone for his sins.

Instead, he strode to the workout room he'd created off the garage, yanked on boxing gloves and began to pound his punching bag. The faces of his bleeding and dying men haunted him, and he hit the bag harder, the rage eating his soul, chipping away at his sanity.

He had to learn to control it. Focus. Forget.

No, he couldn't forget. Forgetting would mean dishonoring the sacrifices they'd made.

He wished to hell they'd just left him to die and saved themselves.

And their wives and families…three wives left alone now because of him.

His sister dead.

His mother gone.

He'd failed them all.

He would not fail Nina Nash.

Her story echoed in his head as he punched and slammed his fists into the bag, over and over, venting his anger over his own past and the anguish he'd heard in her voice.

But you might fail her, a voice taunted. *You might because she wants you to find her daughter alive.*

And you might discover she really is dead.

He slammed the bag so hard it swung back wildly, then came toward him and he punched it again. Again and again and again until sweat poured down his back and face, until his body ached and blood oozed from beneath the gloves.

Finally, when he'd purged his anger, he ripped off the gloves, went to the bathroom, showered then booted up his computer. He nuked a slice of leftover pizza and wolfed it down with a bottle of vitamin water while he searched news reports regarding infants' and children's deaths reported during the past eight years.

He specifically searched for any cases regarding premature births or babies found dead following the hospital fire.

Three different cases caught his eye, one baby who'd been found in a Dumpster two weeks to the day after Peyton had gone missing.

NINA JERKED AWAKE, the sound of the little girl's singing echoing in her head.

The angelic voice… A song from *Mary Poppins*…

It had to belong to her daughter.

Or was she imagining it as the therapist had said? Creating a voice that she thought her daughter might sound like and playing it in her head because she couldn't bear to let her go?

She closed her eyes and burrowed beneath the quilt, willing herself to fall back asleep so she could hear the voice again. Sometimes, the little voice sounded so close that it seemed the child was in the room with her. Sometimes, she knew that if she slept long enough, she would see her face in her dreams, that maybe Peyton could tell her where she was so she could find her.

Instead of the beautiful little girl's song though, William's threat reverberated in her head. Dr. Emery had wasted no time in calling him. He'd probably phoned her father, as well.

They'd probably all sighed and made sympathetic noises and lamented over her mental state. For all she knew, they were planning another intervention to convince her to check herself back in to the loony bin.

She would not go back there. She wasn't crazy or demented.

She was simply a mother who needed to find her child.

A noise startled her, and she clenched the covers, certain she'd heard someone outside. The wind whistled, a tree limb scraped her window and an animal howled somewhere in the distance.

She sighed, willing herself to calm down.

She couldn't lapse into paranoia again, not the way she had after she'd lost Peyton.

But another noise, a creaking sound on the front porch, sent her vaulting up from bed. Outside, thunder rumbled, and the trees shook violently, the sound of rain splattering the windowpanes, making a staticky sound like drums beating in the night.

She grabbed her robe, tied it around her waist and tiptoed to the den, shivering as the air conditioner kicked on. Darkness bathed the room, but a streak of lightning flashed in a jagged line and she froze, her heart pounding.

Had she seen someone on her porch? The silhouette of a shadow?

Fear surged through her, and she reached for the phone.

But the times when she'd called the sheriff flashed back. The way he'd dismissed her fears and ordered her to get some help, then claimed she was inventing shadows in the night.

His calls to her father...the never-ending cycle of his disdainful looks...

She dropped the phone in its cradle, grabbed the umbrella from the stand by the door then slipped the edge of the curtain sheer aside and searched the darkness.

Rain pounded the roof and porch, running in rivulets down the sides of the awning, and down the street a car's lights floated through the fog, disappearing into the blur.

The streetlight in the cul-de-sac on the other end of the street illuminated wet pavement and another house but its lights were off.

Holding her breath, she listened for signs of someone outside, but the storm raged on, the sound of a cat screeching echoing above the rain. Her heart squeezed, and she slowly unlocked the door.

Keeping the umbrella poised in case someone had been on the porch, she pulled the door ajar and the dripping cat darted down the steps.

Then her eyes widened and a sob gurgled in her throat.

God, no...

A small rag doll lay on the porch in front of the door, a knife sticking through its heart.

A doll just like the one she'd found right before she'd had her breakdown, a doll her father and the psychiatrist had insisted she'd put there as some sort of manifestation of her grief and guilt.

SLADE RARELY SLEPT and this night was no different. When he did, the nightmares came.

He'd choose fatigue over the memories haunting him any day.

Antsy to get started, he brewed a pot of coffee and was at the phone by six.

The reporter, a guy named Hewey Darby, had quoted a Detective Swarnson from the neighboring county as the lead detective on the Dumpster case, so he punched in his number, anxious to hear what the man had to say.

When the receptionist for the police department answered, he asked to speak to Swarnson. "I'm sorry, sir, but Detective Swarnson is no longer with us."

"Where can I get in touch with him?"

A moment of hesitation. "I'm afraid you can't. He was killed last year in a random shooting. What is this about?"

He explained that he wanted information on the Dumpster-baby case. "Oh, then you can speak with his partner, Detective Little. I'll connect you to her office."

"Thank you."

A minute later, a woman's voice echoed back. "Detective Little."

"This is Slade Blackburn, Guardian Angel Investigations. I'm investigating the case of an infant who went missing eight years ago in Sanctuary, the same night as the deadly fire and explosion that caused numerous deaths."

"Right. I read about the arrests."

"One of the patients in the hospital at the time was told that her baby died, but her body was never recovered, so I'm investigating the possibility that the child might have been kidnapped."

"I'm not sure how I can help."

"Actually, I'm not sure you can either, but I'm exploring every possible lead. I found records of a case you and your partner investigated where an infant was found in a Dumpster approximately two weeks after the child in question went missing."

"Oh, right, I remember that case."

"What can you tell me about it? Did you ID the child?"

"As a matter of fact, we did." Her voice warbled. "The

mother was a crack addict. She delivered early, but the child wasn't breathing so she freaked out and decided to get rid of it for fear she'd be caught."

"Did you arrest her?"

"She's in prison now." A long sigh. "I'm sorry. I guess that's not much help."

"No, it means that the child I'm looking for might be alive."

"If it's been eight years..." Detective Little said. "You know the chances are slim that you'll find her."

Slade gritted his teeth. "I know. But everyone assumed she died in that fire. The fact that there was no body or proof means there might have been foul play."

"Good luck, Mr. Blackburn. I have a soft spot for kids myself, that's why I work Special Victims. If I can help you any other way, just let me know."

He thanked her, then spent the next hour chasing down the other two instances he'd read about, but both turned out to be dead ends, too.

The rain died, the morning sun fighting through the storm clouds. His phone buzzed, and he checked the number. Nina.

He punched the connect button. "Nina?"

"Slade...can you come over?"

"What's wrong?"

"Someone left a rag doll with a knife in its heart on my doorstep."

Slade cursed, grabbed his weapon, shoved it in his holster, threw on a jacket and rushed outside.

NINA'S HAND TREMBLED as she hung up the phone. Nausea rolled through her as she stared at the doll, and her chest ached so badly it was as if that knife had been plunged into her own heart.

Someone had put the doll on her doorstep to taunt her with the past.

Who would be so cruel?

She rushed upstairs and threw on some clothes, then made coffee and tried to sip it while she waited.

Five minutes later, Slade's SUV rumbled up the drive and she inhaled deeply. She had to pull herself together. She finally had someone on her side, and she couldn't chance losing his services now.

Brushing her hair back into a ponytail, she rushed to the door. The sight of Slade Blackburn on her front porch sent a surge of relief through her.

The wind tousled his hair around his broad face, and the trees shook raindrops from the branches, scattering them across the ground. "Are you all right?" he asked.

She nodded. "Yes, just shaken."

"Tell me what happened."

"Before dawn, I heard a noise outside." She led him to the sofa table. Her hand shook as she picked up the doll. "Then I found this on my porch."

His eyes flashed with anger. "Damn sicko. Did you see who put it on your porch?"

"No, but I saw a shadow outside. Then I heard a car leaving down the street."

Slade's jaw tightened. "Do you have a bag I can put it in? I'll send it to the lab for prints and DNA."

"Sure." She rushed to the kitchen and returned with one, and he used his handkerchief to seal it in the bag.

The temptation to share what happened in the past taunted her, but she decided to hold off.

Maybe he'd find a lead from the doll and she wouldn't have to divulge the humiliating details of her breakdown.

CHAPTER FIVE

SLADE GRITTED HIS TEETH. Nina looked shaken, fragile and exhausted, like a delicate flower that had been crushed in the wind.

But dammit, she also looked beautiful in that pale blue cotton blouse and that flowing black skirt. He itched to pull her into his arms and comfort her but gripped his hands by his sides to keep from touching her.

Someone, whoever had put that doll on her porch, had meant to torment her.

Or maybe the doll had been left as a warning. If she kept asking questions, the same thing would happen to her...

Hopefully Amanda could lift some prints. If not, she might be able to track down where the doll and knife were bought and the buyer.

Slade gritted his teeth. The fact that she'd received it the day after she'd hired him was significant.

Dammit, he didn't like the fact that someone was watching her. Someone who obviously didn't want her asking questions. That fact alone roused his suspicions and gave credence to her case.

The first suspect who came to mind was the doctor. But surely the man was too smart to pull such a stunt. He'd have to know that he would be the first person Slade would question.

"Other than Dr. Emery, who else knows that you hired me?" Slade asked.

Nina ran a hand over her forehead. "William."

His gaze shot to hers. "Peyton's father?"

She nodded and folded her arms across her chest. "He phoned last night."

Slade growled, "How did he find out?"

"Dr. Emery called him."

"Son of a bitch."

Nina's gaze jerked to his, and he forced himself to tamp his anger. "What did he say?"

"He was upset," Nina said. "William doesn't want anyone messing up his life by dredging up his past. Especially me."

Slade frowned. "I don't give a damn what he wants. He's going to talk to me. And I'll get the truth out of him one way or another."

NINA'S HEART WARMED. For the first time in eight years, she actually felt as if someone believed her.

That someone else might care that her daughter had gone missing, when her father and Peyton's own father had accepted her disappearance as if it had been a blessing in disguise.

"Do you want me to call William and tell him we're coming?" Nina asked.

"No, I want the element of surprise on our side when I confront him."

Our side? A warmth spread through Nina at the thought of this man defending her. For so long, she felt as if she'd been waging an uphill battle all alone.

The sun glinted through the clouds, the traffic thick as they left the mountain roads and turned onto the highway toward Winston-Salem. The interstate buzzed with early-morning traffic and commuters.

"Did you grow up in Sanctuary?" Slade asked.

"No, in Raleigh. I attended a private school. That's where I met William. His father lived there before opening a practice in Winston-Salem."

"So how did you end up in Sanctuary?"

Nina sighed. "When I got pregnant, my father rented a small house in town. He wanted to hide me away from the people he knew in Raleigh, especially his business colleagues. I stayed in the house until after Peyton was born, then Daddy wanted me to come back and live with him, but I…couldn't."

Slade's thick, dark brows furrowed. "Let me get this straight. He moved you to a different town and left you alone when you were pregnant and just a teenager?"

Nina shrugged at the censure in his voice. "It was better that way. We weren't exactly getting along back then." She stroked the sides of her arms with her hands, shaking off the memories. "What about you? Where are you from?"

Slade's jaw tightened. "All around. My dad was in the military. He died in combat."

Nina wanted to soothe the anguish she heard beneath his calm veneer but sensed he wouldn't welcome her touch, so she held herself back. "I'm sorry, Slade. How old were you?"

He maneuvered around an eighteen-wheeler. "Thirteen."

"I'm sure that was difficult on everyone."

He made a grunting sound. "Yeah. Two years later my sister disappeared, and my mother totally lost it."

Just as she had when Peyton first went missing.

But she hadn't abandoned a second child who needed

her. "And they left you to fend for yourself," Nina said softly.

Slade stiffened. "I was the man of the family," he said. "I was supposed to take care of them and I failed."

"Slade…"

"Drop it, Nina." His expression warned her not to push. "Where does William live?"

"Downtown. He bought a half-million-dollar condo directly across the street from his law office."

"He must be doing well."

"Yes. Losing Peyton wasn't even a blip on the radar for him," she said, fighting bitterness.

He found a parking spot, parked and they climbed out and walked over to the condo complex. People clogged the sidewalk, walking to work; the coffee shop was overflowing with early-morning patrons and horns and traffic noises filled the air.

They stepped into the entryway of the high-rise building, then stopped at the front desk to speak to security. "We're here to see William Hood."

A middle-aged dark-haired woman greeted them. "Is Mr. Hood expecting you?"

"No," Slade said. "But it's important."

Nina cleared her throat. "Just tell him that Nina Nash needs to see him."

The woman buzzed his condo, announced their arrival then spoke quietly into the headset. A second later, she turned back to them with a frown. "I'm sorry, but he says he doesn't want to see you."

Slade slapped his hand on the counter. "Tell him he can talk to us now or we'll be waiting at his office."

The woman's brows rose, then she spoke into the headset again. This time curiosity lined her face when she glanced back up. "He's in the penthouse."

Slade harrumphed. "Of course."

The woman frowned again as they made their way to the elevator. Nina's stomach thrashed as the elevator carried them up, her ears popping as they climbed to the twenty-ninth floor. The doors finally swished open, and she swayed slightly. Silently Slade took her elbow and guided her to the door, then punched the doorbell.

A snarling William opened the door dressed in a three-piece suit, his sandy-blond hair combed back from his forehead and set with gel, his blue eyes like ice chips. Looking at him compared to Slade made her wonder why she'd been stupid enough to give him her virginity.

"Nina, what in the hell do you think you're doing?" William barked. "Didn't you understand my warning last night?"

"Warning?" Slade asked in a lethal tone.

Nina shifted. "William threatened to tell my coworkers at school that I'm crazy."

"Is that so?" Slade glared at William. "Well, I'm working for Nina now, Hood, and I don't like bullies."

A vein throbbed in William's forehead. "And I don't like smarmy P.I.'s nosing into my business."

A nasty grin slid onto Slade's face. "You don't, huh? Well, you'd better get used to it, because I'm just getting started." He shouldered his way past William into the foyer of the condo. "And no one, especially some skinny-assed lawyer, is going to stop me."

SLADE GROUND HIS TEETH in an attempt to rein in his temper. He couldn't tolerate any man who'd abandon his own child, and this man had rejected his before his baby had even been born.

To think that Hood would use his money, status and weight to intimidate Nina infuriated him.

If it were his own child and he were in Nina's situation, he'd move hell and high water to find out the truth, just as she was.

"Mister—"

"Blackburn," Slade cut in.

"Either leave or I'm going to call security."

"William, please," Nina interjected. "All we want is a few minutes."

William gave her a seething look. "There's nothing to talk about, Nina. We've been over this a thousand times."

"You never wanted to have a child, did you?" Slade asked.

William glared at him but drew a breath, adopting a professional mask that Slade was sure he used in court. Probably to free any lowlife slimeball who paid his salary.

And judging from the condo and the pricey modern furnishings, he either had a lot of clients or his fees were enormous.

Hood checked his Rolex. "Excuse me now, I have work to do."

Slade caught his arm. "First you're going to answer some questions."

Hood jerked free of Slade, his suit jacket crinkling as he squared his shoulders. Finally he gave a labored sigh. "Five minutes."

The temptation to hit the bastard was so strong, Slade rolled his hands into fists. "What makes you so sure that your baby died in the fire in Sanctuary?"

A cold look settled in Hood's eyes. "If you'd seen that explosion, the chaos, the debris...you'd know there's no way that anyone left inside survived." He paused. "And Nina and the sheriff certainly questioned everyone at the hospital."

"Maybe not," Slade said. "You're a lawyer. Kidnappings happen in hospitals all the time. Can you honestly say that it wasn't possible for someone to have carried your baby outside and disappeared with her?"

For the briefest of moments, Slade saw Hood's mind working, saw the hesitation in his eyes, a moment where he actually considered the possibility. But it quickly disappeared, and the uncaring façade returned, his skepticism firmly tucked in place.

"Even if it were possible, it didn't happen," Hood said. "According to the police, every other baby was accounted for. The unit exploded before the rescue workers could save Nina's child."

"She was your child, too," Slade pointed out.

Beside him, he felt Nina's wave of pain as if it had washed through him. But she didn't react. In fact, he admired the way she maintained her composure.

"Nina and I came to an agreement before the child was born," Hood said sharply.

Slade gave a sarcastic laugh. "You came to an agreement? You mean you acted like a spoiled, selfish prick and declared that you didn't want the child."

"I was only nineteen," Hood said defensively. "I had plans."

Nina folded her arms. "So did I. But that didn't mean that I could walk away from our baby."

"That's right, Nina. You're such a damn saint," Hood bit out. "You can't even let the child go when everyone has told you she's dead."

A brunette with wavy hair and catlike eyes appeared with a frown, her silk pantsuit flowing freely. "What's going on, honey?"

Hood jerked his head toward her. "Mitzi, we have

company," Hood said. "Nina and her new detective, Mr. Blackburn."

"God, Nina," the woman muttered. "Don't tell me you're nagging William again."

Hood wrapped his arm around Mitzi's shoulders. "Sorry, sweetheart, but she's still as crazy as ever."

"We were discussing the night of the fire in Sanctuary," Slade cut in. "You seem certain of the facts, Hood, but I spoke with Dr. Emery, the ob-gyn, and I think the case is worth investigating."

Slade removed the bagged doll from inside his jacket and held it up. "In fact, last night someone left this on Nina's doorstep."

Mitzi made a shocked sound, then clung to William's arm as if she feared Slade had stabbed the doll himself just for effect.

Slade directed his comment to Hood. "Where were you last night?"

Mitzi answered before Hood could respond. "He was with me. All night," she said with a suggestive smile.

Hood made a clicking sound with his teeth. "Blackburn, you poor, dumb sucker. Obviously Nina forgot to mention a few details about her past."

"William, don't," Nina said in a choked whisper.

"Don't what, Nina?" Hood scowled at her. "Tell him the truth, that you've pulled this same stunt before?"

Slade shot Hood an angry look, but something about the guilt in Nina's eyes warned him to tread slowly. He was here to investigate, find out the truth, whether or not Nina liked it.

Whether or not he did.

"What are you talking about?" Slade asked.

William's expression turned pitying. "Nina has a habit

of suckering people in with her sweet smile and big, sad eyes. But she's unstable. She has been for a long time."

"If you're referring to the fact that she had a breakdown after her baby went missing, then yes. I am aware of that."

Hood arched a brow. "So she explained the details of her psychosis?"

Guilt and worry slashed her face. "William, don't—"

The look Nina exchanged with Hood made apprehension knot Slade's belly. He'd insisted Nina be honest with him, but apparently she hadn't shared everything.

"After Nina lost the baby, she did things like this. She bought a rag doll like this one, then claimed that someone stuck a knife in its heart and left it on her doorstep."

Slade stood ramrod still, forcing himself not to react.

Hood continued, "She also said that she packed up the baby things and stored them in the attic, but then insisted she came home one night and found them scattered across her bedroom."

"I didn't scatter those baby things around," Nina argued. "They were packed away in my closet."

"That's not what the psychiatrist reported," William said, then turned back to Slade. "Nina also swore that someone put a CD of lullabies in her car and that sometimes she'd wake up at night and one would be playing but that she hadn't started it."

Nina started to speak, but Hood was on a roll and sneered down at her. "Oh, and did she tell you about the voices? She swears she hears her little girl singing to her at night. A *Mary Poppins* song, right, Nina?"

"Stop it!" Nina turned and ran from the condo, her sob echoing in the air behind her.

Slade didn't know what to believe. But he didn't like Hood and refused to let him bait him, so he gave him a steely look. "If I discover you had anything to do with your child's disappearance or those things happening to Nina, you'll pay." He jabbed a finger at Hood's chest. "And no amount of money will save you."

NINA SLAMMED THE SUV door, and leaned her head into her hands. This couldn't be happening again.

Yes, she heard the voices. Her daughter singing. But that was *real*.

Only everyone had made her doubt herself. And then all those creepy things had started happening…and she'd finally broken down.

Heat warmed her cheeks, and she suddenly felt nauseated. The sound of the driver's door opening rent the air, and Slade's masculine scent filled the close confines. This morning she'd felt as if she might have found an ally. Maybe even a friend.

But his anger permeated the tension-filled air as he climbed inside, and she found she'd lost that ally now.

God help her. She had to make him believe her. "Slade—"

He threw up a hand, silently ordering her not to speak. "I warned you yesterday when I took this case that you had to be honest with me."

"But—"

"Stop, Nina," Slade said in a harsh voice. "Don't lie to me now or ever again." He started the engine. "I'm going to talk to your father, and if I discover that you made up the story about this doll to get attention, we're finished."

CHAPTER SIX

HURT KNIFED THROUGH NINA, and she folded her arms and stared out the window as Slade drove toward Raleigh.

Her father would probably verify William's story, paint her as a sad, demented freak just as William had.

She should be used to people's reactions to her breakdown, but she didn't know if she'd ever totally become immune.

She had not stabbed the doll and put it on her porch the night before, just as she hadn't years ago. She also hadn't strewn baby paraphernalia all over the house or put those CDs in her car and house.

Not that she remembered anyway...

No. She wasn't going to doubt herself again. The doctors and therapists had almost convinced her that she was delusional with grief and stress and the effects of the antidepressants. But she wasn't taking antidepressants now, and she had recovered from the breakdown.

Not to mention that the person tormenting her had driven her over the edge.

And now the taunts were starting all over...

Because she'd hired a private investigator.

Couldn't Slade see that that meant someone didn't want her learning the truth?

She opened her mouth to argue, but quickly clamped it shut. Hadn't she learned from experience that protesting and trying to explain only made things worse? Made her sound more pathetic and desperate?

She hated to look pathetic in his eyes.

But how could she explain the voices she heard at night? The little girl's voice singing to her? The sense that she was singing so Nina would come for her...

The words to the song, her soft soprano voice, was like an angel's, the voice mesmerizing her just as the Pied Piper's flute had enthralled the children.

The silence became painful during the drive, Slade's withdrawal hurting more than she could imagine.

"Tell me about Mitzi," he finally said quietly.

Embarrassment heated her cheeks. Mitzi had married William...and made a fool of her.

She licked her dry lips and sucked up her pride. If she wanted his help, and she *did,* she had to be honest. Pride be damned.

"She was Miss Popular in high school and came from a prestigious family. Her father worked abroad so she traveled and studied in prep schools all over the world before they moved back to Raleigh her senior year."

"She seemed to be jealous of you," Slade commented.

Nina gave a sardonic little laugh. "Jealous? Why would she be jealous of me?"

"Because you slept with William and had his baby."

Nina chewed her bottom lip. "*Jealousy* isn't the word I'd use. She hated me."

Memories flooded her. "Mitzi was one of the *it* girls. Plastic, if you know what I mean. She served on every school committee, led the dance squad and was voted prom queen." She sighed. "All the boys wanted Mitzi."

"And Mitzi?"

"She wanted William." Nina picked at a piece of lint on her shirt. It was so long ago, it shouldn't still hurt. But she'd been young and foolish and naive.

"So you fought over him?"

Nina laughed. "Not really. In fact, William never showed any interest in me until after Mitzi broke up with him."

"*She* broke up with *him?*"

"They had some kind of stupid fight a week before prom, and so he asked me. I realize now he only wanted to get back at her."

She felt his eyes boring into her face, but she couldn't quite look at him. "It's really such a cliché. Shy girl goes to prom with the big guy on campus. Gets pregnant. He goes back to the girl he really loves."

Slade muttered an obscenity. "But Mitzi didn't take the pregnancy so well?"

She laughed again. It was either laugh or cry. And she would never cry again over Mitzi or William Hood. "No. She spread the word at school that I was a whore. That I'd thrown myself at William and promised him sex if he'd take me to the prom."

In spite of her resolve to overcome the bitterness, it resonated in her voice. "That's when my father moved me out of town."

Another dark, seething look passed over his face, settling into his deep brown eyes. Eyes that looked permanently angry at the world.

And now angry at her.

She stiffened her spine. She didn't give a damn if he was angry with her or not. She'd hired him to do a job.

And she'd put up with anything he threw at her, even

his ridicule, his pity, his disbelief, as long as he followed through.

Finding out the truth about Peyton was the only thing that mattered.

SLADE CONTEMPLATED WHAT he'd learned about Nina, William Hood and his wife, as they wound up the mile-long drive to Nina's father's estate.

Hood was a first-class bastard, his wife a major bitch.

But that didn't necessarily mean they were lying, just that they'd been young, selfish, immature and relieved to be free of an unwanted child.

He tried to put himself in their places, but empathy wasn't his style, not for spoiled rich kids whose priorities were majorly skewed.

And not when they were so callous toward an innocent baby.

Especially Hood, who'd shared the child's blood.

Slade surveyed Nash's house as he pulled in front of the circular drive. Pristine gardens, sculpted bushes, ornately carved molding and granite lion statues adorned the front of the mansion, a massive white antebellum reproduction set in the midst of ancient oaks and a pond complete with ducks, as well as a massive outdoor patio obviously designed for entertaining.

"Your father must be doing quite well."

"I suppose," Nina said in an oddly distant voice.

"You don't know?"

"He's in banking, finance, stocks. He did well in the past, but I haven't kept up with him in a few years."

He narrowed his eyes. "You don't see each other regularly?"

A sad look flickered in her eyes. "No. As a matter of fact, we haven't talked in…months."

Slade's opinion of the man slipped another notch. "Then he's going to be surprised to see us," he said.

Nina opened her car door and climbed out before he could reach it, but the shudder that coursed up her body confirmed that she dreaded this confrontation.

After the ordeal with Hood, he understood her anxiety.

He'd been rough on her in the car, as well. But dammit, he didn't want to be made a fool of or go on a wild chase.

Instincts urged him to pursue the case anyway, to find out the truth for Nina once and for all.

Then he could walk away with a clear conscience.

NINA WILLED HERSELF to be strong as they walked up the immaculate drive to the steps to her father's house. This place had never been her home.

Her home was the bungalow in Sanctuary where she'd hoped to raise her little girl.

Slade punched the doorbell, and she breathed deeply, desperately relying on the relaxation exercises she'd learned in therapy. But her palms were sweating, her heart racing, painful memories assaulting her like a knife digging into her heart.

Just like the knife in the doll's chest…

The door opened, and Miss Mosey, the housekeeper her father had kept for the past twelve years, looked shocked as she spotted Nina.

"Miss Nash, we…had no idea you were coming."

"I know, Miss Mosey," Nina said softly. "Is Father here?"

The woman's brows pinched together. Nina had once had affection for the older woman, and thought she might be an ally when she'd discovered her pregnancy, but her father's money had obviously meant more to her than Nina's feelings.

"I'm afraid he just left for the office. He had a luncheon at two and wanted to tie up some things there first."

"Thanks," Nina said. "We'll stop there then." She started to turn to leave, then paused and touched the woman's hand. One of her therapists had suggested that forgiveness would help her heal. "It's good to see you again. I hope you're doing well."

Tears suddenly glittered in the woman's eyes, and she surprised Nina by pulling her into a hug. "I hope you are, too, dear. You and your father should make peace. He misses you so much."

Nina's pulse stuttered, and she hugged the woman back then turned to leave, unable to speak.

By rote, she recited directions to her father's office, contemplating Miss Mosey's comment as Slade crossed traffic into town. Did her father really miss her? If so, why hadn't he tried to contact her?

Slade turned onto Glenwood Avenue, then located Nash's office, a two-story brick building in the heart of the downtown area. He parked in the adjacent parking lot, and they walked to the entrance in silence. Her father hated to be interrupted during business, and Nina considered turning around, but Slade took her arm as if he sensed her anxiety and they went inside the building.

A pretty red-haired receptionist wearing a short, black pencil skirt greeted them from the counter where she was pouring coffee. "Can I help you?"

"Yes, I'm Nina Nash. I'm here to see my father."

"Oh, you're Mr. Nash's daughter," the young woman said with a startled look. "I'm Rochelle. It's nice to meet you. I'll tell him you're here."

Nina wondered faintly if her father was sleeping with the young woman but dismissed the thought. She didn't really care about his personal life. He'd dated dozens of women since her mother's death, but never committed to anyone.

Nina watched Rochelle disappear up the steps with the coffee, her long legs stretching beneath the skirt. A minute later, she returned with a wary smile. "He says to go on up."

Slade placed his hand on the small of her back as she climbed the steps, but her stomach fluttered with nerves. Her father's diplomas, photos of business acquaintances and newspaper clippings about his deals lined the walls.

The door stood ajar, and Nina squared her shoulders, determined not to crumble in front of her father no matter how he reacted to her visit.

SLADE IMMEDIATELY SIZED up Mr. Nash from the edge of his office doorway. A compulsive, anal workaholic. His office was neat and orderly, dominated by a walnut desk and credenza with a stocked bar at one end. Dark leather furniture created a seating arrangement around a fireplace near the bar. Books on finance and business filled a bookshelf on the opposite wall. And Nash was dressed in a three-piece suit that probably cost more than Slade's monthly salary.

The man was lean and tall with light brown hair, an angular face and hands that had probably never touched dirt in his life. He looked cool and focused.

Except for the slight hint of emotion that flickered in his eyes the moment he saw Nina.

"Daddy?" Nina said softly.

"Nina." He hesitated, his voice cracking slightly. "This is a surprise."

"I know," she said, then glanced quickly at him. "Can we come in?"

"Of course." Nash gestured toward the seating area, and Slade followed Nina over to the love seat, where she sat down.

"Mr. Nash, my name is Slade Blackburn. I'm with Guardian Angel Investigations."

"I know who you are." Disdain edged Nash's voice, then he turned toward Nina and sympathy softened his expression. "Dr. Emery phoned to tell me you hired another private investigator, Nina."

Nina clasped her trembling hands in her lap. "Yes. I assume you read the papers and know that GAI discovered that the hospital fire and explosion weren't accidental."

Nash gestured to the bar in offering, but Slade shook his head, declining his silent offer of a drink. Still, Nash removed a bottle of water from a small stainless-steel refrigerator and pushed it into Nina's hands. "Yes, I heard the news. But I don't see what that has to do with you."

Nina stiffened but accepted the water bottle and set it on the table. "They uncovered new evidence, proving people were wrong about how the fire started. That means they might be able to find new evidence about Peyton."

"God, Nina." Nash scrubbed a hand over the back of his neck. "You have your teaching degree, a job now. I thought you were finally moving on."

"I've tried," Nina said. "But if there's a chance that the police missed something, I have to at least look into it."

Nash angled his head toward Slade. "I don't know how much my daughter shared with you, Mr. Blackburn, but she can't go through this again. The baby didn't survive, end of story. You're wasting your time and giving her false hope if you continue."

Slade chewed the inside of his cheek. "I've reviewed the details of the case, Mr. Nash. Considering the fact that the baby's body was never recovered, and the chaos that night, there is a possibility that someone could have kidnapped the baby." Slade removed the bagged doll and knife.

"And just last night someone left this for Nina. Doesn't it seem coincidental to you that someone would leave this on her porch only hours after she reopened the investigation?"

"Oh, hell." Nash gave Nina a worried look, and paced back to his desk. Frowning, he opened a drawer, removed a folder and walked back toward them. Then he shoved the file toward Slade.

"This is the report from the psychiatrist who treated Nina after she lost Peyton. Take a look at it and tell me if you really think there's a case here, or if Nina is just unable to accept the truth."

"Dad, you can't show him my medical records." Nina looked appalled. "They're private."

Nina's father stroked her shoulder. "I just don't want to see you put yourself through this kind of pain again." His voice dropped a decibel. "And I certainly don't want you to have another breakdown, Nina. I want to see you happy and building a new life."

Slade's hands tightened around the folder at the sincerity in Nash's voice. For a moment he debated looking at the file, but he'd vowed to find out the truth, and he'd told Nina she had to be completely honest with him.

So he flipped open the folder and skimmed the report. It corroborated Hood's story. According to the psychiatrist's notes, Nina had been in denial, depressed and delusional. The episode with the doll and the knife through its heart symbolized her guilt and grief over not saving her child, and the anguish in her own heart.

Slade's stomach knotted. Had he been a fool to believe her? Was Hood right—had he fallen for her big, anguished eyes because he wanted to be her hero?

A hero for someone because he'd failed time after time after time...

"I AM NOT DELUSIONAL," Nina said emphatically. "Yes, I was grieving, sad, even depressed but not delusional."

"Are you taking antidepressants again?" her father asked.

"No," Nina said. "I didn't want to take them years ago, and I don't intend to ever again." She jutted up her chin, forcing conviction into her voice. "I'm perfectly rational, and I did not stab that doll and put it on my porch. I heard a noise in the night, then got up and saw a shadow outside." Her voice grew stronger. "Don't you care that someone is tormenting me, Dad?"

"This is the way it all started." Her father gave Slade a disgruntled look, then lowered himself into the chair opposite her and pulled her hands into his. "Please go see the therapist again, Nina."

She cast a sideways look at Slade, but his dark eyes probed hers as if she were a bug he was trying to dissect.

Anger fueled her temper. She could handle whatever she discovered about her daughter, but she didn't know if she could tolerate the pitying or condescending looks again. "I should have known that you wouldn't help me, that you wouldn't believe me. You don't want anything to mess up your perfect world, do you, Dad?" She jerked her hands away and stood. "You didn't want a pregnant daughter, or an illegitimate child, and you certainly wouldn't have wanted a preemie who might have been handicapped."

"That's enough, Nina." Her father's eyes glittered with rage. "I love you. Everything I've ever done has been with your best interests in mind."

Nina gripped her shoulder bag, and faced her father. "If you wanted what was best for me, you'd believe me. You would have helped me search for my baby instead of abandoning me and making me feel like I was crazy."

Grief swelled inside her at the realization that she and her father would never get along. Never be close.

She had disappointed him.

But he had disappointed her, too.

He was the one person she'd thought would have had faith in her. But he hadn't trusted in her when she'd needed him most.

She spun around and walked out of the office, knowing she'd never be back.

REBECCA DANGLED HER FEET below the swing, pumping her legs hard to make the swing move back and forth. She was too short to touch the ground, and her legs were weak so it took a bunch of tries, but finally the swing moved.

She didn't care if the kids laughed at her.

She would learn to pump herself even if they teased her until school was out. When her mommy came to get her, she was going to show her everything she'd learned.

A black car drove by the fence near the parking lot, and someone rolled down the window. The sun nearly blinded her, and she scrunched her nose, her glasses slipping down.

But someone in the car pushed a camera out the window and began to snap pictures.

Her stomach spasmed. Why were strangers watching the school? She'd heard other foster kids talk about the news and how kids went missing every day.

That men stole them and did mean things to them, and the kids never came back.

She jumped from the swing to go tell the teacher, but she stumbled again and her knee hit the ground. A big boy with a ball cap on laughed, and she frowned at him as she tried to get up.

Then the flash of the camera blinded her once more. When she finally could see again, the boy had run off and she was alone on the playground.

Alone except for the man in the car watching her... Was he one of the bad men the other fosters talked about?

CHAPTER SEVEN

QUESTIONS AND DOUBTS assailed Slade as they left Raleigh and headed back toward Sanctuary. Nash had seemed sincere in his concern for Nina.

But his condescending attitude had irritated the hell out of him.

Even though Nina had put on a brave face, hurt had laced her voice when she'd stood up to her father.

If anyone should have believed her, her own father should have. So why hadn't he?

Nina might be slightly obsessed over finding the truth about her daughter, but she didn't seem irrational or delusional. She also didn't appear to be taking drugs as her father had suggested.

And dammit, he understood her single-minded focus and the reason she'd asked questions. Obsession had driven him to keep looking for his sister until he'd located her. And although he hadn't liked the outcome, at least he had closure. And his sister had received a decent burial.

Nina deserved to have closure, too.

Considering the fact that Nina was the only one who'd wanted the child, that left plenty of suspects. All who had means, motive and opportunity.

Her father. William Hood. Hood's mother.

Any one of them could have paid someone to kidnap the baby.

But they couldn't have predicted that the fire would break out the night Nina had delivered. Still, Nina's father and Hood might have come to the hospital when the baby was born, and jumped on the opportunity.

He frowned and maneuvered around traffic. And Hood's wife, Mitzi, topped his suspect list. Mitzi was upset about Nina's pregnancy. What if she'd been afraid William would change his mind after the baby was born and decide he wanted Nina and his daughter in his life?

Would she have been desperate enough to steal the baby?

Hood's mother was an even bigger question mark in his mind. She'd tried to bribe Nina to have an abortion. Had she kidnapped the baby so she wouldn't have to live with the stigma of an illegitimate child in the family? Or maybe she'd been worried that Nina might demand money. The baby would have had legal rights to the Hood fortune....

NINA STARED AT THE passing scenery, desperately trying to wrestle control over her ping-ponging emotions. She would not behave like the delusional psychotic her father and William had described.

"Nina?

She braced herself for Slade to announce he was dropping the case. "What?"

Slade slanted her a sideways look as he changed lanes. "Did your father come to the hospital when the baby was born?"

Fresh pain squeezed her heart. "The doctor called him. He was on his way when I went in to have the C-section."

"Did he see the baby?"

Emotions threatened to choke her as she remembered

the harrowing birth. "No." She rubbed her temple in thought. "He didn't arrive until later, after the fire had broken out."

Slade twisted his mouth sideways. "What about Hood or any of his family members? Did they come to the hospital?"

She heaved a breath. "It may sound crazy after the way William treated me, but I did call him when I went into labor. I thought he had a right to know that his daughter was about to be born, that he might change his mind when he saw her."

A muscle ticked in his jaw. "But he didn't?"

"No. He ordered me to sign the papers and give her away, and not to ever bother him again."

"Cold son of a bitch," Slade muttered.

His comment eased some of the tension knotting her shoulders. "I remember thinking that myself. How could anyone be so unfeeling about their own child?"

A heartbeat of silence passed between them. "I don't know either," he said in a gruff voice. "But that apathy gives him motive."

"Does that mean that you're not dropping the investigation?"

The air vibrated with uncertainty and questions. "No, I'm not dropping it," he said. "I may not find the answers you want, but I am a man of my word, and I will get you answers."

SLADE REQUIRED VERY little sleep, but food was a different story. He pulled into the diner in town for a late lunch before heading to the hospital. He wanted to question the nurse on duty the night Nina had given birth.

It was way past the lunch hour, and the diner was nearly deserted, so they slid into a booth in the back.

Slade ordered the deluxe burger and fries, and Nina a bowl of homemade soup. But she barely touched it.

"Have you had contact with William over the years?" he asked as he bit into his burger.

She sipped her tea. "Not really. I heard things through the gossip vine in town. About his graduation from law school, when he took over his Dad's practice. And I saw a write-up in the paper about his country-club wedding. Apparently it made the society page."

Climbing the social ladder seemed to be a high priority to the Hoods. But at what cost?

"You were in love with William?"

She shook her head and leaned her head on her hand, looking exhausted.

"No. I was young, Slade. Trying to fit in. Shy. And I was trying to impress my father."

"You went out with William to impress your father?"

A sarcastic laugh escaped her. "I realize that sounds ridiculous. But I was seventeen with no mother. More than anything I wanted my father to be proud. And the Hoods were the type of prestigious family he wanted me to end up with." She offered a self-deprecating smile. "So I was flattered when he asked me to prom. Then later…"

"Later what?"

"Later, I saw how selfish and conceited he was, and I didn't even like him, much less love him."

Slade ordered himself to resist the temptation to cover her hand with his, to soothe her distress.

But he lost the battle and did just as his heart commanded. Her hand felt small and cold and in need of a big one to cling to, and something twitched inside him urging him to be that someone. That everyone else in her life had let her down.

You might, too, a voice inside his head taunted.

Her fingers curled beneath the weight of his hand as if grasping on, and panic set in. He couldn't make promises to a vulnerable woman like her.

Not when he knew he'd walk away in the end.

He was too damn broken to be any good to anyone long-term.

She deserved someone better. A savior who'd stick around.

So he pulled his hand away and finished his burger in silence, determined to tie up the case so he didn't have to be tortured by her big, sad eyes, and by things he could never have or give her.

His cell phone buzzed as he was paying the bill, and he checked the number, saw it was GAI and connected the call. "Blackburn speaking."

"Slade, it's Amanda Peterson from GAI."

"Yeah?"

"Gage managed to get a copy of all the forensics reports from the hospital fire, including copies of the bodies found after the fire."

Slade's gut tightened. "And?"

"It was a mess," she said. "I can see why forensics and the cops had trouble sorting out the truth. Bodies were dismembered, literally blown apart. The chemicals ate away skin, bone and tissue, making identities impossible. The small town just didn't have the manpower at the time to handle such a large investigation, and the feds that came in wrote it off as a tragic accident and told families they had to accept the loss."

Slade saw Nina watching and adopted a poker face. "So what can you tell me?"

"They did take photographs of the bones and recorded the unidentified ones. Unfortunately hospital records were also destroyed that night, so any records of Peyton Nash, including her footprints and handprints, were lost in the fire."

"Damn."

A moment of silence, then Amanda continued. "But there were a couple of infant bones in the mix. I'm trying to see if they belong to Peyton now, but getting the results may take time."

"How about patient files of other births, infants in the hospital for other procedures, tests or treatments that night?"

"Gage already put Benjamin Camp on it."

Slade's admiration for McDermont rose. "Thanks. I'll fish around at the hospital. Keep me posted."

She agreed and he snapped his phone closed. Nina was watching with anticipation.

"What?"

"I told you I wouldn't mince words," Slade begun.

Her face paled slightly. "All right."

"The forensics expert at GAI is studying copies of the forensics reports. I'm sorry to say, but there were infant bones in the mix."

Her breath hitched out. "Did they identify them?"

"No, they're working on that now. But I want to question Dr. Emery again. According to him, there weren't any babies other than Peyton lost that night."

Tears glittered in her eyes before she blinked them away. "Then he lied," she said with a strength to her voice that surprised him.

"Gage is going to request copies of hospital records from that night, but most were destroyed in the fire."

"Didn't they have some kind of back-up system?" Nina asked.

"Our computer guy is working on that angle." Slade

reached for the bill. "Let's go talk to the nurse on duty that night and find out what she remembers."

THE IMPLICATIONS THAT there had been an infant's bones in the fire made Nina's stomach protest, and for a moment she'd thought she might lose the lunch she'd barely touched.

But she swallowed hard to stem the nausea. At least Slade hadn't given up. She'd asked for answers and she was grateful he was being honest with her, not treating her as if she were a crazy woman who might flip out if he didn't walk on eggshells around her.

The wind ruffled her hair as they entered the hospital and rode the elevator to the maternity floor. Nurses bustled up and down the halls, orderlies were picking up food trays, a woman in a robe strolled toward the nursery and voices echoed from the closest room nearby just as an older couple, probably grandparents, rushed down the hallway carrying flowers and a blue stuffed teddy bear.

Nina's experience had been so different, yet she had to smile at the thought of the happy couple and grandparents celebrating a new life.

"Excuse me," Slade said to a curly-haired nurse wearing pink scrubs at the nurses' station. "Is Carrie Poole here?"

The woman nodded. "She's in the NICU."

"Can you ask her if she can speak with us?" Slade asked.

The woman glanced at Nina with a frown. "Regarding what?"

Nina cleared her throat. "I just want to ask her a couple of questions. She took care of my baby when I was here a long time ago."

"You're Nina Nash, aren't you?" the woman asked.

Nina stiffened. "Yes."

"Dr. Emery said you hired a private investigator and were asking questions." A wariness tinged her eyes. "I wasn't here back then, but I've heard how horrible it was. I can't imagine…"

"I'm not here to cause trouble for the staff, or blame anyone for that night," Nina said. "In fact Carrie was so sweet to me, that I just want to talk to her, that's all. Please."

The woman's expression softened. "All right, sugar. I'll let her know."

She rose from the desk, exited on the opposite side and walked down the hallway.

Voices sounded, and she glanced to the left and saw a new mother cradling her baby as the nurse pushed her in a wheelchair toward the elevator. The father walked behind, carrying a bouquet of balloons and pink roses. As they reached the elevator, he leaned over and kissed his wife and baby girl. Tears stung Nina's eyes.

Slade's hand stroked her shoulder as if he understood how the scene affected her. A minute later, the nurse returned and pointed them to a waiting room. The bubbly red-haired nurse Nina remembered popped into the room a second later, and Nina made the introductions.

"I don't know if you remember me or not," Nina began.

"Of course I do." Carrie sat down and took her hands in hers. "I've thought about you a lot over the years. I'm sorry for all you've been through."

Her kindness touched Nina. "You were so sweet to me and my baby," Nina said. "I want to thank you for that."

Carrie smiled. "I can still see her little face, all scrunched up and fussing. She was a real fighter. I…

thought she had a good chance." Carrie's voice cracked. "And then everything went wrong."

"Can you tell us exactly what you remember about that night?" Slade said.

She bit her lip as she looked at him, then nodded. "I wasn't in the nursery when the fire broke out. I was down the hall with another patient. I helped them to get out, then rushed back to help clear the babies. Two other nurses from the regular unit had infants in their arms, and rescue workers were rushing toward them to help. I ran to the NICU. There were only two babies in there that night, and Jane had the little boy. I went to get Peyton, but she wasn't in the bassinet."

"No one saw anyone take her?"

Carrie shook her head. "Dr. Emery had ordered tests for the baby, and I assumed that someone had taken her to another wing to administer them."

"Carrie, I know it's been a long time," Slade said. "But do you remember anyone odd hanging around the nursery, someone who looked out of place?"

She fidgeted with the pocket of her scrubs jacket. "No, not that I can think of."

Slade hesitated. "How about other births that might have gone wrong that night or week? Maybe someone who had a miscarriage?"

Carrie drew her shoulders back. "That information is restricted for the patient's privacy."

"Please," Nina said. "If there's a chance another patient kidnapped my baby, you have to help me."

Her eyes flickered sideways nervously. "Well, there was one woman… She gave birth to a stillborn that afternoon. A baby boy."

Nina's chest constricted. "Do you remember her name?"

Carrie chewed her bottom lip. "I'm really not supposed to divulge that information. I could get fired." She fidgeted. "Besides, the poor woman suffered a terrible tragedy herself."

"I understand," Nina said. "What happened to the baby?"

"I don't know. He was probably taken for an autopsy."

"The woman's name?" Slade pressed.

"Gwen Waldorp," Carrie said. "I think she moved to Kings Mountain." Carrie glanced at her watch. "If that's all, I need to get back to work."

"One more question," Slade asked. "Do you know William Hood and his family?"

Carrie nodded. "I've seen their pictures in the newspaper."

"Were either William or his mother at the hospital the night Peyton was born?"

She backed away, fidgeting with her hair again. "I don't remember seeing them."

"How about William's wife? Her name is Mitzi."

"I told you I don't remember. It was madness here, everyone in a panic." She tapped her watch. "Now I really have to get back to work." Her ponytail swung behind her as she turned and rushed down the hall.

"What do you think?" Nina asked.

Slade frowned. "I think that nurse knows something she's not telling us." He gestured toward the elevator.

"That bone your forensics person found, it could have belonged to the stillborn," Nina suggested.

He gave a clipped nod. "I'm going to check out this Waldorp woman and have a chat with William's mother."

Nina's thoughts raced as they took the elevator to the main floor, and Slade drove back to her house. Compassion for the woman who'd given birth to the stillborn baby squeezed her heart. Could she have been distraught enough to have kidnapped Peyton?

And William's mother…she'd been adamant that she should get rid of her baby. Could she have stolen her or hired someone else to and arranged for an adoption?

"Does Mrs. Hood live in Winston-Salem, too?"

Nina nodded.

"I'll question her tomorrow, but first I want to do some background work. I'm going to take that doll to the lab." Slade maneuvered around traffic through town, flipping on his windshield wipers as a light rain began to fall. "I'll also see if I can get an address for the Waldorp woman. I'll call you if I find anything."

Shadows flickered along the sidewalk, night setting in, the rain clouds adding to the gray fog over her house as he pulled into her drive.

Nina grasped on to hope as she climbed out and hurried up to her door. She went inside, flipped on the lights, then went upstairs to shower. A few minutes later, she dried off and pulled on a loose warm-up suit.

But the moment she went downstairs, the hair on the back of her neck stood on end, and panic hit her.

The CD of lullabies she'd bought for Peyton was playing.

And the baby blanket she'd crocheted and stored in the blanket chest in the attic was wrapped around another rag doll that had been stabbed just like the first.

CHAPTER EIGHT

SLADE STOPPED BY GAI and found Amanda Peterson still poring over forensics files. Benjamin Camp poked his head in when he saw Slade, and he brought them both up to speed on what he'd learned so far.

"You said a baby was stillborn that same day," Amanda said. "I'll find out if this bone could have belonged to that child instead of the Nash baby."

"Thanks," Slade said. "I'm sure it won't be easy."

Amanda grinned. "That's what I do," she said confidently. "Besides, if I can find out where the bone was located, that might help. And you said the stillborn was a baby boy?"

Slade nodded. "That will narrow things down. I'll make a phone call to the medical examiner and find out the names of any forensic specialists brought in to study the bones. If they had a forensic anthropologist working with them, we should get some answers."

"I've been trying to dig up records on all the employees who worked at the hospital at the time," Benjamin said. "If the Hoods or Mr. Nash decided to arrange for an adoption, they might have hired someone to kidnap the baby."

"That's definitely a possibility." Slade heaved a breath. "Look for anyone with a shady past, a record, financial problems, anything that throws up a red flag." He remembered Carrie's nervous fidgeting. "Be sure to check out a nurse named Carrie Poole. She was on duty that night in the NICU."

"What's your next step?" Amanda asked.

"I'm going to investigate the Hoods, and William's wife, Mitzi. She dated William before Nina and was pissed when Nina turned up pregnant with his child."

"Sounds like motive to me," Benjamin muttered.

Slade sighed. "Yeah, although the nurse didn't remember seeing William or Mitzi at the hospital that night."

"You said yourself it was total chaos," Amanda commented. "With all the panic and rescue workers scrambling about, anyone could have slipped through and no one would have noticed."

"Something else is bugging me," Slade said. He removed the doll and showed it to them, then explained about the psychiatrist's report.

"Do you think she's unstable, that she put it there herself?" Benjamin asked.

Slade shifted on the balls of his feet. "No. At least she doesn't appear to be delusional." He decided to run with a theory. "But what if someone wanted everyone to think she was?"

Amanda drummed her fingers on the desk. "Then putting things in her apartment, like the lullaby CD and doll, that would remind her of her loss would do the trick."

Slade ran a hand over the back of his neck. It was devious, effective and cruel.

And he intended to find the son of a bitch who'd tormented her and make him suffer.

INSTINCTIVELY NINA REACHED inside her purse for her cell phone. She had to call Slade.

But after her father's comment and seeing the psychiatrist's report, she was afraid Slade wouldn't believe her.

The windowpane rattled upstairs, the floor creaking, and pure panic seized her.

What if the person who'd put the blanket on the rocker and started the CD was still inside?

The rain pounded harder, beating the roof, and suddenly the lights flickered off. Nina froze, listening, waiting.

But common sense kicked in, and she slowly slipped into the kitchen, pausing to listen for an intruder. The wind whistled through the eaves, the rain intensifying, and she eased open the door to the garage, scanning the darkness. A streak of lightning illuminated the interior, then suddenly a shadow moved across the window.

Terror streaked through her, and she ran to her car, jumped inside and locked the doors. Her hands shook as she dug her phone from her purse and tried to punch Slade's number. But she was trembling so badly she dropped the phone. She glanced at the window and saw a hand scraping across the fog-coated pane as if the man was reaching for her.

She screamed, bent to snap up the phone again then inhaled a deep breath to calm her nerves. She was locked in the car. The man was outside.

She was safe.

Finally she managed to punch in Slade's number. Again, she thought she saw the silhouette of the man race across the window, and her lungs squeezed, begging for air. The phone rang once, twice, then Slade's husky voice echoed over the line.

She clenched the phone close to her mouth. "Slade, someone was in my house," she whispered. "They're outside now."

"Where are you?"

"The garage." She scanned the window again. "In my car."

"I'll be right there."

The line went dead, and she clawed inside her purse and found her mace, bracing herself in case the man attacked.

SLADE SLAMMED ON his horn, yelling at the cars to get out of the way. He wished to hell he had a siren to make the traffic move faster.

Nina might be in danger. He had to get to her, find out who was at her house.

Rainwater spewed from his tires, and he ground gears as he rounded a curve and sped onto the street leading to her house. As he neared the cul-de-sac, he searched the street and surrounding property.

His headlights flickered across the lawn, and he spotted a dog trotting by the mailbox. Darkness shrouded Nina's house inside and out, sending alarm bells clanging in his head.

The rest of the neighborhood had lights.

Slowing, he pulled to the side and parked along the street, removed his weapon and crept toward her drive, glancing left and right in search of the intruder. The wind was blowing, tree branches swaying beneath the force, but the rain began to die down, turning to a drizzle.

His boots crunched wet leaves and twigs that had blown down in the storm as he inched forward. Moving slowly, instincts alert, he checked the front of the house. A streak of lightning zigzagged across the lawn, allowing him to see that no windows had been broken.

The intruder could have gotten in around back.

Slipping sideways, he padded around the outside of

the house to the backyard. Woods backed up to the property, trees providing cover for someone who might have been inside and escaped.

He scanned the distance, but it was too dark to see into the trees. A twig snapping to the left made him jerk his head sideways, and a shadow moved. He raised his gun to fire, but a dog suddenly ran past, and he cursed. Dammit, he could have shot the animal....

Still tense, he made his way around the house, passing in front of the windows in the garage. Nina's car was parked inside, but the interior was dark and he couldn't see if she was still there.

Knowing he'd spook her if he knocked, he removed his phone and called her number.

She answered on the first ring. "Slade?"

"I'm outside. It's clear out here. Open the garage door and I'll search the house."

"I can't. It's electric," Nina said.

"There should be a button to switch it to manual."

"Yes," Nina said. "Let me find it."

A minute later, the garage door slid upward. Nina looked pale and shaken, and she was clenching a vial of mace in her trembling hands.

At least she'd had something to protect herself.

"You didn't find him?" she whispered.

"The only thing I saw was a dog."

"It wasn't a dog, Slade," Nina cried. "It was a man. I saw his hand on the window."

"How did you know he'd been inside?"

Pain flickered in her eyes. "He left me another present."

A curse rolled from his lips. "Stay here and let me make sure he's not still in the house."

She nodded, and he urged her inside the car again,

then waited until he heard the lock click into place. Then he slipped inside the house to see what the bastard had left this time.

NINA RAKED HER fingernails up and down her arms, her nerves on edge as she waited for Slade to search the house. If the person who'd broken in and left that doll intended to scare her off, he was wrong.

She was stronger than she'd been eight years ago. And the fact that someone was tormenting her only made her believe that she was right about her daughter. That someone was scared she might discover the truth.

Because that person knew where her daughter was.

She glanced back and forth between the windows and door to the inside, her breath hitching when the door squeaked open. It was so dark, the only thing she could make out was the outline of a man's big body. Then the lights suddenly flickered on, and she recognized Slade.

He looked big and feral, his face chiseled into a hard mask. She flung open the car door, jumped out and hurried toward him.

He jammed his gun inside his jacket pocket and gripped her by the arms. "It's clear. The main breaker had been flipped. That's why the lights went out."

She nodded numbly, and allowed him to guide her into the kitchen, then into the den. Her gaze flew to the rocking chair and the doll wrapped in the baby blanket.

The lullaby CD was still playing, taunting her.

Slade clenched his jaw, then walked over and switched off the CD. "I'm going to send it to the lab although I doubt we'll get anything. Whoever did this probably wore gloves, but I'm still going to dust for prints."

Nina stared up at him, her heart racing. "Then you believe me? That I didn't put that creepy doll in the rocker or make up the intruder?"

His gaze met hers, emotions flickering in his brown eyes. Eyes that could dissect a person in seconds, eyes that could look cold and intimidating. Eyes that said he'd seen too much death and violence in his life.

She thought he wasn't going to answer, then he cleared his throat. "Yes, Nina, I believe you."

His gruffly spoken words made her heart twinge, and suddenly tears filled her eyes. She'd been alone so long, had faced scorn and animosity and pity. She knew how to handle those.

She didn't know how to handle having someone believe in her again.

"God, Nina…" A groan ripped from his throat, then he pulled her in his arms and pressed her head to his chest.

Nina collapsed against him, savoring the feel of his strong arms embracing her. His heart thudded beneath her ear, his chest rose and fell with a labored breath and he gently stroked her hair. His touch felt so intimate that she clung to him, a flutter of arousal tickling her stomach.

Her breathing became raspy, her breasts tingled and she had the insane urge to press a kiss to his chest.

But that would be foolish. Just because he was being nice didn't mean he was attracted to her, or that he wanted her. He was simply being human, compassionate.

And she couldn't allow herself to lean on him or become dependent. She'd learned long ago that men couldn't be counted on or trusted.

SLADE'S PULSE RACED. He shouldn't have pulled Nina up against him. It had been too damn long since he'd held a woman. Since he'd been with one.

Since he'd even wanted to.

But Nina had been trembling and afraid, and he'd seen the relief in her eyes that finally someone believed her story, and he couldn't resist.

Oh, hell... It was more than that.

She'd fought against all odds to find out what happened to her baby girl. How could he not admire her dedication and determination?

And now...one touch wasn't enough. Nina felt so small and sweet and precious in his arms that his body hardened, need ripping through him.

He traced his hand down her hair, then along her cheek. Her skin felt so soft that he wanted to put his lips where his fingers had just touched.

She tensed slightly as if to pull away, and he tilted her chin up with his thumb.

"I promise you I'll find out who's doing this," he said in a deep voice.

She nodded, her lower lip quivering. He traced his finger over her mouth, and her breath hitched, desire flaring in her eyes. "Slade..."

Her raspy sigh was his undoing.

He groaned, then lowered his head, angled his mouth and closed his lips over hers.

CHAPTER NINE

SLADE TRACED HIS TONGUE along the seam of Nina's lips, urging her to open for him, and she complied. Her fingers tiptoed up his arm, and she threaded them in his hair, urging him closer, and another groan ripped from his gut.

Aching with the need to have her, he deepened the kiss, savoring the scent of her sweet body as she moved against him. Her lips tasted like berries and hunger, her kiss so erotic that flames of desire shot through him.

She moaned softly, her breasts brushing his chest in an erotic tease, and his hands slid downward to pull her hips deeper into the V between his thighs. He sucked her tongue into his mouth, greedy for more, and she trailed her hands down his arms to his back again, then slid one over his hip.

He wanted her to move that hand lower.

Then she pressed her lips over the scar on his cheek, and something moved inside him.

"What happened?" she whispered.

The images of his dying men flashed in his head. "Iraq."

"I'm sorry," she said, then traced her finger over the puckered skin.

Dammit. What the hell was he doing?

He tore himself away from her, well aware that they

were both breathing heavily, on the verge of doing something each of them would regret.

"This is insane," he said, then forced himself to look away from the stormy heat in her eyes. If he didn't, he'd haul her back into his arms and this time he wouldn't stop. He'd carry her up the stairs, throw her down on the bed and make love to her until neither one of them could remember their names.

"Why is it insane?" Nina asked in such a sultry voice that he had to close his eyes to regain control.

"It just is."

"Why?" she asked again, this time hurt lacing her tone. "Because you think I'm unstable?"

God, he couldn't let her think that. "No. Because I'm working for you. This is a job, Nina. It can't be anything more."

Disappointment darkened her eyes, but he steeled himself and shut down.

He couldn't allow himself to care. Couldn't give her false promises or the impression that he'd stick around, that he was any kind of family man.

He didn't deserve a family, not after all the people he'd failed.

NINA SWALLOWED BACK her hurt. Slade was right.

They were working together, and she'd been frightened and had forgotten her senses for a moment.

It couldn't happen again.

Still, need and desire heated her blood, and she wished for once that she could feel something besides anguish and worry and the never-ending pit of emptiness inside her.

That she could feel loved.

But loving was dangerous. And the only person she

had room for in her heart was Peyton. If—no *when*—she found her, her daughter would need all of her attention and time.

But what if she's happy with a loving family? Can you tear her away from a good home?

Her chest clenched, but she pushed away the thoughts. She'd face that decision if it came down to it.

But the sound of Peyton's little voice taunted her. She wouldn't be able to hear that voice if Peyton wasn't calling out to her....

"Where did the baby blanket come from?" Slade asked, jarring her back to the present.

"I crocheted it for Peyton before she was born," Nina said. "But I packed it away in the storage closet in the guest room. That's where I stored all the baby things."

He narrowed his eyes. "So the intruder was in that room, and dug through your closet. I'll look for prints in there, too."

She nodded, then shivered at the thought of someone pawing through her precious baby items.

"Was there something special about that blanket?" Slade asked.

Nina pressed a hand to her mouth. "I was going to bring Peyton home in it."

A troubled look passed across his face. "Who knew about it?"

Nina frowned, trying to think back. "No one. At least I don't think anyone did. I made it when I lived alone here in Sanctuary."

"How about the CD?"

"One of the nurses who taught the prenatal classes gave each of the women a copy."

"What was the nurse's name?"

"Charlie," Nina said. "Why?"

"I'm just looking for a connection between the items and the person who broke in. For some significance."

Nina gave a small laugh. "Well, the psychiatrist said I played the CDs to soothe my grief, and the blanket to wrap my lost child in my love."

He slanted her an odd look. "I'm not sure I buy into that psychobabble."

"Thank you," she said softly. "That's the nicest thing anyone has said to me in years."

Her gaze locked with his, hope bubbling in her chest.

Hope and desire so strong that it scared her to death.

FOR A MOMENT, desire flickered in Nina's eyes again, and Slade was tempted to pull her into his arms once more.

But his body still burned with need from her earlier touch, and his willpower couldn't tolerate the temptation. So he took a step back. "We should report this break-in to the sheriff."

"No." Panic tinged her voice. "I did that years ago, and look where it got me. Skepticism from everyone I talked to."

Slade hesitated. "All right. Let me retrieve the kit in my car and look for prints. I also want to figure out how the bastard got in here. And, Nina?"

"Yes?"

"Look around upstairs. Make sure nothing is missing."

She folded and unfolded her hands, her face strained. Looking at the baby items had to dredge up bad memories.

Which was exactly what her tormentor intended.

But she squared her shoulders and disappeared up the stairs. He strode out to his car and retrieved the crime kit

GAI supplied. He'd take prints and if he found other evidence, he'd collect everything and send it all to the lab.

He grabbed a flashlight, and examined the front door, windows and back door and discovered that one of the locks on the window in the laundry room was broken. The intruder could easily have crawled in through the window.

Running the flashlight across the ground, he searched for footprints, but the rain had washed away any that might have been made earlier, and he didn't find any stray hairs or clothing fibers. Damn.

Next, he dusted the breaker box for prints, and found an index fingerprint. But it looked too small to be a man's. Probably Nina's. Still, he lifted it for comparison. He dusted the window in the laundry room from the outside, then inside, but again found nothing.

This guy was obviously smart enough to cover his tracks. After all, he'd done the same thing to Nina years ago.

It could be a woman, he reminded himself.

Or a hired crony.

Wiping perspiration from his forehead, he strode up the steps to the second floor and found Nina staring at a tiny pair of pink booties and a dress. God…

"Are you all right?"

"I'm fine," she said in a soft whisper. "I don't see anything missing."

A bittersweet look filled her eyes as she placed the dress back inside a plastic storage bin, and closed it. He dusted the closet door for prints, then the bin. Only one set, which he assumed belonged to Nina.

"Did you find anything outside?" she asked.

"The lock on the window in your laundry room is broken. The intruder must have climbed through it."

Nina nodded. "I didn't realize. I'll go fix it now."

He caught her arm as she stood and stopped her before she could go down the steps. "No, you look exhausted. Go lie down. I'll fix the window and stay on the couch tonight."

Nina rubbed her forehead. "You don't have to do that, Slade."

"Yes, I do," he said. "This guy might come back."

A shudder coursed through her, and he hated himself for scaring her.

"Thank you," she said softly.

"Stop thanking me," he muttered. "I'm just doing my job."

She shifted, her mouth tightening. "Right." Then she rushed into her own room and shut the door. For a moment, he stood rooted to the spot. The temptation to go inside with her taunted him.

What would she do if he knocked and asked to join her? Would she let him hold her? Kiss her? Make love to her?

Damn. This case was starting to feel like more than just a job. He didn't want to see her hurt anymore. And seeing that tiny little dress made him want to bring her child home to her.

But he couldn't get physically involved with her any more than he could emotionally. That would distract him from the case. And knowing that an intruder had broken in and might return meant he had to stay sharp and focused.

He took the steps two at a time, found a tool kit in the garage and repaired the broken lock. Then he retrieved his computer from his SUV, and booted it up at her kitchen table.

He'd set up watch for the night. And if the intruder

came back, he'd catch the son of a bitch and make him sorry for tormenting Nina.

NINA WRESTLED WITH SLEEP, the images of the doll wrapped in Peyton's baby blanket haunting her.

She pulled the covers to her chin, hating the silence. But knowing Slade was downstairs made her feel safer.

Don't get used to it, she reminded herself. *When you find your daughter, he'll leave and you'll be alone again.*

No, she wouldn't. She'd have her little girl, and that would be enough.

With that thought on her mind, she finally fell asleep and dreamed that she had Peyton back, and that she'd taken her to the zoo. Peyton's blond curls bounced around her face as she giggled at the chimpanzees squawking and jumping up and down and chomping on bananas.

The lions' roar frightened her, and she scrunched close to Nina, and Nina smoothed her hair down and hugged her. Then a crowd gathered by the giraffes and they walked over to join them.

Suddenly Slade appeared, the sunlight gleaming off his strong jaw and rugged body. He smiled at her, then swung Peyton up onto his shoulders so she could see over the crowd.

Peyton clapped her hands and shrieked with glee. "I'm almost as tall as the giraffes," Peyton said. "Lift me higher, Daddy, and I can eat from the treetops."

Slade chuckled and pulled Nina next to him, and a warmth enveloped her. She loved her husband and her daughter and finally had the family she'd always wanted.

Then suddenly a dark cloud fell over the crowd, and she looked up and Peyton and Slade were gone. She cried out their names, frantically searching, but she'd lost them....

No, she heard Peyton singing again.

She jerked awake, the sound of her daughter's voice echoing through the room and sending a blinding pain through her chest.

Her breathing was ragged, and she crawled from the bed, walked to the window and looked up at the moon. "I'm going to find you, baby," Nina whispered. "I promise. I'll find you and bring you home and one day we'll take that trip to the zoo."

Only Slade wouldn't be around. Peyton wouldn't have a daddy.

But she would make up for it by loving her enough for two parents.

SLADE LOOKED UP the Hood family and found numerous articles on William's father's law practice, his tragic death from cancer, and articles featuring William's graduation from law school, the honors he'd received and the cases he'd handled.

Apparently, William was a cutthroat lawyer who handled high-finance and tax cases and had made a fortune. Photographs of his society wedding to Mitzi Raynor, the daughter of a prominent judge, highlighted the young couple's budding social life.

Another photo depicted the celebration of Mrs. Hood's fiftieth birthday celebration a few months before. Slade studied the brassy-haired woman in her perfect outfit with her perfect smile, perfect face and perfect family.

Beneath that perfect veneer, beat the heart of an ugly barracuda.

The woman had tried to bribe Nina to abort her own grandchild, then urged her to give the baby up for adoption. Was she cunning enough to plan a kidnapping to spare the family the stigma of an illegitimate child?

His frown deepened as he scrolled farther down and zeroed in on a photo—one that included William, his sister, Diane, and her husband, Dennis, and their daughter.

His shoulders cramped with tension as he studied the little girl huddled between Diane and her husband. A little girl who looked about eight years old. A blonde...

The same age as Peyton...

REBECCA WAS RUNNING, running, running, as fast as she could. She had to get away from the bad men.

He'd watched her at school and taken pictures. And now he'd followed her to the house.

But her legs were weak, and she stumbled. He snagged her arm, and she screamed, beating her fists against him. "Let me go, let me go."

He shook her. "Stop it!"

"No, let me go!"

"Rebecca, wake up."

"No, they're going to get me..."

He shook her harder, so hard her teeth rattled. "Wake up. You just scratched me, you little twerp."

Rebecca jerked her eyes open and stared at the darkness. The voice...it belonged to her foster father. His breath smelled nasty as he glared at her.

"You were dreaming, kid, screaming and carrying on." He released her and she fell back against the bed as he stood. "I don't want to hear any more from you, you hear me?"

"But the man from school, he was watching and he came after me..."

"I said hush." He raised one fist as if he was going to hit her. "Do you hear me?"

Terrified, Rebecca bit her tongue to keep from screaming, then slowly nodded.

The bed creaked as he lifted his bulk. Then the floor squeaked as he shuffled back to the door. He stopped at the doorway and turned back to her. "I mean it, kid. I'd better not hear another sound out of you."

Rebecca clenched the covers to her neck and nodded again, holding her breath until he shut the door.

She blinked hard, and pressed her hands to her eyes to keep from crying. She wouldn't cry. She was a big girl now.

A scraping sound echoed in the room, and she gripped the covers and slowly twisted her head sideways to look at the window.

Scrape. Scrape. Scrape. Something was out there. Something that sounded like claws.

Was it a wild animal? Or had the mean man in her nightmares really found her?

CHAPTER TEN

NINA SAT UP and stared into the darkness. Peyton's singing had stopped.

In fact she was crying. Peyton was scared of something—or someone.

A helpless ache engulfed her, fueling her anger, and she turned her face up to the heavens. "Where is she? God, please, I'm not crazy, am I? My daughter needs me."

Downstairs, she heard footsteps, remembered Slade and breathed in relief.

More determined than ever, she quickly showered, then hurried down the steps. The scent of coffee wafted toward her, and she found Slade gripping a mug in his hand when she entered the kitchen.

His gaze raked over her and made her body tingle. "Did you sleep?"

"A little," she admitted. "But then the nightmares came."

He nodded, his expression hooded, then stepped aside while she poured herself a cup of coffee.

Last night she'd lost her head and let her emotions overwhelm her. Today, she'd keep their conversation focused on the investigation.

And she'd keep her hands to herself. No more reaching for him or letting him hold her. No more kisses.

No use in fantasizing about something that she could never have.

"I located an address for Gwen Waldorp," Slade said. "I'm going to see her this morning."

Nina sipped her coffee, her stomach churning. Questioning Gwen would resurrect painful memories for her. But if she hadn't kidnapped Peyton, she might have seen something, heard something… "All right."

"Then we'll go see William's mother and sister."

Nina narrowed her eyes. "His sister?"

He gestured toward his computer, and she glanced at the photos he'd accessed. "She has a daughter the same age as Peyton."

Nina studied the photo of the little blonde, her mind racing. "No wonder Mrs. Hood was so callous about William having an illegitimate child. She was already going to be a grandmother."

Slade shrugged. "Maybe."

His tone made her pause, and she glanced at the child again. Blond hair, freckles…the same age as Peyton.

Her breath stammered in her chest. What was Slade thinking? Did he suspect that little girl might be Peyton?

"Did you know Diane?" Slade asked.

She shook her head. "No, she was four years older than me and already married."

"Were you aware she was expecting a baby the same time you were?"

Nina swallowed. "No. William never mentioned it…" Her voice warbled. "Slade, do you think…?"

"I don't know," he said, obviously reading her mind. "But it's worth looking into."

Nina agreed, placed her coffee cup in the sink and went to retrieve her purse. She locked the house securely, and she and Slade drove to the mountains. Antique stores, craft shops, a diner, a candy shop and majestic scenery gave the town a quaint feel.

Gwen Waldorp lived in a cottage-style house with white latticework, a glider on the front porch and a bird feeder in the yard. Evidence that kids lived there was everywhere, from the tricycle to the football to the pink scooter.

A pink scooter—Gwen had a little girl, too....

Nerves fluttered in Nina's stomach as she walked up the flower-lined path to the front door. Slade punched the bell, and a moment later, the patter of little feet sounded from inside.

Then the door opened, and her heart squeezed at the sight of the child.

A towheaded little boy about three with bright green eyes.

"Who're you?" He scrunched his nose, revealing a missing front tooth.

"We'd like to see your mommy," Slade asked. "Is she here?"

"Mommy!" the boy shouted. "A giant man and a wady are here!"

"Bobby, I told you not to open the door to strangers," the woman called as she rushed into the room. A dark-haired little girl tagged close behind her, her face streaked with something that looked like chocolate pudding.

"Hi," Nina said, smiling at the little girl. "My name is Nina. What's yours, honey?"

The little girl bobbed from foot to foot, then whispered, "Judy."

"How old are you, Judy?" Nina asked.

Judy smiled. "Eight. I just had a birthday and got a new bike."

Gwen pushed the child behind her like a mother protecting her cub. "Who are you and what do you want?"

Nina scrutinized the child's features, comparing her heart-shaped face to Gwen's, and trying to remember what her own childhood photographs had looked like. Judy's hair was slightly darker than her mother's sandy color, but she didn't have Nina's blond hair either, and her eyes were hazel, not blue.

Still... Could Judy possibly be her daughter?

"Mrs. Waldorp," Slade began. "This is Nina Nash, and my name is Slade Blackburn with Guardian Angel Investigations."

A frown creased Gwen's forehead. "How can I help you?"

Nina wet her dry lips with her tongue. "I'd like to talk to you about the hospital fire in Sanctuary eight years ago. You probably read that the sheriff arrested the men responsible for the explosion."

Gwen's face blanched. "Yes, but what does that have to do with me? I didn't know any of them."

"We're not accusing you of having anything to do with the fire," Slade said.

"Then what's going on?" Gwen asked. "Why dredge up that night? It was a bad time for me."

Nina pressed her hand over the woman's. "I understand, but this is important. Please."

Grief darkened Gwen's eyes, and she seemed to be debating on whether to continue. But then she leaned down and stroked her daughter's hair. "Judy, why don't you take Bobby into the den and watch cartoons. Mommy will be there in a minute."

"'Kay, Mommy." The little girl had been watching

with avid curiosity, but she grabbed her brother's hand and they raced away.

"Come in," Gwen said, then gestured toward the kitchen. The room adjoined the den so she could keep an eye on the kids. She offered them coffee, and Slade accepted although Nina's stomach was somersaulting so she declined.

"We understand that you lost a child the same night as the fire," Nina said. "Your baby was stillborn."

Gwen massaged her temple as if the memory were still raw. "Yes. How did you know?"

"Because I was there. I lost a child that night, as well." Nina explained about her own labor and delivery, and her frantic search to find her daughter.

"I'm sorry." Gwen's voice trembled. "But what does this have to do with me?"

"Forensics never found my baby's body," Nina said. "I think she might still be alive."

Suddenly the woman's eyes flashed with surprise. "What?"

"I know it's a long shot," Nina continued. "But in the chaos, I think someone might have taken her."

Gwen's expression shifted from curiosity to anger at the sudden realization of their implications. "Oh, my God. You think I stole your baby?" she asked in an incredulous tone. She glanced at her daughter. "That's why you asked Judy how old she was."

Slade planted his hands on the table. "We're exploring every angle, no matter how remote," Slade said.

Gwen stood with a hiss. "I think you'd better leave."

"Mrs. Waldorp," Slade said calmly. "We've reviewed the forensics reports. There is an infant's bone in the report, but no ID. What happened to your child? Was your baby's body recovered?"

Anguish flashed on Gwen's face. "No, I...didn't even get to bury him..." She inhaled a deep breath, then straightened as if logging the memory away.

"Judy is eight," Slade pointed out. "You couldn't have given birth to her."

"She's adopted, isn't she?" Nina asked.

Gwen's lips compressed. "That's none of your business."

"Please," Nina pleaded.

Gwen sank back into the chair and fiddled with a napkin on the table. "Yes, she's adopted. But we went through the lawyer in town, and it was perfectly legal."

"Do you know who Judy's birth parents are?" Slade asked.

She lowered her voice. "Yes. The baby's mother died in the fire that night. When we heard about the baby, and learned the woman had no family, we jumped in to take Judy. She needed us and we needed her."

"She seems small for her age," Slade said. "Did she have any health problems when she was born?"

Gwen glanced at her daughter, concern on her face. "She has asthma. Why?"

"My baby was premature," Nina said. "She was in the NICU."

"Judy is not your child, Miss Nash." Gwen folded her arms, her expression shutting down. "Now, I've answered your questions because I feel sorry for you. But I think it's time for you to leave."

"I'm sorry," Nina said. "But I'm desperate to find out what happened to my baby. Do you think it's possible that the lawyer lied to you when he claimed Judy's mother died in the fire?"

Gwen ripped the napkin in two. "Why would he do that?"

Nina explained about the Hoods' reactions to her pregnancy.

Gwen's eyes widened. "You're suggesting that one of them kidnapped your baby, then gave her to me?"

"It's one theory," Slade said matter-of-factly.

Gwen stood. "Well, that's just not possible. Judy can't be your child. Her mother is dead."

Nina glanced back at the little girl. She was precious, but she didn't feel the connection she'd expected to feel when she saw her child again for the first time. Did that mean Judy wasn't hers? That Gwen was telling the truth?

"Then maybe you saw something that night that can help me," Nina continued. "Maybe you saw someone strange hanging around the nursery…"

Gwen folded her arms, then cast her a belligerent look. "I'm afraid I can't help you. I was so distraught over my loss that the nurses gave me a sedative. I barely remember the fire, only that someone carried me outside."

She ran a shaky hand through her hair. "Now, I really do want you to leave. I have my family to take care of."

NINA'S SILENCE DURING the drive toward Winston-Salem worried Slade. He understood that the interview with the Waldorp woman was uncomfortable, but asking questions always caused some kind of emotional reaction. It was part of the job.

Besides, he didn't give a damn what anyone thought of him. He had to ask questions, probe, pry, piss off people, sometimes lie or treat them harshly to get answers.

But Nina had a compassionate nature, and her empathy for the other woman would have clouded her judgment.

"Do you believe her story?" Slade asked.

Nina shrugged. "It sounds plausible."

"Yeah," Slade said. "But she might not know the truth herself. If someone paid the doctor enough, he could have fabricated that story and given her your baby and merely told her the baby's mother died to avoid questions and to push the adoption through without questions."

Nina leaned her head into her hands. "It's hard for me to wrap my mind around the fact that someone could be that devious." Her expression grew more strained. "And the little girl did look happy. Gwen obviously loves her like she was her own."

Slade gritted his teeth. Yes, the woman did. But was the child Nina's? He needed DNA for verification, and Gwen Waldorp wouldn't give that up easily.

Nina looked so distraught he wanted to take her in his arms and hold her again, assure her everything was all right. But if that child was Nina's, then she would be torn over what to do.

And ripping the child away from the only mother she'd ever known, and her father and baby brother, would be hell for everyone.

Dammit.

He glanced at Nina again. How was she going to handle a confrontation with Mrs. Hood, the woman who'd tried to pay her to get rid of her child?

Slade's cell phone buzzed, and he connected the call. "Blackburn."

"It's Amanda. I talked to the forensic anthropologist and she reviewed her files. That infant bone belonged to a baby boy, not Peyton Nash."

Probably Gwen's stillborn child. Slade thanked her again and disconnected the call, then relayed the forensics findings.

Nina chewed her bottom lip. "Then it wasn't Peyton. That means she's alive."

Slade slanted her a warning look. "It means there's no proof that she was caught in the fire, Nina." And he needed more before a judge would grant a request for Judy Waldorp's DNA.

"She's alive," Nina said with such certainty that he almost believed that she really knew, that she might have some kind of connection to her daughter.

But he had long ago lost faith in anything, much less something intangible like love or a connection between two people. Even a mother and daughter.

He found the country-club community where William's mother lived, stopped at the security gate, showed his ID, then drove past the manicured golf course to the Hood estate, a massive English Tudor house that looked more like a hotel than a home.

A crew of workers were busy tending the lawn and flower beds and looked up when he parked, but didn't comment as he and Nina walked up the walkway.

He rang the doorbell, tapping his foot as he waited. Finally a woman in a uniform answered. "Is Mrs. Hood in?" Slade asked.

"No, sir, I'm sorry. May I tell her who was inquiring?"

"Where is she?" Slade asked.

The woman frowned. "I don't give out her where-abouts to just anyone."

"Please," Nina said, then introduced the two of them. "It's important I talk to her."

The woman hesitated but her look softened. "She's at the country club having lunch."

Nina thanked her, and the two of them returned to the SUV. Slade circled back the way they'd come and pulled into the parking lot of the country club.

"Mrs. Hood won't be pleased to see us," Nina said.

Slade grunted. "I don't give a damn. From what I've

heard about this lady, she deserves to be knocked down a peg or two."

A small smile curved Nina's mouth, making him see for the first time how beautiful she would be if she were happy. He wanted to see her smile again.

Marble floors gleamed as they walked in, the scent of fresh flowers filling the entry. Beveled mirrors, expensive paintings and vases decorated the walls, and heavy, red velvet curtains covered the windows.

To the right, he spotted a plush dining room, and he and Nina walked to the doorway. The room was packed with women's groups, couples and businessmen, most dressed to the nines. An outdoor patio held other tables where the tennis and golf crowd seemed to have gathered.

"She's in the far-right corner," Nina said, pointing to a small table of four women.

Slade gestured for her to lead the way, and she crossed the room, silently willing herself to remain strong and not let the woman rattle her. When Mrs. Hood noticed them, she jumped up, shock and anger drawing her face into a scowl. She tossed down her napkin and strode briskly from her party, weaving between white-linen-clothed tables until she reached them.

She stopped and glared at Nina, her diamonds twinkling beneath the crystal chandelier. "What are *you* doing here?"

Nina squared her shoulders. "Trying to find my daughter."

Mrs. Hood rolled her eyes. "My God, it's true," she huffed. "William called and warned me you'd hired another P.I."

"Yes, I have," Nina said flatly. "And I'm not going to give up until I learn the truth."

The woman's eyes spewed rage as she tossed her head back. "Well, I have *nothing* to say to you."

Slade cleared his throat. "We can talk here, lady, in front of your friends or step into the hall for privacy. Your choice. But we will talk."

Mrs. Hood snarled then strutted toward the lobby, her heels clicking on the polished marble floors. Obviously determined to avoid a scene, she led them to a small alcove, then folded her arms, gold bracelets clinking on her wrists. "You have five minutes before I call security and have you removed from the premises."

Nina pressed her lips into a tight line, and Slade gritted his teeth. He'd never hit a woman before, but he felt like slugging this one. "Where were you last night, Mrs. Hood?"

An appalled gasp escaped her. "At the club. Why?"

"Because since I started investigating this case, someone has started taunting Nina."

"Don't let her fool you, Mr. Blackburn. She's delusional and can't accept the fact that her child died."

Slade straightened to his full height, towering over her and pinning her with an intimidating stare. "I think she has good reason to suspect that her daughter might have survived."

"What are you talking about? The police turned up nothing—"

"Exactly," Slade said. "They never found a body."

"Good heavens," Mrs. Hood said, sounding exasperated. "Just look at the horrible pictures from that fire. The baby certainly didn't walk out alive on her own."

Slade shoved his face into hers. "No, she didn't. I think you or someone you hired carried her out."

CHAPTER ELEVEN

AT ONE TIME the vehemence in William's mother's voice would have bothered Nina, but she no longer cared about the woman's opinion.

And if she had been responsible for Peyton's disappearance, she would never forgive her.

Mrs. Hood's eyes widened. "How dare you imply such a thing?"

"You tried to bribe Nina to have an abortion," Slade continued. "And when she refused, you tried to convince her to give the baby up for adoption."

"She was just a child herself, a little tramp, not equipped to take care of a baby," Mrs. Hood said icily.

"Oh, come on," Slade said in a tone that matched the woman's. "You weren't concerned about the baby, or you would have offered to help raise her. You just didn't want a reminder that your son had an illegitimate child."

She batted her false eyelashes. "That's ridiculous."

Slade arched a brow. "Is it? Or does the truth sound as ugly as it is, because it certainly sounds like you had motive for kidnapping."

"I did not kidnap that child," Mrs. Hood said vehemently.

"Then tell me where you were the night the baby disappeared."

"I don't know who you think you are, Mister, but I don't have to tell you anything."

Slade shifted and crossed his arms. "Were you at the hospital the night Nina gave birth?"

Mrs. Hood lifted her chin haughtily. "Either leave now, or I'm calling security."

Nina touched her arm. "Were you at the hospital, Eileen?"

"No." Mrs. Hood jerked her arm away from Nina's hand. "For heaven's sakes, stop harassing me."

"Then you hired someone," Slade suggested. "Did you arrange for an adoption or did your own daughter take the baby and raise her?"

Mrs. Hood gasped and raised her hand as if she might slap Slade. "You leave my daughter and grandchild out of this. Now get out!"

Her raised voice and demeanor caught a security guard's attention and he strode toward them.

Slade made a sarcastic sound low in his throat. "Lady, you don't scare me."

"You should be scared, Mr. Blackburn. I have a lot of money and power in this town, and I can sue you for harassment."

Slade held up a hand to the approaching security guard, indicating that force wasn't necessary. "I don't give a damn who you are or how much money you have, Mrs. Hood. If you did something to Nina's child, I'll find out, and you will rot in prison." He glanced across the ballroom with disdain. "And you won't be dining on caviar or wearing diamonds there."

"THANK YOU FOR standing up for me in there," Nina said as they walked out to his SUV.

Slade grimaced as he climbed inside and started the engine. "That woman is a snotty bitch."

Nina laughed, a musical sound that made Slade pause

and look at her. With the afternoon sunlight dancing through the silky strands of her blond hair and that smile, she looked radiant.

His gut pinched, his body hardening instantly. He wanted to touch her hair again, kiss those perfect, ripe lips and run his hands over her body.

He wanted to solve all her problems.

That thought sent a surge of fear through him. He was getting too close to her, starting to care.

Caring was dangerous.

Gritting his teeth, his resolve set in. *Stay focused. Keep your mind on the case.*

Find the little girl and get away from Nina.

He just hoped to hell he found her alive....

His stomach growled, and he drove to downtown Winston-Salem, and found a café for lunch. Nina ordered a salad and he wolfed down a burger.

"I still can't believe Mrs. Hood would kidnap my baby and keep her from me all these years."

"I can't believe you'd even doubt it. The woman is obsessed with money and her image."

"That's true." Nina nodded and sipped her water. "And she definitely wanted me out of her life."

"If you'd kept the baby, she was probably afraid you'd try to milk the family for money."

Nina gasped. "I would never have done that, Slade."

"I didn't mean to imply you would. But your child would have been a rightful heir to the Hood fortune, and William would have owed you child support for years." He lifted a brow. "This way, they were free and clear."

"She didn't care how much she hurt me," Nina said quietly. "And those dolls...do you think she could have put them in my house?"

"I doubt she'd dirty her own fingers," Slade said. "But

with her money, she could have hired someone to make you look crazy so no one would believe you."

"And it worked," Nina said. "Even my father thought I'd lost my mind, that I did those things myself."

Slade shrugged, then settled the bill, and they went back to the car and headed toward William's sister's house.

"If Mrs. Hood is guilty, I wonder if William knew what she did," Nina said.

Slade gritted his teeth. "If he did, they'll all pay for it."

Nina lapsed into silence until they reached their destination, a modern brick two-story in an upper-class neighborhood. The Lucases were obviously doing well for themselves. From the article he'd read online, he'd learned that Mr. Lucas was a physician at the local hospital.

Slade punched the doorbell, and the sound of footsteps echoed from inside. A thin blonde wearing shorts and a tank top answered the door.

"Mrs. Lucas?" Slade said.

The woman's expression was wary. "Yes. My mother called. I've been expecting you, Nina." She gestured for them to come in. "Let's go out back. Tiff is in the pool, and I need to watch her."

"Of course," Nina and Slade said at the same time.

They followed her through an immaculate kitchen and sunroom to a brick patio and pool. The little girl was playing with a dinosaur raft in the water. Longing swelled in Nina's eyes.

"Mother claims that you accused her of kidnapping your baby eight years ago," Diane said. "Is that true?"

"We just wanted to ask her some questions," Slade began, then explained their reasoning behind believing Peyton might still be alive.

"I see." Diane gave Nina a sympathetic look. "I can't imagine what you've been through," she said in a low voice then turned to look at her daughter who was laughing as she struggled to climb on the raft. "I don't know what I would have done if I were in your shoes, but I'd probably be asking the same questions."

Slade was surprised at her calm sensitivity. This woman seemed nothing like her mother.

"Diane," Nina said, "I hate to ask you this, but your mother hated me back then, and she didn't want me to have the baby. She offered me a bribe to have an abortion."

Diane sighed and glanced down at her hands, then looked back up. "I know. William told me. And I have to admit that I wasn't surprised. Mother has always been obsessed about her reputation and climbing the social ladder."

"In light of how she felt," Slade said, "do you think she might have arranged for someone to take the baby?"

The little girl squealed and Diane glanced at her to make sure she was okay. But Tiff had managed to straddle the dinosaur and was laughing with glee, splashing and paddling with all her might.

"I don't know," Diane said. "I'd hate to think my mother would do something that devious. I...just can't imagine."

A car sounded in the drive out front, and footsteps pounded through the house. A moment later, a dark-haired man in a suit appeared through the French doors, looking furious.

"Diane, what in the hell are you doing letting these people in our house?"

Diane stood. "Calm down, Dennis. There's no reason I shouldn't talk to them."

Dennis stormed over to the patio table where they were sitting. "This is outrageous. Your mother called me, hysterical. She said they accused her of kidnapping a child and then giving the baby to us to raise."

"I'm sorry," Nina said. "I'm just trying to piece together what happened to my little girl."

"Look, Miss Nash," Dennis said, lowering his tone. "Your baby died. It was sad, tragic even, but you have no right to accuse us of kidnapping."

"Can you prove that little girl is your birth child?" Slade asked.

Fury radiated from Lucas's pores. "Of course I can. She was born in the same hospital where I work. I was a resident then and helped deliver her myself." He jammed his hands on his hips. "And before you ask, yes, I have the birth certificate to prove it."

"Papers can be doctored," Slade said with an eyebrow raised. "You're a doctor. You certainly have the power and connections to do it."

"This is unbelievable," Dennis shouted.

The little girl stopped splashing and stared at them, and Diane grabbed her husband's arms. "Calm down, Dennis. You're scaring Tiff."

Dennis cut his eyes toward the little girl, then inhaled a calming breath and spoke through clenched teeth. "I'll calm down when these people get off my property."

"If the little girl is yours," Slade said in a low voice, "then you can easily prove it by giving us a DNA sample."

"I'll do no such thing," Dennis snarled. "Now leave before I call the police and file harassment charges."

Slade returned his stare with a cool mask. "We'll leave for now. But your decision not to cooperate only makes you look guilty."

"I'm protecting my family and well within my rights," Dennis said. "Now get out before I throw you out myself."

NINA BACKED AWAY at the rage in Dennis Lucas's eyes.

Diane placed her hand on her husband's shoulder. "I'll walk them to the door, Dennis. Stay here, have a beer and watch Tiff."

He stared at them for another long moment. "You don't need a P.I., you need a shrink, Miss Nash. Go see one, and don't bother us again."

Slade started to speak, but Nina took his arm. "Let's go, Slade."

The men continued the silent stare-off for another second, then Slade conceded with a nod. "If I find out you're lying about any of this," he said, "I'll be back."

Nina tugged him through the sunroom door, then Diane guided them back into the kitchen. But she stopped and picked up a hairbrush, then gave Nina a sympathetic look.

"This brush belongs to Tiff. Take your DNA and you'll see that Tiff is not Nina's child."

Nina gasped in surprise. "Why are you helping us?"

Diane squeezed Nina's arm. "Because I'm a mother, and if it will put your mind to rest, then I understand. I never approved of the way my mother and brother treated you."

Tears burned the back of Nina's eyes. "I...don't know what to say." She glanced at Slade, thinking they didn't need to take the sample.

But Slade plucked a couple of hair strands from the brush and dropped them into a small envelope he had inside his jacket before she could respond, then Diane escorted them to the front door.

"I hope you find what you're looking for," Diane said.

Nina thanked her again, moved by her understanding and compassion.

She and Slade walked back to his SUV in silence, but as soon as she settled in the passenger seat, she spoke. "I don't think Diane had anything to do with Peyton's disappearance."

"You're too trusting, Nina."

She gave a self-deprecating laugh. "Not really. But she seemed genuine, and she did offer up the DNA."

Slade started the engine, and pulled out into the subdivision and headed back toward Sanctuary. "Still, her husband's reaction made me wonder."

"Wonder what?"

"Even if Tiff is theirs, he might know something. Mrs. Hood could have asked for his help in doctoring paperwork or arranging for an adoption."

Nina leaned her head against the headrest. "And if Peyton was adopted, the records are probably sealed, so I may never know where she is."

Slade covered her hand with his. "If Lucas was complicit, I'll force him to talk. Finding out which adoption agency, especially if it's a private agency, and the name of the lawyer who handled the adoption, would be a lead."

Nina's emotions bounced between hope and despair. "That is, if they used a lawyer. For all we know, Mrs. Hood paid someone to steal Peyton and take her away. She might not even be in the country." Nina's throat clogged with fear. She'd tried not to let her imagination travel that route, but she had to face reality.

Slade's closed look confirmed she could be right. This investigation might only lead them to a certain point, and then the trail could turn cold.

She closed her eyes, willing her courage to return. But suddenly Slade cursed, and yanked the SUV sideways.

She jerked her eyes open, and saw a car racing up too close behind them.

"What's wrong?" Nina asked.

"That car nearly hit us a minute ago."

They were approaching a bridge over a bypass, and suddenly the car roared closer again, and this time sped up and passed them.

"Dammit," Slade muttered as he hit the brakes to avoid slamming into it. But instead of slowing, his car accelerated.

He pumped the brakes, tightening his fingers around the steering wheel in a white-knuckled grip. But the SUV flipped up on two wheels, tires squealing.

"Slade—"

"Hold on, the brakes aren't working!"

An oncoming car blared its horn when he crossed the line, and Slade jerked the car to the right, skimming the guardrail.

Sparks flew, the sound of metal scrunching rent the air, then the SUV slammed into the side and spun out of control.

Nina screamed and Slade cursed as they careened over the side of the bridge, hit the pavement below and began to roll.

CHAPTER TWELVE

Slade's chest pounded as the car spun upside down and skidded toward another vehicle. Metal screeched. Glass shattered. The air bags exploded, popping him in the face and chest, and the front of the car was crunched so tight, he couldn't move his legs.

Dammit. He needed to get them out.

He glanced sideways to see if Nina was all right, but she wasn't moving.

"Nina, honey, are you okay?" He struggled to find her hand and squeezed her fingers. "Nina, talk to me. Are you all right?"

Fear seized him when she didn't respond.

He dug in his pocket, found his Swiss army knife, flipped it open and ripped at his air bag, then hers until he could see her face. She looked so pale that sweat beaded on his skin. A scrape marred one cheek, and blood dotted her forehead. "Nina, baby, you have to talk to me."

But she still didn't respond.

Frantically he felt for his phone, but before he could punch 9-1-1, a siren wailed, and he realized someone else had called in the accident.

Or had it been an accident? His brakes had completely failed....

Nina moaned, and he angled his upper body sideways. His legs were trapped, his right knee throbbing, but at least he could feel them, so that was a good sign. He gently stroked her cheek.

"Nina, wake up, honey. We've been in an accident."

Slowly she opened her eyes, but they looked glazed and disoriented.

"We crashed," Slade said. "But I hear sirens, so an ambulance will be here soon. Where are you hurt?"

She frowned, lifted a scraped hand and pushed the tangled hair from her face. "What?"

"Are you in pain?"

Her brows furrowed, and she shifted slightly.

"Stay still," he said. "Wait until the medics check you out."

"My legs…" she whispered, panic lighting her face. "I can't move them."

TERROR SEIZED NINA. Her head was aching, but she couldn't feel her legs. "Slade, I can't move…"

"Shh, don't panic. The front end of the car is crunched," he said. "The rescue workers will have to cut us out."

Outside, sirens screeched, the fire truck roared to a stop, footsteps pounded on the asphalt and voices shouted.

Slade glanced up to see a firefighter and policeman kneeling and looking through his shattered window. "Are you two hurt?"

"We're trapped," Slade said.

The men exchanged concerned looks. "The ambulance is on its way."

Slade pulled Nina's hand in his and squeezed it between both of his. "Hang in there, Nina."

She clung to his hand, desperately holding on to her composure while she heard the men outside shouting orders. Noises sounded, more voices yelling. The ambulance arrived, the rescue workers manipulating the Jaws of Life, and someone shouted that a news crew had arrived.

The next hour blurred as the firemen worked to release them. Metal scraped, machinery ground and sawed through metal, jarring the car and her aching head and body.

Slade cradled her hand against his chest, kissed her palms and stroked her face, talking to her the entire time the firemen worked. His gruff voice helped calm her, and finally she heard voices murmuring they almost had them out.

Her breathing hitched as the metal gave way, and her legs were freed. Numbness had crept in, but pinpoints of pain stabbed her as feeling began to return.

"Nina?" Slade asked.

She massaged her leg with her hands. "My ankle hurts."

A small smile tilted his mouth. "That's actually good news."

Relief poured through her, but the medics insisted she shouldn't move.

"We have to board you until we transport you to the hospital and the doctors check you out."

She nodded, sucking in a sharp breath and closing her eyes as they secured her neck and body on the board and carried her to the ambulance. A camera flashed in her face, a half-dozen people scrambling around, and she tried to see Slade, but lost him in the commotion.

More voices drifted through the haze.

"My name is Sheriff Driscill," a male voice said. "What happened?"

"My brakes failed," Slade said. "Examine the SUV and see if they were tampered with."

Nina gripped the sides of the stretcher. Was it possible someone had tried to kill them?

FURY ROLLED THROUGH SLADE. He wanted to know why the hell his brakes had failed and, if there was foul play, who was responsible.

They both could have died.

Maybe that had been the plan....

"Why do you suspect foul play?" the sheriff asked.

"I'm a private investigator," Slade explained. "And I've been working a case."

Sheriff Driscill scratched his head. "What case?"

Slade explained about the investigation.

Driscill made some notes in a pad he pulled from his pocket. "I'll have a crime unit take a look."

Slade thanked him. "I'd like to ride to the hospital with Nina."

The sheriff took Slade's business card, then Slade joined the medics. His knee was throbbing, and he had a cut on his arm he'd let them take care of when they arrived at the hospital, but he had to make sure Nina was all right.

She opened her eyes when he climbed in the back of the ambulance, and he perched on the stretcher across from her and cradled her hand in his.

"Slade?"

Dammit, he hated to see her beautiful face bruised. "Are you in pain?"

"My ankle and head hurt, but I'm okay." She licked her lips. "What about you?"

He shrugged. "I've had worse."

Her breathing hitched. "You said the brakes failed?"

He clenched his jaw. "Yes."

"You think they were tampered with?"

"I'd bet my life on it," Slade said bitterly. "And if who-ever did this thought they'd scare me away or kill us, the only thing they did was piss me off."

She smiled, although she winced in pain, and he squeezed her hand. "It's going to be all right, Nina," he said softly. "Just rest. I'll take care of everything."

Protective instincts pulsed through him. He wanted to hold her, kiss her, remind himself that they were both alive.

He wanted to strangle the son of a bitch who'd tried to kill them.

The siren began to wail, the ambulance roared away and he vowed to get vengeance and find Nina's little girl.

THE NEXT TWENTY-FOUR hours became a fog of blurred memories in Nina's mind. The doctors and nurses treated her cuts and abrasions, wrapped her ankle, which thank-fully wasn't broken but sprained, took X-rays, an MRI and a CAT scan and decided she was lucky.

But every bone in her body ached. And nightmares of careening off that bridge filled her restless sleep.

Other times, she saw Peyton standing a few feet away, so close she could almost touch her, but each time she reached out her fingers, her little girl slipped away.

She woke with tears on her cheeks, her chest hurting.

Slade sat beside her, looking rugged and angry, his clothes tattered from the accident, and a bruise discolor-ing his scarred cheek. But he'd stayed with her all night around the clock, and even exhausted, he was the most handsome man she'd ever seen.

"How are you feeling?" he asked in a gruff voice.

She pushed her hair from her face, wincing as she attempted to sit up. He yanked another pillow from the closet and eased it behind her back.

"Thanks." Glancing down, she realized the hospital gown had slipped off her shoulder, and she adjusted it, feeling naked and vulnerable.

"You didn't have to stay," she said.

His frown deepened. "The sheriff called. The brake lines to my SUV were definitely cut."

A small gasp escaped her. "So someone intentionally caused us to crash."

He nodded. "That means we must be getting close, that we've got someone worried."

"So you think Peyton might be alive?"

He was so quiet she didn't think he was going to answer. Finally, when he did, his tone was flat. "I don't know. But obviously someone knows what happened to her and doesn't want us to uncover the truth."

SLADE'S CELL PHONE buzzed, and he flipped the phone open. "Blackburn."

"This is Roan Waldorp, Mr. Blackburn. I want you to leave my family alone."

Slade frowned. "I'm conducting an investigation into a missing child, Mr. Waldorp, so I'm questioning everyone connected to the hospital fire eight years ago."

"I know exactly what you're doing. My wife suffered enough trauma back then, and I won't allow you to come to our home and upset her by implying that we did anything illegal."

"Mr. Waldorp," Slade cut in. "Who arranged for you to adopt that little girl?"

"That's none of your business. My wife and I lost a child, then were lucky enough to adopt another one. A perfect little girl and she's ours, so leave us alone."

He slammed down the phone, and Slade gritted his

teeth. A perfect family. One the man didn't want disturbed.

"What was that about?" Nina asked.

"Waldorp warned me to stay out of his life."

Nina sucked in a harsh breath, and Slade punched in the number for GAI. While Nina had slept, he'd phoned to inform him of the accident—and the brakes being tampered with.

"Gage, it's Slade again."

"How's Nina?"

"Awake now, and feeling better, I think. But Waldorp was pissed that we'd questioned his wife about their adopted daughter. Can you ask Ben or Derrick to check into that adoption?"

"Sure. As a matter of fact, Derrick said that Brianna arranged a meeting with one of the social workers from the state adoption agency."

"I'll be there. Anything else?"

Gage made a sound of frustration. "I checked out the Hood family's alibis for the night of the fire. Two of William's buddies confirmed he was in a bar with them that night until midnight."

"His buddies could be lying for him."

"It's possible," Gage conceded. "Mrs. Hood's alibi holds up, as well. I found an article about the society party she attended, and phoned three of the people in attendance. They all corroborated her story."

"But she could have hired someone to kidnap the baby and paid for the adoption."

"True. But we have no proof yet."

"How about William's wife, Mitzi?"

"According to her father, she was home all night."

Like a father wouldn't lie to protect his daughter.

Another voice echoed in the room, and Gage paused,

then spoke a second later. "Ben wants to talk to you about something he found." Gage transferred the call, and a second later, Camp's voice echoed over the line.

"Blackburn, I've been checking into Nash and the Hood family, digging up old phone records. It might not be anything, but Mr. Nash made several phone calls to a lawyer in Sanctuary in the weeks before and after Nina gave birth."

Slade's suspicions rose. "Calls that could have indicated he was arranging an adoption?"

"That's what I was thinking. Do you want me to talk to the lawyer?"

"No, thanks. I'll pay him a visit. What's his name?"

"Stanford Mansfield." Camp paused, and Slade heard him pop his knuckles. "Blackburn, this is interesting, too. Mansfield's father and Nina's father attended college together. They also belong to the same Rotary club."

Slade stewed over the connection. A coincidence maybe, but if the men were friends, they might have exchanged favors.

"Check out his financials around that time period," Slade said. "See if Nash made any large withdrawals."

"I'm on it."

"Thanks. Good work." Slade disconnected the call and saw Nina watching him. She looked tired and pale, the bruises on her cheeks and arms more pronounced in the daylight.

"What's going on?"

Slade swallowed hard. He had to tell Nina the truth—he'd promised her he would, no matter what he learned.

But how could he tell her that her father might have arranged for an adoption behind her back? That he might be responsible for taking away her child?

NINA NOTICED THE SUBTLE tension lining Slade's jaw. Something was wrong.

"Slade?"

He shifted. "I need to go question a lawyer named Stanford Mansfield."

Nina sensed he was avoiding her gaze. "What does he have to do with this?"

Slade hesitated. "There were several phone calls between him and your father around the time Peyton went missing."

"You think my father paid this lawyer to arrange for an adoption behind my back?"

Slade's eyes darkened. "I don't know, Nina. I'm just following the leads. That's why I want to talk to Mansfield."

She threw off the covers, searching for her clothes. "Let me get dressed. I'm going with you." But pain sliced through her ankle, and she winced and gripped the bed to keep from falling.

Slade caught her in one arm. "Whoa, you aren't going anywhere. You need to rest."

Nina angled her face toward him. "I can't just lie here in bed, not when we're getting so close." She pulled away, hobbled to the closet and dug out her clothes.

"Nina, please stay here and rest."

She ignored him and reached to untie the gown, but realized Slade was watching.

His gaze skated over her, and a tingle traveled up her spine. "Go ask the doctor for my release papers and let's get out of here."

"I can do this on my own," Slade said quietly. "You look—"

"As if I've been beaten up," Nina said with an eyebrow raise.

"Yes," he said tightly.

She offered him a smile. "I know. But so do you."

"I'm used to it," Slade said.

She laughed. "Maybe. But that's not the point. If this lawyer helped steal my baby from me, he needs to see me like this. And I want to tell him that I'm not giving up. Not now. Not ever."

REBECCA HAD TO DO something to make the man and woman like her. They stayed mad all the time, and if they were mad, they'd send her back to the orphanage.

She closed her book, *Pippi Longstocking,* and stuffed it into her tote bag. Pippi was her favorite character in the whole wide world. She wanted to be just like her.

Mama Reese kept complaining about the kitchen floor being dirty. Rebecca would clean it. And if she used Pippi's way, she could do it fast before the old woman woke up.

Her snores echoed from the couch, and Rebecca found the dust mop and a pair of scissors. It took her almost twenty minutes to cut off the ends and divide it in two. Then she dragged the plastic bucket inside, pulled over a chair and climbed in it to reach the sink. She dumped dishsoap inside, then let water run in the bucket.

The handle was wobbly, and the bucket swung back and forth as she tried to climb down from the chair. Then the bucket slipped and water poured over the sides.

She started to yell out, but she couldn't wake Mama Reese. No, she had to clean up the mess.

Soapy water ran across the floor, and she skated across it, sloshing soap across the floor in her path. She nearly slipped twice, but grabbed the table edge, spun around and skated back the other way, zigzagging back and forth.

Suddenly the old woman shrieked. "What are you doing?"

Rebecca stopped and smiled. "Cleaning the floor for you."

But the old woman didn't smile back. She bared her teeth and bunched her hands into fists.

"Look at the mess you've made!" Mama Reese stormed toward her, jerked her arm so hard it hurt and shoved her into the chair.

Rebecca gripped the edge of the chair, her heart thudding. "I'm sorry…"

"You ruined my mop and now you made a big mess for me to clean up." The woman's fingernails dug into her arms. "I don't know what I'm going to do with you, you little brat. You're not worth the pitiful amount of money they give us every month."

Tears pricked Rebecca's eyes, then the woman jerked the mop pieces from her feet and dragged her toward the bedroom. Cursing beneath her breath, she threw open the closet door, shoved her inside then slammed the door.

"We're going to get rid of you," the woman yelled. "I don't want you here anymore!"

Rebecca reached for the doorknob, but the lock clicked in place and she was pitched into the dark. Tears burned her eyes and rolled down her cheeks as she pulled her knees to her chest, hugging them.

What would happen to her now? No one wanted her.…

CHAPTER THIRTEEN

SLADE INSISTED THEY return to their houses and shower before confronting the lawyer. Nina was relieved to have some time to prepare herself for the visit.

If her father was connected... No, she couldn't believe that he would hurt her by deceiving her so ruthlessly.

Gage had dropped off a rental car, and they drove to Slade's place first since hers was closer to the lawyer's office.

"You own the house?" Nina asked.

"Yeah. It needs some work, but I liked the location," he said as he guided her up the steps to the porch and inside.

"It has charm," she said, admiring the two-story with the big front porch. "And the view of the mountains is spectacular. It's so private, too..."

"That was another plus," Slade said. "I like the solace."

She imagined the house with fresh white paint, flower boxes on the windowsills, a garden out back, and knew it would make a beautiful home once he finished renovations. She envisioned a passel of little children running around in the yard.

But Slade liked the peace and quiet—he wanted to be alone, not have a family. And she had to remember that.

As they stepped inside, she noted the sparse furnishings. A comfortable leather couch and throw rug, a big club chair, stereo, but no pictures on the walls or mantel.

Then she noticed the photograph of a young girl about ten and a brunette woman perched on the desk in the corner. It had to be his mother and sister.

"Do you need anything while I shower? Something to drink?"

"No, thanks, I'm fine. I'll just wait here." She sank onto his overstuffed sofa, and he stared at her for a long moment, then nodded. His boots pounded on the steps, and a second later, the shower water kicked on.

An image of Slade undressing flashed into her mind, and she closed her eyes and groaned. He was tall, broad-shouldered and, she imagined, deeply tanned and mus-cled beneath those clothes. She could almost see the soapy water beading on his skin, see his thick body hard-ening....

She jerked her eyes open, shocked at her train of thought. Good grief, she was not the lustful type. She was a schoolteacher. She'd been alone so long that she hadn't even thought about being with a man.

She'd been solely focused on surviving one day at a time. On school. On teaching. On holding on to faith when her faith had been crushed so many times.

Frustrated, she stood, walked over to the photograph and studied it. The little girl looked happy, the mother smiling, her arm curved protectively around her child.

Only their lives had fallen apart when the girl had become lost.

That was the reason Slade understood her anguish. He'd suffered his own.

Then she spotted a box of things he'd unpacked in the corner by the fireplace and glanced inside. Some plaques from the service, a medal for bravery.

Slade's footsteps sounded, the stairs squeaking as he descended. When he noticed her looking at his things, his jaw clenched.

"Are you ready?"

Nina nodded, but her palms felt sweaty at the sight of him fresh from the shower. His hair was still damp and tousled as if he'd just run the towel through it. And he hadn't buttoned the top button of his denim shirt, which revealed his golden-bronzed chest.

"Nina?" Something hot and sultry smoldered in his eyes, and her belly tickled.

But heat climbed her face as she realized he knew she'd been staring. The moment felt intimate. She had to distract herself, so she gestured toward the photograph.

"You were a war hero. That's impressive."

"Trust me, Nina, I was no hero."

"I don't believe you, Slade."

He gestured toward the scar on his cheek. "See that? I got it escaping while three of my men died saving me."

Anguish and guilt underscored his self-deprecating tone, raising her curiosity. He knew everything about her, all her deep, dark secrets, while she knew very little about him.

She gestured toward the picture. "Your sister was pretty. What happened to her?"

Any heat that had passed between them died, and his expression became closed. "She got mixed up with the wrong crowd, and ran away. Died. End of story."

His cell phone buzzed, abruptly ending the conversation, and he connected it as he gestured toward the door.

"Blackburn." He paused. "Yeah, okay. Thanks."

"Who was that?" Nina asked as they made their way to the sedan.

"Ben Camp again. I asked him to check into your father's financials around the time of the hospital fire."

Nina's pulse rocketed. "And?"

For a brief second, he hesitated as if he didn't want to admit what he'd learned.

"You promised not to keep things from me," she said.

He released a pent-up sigh and started the engine. "He found a large withdrawal from your father's personal account the week before you delivered Peyton."

Nina's stomach sank, and she turned to look out the window as he drove to her house. When they arrived, he strode around to help her from the car. "I'm sorry, Nina. We could be wrong about your father."

She fished for her keys and shook her head. "And you could be right. Daddy likes control. He obviously thought I wasn't mother material back then."

"As a father, he wanted the best for you," Slade said. "A bright future, college."

She frowned. "So you're defending him?"

"No, not at all. I'm just trying to get in his head. Some men want to protect their kids no matter what. Even if they do make the wrong decisions."

She gritted her teeth. He'd described her father to a *T*.

Silently she limped to her bedroom, stripped and climbed in the shower. Battling tears, she stood beneath the shower massage, allowing the warm water to soothe her sore muscles. Her chest was bruised from the air bag, her legs battered from the dash and her face looked as if someone had taken a fist to it.

But her physical injuries didn't matter. Her heart was breaking.

If her father had paid someone to take Peyton away and had lied to her all these years, she would never forgive him.

WHILE NINA SHOWERED, Slade distracted himself from thinking about her being naked and wet by searching the computer for background information on the lawyer.

As a teenager, Mansfield had hidden behind his daddy's money. Was he hiding behind money now?

He found several articles on the lawyer, cases he'd handled, but nothing specific to suggest illegal behavior.

Still, judging from the pricey area where he lived, and his Mercedes, he was rolling in the bucks. And none of the cases Slade noted were impressive enough to make him wealthy. He phoned to verify that the lawyer was in his office, and learned he was working at home for the day.

Nina emerged, looking vulnerable and soft and so damn pretty that something stirred inside him. He knew she was anxious about her father and hoped like hell he hadn't deceived her all these years.

He drove them to Mansfield's, a ten-acre estate on the outskirts of town on the river. "Looks like Mansfield has done well for himself."

The troubled expression on her face indicated she understood his implications. That she knew her father might have padded the man's wallet.

"Are you sure you're up to this?" Slade asked.

Nina nodded. "Yes. We've come this far. I'm not backing down now."

Slade traced a thumb over her wrist, his body instantly reacting to the warmth of her skin. "Not even after that attempt on our lives?"

"Like you said, if whoever did this thought he scared me off, he's wrong. He only made me more determined that I'm right, that Peyton is out there somewhere, that she's alive."

Slade refused to comment. At this point, he knew

something had happened eight years ago that somebody would kill to keep quiet, and he wanted the whole story now.

Her ankle was still slightly swollen, and she had to lean on Slade as they walked to the door. Her injuries only reminded him that they had nearly died the night before, raising his protective instincts. He had the insane urge to whisk her away to bed and protect her from the danger, and whatever they learned.

But she gave him a brave smile, and he punched the doorbell instead. The river gurgled and splashed over rocks behind Mansfield's property, and Slade noted tennis courts to the side, then heard the sound of a match being played on the courts.

So much for Mansfield working at home.

A maid greeted them at the door. "May I help you?"

"We're here to see Mr. Mansfield."

"He's busy at the moment. Can I make an appointment for you?"

Slade produced his ID. "No. We have urgent business. We need to see him now."

A nervous expression flitted across her face, but she gestured for them to follow. "He's having a tennis lesson," she said. "He won't like being disturbed."

"He'll get over it," Slade muttered sarcastically.

Nina leaned on him again, and they followed the maid through the house to a patio overlooking the tennis courts.

Mansfield glanced up and saw him, and missed his shot. The trainer said something to him, then Mansfield motioned that the lesson was over, leaned his racket against the fence and strode toward them, mopping his face with a towel.

His eyes narrowed on Nina as if he recognized her and knew the reason for their visit.

The maid offered an apologetic look. "They insisted it was important, Mr. Mansfield."

Mansfield gestured for her to go inside, sank into a patio chair with a curse then took a long drink from his water bottle. "What the hell do you two want?"

"You know who we are?" Slade asked.

The man wiped his mouth with the back of his hand. "Yes. I saw the news article about your accident this morning in the paper. You're a P.I." He crooked a thumb toward Nina, his breathing labored from the exertion of his tennis lesson. "And everyone in town knows you, Miss Nash."

Anger pulsed inside Slade at the man's abrasive attitude. "I have some questions for you, Mansfield."

Mansfield wiped sweat from his neck with the towel. "You should be asking her the questions. Like why she keeps stirring up trouble."

"If she's stirring up trouble by asking questions, that means someone is keeping secrets." Slade gripped the man's collar. "In fact, some bastard tried to kill her—and me—last night. Was that bastard you, Mansfield?"

"Take your hands off me, Mr. Blackburn," Mansfield said, his eyes fuming.

"You know," Slade said, "for a bunch of innocent people, you and everyone I've talked to certainly are acting defensive."

"Go to hell," Mansfield spat out.

"I've already been there." Nina gestured toward the bruises on her face and arms. "Both physically and mentally."

Slade shoved him back into the chair. "Listen, Mansfield, I know for a fact that you and Nina's father had several phone conversations around the time her baby disappeared. I also know that Mr. Nash made a sizeable withdrawal, as well. My guess is that Nash paid you to arrange an adoption for her baby."

Mansfield released a withering sigh. "Miss Nash, your father approached me about arranging an adoption, but later he phoned me and claimed that you refused to sign the papers."

"That's true," Nina said.

"But he didn't give up, did he?" Slade pressed.

Mansfield drummed his fingers on the table. "He was persistent," Mansfield said. "He thought eventually Miss Nash would agree, but then she delivered the baby prematurely and the fire occurred that night, and the baby died, so the point became moot."

"So my father didn't pay you to find a family for my baby?" Nina asked.

His expression turned chilly. "No."

"What about the Waldorp's adoption?" Slade said. "Did you handle it?"

"Whether I did or did not is none of your business." Mansfield stood and gestured toward the door. "Adoptions are sealed and confidential, and I'm bound by attorney-client privilege. I could be disbarred if I shared any information about them."

"Being disbarred will be the least of your problems if you were complicit in kidnapping and arranging a phony adoption." Slade squared his shoulders. "I'll see that you rot in jail, and your career will be over."

NINA STRUGGLED TO BELIEVE in her father's innocence as they left the lawyer's house and drove to meet Brianna McKinney and the social worker at the adoption agency.

Brianna greeted them with a genuine smile, putting

Nina immediately at ease. "I've heard about your ordeal, Nina, and I can't imagine what you've been through. My adopted son was kidnapped a few months ago, and it was the most harrowing experience of my life."

Nina recalled the story in the paper about the abduction. "I read about you," Nina said. "That case led to the arrests regarding the hospital fire and explosion."

Brianna nodded, and led her and Slade into an office where an auburn-haired woman with freckles sat, studying a file.

"Miriam," Brianna said, "this is Slade Blackburn of GAI, and Nina Nash, the woman I told you about." She gestured toward her and Slade. "This is Miriam Sheppard. She works with the state adoption agency."

They exchanged pleasantries, then Slade spoke. "Miss Sheppard, we're looking into the possibility that Nina's baby was kidnapped, then adopted." He explained the Hoods' and her father's reactions to her pregnancy. "We think Stanford Mansfield might have been paid to arrange the adoption. And it's possible that Gwen and Roan Waldorp took the child. They have an adopted daughter the same age as Nina's child."

"You know adoption records are sealed," Miriam said.

"Please," Nina begged. "Just tell us what you know."

Miriam glanced at Brianna warily then sighed. "All I can tell you, and this is under the table, is that the Waldorp adoption was not a state adoption."

"Meaning it was a private adoption?" Slade asked.

She nodded in confirmation.

"Do you have records of a premature baby being adopted around that time?" Slade asked. "And could that child have been adopted by the Waldorps?"

Miriam spoke quietly. "I have no record of preemie adoptions, or suggestions that the Waldorps have your child, but I'll dig deeper. She could have ended up in foster care."

"My poor little girl," Nina said in a pained whisper. "What if no one adopted her and she's lost in the system?"

Miriam smiled for the first time since they'd entered. "It's possible. I'll search and see if I find a child in foster care who matches that description."

Hope budded in Nina's chest. But it was a long shot. For all she knew, a family had adopted her. If so, she only prayed that they loved her.

But that nagging sensation clawed at her, and she closed her eyes. She could hear her little girl crying again.

She needed her.

Nina would find her no matter what.

SLADE HATED THE DISCOMFORT on Nina's face, but if Peyton was in foster care, it might be easier to track her down than if she had been adopted. But the thought of the little handicapped girl being shuffled from one place to another, knowing she might have suffered God knew what, ripped at his gut.

He knew firsthand what foster care was like. Knew that some people could be loving, but that other times, they could be cruel.

His cell phone buzzed, and he excused himself to answer it. "Slade Blackburn."

"Mr. Blackburn," a woman's voice whispered. "This is Paula Emery."

Slade tensed. "Yes?"

A tension-filled minute stretched between them. Slade thought he heard shuffling, then running. "Mrs. Emery?"

"I have to see you," she cried. "Roan Waldorp called

here a few minutes ago having a fit. I think I may know who kidnapped Nina Nash's child."

He sucked in a sharp breath. "The Waldorps?"

"Not over the phone," she whispered. "Meet me at Caleb's Cabins off Old Canyon Road. The cabin at the end of the road."

A man's voice sounded in the background, and the woman's breath quickened. "I can't talk now. I have to go. Just meet me."

The line went dead, and Slade rushed back in to get Nina. Mrs. Emery sounded scared, nervous.

Did she really know who had kidnapped Peyton, or was this some kind of trap?

CHAPTER FOURTEEN

SLADE STEPPED BACK into the room. "Nina, we need to go. We might have a lead."

Hope brightened her face, and she stood, although her ankle gave way and she gripped his arm to steady herself.

"I can drop you at the agency if you want," he offered.

"No. I'm going with you." She clung to his arm and he helped her out to the rental car. "What happened?" she asked as she fastened her seat belt.

Slade started the engine. "That was Dr. Emery's wife. She said Gwen's husband called, frantic about our visit. Then she claimed she has information about Peyton."

"Oh, my God…" Nina's eyes filled with tears.

"I hope she's telling the truth, Nina," he said, feeling the need to caution her. "But we have to be careful. This could be a trap."

"A trap?"

He squeezed her hand. "Remember, someone tried to kill us already."

"But why would Mrs. Emery want to hurt us?"

"To protect her husband," Slade said matter-of-factly.

Nina thumbed a strand of hair from her cheek and slowly nodded.

A thunderstorm rumbled on the horizon, the clouds thickening as they climbed the mountain toward the rental cabins. Traffic thinned, a single car or truck passing as night fell. The wind whipped leaves from the trees, the temperature dropping, the area becoming more isolated and dense with woods.

Slade checked the rearview mirror a dozen times to make certain no one was following. Lights from an oncoming truck nearly blinded him as he rounded a curve, then a deer raced across the road. The truck's brakes squealed as he swerved to avoid it, and Slade skimmed the side of the road to avoid hitting the truck.

His lights flickered down the embankment, and he caught sight of a car that had nose-dived into the small ravine. The truck raced on, oblivious.

"Damn. There's a car off the road down there," Slade said, righting his vehicle and pulling a few feet ahead to an overhang. "Let me see if anyone is hurt inside."

Nina nodded, and he jumped out. "Lock the door. And if anyone approaches, honk the horn." He didn't wait on a reply. He raced down the embankment, dirt and rocks skidding beneath his boots.

He skated over the rocks but his foot slipped, and he grabbed a tree limb to keep from falling. Cursing, he climbed over a tree stump, and mangled limbs scattered across the terrain from a past storm then placed his hand on the car. It was still warm.

The front end was crunched into the ravine, the windows shattered, the sides dented, and the mirror on the driver's side had been ripped off.

Pushing through the briars and weeds, he looked inside the window at the driver's seat. A body was plastered against the seat, half hidden by the air bag. He used his pocketknife to rip it away, then saw the woman's bloody face. Her skin was ashen, her chest heaving for air.

"Miss, my name is Slade Blackburn. I'll call an ambulance."

"Wait…" she rasped. "She did this…"

"She?" He frowned and tilted her face to see her eyes. "What are you talking about?"

"I called you," she choked out.

Cold fear gripped Slade's belly. "You're Dr. Emery's wife?"

Her body jerked and convulsed, another pain-filled choked sound erupting from her.

"Ye-es," she whispered. "Carrie Poole, nurse…affair with my husband. She…stole the baby."

Slade's heart pounded. He had to get help. "I'm going to call an ambulance."

But suddenly the woman rasped another sound, gripped her chest and panic filled her eyes.

Then she slumped back in the seat, her eyes glazed over and she stopped breathing.

NINA WONDERED WHAT WAS taking so long. Was someone in the car? Maybe hurt…

Suddenly, a shot blasted the front window of the car, and she ducked. Another shot hit the front bumper and pinged off, and she screamed.

Where was the shooter? In the woods? Had he hit Slade?

Panic flooded her. No, Slade couldn't be hurt….

Another shot echoed from the other side, and she heard Slade shouting, "Stay down, Nina!"

She covered her head with her arms and did as he said, while more gunfire exploded around her. Outside the car, footsteps crunched gravel, thunder rumbled then she heard someone scrambling near the passenger door.

Was it the shooter?

Rain began to splatter the windshield, and the door lock clicked then the door swung open.

Nina sighed in relief when she spotted Slade sliding into the seat. "Are you all right?"

"Yes. What about you?"

Another shot pelted the passenger side this time, and he twisted the key in the ignition, punched the accelerator and took off. "Hang on," he shouted.

Nina refastened her seat belt but crouched low as he raced around the curve. He shoved his cell phone toward her.

"Call the sheriff, tell them I found Emery's wife's car crashed." He paused and gave her a troubled look. "And tell him to send the coroner. She's dead."

"Oh, my God…" She started punching in numbers while he maneuvered the curves. "What happened?"

"I don't know," Slade said. "But if that shooter was any indication, she was murdered."

Nina gasped. "She was killed because she was going to talk to me."

Slade pulled her hand into his lap. "This is not your fault, Nina. So don't even go there. For all we know, Mrs. Emery knew who the kidnapper was all along and remained quiet all these years."

A deep-seated trembling overcame Nina, and she gripped his hand tighter. "Did you see the shooter?" she whispered.

Slade shook his head, then veered onto a dirt side road that wound along the creek. Nina spotted the sign for the rental cabins, and realized they were still headed to Emery's cabin.

"What did she say?" Nina asked.

"She claimed her husband and Carrie had an affair."

"Carrie and Dr. Emery?" Nina frowned. "That doesn't seem likely."

Slade shrugged. "Maybe, maybe not. But if Emery didn't know about the kidnapping, and Carrie was responsible for killing his wife, she may be going after him next."

NINA'S HANDS WERE trembling so hard that Slade took the phone. "This is Slade Blackburn of GAI." He relayed what had happened and asked for an ambulance.

"I'm going to check out the doctor's cabin now."

"I'll send someone up there to comb the woods ASAP. Call me if you need backup." Sheriff Driscill paused. "And, Blackburn, remember, you're not a cop. You don't have a warrant so keep it within the law."

Slade gritted his teeth. "Yeah, right." He ended the call with a curse. To hell with the law.

He and Nina had been nearly killed twice. Mrs. Emery was dead.

And someone didn't want them to find out what had happened to Peyton Nash.

He'd do whatever it took to find the truth now. Even if he had to risk his reputation, his job and his life to do so.

He swerved around a pothole, gravel spewing from the tires as he ground his way across the dirt road. Rain pounded the roof of the car, the thunder growing louder, and he slowed slightly, creeping past several cabins until he reached the hollow. A lone cabin sat atop the hill, a small sedan parked outside.

A streak of lightning shot across the sky, illuminating the dark interior of the cabin, and he scanned the perimeter. No lights on inside or outside.

Was anyone home? Or could the shooter be hiding out here?

No. On foot, he couldn't have woven through the woods that quickly.

He threw the car into Park and glanced at Nina. "Stay here with the doors locked. I'll check out the cabin and see if anyone's here."

Nina grabbed his hand. "Slade..."

"Yeah?"

"Be careful." Her lower lip quivered. "Please."

Her eyes were big, beautiful pools of color, filled with fear. Fear for him.

Something deep and untamed moved inside him. Arousal? Need? Hunger?

That and emotions he had never felt or thought he would feel for a woman. God, he didn't want to lose her....

Inhaling a deep breath, he cupped her face in his hands. "I will. Stay put and if you hear or see anyone, hit the horn like I told you earlier."

Slade kissed her deeply, tenderly, urgently. Desire surged through him along with protective instincts and the need to tell her that he cared for her.

No... Too scary.

A dog barked somewhere in the distance, and reality sucker punched him. So he pulled away.

"Hurry," Nina whispered.

He nodded, then opened the door, slid outside and crept up to the house. Rain pelted him, and he scanned the land and exterior, then peered in through the front window. Although the house was dark, and he didn't detect movement, a noise jarred him.

A soft pounding? A knock?

He couldn't quite tell, so he crept to the side of the house, checking the windows there, searching for one that might be open. A deck had been built onto the back, and he padded up the steps, then jiggled the back door.

The noise sounded again. A knocking sound, maybe a fist or a chair? Then another sound...a moan.

His pulse spiked. Someone was inside, someone hurt.

He removed his wallet, removed the small lockpick he kept stored inside, jammed it in the lock and jimmied it open. The scent of coffee and something acrid filled the air, and he frowned and inched inside, keeping his gun at the ready.

Then he heard the moan again, a low, keening sound of pain, and he moved forward, listening for other sounds as he inched through the kitchen into the small hallway leading to the living room. But his foot hit something, and he realized a chair was overturned.

The metallic scent of blood assaulted him, and he glanced down and found a woman lying on the floor. She had one hand wrapped around the chair, either trying to pull herself up or banging it to attract his attention.

"Help me," she whispered in a choked cry.

Slade knelt beside her and checked her pulse. Low but thready. The woman was Carrie Poole, the nurse from the hospital. Blood soaked her blouse, and she tried to raise a trembling hand to reach for him.

But it fell limply to her side, she gasped for a breath and her body convulsed.

NINA HEARD A NOISE near the house, and panic set in. What was taking Slade so long?

Was he all right?

Her heart was pounding so loudly she could almost hear the blood roaring in her ears. She just couldn't sit here. She had to do something.

Then a car raced up the drive, a black Mercedes. Dr. Emery's.

Anxiety choked her, and for a moment, fear. What if Dr. Emery had known what Carrie had done?

But his face looked panicked as he jumped out and ran up to the sedan. The rain was starting to die down, but rivulets trickled down his cheeks as he pounded on the door.

"Nina, what are you doing here?" He frantically pulled at the door. "Open up. Have you seen my wife?"

Nina tensed and gripped the door handle. He didn't know about his wife's accident…that she was dead…

He threw up his hands, his face filled with fear. "Nina, open up, tell me what's going on."

Nina chewed her bottom lip, but opened the car door. If Carrie was inside, she might have laid a trap for the doctor. And Slade might have walked into it, meaning he needed help.

"My wife phoned, frantic," Dr. Emery said. "She claimed she knew who took your baby, that she was scared, for me to meet her here."

Nina inhaled a sharp breath. "I know…she called me, too."

His eyes raked over her, then fell to the empty driver's seat. "Did that P.I. come with you?"

Nina nodded. "He went inside to see if you were there. He thought you might be in danger…" Her voice cracked. "Dr. Emery, I don't know how to tell you this, but we found your wife's car crashed down the road. She didn't make it."

His eyes went flat, and suddenly he gripped her arm. "I know."

Nina stared at him in horror as he yanked her from the car and jammed a gun in her side.

CHAPTER FIFTEEN

SLADE STARTED TO punch 9-1-1, but Carrie grabbed his arm. "I didn't do it..."

"Do what?" Slade asked.

"Didn't have an affair with...Dr. Emery..." Carrie gasped. "And I didn't kidnap the baby..."

"Then who did?" Slade asked.

"Mrs. Emery said I did...that I stole babies for him because I was sleeping with him..." Tears leaked down her pale checks as she struggled for a breath. "That's not true..."

Slade stroked her arm to calm her. "Carrie, do you know what happened to the Nash baby?"

"Adopted...I overheard doctor on the phone yesterday..." Her breathing grew labored, and Slade's jaw hardened.

Dammit. He wanted to know more but he couldn't let the woman die.

He punched in 9-1-1 and asked for an ambulance and the sheriff, but suddenly the door squeaked open and footsteps shuffled in the front room. Alarm shot through him, then Nina's voice called his name.

"Slade?"

He glanced up and saw Nina in the shadow of the doorway, and his blood went cold.

Dr. Emery was standing behind her with a gun aimed at her head.

NINA WAS TREMBLING SO badly her knees were knocking. Carrie Poole lay on the floor, her chest soaked in blood, her breathing labored.

Had Dr. Emery shot her? Was he going to kill all of them?

Slade's eyes settled on her.

"Put your gun on the floor. Slowly," Dr. Emery said in an icy tone. "And if you make any sudden moves, I'll kill her."

"You son of a bitch," Slade growled.

Dr. Emery jerked her arm, and Slade raised his hands in surrender. "All right. Just don't hurt her." Slowly, he lowered his gun hand and placed the piece on the floor.

"Now move away from it," Dr. Emery ordered.

"Why are you doing this?" Nina whispered as Slade inched closer toward them. "You're supposed to save lives, not take them."

Dr. Emery's fingers dug into her arm. "I do save lives. I saved your baby's, didn't I?"

"But you told me she died in that fire," Nina said bitterly. "That's not true, is it?"

"Why couldn't you just move on and forget about her?" Dr. Emery growled. "That's what your father wanted. What everyone wanted."

Slade cleared his throat. "What did you do to Peyton, Emery?"

"You two ask too many damn questions. My wife..." His voice cracked. "She had to die because of you."

Carrie groaned from the floor, and the doctor jerked Nina sideways. "And now she's going to die, too, and it's all your fault."

"My fault," Nina said in a ragged whisper. "You're crazy. I'm just a mother who wants to know what happened to her child."

"What did you do?" Slade asked in a level tone. "Is Peyton still alive?"

"I have no idea where that child is now," Dr. Emery said sharply. "I arranged for her to go to a good home, a home with two parents, two who would know how to raise a handicapped child."

"How could you be so cruel?" Nina said. "I loved my baby. I wouldn't have cared if she had problems. I would have taken care of her—"

"You were too young to have a child," Dr. Emery snapped. "Even your father wanted you to give up the baby."

Nina's lungs tightened so painfully she couldn't breathe. "Did my father have something to do with this?"

The doctor shook his head. "No, but he was happy the child was gone. He wanted you to grow up, move on." He shook her again, and she felt the cold metal of the barrel against her temple. "But you refused to let it go."

"Because my baby is out there and she needs me," Nina argued.

"No, she doesn't. She's better off, just like the others."

A sick feeling swept over Nina.

Slade balled his hands into fists. "What others?"

Sweat trickled down the side of the doctor's face. "The other little whores who got knocked up without being married."

Nina couldn't believe what she was hearing.

"So what do you plan to do, Emery? Kill all of us? You can't believe that you'll get away with it?"

The doctor's hand jerked as he frantically looked around the room. Then a sinister laugh escaped him. "Hell, I'll make it look like Nina killed you both. She had a breakdown before. It won't be hard to make it look like she had another."

He waved the gun toward Slade. "Now get down on your knees."

Nina's heart started racing. She couldn't die, not knowing Peyton had survived.

She had to fight to stay alive so she could find her.

SLADE SAW THE wheels turning in Nina's mind. She didn't intend to give up.

But he didn't want her to do anything stupid that could get her killed. Dammit, he had to save her. Save both of them.

Where was that damn ambulance? And the sheriff?

"I've already phoned the sheriff. And all my people at GAI are on the case, Emery," Slade said calmly. "There's no use in taking any more lives."

"Shut up."

"Killing us will only add more to your sentence," Slade continued. "But if you turn yourself in, you might be able to swing some kind of deal."

"Deal?" Emery barked. "My career, my life will be over."

"Your life will be over anyway," Slade said. "The sheriff is going to be here any moment."

"You're bluffing," Emery bit out.

Slade shrugged. "I called when I found Carrie."

Slade glanced at Nina and saw her eyes flickering sideways toward the fireplace. A fire poker leaned against the brick hearth, and he sensed the direction of her thoughts. He tried to signal her not to risk it, but a siren echoed in the distance, Emery jerked his head toward the door in shock and Nina shoved him away from her.

She wasn't strong enough though, and Emery pistol-whipped her across the face. She screamed and flew backward from the impact, then landed against the hearth with a groan.

Slade cursed and lunged toward the doctor, but the gun went off. The bullet skimmed his arm, and he ducked sideways and rammed his head into the man's stomach.

Emery grunted, and they fell to the floor, struggling for the gun. Another shot pinged into the ceiling, sending plaster raining down. Slade shoved Emery's head against the wall, clawing at Emery's fingers to force him to release his hold on the weapon. Emery kneed him, and he flipped him sideways, then the gun fired another bullet and he heard Nina scream.

Fear shot through him. Had she been shot?

The second he took to look gave Emery an advantage, and he rolled Slade to his back. Determination seized Slade, and he karate-chopped Emery's arm. The blow made Emery yelp and the gun fell to the floor beside them.

Emery's eyes went wild with panic and rage. The siren wailed closer. Nina moaned and tried to get up from the hearth, staggering.

Slade thought of the pain she'd suffered all these years, of her lost little girl, of Emery lying to her and making her think she was crazy, and cold fury empowered him.

He slammed his fist into Emery's face and sent his head rolling back. Another punch and the man fell to his back, but his hand slid around the gun on the floor beside them. Slade lunged for it, but Nina had grabbed the fire poker and swung it down. The poker caught Emery's arm above the wrist, and the bone snapped.

Emery yelped in pain, dropped the gun and Slade grabbed it then stood.

"You're going to jail, Emery," Slade snarled.

His breath gushed out as he reached for Nina. She fell

into his arms, trembling and crying, and he kissed her hair and hugged her to him.

THE NEXT FEW HOURS blurred for Nina. The ambulance and sheriff arrived, along with a crime unit, and they rushed an unconscious Carrie to the hospital. Another team raced up and checked her head for injuries, but she assured them she was fine, then they treated Slade where his arm had been grazed by the bullet.

Sheriff Driscill arrested Dr. Emery, but he refused to talk, insisting that he wanted a lawyer. The medics splinted his arm, then loaded him in the ambulance.

Slade filled the sheriff in on everything that had happened.

"So Emery killed his wife and shot Carrie because they found out what he was doing and threatened to tell?" Sheriff Driscill asked.

"That was my impression," Slade said. "Maybe you can force more information from the doctor."

The sheriff turned to Nina. "And he admitted that he kidnapped your baby?"

"He confirmed that he arranged an adoption," Nina answered.

"I think Stanford Mansfield was involved in the deal," Slade said.

"I'll have him picked up," the sheriff said. "And I'll obtain warrants to subpoena Emery's files."

"Good," Slade said. "Let me know when you bring Mansfield in. I want to be there when you interrogate him."

Driscill agreed then headed to the ambulance to ride with Emery.

Slade cupped Nina's elbow in his hand. "Are you all right?"

She nodded, although she felt numb inside. For so long she'd sensed that her daughter hadn't died in that fire and now to have that fact confirmed created a mixture of emotions. Relief that she'd survived. Hope that she might find her. Anger over the years they'd lost together. Anxiety over where she was and who had been caring for her.

Fear that she still might never find her.

Slade coaxed her back to the car, helped her inside, and she fastened her seat belt. When he settled inside, he gave her a concerned look, then started the engine and drove away from the blinding lights of the police cruiser and the crime scene they'd just been a part of.

"I know a thousand things are going through your mind right now," Slade said gruffly.

She gave a small, sardonic laugh. "Since when did you become a mind reader?"

He chuckled. "Because they're going through my mind, as well."

Could he really understand? No… No one could…

"I guess I should be glad to have answers," she finally said. "And I am. But…"

"But you want to know more?"

"Yes," she said softly. She turned to look out the window, and focused on the rain dripping from the branches, heard the slush of water as the tires rolled over wet pavement. An image of her and her daughter singing in the rain flashed into her mind, and fresh pain rocked through her. She could almost hear Peyton's voice again singing in a low tone.

"Emery indicated that he'd arranged for other babies to be adopted," Slade said, jarring her from her fantasies. "My guess is, the adoptions were all private and he was

paid well, so I intend to have GAI study his financials
and see if they connect with Mansfield's."

Hope bloomed in her chest like a rainbow after a
storm. Slade was on her side now. She wasn't alone.

There was still a chance that she could find Peyton.

She closed her eyes and said a silent prayer. And if
Peyton didn't need her, if she'd found another mother,
somehow she'd find peace in the lies and betrayal she'd
suffered. After all, a mother's love meant being unselfish.

The only thing that mattered was that her daughter
was safe and happy.

REBECCA SAT HUNCHED on the floor, her knees to her
chest, her arms wrapped around herself, rocking back
and forth, back and forth.

How long had she been in this dark closet? Were they
ever going to come back?

She had to stay strong. Be tough. Not be a crybaby.
She pictured Mary Poppins in her mind and heard her
sing, so she joined in in a soft whisper.

Suddenly footsteps pounded in the bedroom. She
held her breath at the stench of cigarette smoke seeping
through the crack in the door. Then the door opened,
and Daddy Reese grabbed her by the wrists and dragged
her toward the kitchen. Her eyes hurt from the sudden,
blinding light.

"We're getting rid of you now," he bellowed. "I can't
stand it anymore."

She bit her lip so as not to cry as he tossed her into
the kitchen, and she fell on the floor. Her chest heaved.

What did he mean? What were they going to do to her?

CHAPTER SIXTEEN

NINA SUDDENLY DOUBLED OVER as she entered her house, a sharp pain wrenching her heart. Something was wrong... She felt it deep in her bones.

Slade gripped her arm. "Nina, what is it?"

She closed her eyes and inhaled deeply, forcing herself to take slow breaths as the therapist had taught her years ago. One, two, three...breathe through the pain...

Slade suddenly swung her up into his arms and carried her toward her bedroom, then into the bath. "You should have let the medics admit you to the hospital."

"No..." Nina whispered. "It's Peyton... Something's wrong, Slade. Something's happening to her. I can feel it."

Slade tensed, but then pulled her into his arms. "Oh, honey..."

She fell against him, inhaled his deeply masculine scent and clung to his strong arms. Slade had stayed with her, had protected her, had fought to find her child when everyone else had insisted she was crazy.

She needed him now. Needed him to hold her until she could pull herself together. Until she could find her daughter.

He cradled her against him, then gestured toward the tub. "I'll run you a hot bath, then fix you a drink. That will help you sleep."

She nodded, although sleep was the last thing on her

mind. Sleep would bring the nightmares, the waking up
to the emptiness, the lonely bed, the dark...

But she felt gritty with dirt and sweat, and needed the
stench of the doctor off her skin, so she nodded, and he
eased her to the floor. A numbness settled over her as
Slade ran the bathwater, a coping mechanism to handle
the shock of all that happened. But her mind kept replay-
ing the past few hours.

Mrs. Emery had died. Carrie was in the hospital. The
doctor she'd once trusted had shoved a gun at her head.

Slade sat on the edge of the tub and dumped in the
bath salts, then brushed her hair back from her cheek.
"I'll be downstairs if you need me."

"Thank you," she said softly.

For a moment, he simply stared at her, the tension
between them palpable, the scent of his body filling the
room and making her think crazy things.

Things like she wanted to ask him to join her in the
bath. To make love to her.

As if he sensed that need and was sending her a silent message, he turned and walked out the door. Tears
pricked her eyes as she undressed and climbed into the
bath. Was she just a case to him, or could he possibly
care?

He'd been so gentle earlier that she'd felt a connection with him. A connection that went deep. A connection that she didn't want to lose...

A connection that terrified her because she not only
wanted him, but also needed him.

SLADE DRAGGED HIMSELF away from the bathroom when he
really wanted to go inside, slowly remove Nina's clothes,
climb in the bath with her and soap her delicate skin, then
stroke her body until she groaned his name in oblivion.

The fact that she was struggling with her feelings over all that happened only endeared her to him. The fact that she'd fought so hard to find her daughter and to save herself and him stirred his admiration...and lust.

But there were more answers he needed to find. Not just for Nina but for himself.

He didn't even know her daughter, but he found himself worrying about her. Wondering how she'd survived. If she was safe and loved.

If someone had taken care of her needs.

Or if her handicaps had caused couples to reject her.

The thought of that made anger rail.

He'd wanted to kill Emery for hurting Nina and depriving her of her child. And of depriving the little girl of her birth mother.

Nina might have been young, but she would never have abandoned her daughter. She would have done everything humanly possible to see that she received the help she needed to thrive.

He heard a splash of water, and envisioned Nina naked, her creamy skin dotted with bubbles, and his body hardened.

He had to get a grip. He still had work to do. They had to break Emery. Interrogate Mansfield.

Forcing the mental picture of Nina naked from his mind, he phoned Gage to fill him in.

"I'll pass the info on to Derrick and Brianna," Gage said. "See if they found a lead with the foster child angle."

"And I'll follow up with Driscill and Carrie Poole. Maybe she knows more than she's telling."

Gage grunted. "I'll be glad to finally nail that sleazebag Mansfield."

"You have history?" Slade asked.

"You could say that," Gage said. "He stood by and watched while a crime happened one night, but he got off scot-free."

It sounded personal, but if Gage wanted to share details he would. "How's Nina?" Gage asked.

Slade's throat felt dry as she slowly descended the stairs. A thin satin robe floated over her curves and made him wonder what she wore beneath it. "Hanging in there. I have to go."

He closed the phone, reminding himself that Nina was a client, and vulnerable.

But the sultry look in her eyes sent his pulse skyrocketing. The bruises from their earlier accident were still dark and purple, and the image of Emery shoving that gun at her head assaulted him, sending fear straight to his heart.

"Nina?" he said gruffly.

"I can't sleep," she whispered hoarsely. "I don't want to be alone, Slade."

Every professional instinct warned him to back off. Every self-preservation instinct ordered him to run like hell.

But the tearstains on her cheeks made his stomach knot. And the creamy cleavage that appeared where her robe fell open made his body harden and need surge in his loins.

"Go to bed," he said, making a last-ditch effort to do the right thing.

She reached out her hand. "Not alone. Not tonight."

"Nina…"

"Don't I deserve one night of pleasure?"

"Yes. Of course you do." Slade gripped his hands by his sides to keep from reaching for her, but his body betrayed him by aching for her, and he lost the battle with his conscience.

Nina was the bravest woman he'd ever met. Far stronger than he was. And he wanted to assuage her pain, to have her in his arms and bed.

So he took her hand and followed her up the steps.

NINA COULDN'T BELIEVE she was being so bold, but the hungry look in Slade's eyes when she'd descended the stairs had sparked her courage. His sultry eyes and mouth aroused her to the point of desperation.

She was tired of being alone. Of shutting herself off from others because she was afraid of loving and losing again.

Not that Slade would promise anything more than tonight.

But she didn't care. She still wanted one night in his bed, in his arms, with his lips and mouth and hands touching her intimately.

"Nina…" he said gruffly.

She offered him her most seductive smile, and his jaw clamped as if he was reining in his control.

Control be damned. She'd kept an ironclad leash on herself for years.

Not anymore. She was tired of the pain, of waiting for tomorrow.

"Nina, we shouldn't do this," Slade said in a husky voice. "You're vulnerable."

Her confidence slipped a notch. "You don't want me, Slade?"

His shoulders drew back as his gaze raked over her, and she noticed the thick bulge in his jeans. His breath quickened at her perusal, and a bead of perspiration dotted his forehead. "Yes, I want you," he said in a voice laden with sexual innuendo. "But—"

She pressed her finger to his lips to shush him. "But nothing. We almost died tonight."

His look darkened, anger radiating from him. "I know, dammit." He stepped toward her, then lifted his hand and stroked her hair from her face.

It was such a tender gesture that her heart swelled with affection, and her body throbbed with longing.

Heaven help her, she was falling in love with him. He could be so tough, so bold...so gentle, that arousal flooded her. Her body tingled, her nipples ached, between her thighs grew moist.

"You deserve more than a broken man like me," he said gruffly. "I'm scarred, inside and out."

"I'm scarred, too," she said softly.

A growl left his throat. "Nina, you're the strongest, most courageous, most beautiful woman I've ever met."

She slid her hand to the back of his neck to urge him toward her. "Then kiss me, dammit."

Slade chuckled, but the heat in his eyes intensified, then he dragged her in his arms, slanted his lips over hers and kissed her so deeply that her heart completely melted.

THE VOICE INSIDE SLADE'S head whispered for him to stop the kiss, but he ignored it. Nina deserved one night of love, a night of pleasure to help her forget all the anguish she'd suffered. And he intended to give it to her.

Her lips tasted like warm sunshine, her purr of arousal as he teased her lips apart with his tongue sending fire straight to his sex. He wanted her more than he'd wanted a woman in a long time.

Maybe more than he ever had.

And not just because of her sexy body. Because he admired her, even liked her.

The emotions pummeling him made her kisses more special, more erotic.

Made him wonder if he'd be able to walk away when the case was over.

Of course, he would. He wasn't a settle-down kind of man. He was a loner. Had to pay for not saving his mother and sister. For not being a better man.

She made a low, throaty sound of need, and he deepened the kiss, threading his fingers into her hair and savoring the erotic scent of her skin as he dipped his head lower to taste her throat. He didn't deserve her or a family, not after his failures.

But he would take tonight for both of them.

He spread kisses around her face, down her neck, dipping his head toward her cleavage, and cupping one breast in his palm.

A surge of excitement shot through him as her nipple stiffened beneath his touch.

That damn satin robe clung to her curves, leaving little to the imagination, but he still wanted more. He wanted it off, her bare skin against his, her body wrapped around his own.

A moment of sanity gripped him, and he realized they were standing in the hall in front of the stairs. He didn't want her on the cold floor—he wanted her in bed lying beneath him.

His heart racing, he swung her up into his arms and climbed the stairs. She clung to him, kissing him greedily, teasing his ear with her tongue then tracing a damp path down his neck where her fingers tugged at the buttons on his shirt.

Hungry for her, he lowered her on the bed, his breathing slashing the silence in the room. The rain had died, and a sliver of moonlight wove through the sheers, illuminating her like an angel lying on the sheets, an angel offering herself to him.

She licked her lips in a devilish grin, her fingers struggling with the buttons. He was tempted to rip the damn thing off, but forced himself to wait. To watch the stormy play of colors in her eyes as she smiled at him, to savor the feel of her fingertips grazing his chest as she slid open the folds of the shirt. Then her hands raked over him, greedily, and she reached for his zipper. His sex was straining to be free, but he caught her hand. "Not yet. I want to see you first," he murmured. Heat seared his blood as he tugged the belt of her robe and opened the satin so he could feast on her naked breasts. They lay like golden globes waiting for him to hold, her nipples taut and rosy in the moonlight, and he lowered his head and traced his tongue over one gorgeous tip, then the other.

She moaned and thrust her hips upward, making his erection strain against his fly. Smiling, he sucked one taut bud into his mouth and suckled her, then rolled the other between his fingers, teasing and taunting her until she groaned his name.

"Please, Slade…" Her fingers fumbled with his belt, and he let her remove it this time, then he stepped back, slipped her robe the rest of the way off and allowed himself the sheer pleasure of looking at her naked and waiting for him on the bed.

A blush stained her cheeks, but she didn't cover herself, she simply let him look his fill.

"You're so damn beautiful," he whispered hoarsely.

"Take off your jeans," she ordered, one eyebrow lifting as she propped herself on her elbows. "I want to watch."

So sweet, vulnerable Nina could be demanding in bed. He shouldn't be surprised. She was a woman who went after what she wanted, and damned if he knew why, but she wanted him.

And he was determined to give her what she wanted. *Everything* she wanted.

At least for tonight.

So he slowly lowered his zipper, the rasp of it crackling in the tension-laden air, then grabbed a condom from his pocket before meeting her back on the bed. She reached for him and he fell into her arms, then kissed her again, deeper, more intimately, tasting the heady scent of her arousal as he dipped down to tease her breasts again, then lower over her belly and to the sweet, honeyed flesh between her thighs.

She was moist with desire, and he breathed in her essence then licked and teased her legs apart until his mouth closed over her sex, swollen with want and need.

A second later, she moaned his name and her body convulsed, the succulent taste of her release flooding his throat. Breathing like a wild man, he lifted his head and stared at her for a moment. Her cheeks were flushed with pleasure, her eyes glazed and hungry.

She wanted more and so did he.

He tore the condom wrapper open with his teeth, and she helped him sheathe himself, then he gripped her hips and teased her legs apart again with his sex. She closed her eyes and groaned, and he lowered his head and kissed her again, then thrust into her. She was small and tight, and he wondered momentarily if she'd been with another man since that creep William, then knew without asking that she hadn't.

The fact that she'd allowed him this guilty pleasure

moved emotions deep inside him, emotions he didn't want to feel or face.

But he felt them anyway, just as he felt her delicious body hugging him inside her, felt her muscles clench and tighten around him. She clung to his arms as he thrust deeper inside her, then pulled out and thrust again and again until she rocked her hips upward, matching his rhythm, and they soared to the heavens together.

NINA SNUGGLED UP to Slade, her body humming with bliss. Slade wrapped his arms around her, and stroked her hair, his breathing heavy in the silence.

She pressed her face against his chest, savoring the euphoria rippling through her body. Emotions welled in her chest and throat and a tear spilled over.

Slade lifted her head back and searched her face. "What's wrong, Nina?"

"I think I'm falling in love with you," she whispered.

Slade tensed, and immediately withdrew from her.

"Slade?"

He sat up, swung his legs over to the side and leaned his head into his hands. She'd made a mistake in blurting out her feelings, but their lovemaking had touched her down to her soul.

She stroked his back, coaxing him to face her. "I'm sorry. I didn't mean that to pressure you."

He angled his head and stared at her, but he was shutting down in front of her eyes, and the hunger she'd seen earlier had vanished. "Nina, you don't love me. You're just grateful that I've been helping you—"

Anger knotted her stomach. "I didn't make love to you out of gratitude."

"You're coming off an adrenaline rush," he said matter-of-factly. "We both are. We almost died tonight."

He gestured toward the rumpled sheets. "That's all this was."

Hurt stabbed Nina, but before she could reply, the doorbell rang.

Slade narrowed his eyes in question, and she clenched the sheets. "I wonder who that is this time of night."

"Maybe the sheriff." Slade stood, grabbed his jeans and shirt and hurriedly dressed. "I'll go find out."

Nina waited until he left the room, then grabbed a pair of shorts and a shirt and tugged them on, and ran a brush through her hair. She heard a woman's then a man's voice from downstairs, then Slade's and rushed down the steps.

She was shocked to see Gwen and Roan Waldorp in the doorway. Gwen's eyes were red-rimmed and swollen, and her husband looked angry.

"Nina, they said they have to talk to you," Slade said.

Dread mushroomed inside Nina. Something was wrong, and she had a sinking feeling it had to do with her daughter.

CHAPTER SEVENTEEN

SLADE MUST HAVE sensed that she was falling apart, because he guided her to the living-room sofa, indicating for the couple to follow.

When they were all seated, Nina blinked, forcing herself to calm down and listen to what they had to say.

"Why did you come?" Slade asked bluntly.

Gwen glanced at her husband, and he cradled her hand in his. Gwen gripped it as if she needed a lifeline.

"I'm sorry," Gwen whispered. "We... I wanted to tell you that day you came to the house, but I...was afraid... and ashamed."

"Then we heard the news about Dr. Emery's arrest," Waldorp said. "And we knew we had to come forward."

"Because you were afraid of being arrested, too?" Slade asked coldly.

Gwen shook her head. "Because it was the right thing to do."

Nina inhaled a deep breath. "What are you talking about?"

Gwen glanced down at her lap where she was clenching her husband's hands. "We were supposed to adopt your baby."

Nina's heart raced. "What do you mean, you were *supposed* to?"

"After we lost our child, we paid Stanford Mansfield

to find us another one," the husband said. "He said he'd let us know when a baby became available."

Slade sat down beside Nina and placed a comforting hand on her shoulder. "Then what?"

"He called a couple of weeks later, and said he'd found a little girl, that her mother abandoned her and she needed someone to adopt her."

"He told you I abandoned her?" Nina said, furious.

Gwen nodded then lifted her head and looked at Nina again. "We honestly didn't know she was your baby. We believed him."

"So he brought my little girl to you?" Nina asked.

"Yes," Roan said.

Gwen's lip trembled. "I'm so sorry, Nina. And so ashamed…"

Nina bit down on her lower lip. "Ashamed? Why?"

"Because we…saw her, and she was so frail and needed physical therapy…so we decided we couldn't keep her." Gwen swiped back a tear that trickled down her cheek. "We didn't know how to handle a handicapped child."

Slade squeezed Nina's shoulder. "What did you do then?"

"We explained our misgivings to Mansfield," Roan said, then gave Nina a pleading look. "You have to understand. We lost one child, and we wanted a perfect one…"

Nina nearly came off the chair. She wanted to scream at them to leave, to tell them they were cruel, but she'd forced herself to school her emotions for so long, that she managed to rein in her temper.

"So what happened to Nina's baby?" Slade asked.

"We have no idea," Waldorp said. "I assumed someone else adopted her, and a week later, Mansfield phoned that he had another child for us."

"We had no idea she was your baby back then," Gwen said shakily. "I was so traumatized from our own ordeal that it never occurred to us that Mr. Mansfield had lied about the mother."

"And when we came to see you the other day?" Slade asked.

Gwen and her husband exchanged a wary look. "We put it all together and we were afraid," Gwen said in a low voice.

"Afraid Nina would blame you?" Slade asked. "That you'd lose your daughter?"

Gwen and Roan nodded miserably. "And that you'd think we had something to do with the kidnapping," Roan said. "But we didn't."

Nina understood their fear, and had no idea if it was founded. All she could think about was that this couple had rejected her daughter.

How else had Peyton suffered? And where was she now?

In a home or somewhere lost, alone, feeling abandoned?

SLADE STRUGGLED TO control his rage as the couple left. They wanted a *perfect* child.

Peyton hadn't been perfect.

So if they had given birth to a handicapped child, what would they have done—given that baby away, too?

Nina obviously didn't feel that way.

Dammit. He wanted to put her child back in her arms so badly he could taste it.

"Nina?"

"I don't understand people like them," Nina said, her voice laced with sadness.

Just as he couldn't believe it when his own mother

had dropped him off on the doorstep of the orphanage and never returned…

"Not everyone is as strong as you, Nina."

She gave a bitter laugh. "Me? You're forgetting that I'm the one who had the breakdown."

"Under the circumstances, having an emotional breakdown was understandable. You'd not only lost a child, but someone tormented you with that loss." He breathed out deeply to keep from touching her. "I'm going to make some phone calls."

She nodded, but she looked numb as she walked over, picked up the picture of her baby and stared at it. He imagined the train of her thoughts, and forced himself to block out his ping-ponging emotions.

He stepped into the kitchen and punched in the sheriff's number. "It's Slade Blackburn. The Waldorp couple just stopped by and admitted they were supposed to adopt Peyton Nash, that she was alive after that fire. But they declined to keep her because she was handicapped. They also confirmed that Stanford Mansfield handled the adoptions. Have you found him yet?"

"No, I checked his house and it looks like he left in a hurry. I have an APB out on him now."

"Let me know when you track him down. He might be able to lead us to Peyton."

He disconnected the call, then phoned Gage and asked him to have Ben Camp find out if Mansfield had a second house or vacation spot where he might be hiding out.

Then he spoke to Derrick McKinney and explained the latest revelations in the case.

When he ended the call, Slade pocketed his phone then went back to the living room.

Her gaze met his, tension thrumming between them. "I'm going to lie down."

He stared at her for a long moment, the memory of their lovemaking taunting him. He wanted to go back to bed with her.

But she had declared her love and he had thrown it in her face, so he knew he couldn't join her.

Still, he wouldn't give up.

He had to find Peyton for her. He couldn't fail her as he had his sister and mother.

NINA LAY AWAKE, restless and emotionally wrought. She found herself hating the Waldorp couple for giving her daughter back. If they'd kept her in Sanctuary, she might have recognized her, discovered where she was sooner.

All these years wasted.

Stop it, she reminded herself. *When you find her, you'll make up for lost time.* That is, *if* she found her. If she had been adopted, she might never be able to locate her. The people could have moved anywhere, even out of the country....

And if she hadn't? How had her little girl suffered?

Downstairs, she heard Slade moving around and prayed he'd come upstairs, crawl into bed and hold her.

But like so many other times, her prayers went unanswered.

Slade had slept with her because she was available and needy. God, he'd probably felt sorry for her.

Embarrassment flooded her and she vowed not to throw herself at him again.

She'd survived all these years alone. She would survive now.

She closed her eyes and focused, tried to hear her little girl singing to her. But the sound of a child's crying echoed in her head instead.

Peyton was lost and lonely and needed her mommy....

She climbed from bed and retrieved the tiny dress she'd bought years ago and inhaled the scent. Then she crawled back into bed, buried her head in the covers and sobbed her heart out.

Finally dawn streaked the sky, and she forced her achy body from bed and showered. Her face looked puffy, her eyes red-rimmed and swollen, and she made a futile attempt to cover the splotches with powder.

What difference did it make how she looked? Slade wasn't waiting downstairs to tell her he loved her.

She dressed in jeans, a cotton T-shirt and sandals and headed down the steps for coffee. Slade was sitting at the table with a cup already. His gaze met hers, deep and probing, and she wondered if he'd heard her crying.

But if he did, he didn't mention it. "I'm going to the jail to question Emery."

She poured herself a cup of coffee and sipped it. "I'll go with you."

For a moment, he looked as if he intended to tell her no, but she needed to see this through and would refuse to take no for an answer.

The storm clouds from the night before still lingered, painting the sky a dismal, dreary gray and adding a chill to the mountain air that sent a shiver through her as she stepped outside. Traffic was light, but a few shopkeepers were starting to open up, and the diner looked packed with the breakfast crowd.

Slade parked in front of the sheriff's office, and they headed inside silently. Her ankle still ached, but she managed to walk inside without reaching for Slade for help.

No more doing that. Keep it professional.

But as soon as they entered the front office, Nina knew something was wrong. The medical examiner was standing in the front talking to Sheriff Driscill in a hushed voice.

They glanced up, both looking haggard, and the sheriff shook his head as if in disgust.

"What's going on?" Slade asked.

Driscill blew out an exasperated breath. "Dr. Emery is dead."

"What?" Nina gasped.

The medical examiner ran a hand through his gray hair. "He committed suicide sometime in the night. Hanged himself with his own belt and tie."

SLADE GLANCED AT Nina's pale face and cursed. The damn coward had known he'd rot in jail, and couldn't face it. But he'd taken his secrets with him to his grave.

No...maybe not.

"Sheriff, did you get a subpoena for his files? He may have kept a database of the adoptions he arranged."

"I've put in a request," Sheriff Driscill said.

Slade's phone buzzed, and he glanced at the number. GAI. Maybe they had a lead.

"I need to get this." Nina gave him an inquisitive look, and he stepped outside to answer the phone.

"Blackburn, this is Derrick. I just talked to Brianna, and you won't believe this. We may have a lead on Peyton."

"What?"

"The social worker Nina knows called and there's a little girl who was just turned back into the system. She's been in foster care for years, has vision problems, and her latest foster parents say they can't take care of her."

"When and where was she born?"

"Sanctuary Hospital, eight years ago."

Slade scribbled down the address and disconnected

the phone, then turned to Nina. He hoped to hell this little girl was her child, and that she wouldn't have to face another disappointment.

REBECCA HUGGED HER rag doll to her chest, rocking her back and forth, as she sat huddled on the cot in the orphanage. A big girl with a bulldog face stared at her as if she didn't want her around, and downstairs a little boy was crying.

The place smelled dusty and a spider had spun a web above her bed on the dirt-coated window.

"So those people didn't want you?" the girl said with a snarl.

Rebecca shook her head, but clutched the doll tighter.

"You'd better get used to this place," the girl said. "No one wants kids who ain't normal."

Tears pushed at the back of Rebecca's eyes. The girl was right. The old lady had said the same thing. She'd called her a freak, said she knew why no one had ever kept her.

Why no one ever would.

The bulldog-faced girl barreled from the room, leaving her alone, and Rebecca toyed with her doll's pigtails. The doll looked so sad that Rebecca swayed her side to side like a baby. She wanted to sing to her, but her throat wouldn't work, and she was afraid if she tried, she'd start crying.

CHAPTER EIGHTEEN

NINA'S PULSE CLAMORED as they drove to the orphanage in the mountains. Slade had phoned the social worker and asked for all of the records of the little girl to verify that she was Peyton.

So far, the paper trail indicated she was. But DNA would have to be checked to make certain.

The tension that had riddled the air between them ever since they'd made love intensified as they neared the concrete building and parked.

"Nina," Slade said in a thick voice, "if this—"

"Don't," she said, cutting him off. "I know this little girl may or may not be mine. And maybe I won't even know, won't recognize her, but I have to do this."

He stared at her for a heartbeat, then nodded and they climbed out and walked up to the door in silence. Slade knocked, and a plump middle-aged woman with curly hair opened the door.

"I'm Mildred, the house mother," the woman said with a friendly smile. "Brianna McKinney phoned and explained the circumstances and said that you were coming."

Nina cleared her throat, willing herself to be strong when her legs felt like rubber. "Where is the little girl?"

"Up in the dorm room," Mildred said. "Poor little thing has hardly said a word since she arrived. The man and woman who brought her here weren't very nice."

Anguish squeezed Nina's chest, robbing her of breath.

"Can we talk to her?" Slade said.

"Of course." Mildred placed a hand on Nina's arm. "But please... She's been shuffled around a lot. Be gentle with her. I'm not sure how much more the little thing can handle."

Tears threatened to choke Nina, and she couldn't speak. She simply nodded, and she and Slade walked into the office to the right, sat down on the couch and waited while the woman climbed the wooden steps to retrieve the little girl. Anger at the system filled Nina. Her daughter or not, no child should have to suffer and not feel loved or wanted.

Seconds later, the wooden steps creaked, and a tiny girl with sandy-blond pigtails appeared in the doorway, wearing a faded dress that looked two sizes too large for her slender frame. Freckles dotted her nose and she pushed her thick glasses up on her face. She looked timid and scared, and so damn small and unhappy that Nina's heart melted.

"Peyton?"

The child scrunched her nose. "My name is Rebecca."

"Her papers say Rebecca Davis," Mildred interjected.

Nina forced herself to breathe. "Hi, Rebecca." She glanced at Slade, then spoke in a low whisper. "Davis is William's middle name."

His look hardened. "Then William has more questions to answer."

Nina spotted the rag doll in Rebecca's arms, and smiled. "I like your doll. What's her name?"

Rebecca chewed her bottom lip for a moment, then lifted her chin bravely. God help her. Nina wanted to sweep her in her arms and hug her.

"Pippi."

Nina smiled. "After Pippi Longstocking?"

Rebecca slowly nodded. "You know Pippi?"

"She's my favorite." Nina rose, slowly walked over and stooped down to Rebecca's eye level. "I have all the Pippi Longstocking books. I collected them when I was your age, and I read them to my second-grade class every year."

Rebecca pushed her glasses up on her nose again. "Really?"

"Really," Nina said. "When I was little, I used to want to be just like Pippi."

Rebecca's head bobbed up and down. "Me, too."

Nina stroked the doll's pigtails. "I like Mary Poppins, too. I always sing along with the songs. Do you like to sing?"

That wary look crossed her face again. "Yes," she said in a tiny voice. "But the people I stayed with didn't like it."

Protective instincts surged through Nina. She was almost certain this little girl was her long-lost child. But even if she wasn't her blood relative, she would take her home and love her anyway. "Come and sit with me and let me tell you a story."

She reached out her hand and Rebecca slid her small hand inside hers. Trusting but wary.

Nina's chest threatened to explode as she led Rebecca to the sofa. They sat down, her hand still holding Rebecca's.

She felt an instant connection, felt the emptiness inside her bursting with love and happiness. But she didn't want to frighten Rebecca.

Keeping her voice to a soothing pitch, she began, "A long time ago, eight years to be exact, I had a baby girl. But that night there was a terrible fire at the hospital where she was born. I got lost from her, and I've been looking for her ever since."

"I losted my mommy, too." Rebecca sighed. "Did you ever find your little girl?"

"I think so," Nina said softly. "I used to hear her sing to me at night. Do you know what song she would sing?"

Hope lit up the little girl's big blue eyes. "Mary Poppins—"

"Just a spoonful of sugar," Nina said, her throat thickening.

Rebecca gasped. "You heard me?"

Nina nodded, and tears filled her eyes. "Oh, honey, yes, I heard you." She raked a strand of Rebecca's hair from her forehead. "And I want you to come home and live with me forever."

Rebecca's lower lip quivered. "But everybody says I'm too much trouble." Her sweet voice cracked. "I have to have special help in school…and I take medicine for seizures."

Nina wanted to scream and shout and cry against all the injustice her daughter had suffered. "You are the most beautiful little girl I've ever seen," Nina whispered. "And I want to be your mommy forever."

Then she did what she'd wanted to do for years. She pulled her daughter into her arms and hugged her.

EMOTIONS CHOKED SLADE every time he replayed the reunion between Nina and her daughter in his head. Finally Nina had her child, and they could make a family.

A family he would not be a part of.

He clenched his jaw, reminding himself that he didn't want to be part of it. That he liked being alone.

But at night in his big, empty house the past two days, he found himself imagining the pitter-patter of little feet racing across the floor in the morning. Imagined Rebecca running into the bedroom where he and Nina lay cuddling.

Imagined Nina pregnant, her belly swollen with his own child. A brother or sister for Rebecca.

Dammit, he missed Nina. He even missed the little girl and he barely knew her.

Shoving those foolish images out of his mind, he headed toward the sheriff's office.

He'd finally convinced Driscill to bring William Hood and his mother in for questioning on kidnapping charges. He'd also requested Nina's father be present.

Any one of them could have grabbed Rebecca that night—or collaborated together.

But he hadn't told Nina about the meeting. He wanted to spare her.

He entered the sheriff's office, prepared to pound the truth out of the Hoods or Nash, but Nina's father looked distraught already.

"You're telling me that Nina's child did survive the fire?" Nash asked.

Slade nodded. "DNA confirmed she's Nina's daughter."

"My God…" Nash collapsed into one of the wooden chairs. "Nina was right all along…and all this time I didn't believe her." His voice choked. "I thought she just couldn't handle the grief."

"Someone very cruel kidnapped the child, then taunted her by leaving gifts and children's things in her house to drive her over the edge," Slade said stonily.

Nash buried his face in his hands. "Oh, my God, Nina tried to tell me… She must hate me…"

William's face paled. "Where has the child been all this time?"

Slade glared at him and his mother. "Don't pretend like you don't know. One or both of you arranged to have her kidnapped from the hospital. Either that or when the fire broke out, you saw the perfect opportunity."

William shot up. "Look, I admit that I didn't want the baby, but I didn't kidnap her. I honestly thought she died in that fire."

Mrs. Hood fumbled with her hands, and Slade angled himself to her. "But you did know, didn't you?"

"That girl and her illegitimate child were going to ruin our family!" she shrieked.

William suddenly turned on his mother with a shocked look. "Mother, what did you do?"

"I didn't do anything," Mrs. Hood cried. "Except to think of you."

"Mother," William spat out, "what happened?"

Mrs. Hood raked a strand of silver hair from her cheek, her diamonds glittering. "Nothing that was so horrible, so don't look at me like that. I simply paid Stanford Mansfield to arrange an adoption. The baby was supposed to go to a nice young couple who could raise her, one with two parents."

"The Waldorps," Slade filled in. "But when they realized the little girl was handicapped, they decided they didn't want her either."

Mr. Nash jerked his head up. "Then what happened to her?"

"They put her in foster care," Slade said, rage eating at him. "She's been shuffled from one place to another all these years, while you all ignored Nina and her."

Nash paced across the room, his expression miserable. Slade was glad to see that he did care about his daughter. Maybe they could reconcile.

But Mrs. Hood showed no regrets.

Slade turned on her. "Did you steal the baby or did you hire someone?"

The woman's hawklike eyes gleamed. "I refuse to say another word until I have an attorney."

NINA HUNG UP the phone, her emotions on a roller coaster. Getting to know her daughter, shopping for furniture and bedding to decorate her room, laughing and watching movies and cuddling at night had been pure bliss. She couldn't wait until the four-poster white bed she'd ordered arrived and saw Rebecca snuggled up, sleeping under the lacy canopy.

Although occasionally her anger and sadness over the years they'd lost surfaced, she refused to dwell on it. They'd finally found each other and she would never be separated from her daughter again.

She scraped her hand through her hair, staring at the phone in dismay. And now her father had called. He'd apologized for not believing her before, for letting her down, and wanted to make it up to her and her daughter. She'd declined his offer of money, but was overjoyed to know that he wanted to be a grandfather, that he would be a part of her family.

The only thing missing was Slade.

He thought she'd mistaken gratitude for love, but he was wrong. She loved him deeply.

Enough to let him go.

Not every man wanted a ready-made family, especially one with challenges to face.

Rebecca suddenly appeared at the bottom of the steps in her new pink pajamas. "Tuck me in, Mommy."

Nina smiled and took Rebecca's small hand in hers, and they walked to her bedroom. Rebecca climbed in bed and hugged her rag doll, and Nina crawled in bed beside her, then sang to her until Rebecca's eyelids drooped and she drifted asleep. Even then, she lay and watched her daughter for a while, soaking in the fact that she finally had her home.

Finally she fell into a deep sleep, content and dreaming of her first Christmas to come with her daughter home.

But sometime later, she woke to the acrid scent of smoke wafting toward her. A second later, the fire alarm downstairs blared.

Panic assaulted her, and she jumped up and ran to the steps. Dear heavens, the foyer was on fire.

The flames were spreading quickly, eating up the living room and front of the house, completely blocking her path to the door. Smoke clogged her lungs as she raced up the steps.

She had to get Rebecca out.

With one hand, she grabbed the phone and punched 9-1-1. With the other she gently shook her daughter. Smoke was rising and seeping into the hallway, wood crackling downstairs.

The 9-1-1 operator answered. "My house is on fire," Nina said, then recited her address and dropped the phone, pulling Rebecca into her arms. "Wake up, sweetie. We have to get out of here."

Rebecca stirred and rubbed her eyes. "Mommy?"

"Honey, there's a fire downstairs. We have to get out."

Her mind raced for an escape route. The only way out was downstairs, but they couldn't make it through the blaze. They'd have to climb through a window.

Rebecca coughed. "Mommy, I'm scared…"

"I know, sugar." Nina stroked her hair. "But I'll take care of you, I promise." She had to. She couldn't lose her little girl again.

She glanced out the window in her room, but there was nothing to hold on to outside the window, no ledge, no tree, nothing. Pulse pounding, she buried Rebecca's head against her chest to keep her from inhaling smoke and ran to the room she planned to paint for her daughter.

A huge oak tree stood beside the house, its branches massive, one limb touching the glass pane. She and Rebecca had talked about building a tree house in it.

"I'm going to sit you down, honey, and open the window," Nina said. "Then we're going to crawl into the tree. When the firemen arrive, they'll rescue us."

Rebecca's eyes widened. "I can't climb a tree, Mommy."

Nina hated the sound of her daughter's fear and uncertainty, but smoke was beginning to curl into the room, and glass downstairs shattered as the fire spread.

She stooped down and stroked her arms. "Rebecca, remember the story we read last night about the little engine that could?"

Rebecca's head bobbed up and down. "The little engine didn't think he could make it—"

"But he said, 'I think I can, I think I can,' and he did," Nina whispered. "That's what we have to do now."

"All right." Rebecca's chin lifted again, and Nina's heart swelled. Her child wasn't handicapped. She was the bravest, most special little girl in the world.

"Ready?" Nina asked.

Rebecca nodded, and Nina pushed open the window and lifted her in her arms. "Just grab that branch, sweetie, wrap your arms around it and hang on."

Rebecca tried, but her arms were too weak, and Nina gasped as she missed and nearly plunged downward.

Fear threatened to immobilize her, but she refused to give up. She hadn't searched all these years for her child only to lose her now.

She hugged Rebecca to her. "Listen, sweetie, I'm going to climb first, then pull you up."

Rebecca tugged at her arm. "No. Don't leave me, Mommy."

Tears filled Nina's eyes, and she cradled Rebecca's small face between her hands. "Sweetheart, I love you. I will never leave you, you understand?"

Rebecca's chin quivered, but she finally nodded.

Smoke was growing thicker, and the blaze had inched up the steps and was eating at the wooden doorway of the bedroom.

They had to hurry.

She kissed Rebecca's cheek, then released her and dragged a chair to the window. She climbed in the chair, then lifted Rebecca up beside her. Then she hoisted herself through the window. She was shaking all over, but gripped the limb with all her might, testing it to make sure it would hold them.

Satisfied it would, she reached for her daughter. "Come on, sweetie."

Rebecca stood on tiptoes in the chair and held up her arms. "I think I can, I think I can…"

Nina grabbed her and hauled her up beside her. It took every bit of concentration for her to steady them, but she wrapped Rebecca beneath her, and held on for dear life.

FEAR STABBED SLADE AS he raced up Nina's drive. He'd been at the sheriff's waiting on Mrs. Hood's lawyer when the 9-1-1 call had come in.

He'd run out and nearly had a heart attack as he'd driven to her house, afraid he would be too late.

Afraid he might lose her.

God, he loved her.…

He couldn't let her go. And he sure as hell couldn't let her die....

Behind him, a siren wailed, but he beat the fire engine to the house, threw the vehicle into Park, jumped out and raced toward the house. The fire was blazing, the entire front burning wildly, smoke floating in a thick plume.

Where was Nina? Had she and Rebecca escaped?

Frantically he shouted her name over and over as he ran to the side of the house, searching the windows to see if she was trapped inside.

"Nina!" he shouted. "Nina, where are you?"

Wood crackled and popped, glass shattering as the porch collapsed and the fire spread upward. He coughed, the heat scalding him as he checked the back of the house. On fire, too.

Slade shouted Nina's name again, then Rebecca's. Frantically, he raced to the other side of the house and checked the guest bedroom window. It was ajar and flames shot through the opening.

Panic nearly made him collapse. There was no way they could survive....

CHAPTER NINETEEN

"SLADE!"

The fire engine wailed closer, but Slade was certain he'd heard Nina. Where the hell was she?

Suddenly a low, keening sound echoed from somewhere above. The tree branch shook. Leaves rained down.

"Nina?"

"Slade! We're up here! Hurry!"

Slade frowned and peered through the fog of smoke, then spotted Nina cradling her daughter huddled on a tree branch.

Thank God they were alive.

"Hang on, I'll be right there." He studied the tree, gauging his path, then grabbed the lowest branch and hurled himself upward. He climbed as quickly as possible, testing each branch as he climbed to make sure it would hold him.

Rebecca looked pale in the light of the blaze, and both she and Nina were sweating from the heat. One branch, two, another... He climbed until he made it to the branch below them.

"Take Rebecca down first," Nina cried.

Slade's gaze met hers, and he knew that she was afraid the branch was going to catch on fire. The flames were inching out the window toward her.

"I'm going to get you both down," he said through gritted teeth.

"Please, Slade, take her," Nina whispered.

"Mommy, I don't want to leave you," Rebecca sobbed.

"I'll be right behind you," Nina said softly. "I promise."

Rebecca's fingers tightened around her for a second, then Slade stroked her hair.

"Rebecca, honey, listen to me. I'm going to save you and your mommy, but you have to trust me."

Terror darkened her eyes as she clung to Nina. "Mommy…"

Nina lifted her daughter's chin and forced her to look at her. "You can trust Slade, honey. I'll be right behind you, I promise. But we have to hurry."

Rebecca bit down on her lip. "'Kay."

Slade smiled at her. "That's good, honey. Now I want you to climb on my back, and wrap your arms around my neck like a monkey. Then put your legs around me, too, and hold on as tight as you can."

"Remember the little engine," Nina said softly.

Nina helped her daughter wind her arms around his neck, then Rebecca squeezed her little legs to his waist, and he began climbing down.

The fire engine finally arrived and careened to a stop, and he shouted for them to help him. The men jumped into motion. Two men dragged a hose to douse the flames while another spotted him as he dropped to the ground with Rebecca and raced over with a ladder.

"I'll get Nina, you try to save the house," Slade shouted. He didn't wait on a response, but gripped the ladder and began climbing. Nina was trying to make her way down, but slipped and dangled from a branch above him. Rebecca screamed, and Nina looked down, hanging on to the branch with one hand and clawing to reach it with the other.

"Hurry, I'm slipping," Nina cried.

"Hang on, honey." Slade grabbed her just before she plunged to the ground.

Fear shot through him as he pulled her to him, and he silently vowed never to leave her again. Then together they climbed down the ladder.

The firefighter helped her off the ladder first, then Slade jumped to the ground.

Nina pulled Rebecca into her arms, and the little girl clung to her, both of them trembling. He ushered them away from the heat of the burning house.

Another siren screeched, and suddenly the sheriff's car roared to a stop. Sheriff Driscill climbed out and strode toward them. Slade saw someone in the back of the squad car and frowned.

"You all okay?" Sheriff Driscill asked.

Slade nodded. "It was close, but yeah."

"I know who started the fire." Driscill jerked his thumb toward the car. "The same person who kidnapped the baby."

Nina pressed her daughter tighter into her embrace, and glanced at the police car. Slade saw the woman beating at the glass, screaming and crying.

"Mitzi..." Nina said in a stunned voice.

"I caught her racing away around the corner. She was hysterical, screaming that she had to do it. That she was afraid William would want you back now you found the child."

"William gave up his rights a long time ago," Nina said stiffly.

The sheriff nodded. "She also admitted that Hood's mother was in cahoots with her. Mitzi actually kidnapped the baby from the hospital, but Hood's mother paid for the adoption. They'll both serve time for this." He paused. "And one of my deputies found Mansfield. He's bringing him in, as well. He'll be charged with conspiracy."

Nina glanced at her house, the flames bursting higher.

"I'm sorry you lost the house," Slade said.

"It doesn't matter." Nina scooped Rebecca into her arms and hugged her. "I have all that's important right here."

Slade's resistance completely shattered. How could he not love a woman like her? She knew her priorities and fought for them.

"Thank you for saving us, Slade," she whispered.

He hesitated, remembered that he'd accused her of gratitude instead of love before, and shame filled him. He'd been a coward, had thought by punishing himself by being alone and denying himself happiness that he could atone for his guilt.

But Nina had taught him about courage. About really loving... "I don't want your gratitude, Nina."

Fire crackled and popped, illuminating her beautiful face. But a puzzled look darkened her eyes. "Then what do you want, Slade?"

His throat thickened, and he knew he was taking a chance. Knew that he still might fail sometimes or lose them one day.

But he didn't want to lose them now.

"I want your love," he said in a husky voice.

A slow smile softened her mouth, and she placed a hand against his chest. "You have that already."

"And you have mine," Slade said gruffly.

Nina smiled, a radiant look that he knew would be

imprinted in his mind forever. A look filled with love and hope and promises of a happily-ever-after.

Then she glanced down at her daughter, who was watching them with big eyes.

Slade gently stroked Rebecca's hair. "You have a mommy now, Rebecca. How would you feel about having a daddy, too?"

Her eyes lit up and she nodded wildly. Moved beyond speech, he wrapped his arms around both of them.

"I love you, Nina," he said against her hair. "And I will love you and your daughter forever, I promise."

"I love you, too," Nina whispered.

Then she closed her mouth over his and kissed him.

* * * * *

THE MISSING TWIN

To Mother for all the love she gave her own twins...

CHAPTER ONE

FEAR CLOGGED FIVE-YEAR-OLD Sara Andrews's throat. She could see her twin sister running from the old wooden house, stumbling down the porch steps, crying as she raced toward the woods.

"Help me," Cissy cried. "He's gonna hurt Mommy!"

The wind whistled, shaking the trees. Leaves swirled and rained down. A dog howled in the distance.

Then thunder boomed.

No, not thunder.

It was the big, hulking man storming down the steps. "Cissy!" the monster bellowed. "Come back here."

He slapped at the branches with his beefy fists, moving so fast he was nearly on top of her. Then he lunged for her.

Cissy screamed and darted to the right, running, running, running into the darkness....

The monster reached a pawlike hand toward her and snatched her jacket. Cissy screamed again, stumbled and fell to the ground. But her jacket slid off in the man's hands, and he cursed.

Sweat slid down Sara's temple. Her heart was pounding so loud she could hear it beating in her ears. "Get up," Sara whispered. "Get up and run, Cissy."

As if Cissy heard her, she took a deep breath, grabbed a fistful of dirt and hurled it at the man.

The dust sprayed his eyes and he cursed, then swung

one fist toward Cissy. Cissy dodged the blow, pushed herself to her hands and knees and stood. Tree branches cracked. The wind screeched.

The monster roared and dove for her.

"No!" Sara cried. "Run, Cissy, run."

Tears streamed down her sister's cheeks as Cissy tried to run, but the monster yanked her by the hair and dragged her back toward the house.

"Help me!" Cissy cried. "Please, help me!"

"No!" Sara screamed. "Let her go…."

MADELYN ANDREWS RACED toward her daughter's bedroom, her lungs tightening at the sound of her daughter's terrified sobs. Outside, the wind roared off the mountain and sleet pelted the window, reminding her that a late winter storm raged around the small town of Sanctuary, North Carolina.

Shivering with the cold, she threw open the door, flipped on the sunflower lamp Sara had begged for and crossed the distance to her little girl's bed. Sara was thrashing around, tangled in the bright green comforter, sobbing and shaking.

"No, don't hurt her, don't hurt Cissy…"

Madelyn's heart broke, worry throbbing inside her as she eased herself onto the mattress and gently shook Sara.

"Honey, wake up. It's just a nightmare," she whispered. Although Sara would insist that it was real.

Sara sobbed harder, swinging out her hands as if fighting off an invisible monster, and Madelyn pulled her into her arms. Tears blurred her own eyes as she rocked her back and forth. "Shh, honey, Mommy's here. It's all right."

"Gonna hurt Mommy…" Sara wailed. "Help Cissy. We have to help Cissy!"

"Shh, baby." Madelyn stroked Sara's fine, blond hair. "No one is going to hurt Mommy. I'm right here."

Sara jerked her eyes open, her pupils distorted, her lower lip quivering. For a moment, she stared at Madelyn as if she didn't recognize her.

"But Cissy's mommy is hurt," Sara said in a shaky voice. "The bad man chased Cissy into the woods and he catched her, and…"

"It was a dream." Madelyn cupped Sara's face between her hands, imploring her to believe her. "A really bad dream, sweetheart, but it was just a nightmare."

"No," Sara choked out. "It was real. Cissy's in trouble and we gots to help her or he's gonna hurt her…"

"Oh, honey," Madelyn said softly.

Sara gulped. "It *was* real, Mommy. I saw Cissy." Tears rolled down her face. "And she saw me. She begged me to help her. I tolded her to get up and run, but he caught her and dragged her back to the house…."

Shaken by the horror in Sara's voice, Madelyn took a deep breath, desperately trying to calm the anxiety bleeding through her.

She dried Sara's tears with her fingers. "Sara, I told you that we lost Cissy a long time ago."

"No," Sara said with a firm shake of her head. "She lives with that other mommy. But if we don't helps her, that mean man's gonna kill 'em both."

Madelyn hugged Sara to her, lost in turmoil.

Something was very wrong with her little girl. She'd been having these nightmares for the past two months, ever since they'd moved back to Sanctuary, and nothing Madelyn had done or said had helped. Not her long talks with her about Cissy, Sara's twin who they'd lost at birth, or the therapists Madelyn had consulted for assistance.

"Please, Mommy," Sara cried. "We gots to do something."

A tear slid down Madelyn's cheek. The day the twins had been born was the happiest and saddest day of her life. She'd gotten Sara but lost her sister.

She'd heard that twins had a special connection, but why was Sara still dreaming that Cissy had survived?

Knowing neither she nor Sara would sleep well the rest of the night, she carried Sara to her bed, then snuggled beside her. Sara lay on her side, sniffling for another hour, then finally drifted into an exhausted sleep.

Madelyn's heart wrenched, and she lay and watched her daughter, unable to sleep. Just as dawn streaked the sky, her telephone jangled. Who could be calling at this hour? She checked the caller ID. Her mother.

She grabbed the handset, then slid from the bed, walked to the window and connected the call.

"Mom? What's wrong? Are you all right?"

"Yes, honey, I'm fine. Have you seen the news?"

"No, why? What's going on?"

"A big story aired about a doctor in Sanctuary who stole babies and sold them. His name was Dr. Emery. Isn't that the doctor who delivered the twins?"

"Yes. Oh, my god. What else did the story say?"

"This lady named Nina Nash thought her baby died in that big hospital fire eight years ago but discovered her child was alive. She hired these detectives at an agency called Guardian Angel Investigations there in Sanctuary. These men are all dedicated to finding missing children and they found her little girl."

A cold chill swept up Madelyn's spine. She glanced back at the bed where Sara was sleeping.

Dear God.

Was it possible that Cissy could have survived?

CALEB WALKER ENTERED the offices of GAI, his neck knotted with nerves. He hadn't liked the sound of his boss's voice when he called. The urgency had him postponing his visit to the cemetery to visit his wife's grave this morning, and that pissed him off. He'd wanted to go by first thing, to pay his respects, leave Mara's flowers, talk to her and beg her forgiveness one more time....

Gage's voice rose from his office, breaking into his thoughts, and Caleb forced himself to focus. There would be time for seeing Mara later. Time to drown his sorrows and guilt.

He climbed the steps to Gage's office, his mind racing. Had another child gone missing?

Or was there another case related to Sanctuary Hospital? Ever since the news had broken about the recovery of Nina Nash's daughter and Dr. Emery's arrest for selling babies, the phones had gone crazy.

People from all over were demanding to know if their adoptions were legal. GAI had been plagued by crank calls, as well, two from distraught women whose accusations of baby kidnapping had turned out to be false. The women had been so desperate for a child they'd tried to use the illegal adoptions to claim one for themselves.

Caleb twisted the hand-carved arrowhead around his neck to calm himself as he knocked on his boss's office door.

"Come in."

Caleb opened the door and Gage stood.

"I'm glad you're here," Gage said without preamble. "We have a new client. One I'd like for you to handle."

Caleb narrowed his eyes. "Why me?"

Gage's eyes darkened. "You'll know after you meet her and her five-year-old daughter, Sara. Sara insists she sees her twin in her nightmares, that her sister is in trouble."

"I don't understand," Caleb said. "Sounds like a child having bad dreams, not a missing person case."

"It gets even more interesting." Gage flicked his gaze to the conference room across the hall. "The mother claims the twin died at birth, but Sara insists she's alive."

Damn. Gage requested him because of his so-called sixth sense. He wished to hell he'd never divulged that detail.

But Gage had caught him in a weak moment.

Gage motioned for him to follow. "Come on, they're waiting."

Caleb rolled his hands into fists, then forced himself to flex them again, struggling to control his emotions. Emotions had no place in business. And business was his life now.

The moment Caleb entered the conference room, he spotted the woman sitting in a wing chair cradling the little girl in her lap. Gage had purposely designed the room with cozy seating nooks to put clients at ease.

But nothing about this woman appeared to be at ease.

Her slender body radiated with tension, her eyes looked haunted, her expression wary.

Yet he was also struck by her startling beauty. Copper-colored hair draped her shoulders and flowed like silk around a heart-shaped face. Big, green eyes gazed at him as if she desperately needed a friend, and freckles dotted her fair skin, making her look young and vulnerable. Her outfit was simple, too, not meant to be enticing—long denim skirt, peasant blouse—yet the soft colors made her look utterly feminine.

And downright earthy.

Earthy in his book meant sexy. Lethal combinations to a man who had been celibate for the past three years.

Dammit. He hadn't been attracted to another woman since Mara. He sure as hell didn't want to be attracted to a client. Not one with a kid who claimed to see her dead sister.

Then his gaze fell to the little blonde munchkin, and his lungs tightened. She looked tiny and frail and terrified and so lost that his protective instincts kicked in.

"Ms. Andrews," Gage began. "This is Caleb Walker. He's one of our agents at GAI. I'd like for him to hear your story."

The woman squared her shoulders as if anticipating a confrontation. She expected skepticism.

"You can call me Madelyn," she said in a husky voice that sounded as if it was laced with whiskey.

Gage claimed the love seat, leaving the other wing chair nearest Madelyn for him. Caleb lowered himself into it, aware his size might intimidate the little girl.

"What's your name?" he asked in a gentle tone.

Eyes that mirrored her mother's stared up at him as if she was trying to decide if he was friend or foe. Smart kid. She should be wary of strangers.

He smiled slowly, trying to ease her discomfort. But his senses prickled, suggesting she was special in some way. That she possessed a sixth sense herself.

Not that he would wish that on anyone, especially a kid.

"Let's see," he said, a smile quirking his mouth. "Are you Little Miss Sunshine?"

A tiny smile lit her eyes, and she relaxed slightly and loosened her grip on her blanket. "No, silly. I'm Sara."

"Hi, Sara," he said gruffly. "That's a pretty name."

"Thank you," she said, her tone sounding grown up for such a little bitty thing. "It's my Gran's middle name."

"Okay, Sara. Tell me what's going on so I can help you."

Madelyn stroked her daughter's hair. "Sara's been having nightmares for the past two months, ever since we moved back to town."

"Where are you from?" Caleb asked, probing for background information.

Madelyn hugged Sara closer. "We moved to Charlotte four years ago to be near my mom, but Sara was born in Sanctuary. Recently my mother suffered a stroke, and I found a nursing facility here that she liked, so I bought the craft shop in town, and we packed up and moved back."

"I see," Caleb said. Had the move triggered these nightmares? "Sara, did you have dreams of your sister when you lived in Charlotte?"

Sara nodded and twirled a strand of hair around her finger. "We talked and sang songs and told secrets."

Caleb narrowed his eyes. "What kinds of secrets?"

Sara pursed her mouth. "They're not secrets if I tell."

Hmm. She was loyal to her sister. But those secrets might be important.

"She has dreamed about her twin all her life," Madelyn confirmed. "But lately those dreams have been disturbing."

Sara piped up. "Her name is Cissy, and she looks just like me."

Caleb nodded, aware that she used the present tense. "Sara and Cissy. How old are you?"

"Five," Sara said and held up five fingers. "Cissy's five, too."

He smiled again. "You're identical twins?"

She swung her feet. "Yep, 'cept I gots a birthmark on my right arm and hers is on the other side." She pointed to a small, pale, crescent-moon shape on her forearm.

Caleb folded his hands. He needed to keep Sara talking. "Tell me what happens in your dreams, Sara."

Terror darkened the little girl's face. "Cissy is scared and she's screamin' and she runned into the woods."

Damn. He understood about nightmares, how real and haunting they could seem. "Who is she running from?" Caleb asked.

"From a big, mean man. He screamed at her mommy," Sara said with conviction. "Cissy says he's gonna kill them."

Caleb intentionally lowered his voice. "Can you see his face? Does she call him by name?"

Sara chewed on her thumb for a moment as if trying to picture the man in her mind. "No, I can't see him." Her voice rose with anxiety. "But I saw Cissy running and crying."

Caleb clenched his hands, listening, hating the terror in the little girl's voice. The last thing he wanted to do was traumatize a troubled child by doubting her or confirming her fears. And she was genuinely afraid and believed what she was telling him.

His sixth sense kicked in. This little girl was...different. Did she truly have a psychic connection to her twin?

Other questions bombarded him: If her sister was dead, was Sara seeing and conversing with her spirit? Was Sara a medium? If so, why was she seeing images of Cissy at the same age as herself instead of the infant she'd been when she died? Was Cissy's growth a figment of Sara's imagination?

Another theory rattled through his head. Or could Sara be experiencing premonitions? Could Cissy's spirit be trying to warn Sara that Sara was in danger from some future attacker?

"You're a brave girl," Caleb said, then patted Sara's arm. "And if you see anything else—the man's face, or the mommy's—I want you to tell me. Okay?"

Sara bobbed her little head up and down, although she looked wrung out now, as if relaying her nightmare had drained her. Or maybe she was worried that describing the terrifying ordeal might make it come true.

He lifted his gaze to Madelyn. "Can we talk alone?"

Her wary gaze flew to his. "I don't like to leave Sara by herself."

Gage retrieved a pad of paper and some crayons and gestured to the coffee table. "It's okay, Madelyn. I have a little girl, too. Her name is Ruby and she likes to draw when she comes to the office." He stooped down and handed the crayons to Sara. "Would you like to use Ruby's crayons to draw a picture of Cissy while Caleb talks to your mother?"

Sara studied him for a long moment, then nodded. Madelyn reluctantly stood and settled Sara on the floor in front of the coffee table. Caleb gestured to the door, and she led the way out into the hallway.

The moment he closed the door, she whirled on him, arms crossed. "Listen, Mr. Walker, I know you probably think that Sara is disturbed, and believe me, I've taken her to shrinks, consulted with specialists, tried to talk to her myself, but these nightmares keep reoccurring, and there has to be a reason."

Caleb shifted. "Did these doctors make a diagnosis?"

Madelyn sighed, her expression strained. "Oh, yes, lots of them. The first doctor suggested Sara was seeing herself, that the twin was a mirror image. Doctor Number Two implied that she was terrified because she had no father, then suggested she made up the bizarre connection with Cissy to get attention. His colleague indicated Sara might be bipolar and wanted to put her in a special twin study, run a mountain of tests and analyze her brain." She blew out a breath, sending her bangs fluttering. "The last one suggested she was schizophrenic and advised me to let him prescribe drugs."

Caleb frowned. "Did you try medication?"

"No," Madelyn said emphatically. "She's only five years old." She paced across the hall, her hands knotting in the folds of her skirt. "I really hoped that I could handle it, that if I carried Sara to see Cissy's grave she'd accept that her sister is gone."

"What happened at the cemetery?" Caleb asked. "Did she see Cissy?"

Madelyn cleared her throat. "She insisted that Cissy wasn't buried in the grave. That it was empty."

Tears filled Madelyn's eyes, making Caleb's gut clench.

"But I know she is," Madelyn said in a haunted whisper. "Because I buried her myself."

CHAPTER TWO

SARA'S WORDS HAUNTED Madelyn as Caleb coaxed her into his office.

"Cissy's not dead, Mommy. She gots another mommy, and she likes to play dolls and read stories just like me." Then Sara had started to cry. *"But her mommy's in trouble and this mean man's gonna hurt her and Cissy."*

Only she *had* buried Cissy five years ago.

Caleb propped himself against the desk edge while she sank onto a chair.

"If you're so sure Sara is wrong, why did you come to GAI?" Caleb asked.

Madelyn desperately tried to decipher the intensity in his deep brown eyes. The man scared the hell out of her.

He was huge, broad-shouldered, muscular, dark-skinned, with shoulder-length thick, black hair, and had the gruffest voice she'd ever heard. His Native American roots ran deep and infused him with a quiet strength that radiated from his every pore but also made him appear dangerous, like a warrior from the past.

Yet he had been gentle with Sara and obviously the head of GAI trusted him.

"My mother phoned. She heard a news story about GAI uncovering some illegal adoptions associated with Dr. Emery, babies he delivered at Sanctuary Hospital."

"You delivered the twins there?"

"Yes."

"What about the father?" Caleb asked.

Madelyn chewed her bottom lip. "He left us when Sara started calling her dead sister's name. I haven't seen him or heard from him since."

Caleb frowned. "He doesn't send child support?"

"I didn't want it," Madelyn said. "Not that he would have come through. He was having financial problems back then, his business failing."

Caleb sighed. "I'm sorry. Tell me about the delivery."

Grief welled inside Madelyn. "The night I went into labor, I had a car accident," Madelyn began. "I was going to the store when a car sideswiped me. I lost control and careened into a ditch." She knotted her hands. "My water broke and I went into labor."

Caleb narrowed his eyes. "What happened to the driver?"

Anger surged through Madelyn at the reminder. "He left the scene."

Caleb's big body tensed. "He didn't stop to see if you were okay or call an ambulance?"

"No." Madelyn rubbed her hands up and down her arms. "And the police never caught him." Not that they'd looked very hard. And she hadn't seen the vehicle so she hadn't been able to give them a description of it or the driver.

Caleb's expression darkened. "So the accident triggered your labor?"

Madelyn nodded.

"Were you injured anywhere else?"

She shrugged. "Some bruises and contusions. I lost consciousness and the doctor said I was hemorrhaging, so he did an emergency C-section and took the babies."

Caleb's jaw clenched. "You weren't awake during the delivery?"

"No," Madelyn said, fidgeting.

"But you held the babies when you regained consciousness?"

"I was out for a couple of hours. When I came to, I got to hold Sara for a minute. She'd been in ICU, being monitored." Madelyn ran a hand through her hair. "But Cissy... No, I never held her. Dr. Emery said...she was deformed, stillborn, that it was better that I not remember her that way."

Caleb arched a thick, black brow. "So you never actually saw your other baby?"

"No..." Emotions welled in her throat. She tried to steel herself against them, but memories of that night crashed around her. The fear, the disorientation, the joy, the loss... "I...was so distraught, so grief-stricken that the doctor sedated me." She wiped at a tear slipping down her cheek. "Besides I...I believed Dr. Emery. Then there was Sara, and she was so beautiful and tiny, and I was so glad she'd survived. And she needed me...."

Caleb's silence made her rethink that night, and questions nagged at her. If she hadn't seen Cissy, maybe she hadn't died or been deformed at all.

"Did the medical examiner perform an autopsy on the baby?" Caleb asked.

"No." Tears burned the backs of her eyelids. "I... didn't want it. Didn't want to put her through it."

Although maybe she should have insisted. Then she'd have proof that her baby hadn't survived, and she'd know exactly what had been wrong with her.

Sara's insistence that she saw Cissy in her visions taunted her. If Dr. Emery had lied to other people, perhaps he'd lied to her. "We have to talk to Dr. Emery and force him to tell me the truth about Cissy."

"I'm afraid that's impossible," Caleb said quietly. "Dr. Emery hanged himself the day after he was arrested."

A desolate feeling engulfed Madelyn. "If he's dead, how will we ever learn the truth?"

Caleb's intense gaze settled on her. "Trust me. We'll find the truth."

"Then you'll investigate?"

"Yes." He gestured toward the conference room and pushed open the door to where Sara was drawing.

The childlike sketch showed Sara and her twin sister displaying their birthmarks. A second picture revealed a greenhouse full of sunflowers, and a tire swing hanging from a big tree in the yard.

Sara had also drawn an ugly, hairy, monsterlike man with jagged teeth and pawlike hands. "That's the meanie gonna hurt Cissy and her mommy," Sara said.

She turned her big, green eyes toward Caleb. "Will you stop him, Mister?"

ANXIETY KNOTTED CALEB'S SHOULDERS. How could he say no to this innocent little girl? She seemed so terrified....

But if he promised to save her sister and this woman and failed, he wouldn't be able to live with himself. Not after failing Mara and his own son.

Hell, he was getting way ahead of himself. First, he had to determine if Cissy Andrews was actually alive.

The fact that Sara truly believed that she was real was obvious. But he couldn't dismiss the shrinks' theories, either. Not yet.

Gage glanced at the sketch, then at him as if silently asking his opinion.

He gave him a noncommittal look. "We need access to Emery's records."

"Afraid that's not going to happen," Gage said. "He destroyed them before he killed himself."

Damn. So they had no records, and he couldn't push a dead man for answers. His visions didn't work that way.

"What about the lawyer who handled the adoptions?" Caleb asked. "Wasn't his name Mansfield?"

"Yeah. The sheriff brought him in for questioning. He's facing charges, but his case is still pending, so he was released on bail."

"Then we look at his records," Caleb said.

"D.A. already confiscated them," Gage said. "And she's not sharing. Not with privacy issues and the legal and moral rights regarding adoptions."

Caleb stewed over that problem. They didn't work for the cops or have to follow the rules. If he knew where those records were, he'd find a way to search them.

But talking to Mansfield would be faster.

First, there was something else that had to be done. Something that would be painful for Madelyn. But a task that was necessary in order to verify whether or not that grave held a baby.

"Madelyn," he said in a voice low enough not to reach Sara's ears. "We need to exhume the casket you buried."

Grief flickered in her eyes as she glanced at Sara who was madly coloring another picture of her and Cissy. This time they were holding hands, dancing in the middle of a sea of sunflowers.

"All right," Madelyn said firmly. "If it'll help us learn the truth, then let's do it as soon as possible."

MADELYN PICTURED THE Lost Angels section at Sanctuary Gardens where they'd held Cissy's memorial service in her mind and nausea flooded her. Still, with the questions Caleb had raised, Sara's nightmares, and the revelations about Dr. Emery, she wouldn't rest until she knew if Cissy was really buried in that grave.

Compassion darkened Caleb's eyes. "Okay. We'll get the ball rolling."

Madelyn nodded, gripping her emotions with a firm hand. For so long she had accepted that Cissy was dead that it was hard for her to wrap her mind around the fact that she might have survived. That she might be living somewhere with another family. That a physician would actually deceive his patients and sell their babies.

But the doctor's arrest was proof of the possibility, creating doubts, and she had to investigate or she would always wonder.

Sara ran to her, waving her drawing, her ponytail bobbing. "Look, Mommy, Cissy's gonna be so happy when we brings her home with us. She loves sunflowers. They're all around her."

"The sunflowers are beautiful," Madelyn said, her heart aching as worry knotted her insides. Was it true that twins were only half of a whole? What if they didn't find out Cissy was alive and bring her home? How would Sara take the news?

Would she be able to move on and finally be happy?

Sara tugged at Madelyn's hand. "We gots to hurry, Mommy."

Madelyn stroked Sara's hair away from her forehead. "Sweetheart, that's why we're here. Caleb—Mr. Walker—is going to investigate and find out why you're seeing these scary things."

Sara angled her face toward Caleb. "Thank you for 'vestigatin', Mister."

Madelyn smiled in spite of her turmoil because, after all, Sara was a charmer. Caleb knelt and extended his hand to Sara, and Madelyn couldn't help but notice how strong and calloused and tanned his fingers were, how masculine.

"I promise I'll do whatever I can to help you, Sara."

An odd look crossed Sara's face, then she took Caleb's hand and turned it over in her own small one and studied his palm as if she could see inside the man through his fingers. Madelyn noted the breadth of his palm against Sara's tiny one and thought that Sara might be frightened of him, but she seemed to immediately trust him.

In fact, neither one spoke for a moment. They simply stared at each other, silent, assessing, as if sharing some private moment.

"You gots an Indian name?" Sara asked in a whisper.

Caleb nodded. "Firewalker."

Sara's eyes widened. "You walks on fire? Does it hurt?"

Caleb shook his head then pressed a hand to his chest. "No. Not if you hone in on your inner strength and power. On peace and faith."

Sara smiled. "I gots faith that you're gonna find Cissy."

A pained look crossed Caleb's face. "I will do my best, Sara," he said gruffly.

Madelyn's heart melted. Sara had not only missed her twin sister, but she'd missed having a father, as well. And she had been so caught up in raising her little girl, on being a single mother, surviving the loss of her husband and Cissy and making ends meet, that Madelyn hadn't once considered a personal relationship with a man.

Or finding a father for Sara.

She didn't need a man, she'd decided long ago. Sara had her, and she would be enough.

Only she wasn't enough. And now she needed this detective's help.

Her breath fluttered as he swung his gaze up to her.

His dark eyes sparkled with questions, yet she also sensed that she could trust him.

She hoped to hell that was true.

Sara dropped his hand and skipped to the door.

"Caleb, you'll let me know what you find." She didn't know if she could bear to be at the exhumation.

He nodded, then extended his hand to her this time. Wariness filled Madelyn, but she slid her hand into his. An odd sensation rippled through her at the feel of his rough, leathery skin against her own. It had been so long since she'd touched a man that her belly fluttered with awareness.

She pulled away immediately. She couldn't afford to indulge in a romantic flirtation. Finding out the truth about Cissy and ending these nightmares for Sara was all that mattered.

As soon as Madelyn left, Caleb set the wheels in motion for the exhumation.

"Sheriff Gray said he expects this won't be the last request for one," Gage said. "Damn Dr. Emery."

"Damn him for killing himself," Caleb said. "He should have to face every patient he deceived and make things right." Although there was no restitution, nothing that could make up for the loss of a child.

"The sheriff said workers will be meeting at the cemetery early in the morning for the exhumation. They want to make sure it's as private as possible," Gage said.

Caleb nodded. "I'll meet them there."

Yanking on his rawhide jacket, he headed outside. Time to pay his respects to Mara.

Wind battered his Jeep as he plowed across the mountain toward the Native American burial grounds. As he parked and climbed out, the sounds of ancient war drums and echoes of fallen friends bombarded him. Stones and wooden markers etched with family names stood in honor of loved ones, while handmade Native American beads and baskets decorated others, holding treasures.

Gripping a bouquet of lilies in one hand, he crossed the graveyard, grateful he'd managed to bring Mara here where her own parents were also buried. He paused at their markers, then stopped in front of Mara's, his heart heavy as he placed the flowers on her grave.

Today would have been Mara's twenty-eighth birthday. If she had lived.

And his son, if he'd been born, would have been two.

That hollowness he'd lived with since Mara's murder gnawed at him, and he traced a finger over Mara's name. His throat tightened as an image of what his son might have looked like materialized in his mind.

A toddler with chubby cheeks, thick, black hair, dark skin, and brown eyes like Mara's. His son would have been walking and climbing onto everything now.

But his little boy had never had a chance...

The icy cold of the winter wind seeped through him, adding to the chill he'd felt for the past three years. Three years of living alone. Of wondering why Mara and his unborn child had been taken instead of him.

Three years of living with the guilt.

Gritting his teeth, he stood, the vision of his son disappearing in the foggy haze. But Mara waited, an ethereal beauty in her traditional white wedding dress.

Although each day he sensed her fading. That her soul was preparing to move on. That she was waiting on something...something she needed from him...

For him to let her go? He wasn't sure that was possible. The guilt alone kept him coming back, kept him praying, kept him...prisoner.

Why couldn't it have been him instead of her?

Sara's insistence that her sister was still alive echoed in his mind. He understood the draw Sara felt, the difficulty in letting a loved one go. Did Sara suffer from survivor guilt as he did?

The sound of a flute echoed in the wind, and he closed his eyes, remembering their marriage ceremony. The traditional Love Flute playing, the fire ceremony with the golden glow illuminating Mara's beautiful face, the Rite of Seven Steps, the moment the traditional blue blanket had been removed from around them and the white one enfolded them, signifying their new ways of happiness and peace.

Yet that happiness and peace had been shattered a month later with bullets that had been meant for him. Mara had been struck instead and died in his place.

Hell. A fat lot of good his vision or gift, whatever the hell it was, had done him.

He hadn't foreseen Mara's death or he might have been able to stop it.

"What should I do, Mara? I don't want this gift, and I sure as hell don't want that little girl to have it."

But he had felt something kinetic pass between them when he'd touched Sara's tiny hand. He'd seen the dark images in her mind. Felt the violence she felt.

And he'd witnessed a little girl identical to Sara running for her life, disappearing into the dark woods just as Sara had described....

What if Sara was right? What if her sister was alive and in trouble?

"I know I failed you," Caleb said in a pained voice. "I just pray I do not fail this little girl."

Madelyn's big, green eyes and frail smile flashed in his head, and a twinge of guilt assaulted him. He had also experienced a faint flicker of awareness when he'd touched Madelyn, a current of desire he hadn't felt since Mara.

But that was wrong. Mara had been his wife. He owed her his dedication. His life.

The wind suddenly whipped through the trees, hissing as it tossed dry leaves to the ground and sent them swirling across the cemetery. The scent of wilted roses filled the air, the sound of broken limbs snapping mingled with the echoes of the dead.

He waited, hoped, prayed he would hear Mara's voice one more time, but a bleak silence followed.

He turned and hurried back to his Jeep, started the engine and peeled from the parking lot. Tomorrow was the exhumation. It wouldn't be easy for Madelyn.

But nothing personal could or would happen between them.

Not ever.

NIGHTMARES OF MARA and his son tormented Caleb all night. He woke drenched in sweat. No wonder he had connected with Madelyn and her daughter.

He and Madelyn had both lost a child.

A five-mile run and shower, then he grabbed a Thermos of coffee and jumped in his Jeep. But dread filled him as he drove across the mountain to Sanctuary Gardens. The sheriff's car was parked in the cemetery parking lot, a crew of men a few feet away preparing to exhume the body.

Anxiety needled him as he swerved in beside the patrol car, jammed his hands in the pockets of his jacket and strode toward the sheriff.

Sheriff Gray extended his hand. "You must be Caleb Walker?"

Caleb nodded. "Thanks for arranging this so quickly. You have the paperwork in order?"

Gray indicated the envelope in his hand. "Signature from Madelyn Andrews giving us permission. The license. And—" he gestured toward a tall, white-haired man with glasses wearing a lab coat "—Environmental Health Officer present, as required by law."

Caleb glanced at the E.H. Officer as he met up with the men designated to dig the grave. The transport service with the second coffin arrived and the driver stepped out, then crossed the graveyard to speak to the sheriff while two men from the funeral home erected a tent around the grave for privacy and to show respect for the grave while the exhumation took place.

Sheriff Gray introduced him to the medical examiner, Dr. Hal Rollo, who seemed pensive as he waited to do his job.

Caleb had witnessed a couple of exhumations before, but none for a child.

The thought made his stomach knot.

"You really believe there's truth to the woman's story?" Sheriff Gray asked. "I heard her kid is the one stirring things up, that she claims she sees her dead twin."

So much for keeping that part of the story under wraps to avoid skepticism. "I guess we'll know soon enough."

He followed Gray over to the Lost Angels corner of the cemetery, noting the wrought-iron gate protecting the resting place for the little souls. Ivory doves were perched above a bubbling fountain, and a statue of Jesus, hands folded in prayer as he looked toward the heavens, sat at the head of the plots as if guarding the angels below. Bright flowers, toy trucks, teddy bears, dolls and various other toys had been left as if to keep the children company, marking birthdays and holidays. His throat tightened at the sight. Two rows back, he spotted the marker for Cissy Andrews.

The plot had been well maintained, her marker adorned with plastic sunflowers. A small photo of Madelyn and Sara also sat at the head as if to reassure Cissy she wasn't forgotten or alone.

Drawn to the spot, he walked over and knelt beside it, his vision blurring as he studied Cissy's name and birth date. Sometimes touching objects, items of clothing, people triggered his visions.

His hands shook as he reached out to press them over the small grave. Behind him the other men's voices faded to a distant hum. He hesitated, a sliver of apprehension needling him. He might see nothing.

Or he might see the child's small body in the ground.

Sucking in a sharp breath, he told himself he had to do this.

Reality slipped away and the wind screamed through the trees as he laid his hand on the mound.

CHAPTER THREE

MADELYN'S EMOTIONS PINGED back and forth as she drove
Sara to her mother's home. She had already called her
assistant at the craft shop and asked her to cover for her
for a few days. She needed time to see this through, and
Sara needed her.

She so did not want to see Cissy's grave upturned. Or
her body desecrated.

But she'd trusted Dr. Emery and the hospital staff,
virtual strangers, with her daughter before, because of
her vulnerable emotional state, and she refused to do
that now.

She had to know for sure if Cissy was buried and, if
not, where she was.

The images Sara had painted tormented her.

Please dear God, if she did survive, let her be okay.

She glanced at Sara who gripped her blanket in one
hand, a bouquet of sunflowers in her other for her grandmother. Sara never visited without a bouquet, and she
always insisted they were from her and Cissy, not just
her. Why was Sara obsessed with sunflowers?

Could her daughter possibly have some kind of psychic ability? Madelyn had never actually believed in anything supernatural, but what if she was wrong?

Perspiration trickled down the back of her neck, and
she gripped the steering wheel tighter, mentally giving
herself a pep talk as she had over the years.

She could do this. She was strong.

She had Sara, and no matter what happened, nothing was going to change that.

"Mommy, I liked Mr. Firewalker."

Madelyn smiled, ignoring the tickle in her belly that the mere mention of the man's name evoked. "I think he liked you, too, sweet pea." She tousled Sara's hair, well aware that Sara didn't always make friends easily. Some of the children in preschool shied away when she boasted about a sister they couldn't see. "After all, how could he not? You're adorable and smart and have that gorgeous smile."

Sara beamed a gap-toothed grin, and Madelyn steered the station wagon into the driveway at the assisted living facility, Sanctuary Seniors, and parked in front of her mother's unit. A few months ago, her mother had suffered a stroke and was partially paralyzed on one side, leaving her confined to a wheelchair. But her mind was quick and seeing Sara always lifted her spirits.

Sara bounded out of the car clutching the flowers in one hand, raced up to the door and banged on the front. "Gran, guess who's here," she sang. "We gots a surprise for you!"

A second later, Liz Cummings, one of the health care workers, greeted Sara with a big hug.

By the time Madelyn made it inside, Sara was already perched on her mother's lap in the wheelchair, talking in an animated voice about the big, dark-skinned Indian who could walk on fire, and Liz was putting the flowers in a vase on the window ledge so her mother could enjoy them.

Sara's mother arched a brow as Madelyn entered. "So is this young man handsome, dear?"

Madelyn blushed. Her mother never ceased to play

matchmaker. So far, Madelyn had managed to avoid a real date with the men her mother had thrown in front of her.

"He's big, so biggg, Gran." Sara threw up her hands indicating that he was gigantic, and Madelyn bit back a laugh. "And he's gonna find Cissy. He promised."

Madelyn's smile faded. She hated to give Sara false hopes and then have her be even more devastated if things fell through. "Honey, he's investigating, but we can't be sure what we'll find."

"He will find her," Sara insisted stubbornly. "He said he would and he can walk on fire so he can do anything."

Madelyn's mother, Cora, stroked Sara's hair. "I'm sure he'll do his best, pumpkin. Now, why don't we have a tea party while your mommy does her errands? Liz brought us some cookies, but they look pretty bare to me."

Sara clapped her hands. "We can decorate them, Gran! We'll make 'em look like sunflowers for Cissy!"

"That sounds like a fabulous idea," her mother said.

"Come on," Liz said. "Help me put out the icing and sprinkles so we can make those cookies pretty."

Sara skipped to the kitchen with Liz but worry knitted Madelyn's brow.

"She'll be all right." Her mother wheeled her chair over and clasped Madelyn's hand. "And so will you."

Madelyn soaked in her mother's smile. She loved her and Sara more than she could say. "I don't know what I'd do without you, Mom. Sara and I...we both need you."

Her mother barked a laugh. "Well, I'm not going anywhere, sugar. Now you go and do what you need to do. I'll take care of Sara while you look for Cissy." She tilted her head toward the sunflowers. "I think Sara is right. Cissy loves sunflowers."

Madelyn's stomach twisted. Apparently her mother trusted Sara's visions.

They exchanged concerned looks. But her mother refrained from commenting further on Sara's recent sunflower obsession. They'd both hoped it would play itself out, but now Madelyn wondered if the sunflowers might be some kind of clue to her other daughter.

Pasting on a brave face, she hugged her mother. "I'll call. You two have fun."

"We always do," her mother said with a beaming smile.

Madelyn's throat thickened, and she nodded, afraid if she spoke, the dam holding back her emotions would break, and she'd fall on the floor in a puddle and start sobbing. Once she started, she might not be able to stop.

The morning sun sliced through the bare trees as she jogged to the minivan, then drove around the mountain. Early morning shadows flickered across the dark asphalt as the sun fought through the storm clouds gathering above. She slowed as she spotted the cemetery, dread flooding her at the sight of the sheriff's car and the hearse.

The day of the funeral threatened to replay through Madelyn's head, but she hit the pause button in her brain and zapped it on hold. She refused to relive that day again now with all these men watching.

Swallowing back nerves, she parked and walked to the top of the hill overlooking the Lost Angels corner where the sheriff and three other men stood conferring. Where was Caleb?

Inhaling a breath to fortify her courage, she stumbled down the hill and through the iron gate. Sheriff Gray gave her a concerned look, but she rushed past them, then looked into the tent protecting the site.

Caleb *was* there, kneeling with his hand on Cissy's grave. His dark skin had drained of color, and an odd mixture of grief and pain marred his face.

What was he doing? Could he see inside the grave?

CALEB'S WORLD SHIMMERED out of control as he felt a vision coming on. Darkness pulled at him, dragging him into an endless tunnel, a pit of silence that stretched below the ground, desolate, screaming with secrets…

"Caleb?"

The sound of a woman's voice jerked him free of the spell.

"What are you doing?"

Twisting his head sideways, he spotted Madelyn staring at him, her arms crossed, her expression troubled.

He stood abruptly, taking a step back, confused by what he'd seen. By what he hadn't seen. He needed more time, dammit. And he wasn't ready to share his gift just yet. "Nothing. Just thinking about the case." He crooked a thumb toward the sheriff. "Are you ready?"

"Yes." Sheriff Gray gestured toward the E.H. Officer. "Madelyn, this is Oliver Gordon, the Environmental Health Officer. He'll oversee the exhumation."

Madelyn nodded in greeting, obviously struggling with the reality of the task to come and its ramifications.

Gordon cleared his throat. "For health reasons, I have to ask everyone to wait a safe distance away. We must respect this grave as well as the surrounding ones."

"Of course." Madelyn folded her arms around her waist as if to hold herself together while the funeral home employees approached with shovels. The distress on her face made Caleb's protective instincts surge. He wished he could spare her this ordeal, but this exhumation was vital to whether or not they moved forward with an investigation.

Amanda Peterson, GAI's resident forensic anthropologist, climbed from a sporty gray sedan at the top of the hill and walked toward them.

Caleb gestured to Madelyn. "Come on, let's take a walk."

Her face paled, but she didn't argue. Instead, she allowed him to guide her up the hill. Fine tremors rippled through her body as she stopped beneath a giant oak. Caleb rubbed a hand along her neck, hoping to calm her.

Amanda approached them, her expression sympathetic. "You must be Madelyn Andrews." She extended her hand. "I'm Amanda Peterson. I work with Caleb and Gage at GAI."

"It's nice to meet you," Madelyn said. "I didn't realize another agent would be present."

Caleb's gut pinched. "Amanda is a forensics anthropologist. We thought she might be helpful today."

Madelyn's eyes widened as the implications registered.

"She's going to oversee the medical examiner's work," Caleb continued, "just so we can verify the findings. In light of Dr. Emery's lies, we can't be too careful."

Amanda tugged her all-weather coat around her. "I'm sorry, Madelyn. I know this is difficult."

"Yes, well, thank you for being here. If I'd had my wits about me five years ago, I would have demanded to see my child before I buried her."

"Don't blame yourself," Amanda said, her voice and smile genuinely understanding. "You were a victim. And we're going to find out just how much of one today."

Amanda's pep talk seemed to give Madelyn strength, because she offered her a tiny smile.

Amanda nudged his arm as she headed down the hill as if silently ordering him to stay with Madelyn. Hell, she didn't have to tell him that Madelyn was vulnerable.

But getting too close to her was dangerous for him.

"You didn't answer me earlier, Caleb," Madelyn said. "What were you doing at Cissy's grave?" Suspicion flared in her eyes. "Do you have some kind of psychic ability that you didn't mention? Is that why you believed Sara? Could you see inside the grave?"

Irritated that she'd caught him when he'd had no intention of revealing his personal visions, he hesitated. Telling her meant opening himself up to scrutiny.

His grandfather's image flashed in his mind. White Feather, a shaman, a man with strong faith and belief in the Cherokee customs, in the healing power of herbs and the earth. And in the healing power of love.

He'd also believed in Caleb, in his visions, because his grandfather simply believed that he was special.

But if he had been so damn special, why hadn't he foreseen the shooter that horrible day?

"Caleb, I'm not going to judge. I saw you with Sara, the look on your face. She trusted you and her trust doesn't come easily." Madelyn laid her palm against his cheek, stirring primal instincts and needs that had lain dormant too long. "Just tell me the truth," she said softly.

His gaze met hers, and something sweet and frightening and sensual rippled between them, a connection he'd never felt, not even with Mara.

Because he had never shared the truth about himself with her. He had tried to be a man she'd approve of. A hard worker, a provider. They'd married because they both wanted to raise a family without the stigma of a mixed race.

But this sensual connection, this drive to be near Madelyn, was foreign and disturbing and heated his blood.

Arousing him.

Arousal and lust had no place in an investigation.

Self-loathing filled him. They were at a graveyard, for God's sake. And Madelyn was inquiring about his gift and how it might impact this case. Not because she was remotely interested in him personally.

"Sometimes I sense things," he said quietly, watching her for a reaction. "It's not an ability I can control or call upon at will. It just…happens."

Her expression softened. "That's the reason you believed Sara? You sensed something when you shook her hand?"

"Yes, I believe that Sara is special," he said by way of an answer. He jammed his hands in his pockets, ignoring the whistle of the wind bringing cries of the dead from the graves. He had to focus on one case here and that was the Andrews child. The other lost spirits would have to find another medium to hear their pleas.

Madelyn shivered and rubbed her hands up and down her arms. Leaves fluttered down from the trees, scattering amongst the markers, adding bold reds, yellows, and oranges to the brittle, brown grass.

Madelyn cleared her throat as if summoning courage. "What did you see when you touched the grave?"

His former vision flashed back. But he wasn't certain it was a vision at all. A world of darkness spun around him, that long empty pit clawing at him.

Madelyn clutched his arm. "Caleb, tell me the truth. Please."

"I didn't see anything," he said gruffly. "It was just dark and…I felt an emptiness. I…can't explain it. Sometimes my senses, my visions aren't correct. Sometimes they don't even make sense."

The heartbeat of silence while Madelyn stared at him felt like an eternity. "Just don't lie to me," she said. "I may seem like a fragile woman to you, but I can handle whatever happens."

Caleb's hearing suddenly seemed more acute. He could hear the scene behind him, the voices of the sheriff and funeral workers. Twigs snapped in the wind, leaves rustled, the shovel crunched dry dirt....

"How long has Sara had these nightmares about Cissy?" he asked.

Madelyn sighed, the weary sound of a worried mother. "I told you, the past two months, ever since we moved back to Sanctuary."

"But you said she talked about her twin before?"

Madelyn nodded. "At eighteen months, she started acting as if she was playing with her. Even now, when she has tea parties, she sets a place for Cissy. When she colors, she draws Cissy and those sunflowers. When she plays on the seesaw, Cissy is always on the other end."

Her voice broke, and she pressed a hand to her mouth to regain control, then forged ahead as if she needed to share her story. "When she was a baby, she'd lay on her side and giggle and reach out as if someone was there."

Caleb's mind raced to paranormal research he'd done. "Parapsychologists believe that children can see ghosts when they're babies. They have a connection then, but once their innocence is lost and society trains them, they no longer believe, so the spirits don't appear to them anymore."

Madelyn chewed her bottom lip. "I read that, too. But Sara never lost that ability. In fact, her connection only seemed to grow stronger. Last year she started insisting that Cissy was alive, telling me stories about things she did, places she went. That's when I got really worried."

Caleb heard the pain in her voice. "When you consulted the shrinks?"

"Yes." The wind swept Madelyn's hair into her face, and she tucked it back with her fingers. "Sara seems so certain that her dreams are real, that her sister is alive, that I started to believe her." Her shoulders fell. "Maybe because I really wanted to so badly."

"That's understandable." Caleb ached to touch her, to soothe the torment in her voice, but the only way to help Madelyn was to uncover the truth.

If Sara was right, then her sister had been kidnapped and adopted by another family, she might be in danger.... And if she was wrong, Sara's visions might be ESP—or she might have some form of mental illness.

Or she might be communing with a dead girl....

A noise down the hill jarred him, and he jerked his head toward the gravesite. Sheriff Gray had stepped outside the tent and was motioning for him.

"Walker, we're ready," Gray shouted.

Madelyn's legs buckled, and he caught her around the waist. "Sit down on that bench by the fountain. Let me see what they found."

Too weak to argue, she nodded and allowed him to guide her to the bench. His heart climbed into his throat as he left her small form hunched inside her coat, shivering on that cold, stone slab.

But he squared his shoulders, determined to end the questions in her mind. It was the only way she and her daughter could find closure and move on.

Clenching his jaw, he raced down the hill and stepped inside the tent beside Amanda. The mood was somber, reverent, racked with tension and dread.

Slowly the E.H. Officer opened the casket.

Caleb braced himself but shock still ripped through him.

The casket was empty.

MADELYN TWISTED HER hands together, willing herself to remain calm as she waited. But every second that ticked by felt like someone was pulling out her fingernails one by one. The sound of a car motor drew her gaze back to the parking lot, and she saw an elderly man exit a sedan and hobble toward a grave near the church. Probably his wife's.

Poor man. How long had they been married before he'd lost her?

She'd thought she and Tim would grow old together, not that he would abandon her and Sara when they needed him most.

Bitterness threatened but she tamped it down. She'd long ago vowed not to indulge herself in that emotion for fear Sara would pick up on it.

She never wanted her daughter to know the truth about her father.

Voices carried in the wind, and she spotted Caleb walking toward her. Her lungs squeezed for air at his bleak expression. A bird chirped from a tree nearby, and leaves fluttered down into the fountain. One landed on the wings of the angel, another at her feet.

She gripped her hands together, waiting, watching for the small casket to appear.

"Madelyn," he said in a gruff voice. "I'm sorry."

She lunged to her feet. "What's wrong?" Her voice cracked, and for the first time, she realized that she'd actually held out hope that Sara might be right. That Cissy was alive.

Suddenly oblivious to her surroundings, she vaulted down the hill, stumbling blindly. Whatever he had seen, she had to know.

"Madelyn, wait!"

Her boots pounded the ground as she ran down the hill. All she could think of was seeing that tiny casket, knowing whether her daughter was in there...

Her pulse pounded, sweat slid down her temple, and she stumbled over a loose rock and felt herself flailing to remain on two feet.

Caleb caught her arm and righted her, then helped her to the tent. Her heart pounded as she stepped beneath the tarp.

Dear God...

She gaped at Caleb. "I don't understand," she whispered.

A muscle ticked in Caleb's jaw. "Someone lied to you, Madelyn. Dr. Emery, the funeral director maybe. But you didn't bury your daughter five years ago. You buried an empty casket."

Anger, shock and betrayal slammed into her along with a million questions. But the one fact that she latched onto was the one she wanted to believe more than anything.

The casket was empty because Sara was right.

Cissy was alive.

CISSY RAN AND HID behind the door between the den and the kitchen clutching her dolly to her chest. They were screaming again. They'd been at it for a long time now.

"How could you do this?" her mama shouted. "Why?"

"Because you wanted a kid, you were grieving over losing Doug."

"I know, but you lied to me."

"Just keep your mouth shut!" the big man yelled.

Cissy peered around the corner and saw her mama reach for the phone. "It's not right," her mama cried. "What you've done… It's not right. No wonder Cissy has bad dreams."

"That kid is crazy. She always has been." He grabbed her mama's shoulders and shook her. "Listen to me. You call, you'll lose her, and I'll go to jail. You wouldn't do that to your own family, would you?"

"But Cissy has a right to know the truth," her mama argued. "And I won't go to jail because I'll tell the truth."

"The truth. Hell, you don't even know the truth, you stupid bitch." He slapped her mother across the face. "You're up to your damn eyeballs in this. The kid is evidence, and we can't leave evidence behind."

"What are you talking about?" Cissy's mama looked terrified as she leaned against the sink.

Terror streaked through Cissy, and she backed into the hallway, but she tripped over a pair of work boots and yelped. He heard the noise and swung around. His face was red, his nostrils wide. His eyes bulged like a madman's.

He was going to kill her.

"Damn kid," he mumbled then turned and stomped toward Cissy, his big footsteps pounding the floor like a giant's.

"No, I won't let you hurt my baby." Her mama grabbed his arm to stop him, but he swung his arm back with such force that he slung her to the floor. Her mama hit her head on the table with a whack and blood spurted and ran down her face.

Cissy bit back a scream. Tears blurred her vision.

His growl dragged her from her stupor though, and

she turned and darted out the back door. The porch door slammed behind her. His loud bellow followed.

"Get back here, kid. Come on, we'll play a little game."

He didn't want to play games, Cissy thought, as she barreled down the steps. He'd hurt her mama and now he was gonna hurt her.

She had to get away.

She dashed down the steps as quick as she could and ran toward the greenhouse and the sunflowers. It was the only place she'd be safe.

Sweat streamed down her face, and she heaved for a breath as she shoved open the heavy door and sneaked inside. She tucked her doll beneath her arm, then pushed with all her might to shut the door, pulling the metal latch. Then she ducked between the rows of sunflowers, weaving her way until she was hidden deep within the rows.

Crouching as low as she could, she hugged her dolly to her, closed her eyes and felt the tears flow.

"Please, Sara, help me," she whispered. "I don't know how much longer I can hide."

The door rattled as he shook it. "Get out here right now, kid!"

Cissy rocked herself back and forth and rolled into a tiny ball. She could see her sister in her mind. She wasn't crazy like the big meanie said.

"Sara, please come and get me," she whispered. "I'm scared. I don't wanna die."

CHAPTER FOUR

CALEB CONTEMPLATED THE implications of the empty grave. He wished like hell Dr. Emery was alive to explain how he could have deceived Madelyn. She was a new mother, had been in labor, suffering from an accident, and he had lied to her about one of her babies. The enormity of that cruelty boggled his mind.

"I can't believe it..." Madelyn murmured. "After all these years of thinking Cissy was gone...of visiting her grave..."

A mixture of grief, shock, rage and desolation spread across her face, and he couldn't resist. He slid an arm around her to support her, wanting to offer comfort. She surprised him by bowing her head and resting it against his chest.

"She could be alive," Madelyn whispered in a tormented voice. "All this time, she could have been out there, alone, hurting, wondering why her mother didn't want her."

Caleb hated to remind her of Dr. Emery's crimes and the other possibilities, but it was inevitable. And she had asked him to be honest.

"Or he could have given her to another family, Madelyn. A couple who wanted a baby and had no idea that Emery was stealing children from unsuspecting mothers." He paused. "A couple who loved her."

Her silent words echoed in his head even though she

didn't speak them. *But she should have been with her mother and her twin.*

Madelyn furrowed her brows. "Except that's not what Sara saw."

He shrugged. "It still could be possible."

Pain flashed in her eyes again. "But if Sara was right about Cissy being alive, then maybe she's right about Cissy being in trouble now." She clutched his arms. "Caleb, we have to find her. Sara says she's in danger and so is her m—the woman who adopted her. We have to hurry."

The E.H. Officer, Sheriff Gray, the men from the funeral home and the medical examiner all filed from the tent.

"What the hell is going on?" one of the funeral workers muttered.

"The fact that there is no body proves Dr. Emery lied to Madelyn," Caleb said, "and that her baby might have been adopted just as little Peyton Nash was."

"But I thought that was an isolated incident," the medical examiner said, "that it was personal. The girlfriend of the baby's father and his mother kidnapped that little girl and arranged the adoption."

"Emery was guilty of more than that," Sheriff Gray said. "According to the files from the former sheriff, he had a problem with single mothers and liked money."

"But I wasn't single at the time," Madelyn pointed out.

Caleb considered that. "Maybe not. But you had two babies, and he was in the business. He probably figured he could take one, and you still had the other baby, so you wouldn't question him."

Madelyn clenched her jaw. "And he was right. But I haven't been okay and neither has Sara."

Questions ticked through Caleb's mind. "Madelyn's

baby did not have an autopsy. Did you know Dr. Emery at the time, Dr. Rollo?"

Dr. Rollo wrinkled his brow. "No, I only came on last year. But I'm surprised the M.E. at the time didn't request one."

"Where is he now?" Madelyn asked.

"He died last year," Dr. Rollo said. "Had an embolism."

Dammit. Dr. Emery was dead and so was the former medical examiner. "I want to talk to that lawyer, now."

Caleb firmly set his jaw. Jameson Stanford Mansfield. According to Gage, Mansfield was a sleaze.

If he knew anything about Madelyn's missing child, he'd find out. No matter what it took.

Madelyn phoned her mother while Caleb studied the grave site and casket. He was examining the site to verify that it hadn't been disturbed by anyone prior to them.

"Yes, Mom, it was empty," she said softly.

"Oh, my God. So little Sara's visions are real?"

Madelyn's chest ached. How many times had her daughter tried to convince her that Cissy was alive, yet she hadn't believed her? "Yes. Maybe. Poor Sara, I should have listened to her before. She kept insisting Cissy wasn't in that cemetery."

Her mother's breath wheezed out. "You know your grandmother had visions."

"What?" This was the first she'd ever heard of it. "Why didn't you ever tell me, Mother?"

A labored sigh echoed back. "Because she didn't like to talk about them, said people thought she was odd because of them." Another wheezed breath. "All this time I hoped...prayed...Sara didn't have them. Although at the same time, I hoped she did."

Madelyn didn't know what to make of that. "How is Sara now?"

"She's okay at the moment, but she became agitated earlier."

"What happened?"

"She and I were drawing. She drew more sunflowers except this time Cissy was hiding in the midst of them."

A cold wave of fear washed over Madelyn. "I planned to go with Caleb to confront the lawyer who arranged adoptions with Dr. Emery, but I can come and pick her up right now."

"No, she's settled down now, honey, and she and Liz are decorating the cookies. Take your time. The sooner you find Cissy, the sooner these disturbing images and nightmares will end for Sara."

"Are you sure you're feeling up to it, Mom? You've had a difficult year."

"Oh, honey," her mother said. "Sara keeps me young. Besides, just knowing Cissy might be out there is enough to make me work harder to free myself of this wheel-chair."

Tears threatened to surface. It would be a miracle if her mother walked again. And another one if she found Cissy and brought her home.

Both seemed light-years away and impossible.

She closed her eyes and sighed, hating that Sara was suffering. And what about Cissy? What was happening to her?

"Sara's calling me to help with the sprinkles." Her mother lowered her voice. "Be careful, honey. When Nina Nash tried to find her child, someone tried to kill her. And if Sara is right about a man threatening her and her adopted mother, going after them could be dangerous."

Chills skated up Madelyn's spine, but she shook off the fear. Nothing was going to stop her now. "I'll be fine, Mom. I'm with Caleb."

"Ahh, yes. That handsome Native American."

"Mother..."

"It's all right to lean on someone, Madelyn. Tim did a number on you, but not every man is a scumbag like him."

Her mother hung up and Madelyn shivered, then opened her eyes and looked across the graveyard. The small town was supposed to be a great place to raise a family, a haven for her and Sara.

But recently the revelations about the hospital fire eight years ago and now babies being sold made her wonder what other secrets lay in the town.

Did someone in Sanctuary know where her daughter was?

"SHERIFF, WE'RE GOING to pay a visit to Mansfield," Caleb said.

Sheriff Gray shrugged. "Good luck. But don't expect a confession from the bastard. He's pleading innocence and lawyered-up."

"Maybe he'll talk to me," Madelyn said.

Gray studied her for a long moment. "It's worth a shot. But Mansfield is shrewd and devious. He also uses his money and his daddy's name to get his way."

"His money and name don't mean crap to me," Caleb muttered, already contemplating ways to force the man to spill the truth if Madelyn's pleas didn't work.

"But what about his records?" Caleb asked. "Is there any way we can look at those?"

Gray shook his head. "District attorney subpoenaed them. You can talk to her, but I doubt she'll share with the case pending. That and adoptions being sealed and the rights of the adopted parents being a priority makes these types of situations almost impossible."

Exactly what Gage had already told him.

Caleb ground his teeth. Then again, he didn't work for the cops or play by their rules. Wasn't that one advantage Gage had pointed out when he'd recruited him for GAI?

Madelyn glanced toward the empty casket. "What are you going to do with that coffin?"

"It appears to be clean." The medical examiner squinted through the sun. "But I'd like a crime unit to process it. All right with you?"

Madelyn nodded.

Caleb placed his hand at the small of her back. "Let's go, Madelyn. I want to pay a surprise visit to Mansfield."

Determination settled on Madelyn's face. "Me, too. If he knows where Cissy is, he'd better tell us."

Caleb rubbed her back. If he didn't, court would be the least of Mansfield's problems.

Caleb walked her to her car, and they agreed to meet back at GAI headquarters. A few minutes later, Caleb led the way inside the agency to Gage's office.

"Amanda filled me in when she called." Gage frowned. "So Emery's adoption ring was bigger than just the Nash case."

"It appears that way," Caleb said.

"I'll talk to Sheila English, the D.A., and see if she'll give us any leads," Gage said. "I also phoned a buddy of mine at the Bureau. I'll let you know if he has any helpful information."

Caleb shifted on the balls of his feet. "Thanks. Since kidnapping is a federal case, we might need him."

Gage punched his intercom button and requested Benjamin Camp and Derrick McKinney come to his office. Five minutes later, Ben Camp, the computer expert, stood with them, arms crossed and solemn as Caleb caught him up on the case. Derrick listened silently as well, his hands jammed in his pockets.

"The sheriff said Mansfield's records have been subpoenaed. It's going to be hell getting access to them," Caleb said.

Ben shrugged, a mischievous smile tugging at his mouth. "I'll see what I can do."

Derrick cleared his throat. "Madelyn, my wife, Brianna, has connections with several adoption agencies and the local orphanage. I'll have her put out some feelers."

"Thank you." Madelyn offered him a tentative smile. "I really appreciate all of your help."

Ben gestured toward Caleb. "Can I see you for a minute? My office."

Caleb nodded. "Wait for me outside, Madelyn."

She gave him a questioning look but did as he said. Caleb followed Ben to his office, curious. He'd heard Ben had been in trouble with the law before, that his expertise had landed him in jail. But he didn't give a damn. "What is it? Did you find something already?"

Ben shook his head, reached inside his desk and slid a small device into Caleb's hand. "It's a bug. Plant it in Mansfield's office."

It was illegal and inadmissible in court, but that was the advantage in working with a private agency. They'd get information any way they could get it.

Caleb tucked the bug in his pocket. "Thanks, Camp. Oh, and see what you can dig up on Madelyn's ex. Tim Andrews."

"You think he's involved?"

Caleb shrugged. "Who knows? But the jerk left when

Sara started calling her dead sister's name. That makes him suspect in my book."

"Sounds like a real winner," Ben muttered. "I'll get on it right away and keep you posted."

Caleb hurried outside and found Madelyn tapping her foot by his Jeep. "What was that about?"

Caleb shrugged and opened the Jeep door. "Just business."

Madelyn caught his arm. "Please, Caleb, tell me the truth. Do you know something about Cissy you're not telling me?"

Caleb covered her hand with his. "No, just speaking to Ben about research."

Her eyes flickered with unease, then trust, making his insides knot. God help him. He didn't want to disappoint her.

Her fingers curled beneath his, her skin soft, her hand small in his. The urge to hold her seized him.

Sensations zinged through him, heating his blood. His mouth watered for hers.

Suddenly the wind whipped her hair around her face, and a drop of rain pinged on the sidewalk. Madelyn clamped her teeth over her bottom lip as she glanced at the mountains.

The fear that stretched across her face jerked him out of his lust-driven stupor, reminding him that a little girl might be out there somewhere in danger.

No time for play. They had work to do.

"Let's go meet Mansfield, Madelyn. Maybe we can convince him to talk and get some answers."

MADELYN CLENCHED HER HANDS in her lap, missing the sweet comfort of her hand cradled inside Caleb's. For a brief moment, she'd felt a frisson of sensual heat rippling between them. But it must have been her imagination.

Caleb was a professional and had only been offering support in a trying time. She could not become dependant on him.

As he drove to Mansfield's office, images of Cissy flashed through her head. Where had she been all these years? Who was raising her? What kind of life had she had? Did she live in North Carolina? Near Sanctuary?

Was she loved?

Did she know that she had a twin or that she was adopted? What had her family told her?

Anger boiled inside her, as well, as picture after picture of Sara and Cissy together surfaced. All the years they could have been together, played together, shared toys and secrets and laughter.

And to think, Sara would have gone without nightmares these past two months.

And if Sara was connected to Cissy, did the connection work both ways? Was Cissy calling out to Sara for help?

Or could Sara be wrong? Only seeing what she wanted to see; that Cissy wanted to be with them because Sara missed her?

She swallowed back tears. No. She would not doubt Sara again.

"Madelyn, if you want me to drive you home first, I can do this alone," Caleb offered as he pulled in front of the lawyer's office and parked. The building was an older, Georgian-style house that had been renovated into an office, but it looked well maintained. She'd heard that Mansfield had family money, and that he used it to throw his weight around.

But she wasn't afraid of the man. And if he'd earned

any part of that money by selling babies, *her* baby, she'd make sure he rotted in jail.

"No." She interjected steel into her voice. "I want to see this man's face when we confront him."

Caleb's gaze locked with hers. "Good. I think he should have to face the people he wronged."

She reached for the door handle and climbed out, then followed Caleb up the steps to the office. Traffic crawled by the downtown area, the sound of tires skating over slushy, wet leaves echoing behind them.

Caleb entered without knocking and she followed him inside. A chunky bottled-blonde with a miniscule skirt and cleavage to spare beamed a smile up at Caleb.

"Hi, Mister, how can we help you?"

"We need to see Mansfield," Caleb said, ignoring her flirtatious smile. "It's urgent."

"Is this a legal matter?"

"I'd rather speak to Mansfield about it in private." Caleb strode toward the door. "Don't bother to get up. We'll let ourselves in."

The woman's expression morphed from solicitous to concerned in a nanosecond, and she rushed toward the lawyer's door, tottering on three-inch heels. But Caleb was already stalking in. Taking his cue, Madelyn elbowed her way past the receptionist.

"What the hell?" A balding man jumped to his feet behind a massive, cherry desk and glared at them. "Brenda, what's going on? I told you no one gets through."

"Don't blame her," Caleb said in a tone that brooked no argument. "No one, especially your receptionist, could stop us from being here, Mansfield."

Mansfield reached for his phone, his scalp reddening. "I'm calling the police."

Their gazes locked in challenge. "Put down the phone," Caleb ordered.

Madelyn barely resisted the urge to pummel the man with her fists. "Tell me what you did with my daughter, Mr. Mansfield."

Mansfield's eyes widened in shock. "I don't know who you are or what you're talking about." He slanted a panicked look toward the doorway where his receptionist still stood. "Get my lawyer here now!"

Madelyn wasn't backing down. Instead, she leaned forward, planted her fists on his desk and gave him an icy look. "Don't pretend innocence, Mr. Mansfield. Just tell me who you sold my little girl to, because I want her back."

CHAPTER FIVE

CALEB NARROWED HIS EYES, scrutinizing Mansfield, as panic etched lines across the lawyer's face. The creep was hiding something. He wasn't as innocent as he and his damn lawyer wanted everyone to believe.

"Tell me," Madelyn said sharply. "Where is my daughter?"

Mansfield shot his receptionist another frantic look indicating for her to hurry and make the phone call.

"You can call your lawyer," Caleb said sharply. "But we're not going away. We know you handled arrangements for Nina Nash's daughter's illegal adoption, and now we suspect that Mrs. Andrews's child was also abducted at birth."

"Like I said, I have no idea what you're talking about." Mansfield ran a shaky hand over his sweating forehead. "I don't even know who you are, Mrs. Andrews, much less anything about your child. And I don't recall seeing anything about a child abduction in the area regarding a baby named Andrews."

"That's because Dr. Emery lied and told me my little girl died at birth." Anger tinged Madelyn's voice. "He said she was deformed and it was better that I not see her."

Mansfield's nostrils flared. "Again, I have no knowledge of improprieties regarding you or your child. If Dr.

Emery deceived you, then he did so without my knowledge."

Caleb cleared his throat. "Oh, come on, Mansfield. The D.A. has your files. She's going to fry your ass and you know it. So why not cooperate and help rectify the damage you did years ago by helping us find Madelyn's baby?" He hesitated, then continued, hoping to drive his point home. "Maybe the D.A. will even cut you a deal for your assistance."

"I did not sell babies!" Mansfield bellowed. "I'm an upstanding member of this town. Do you know who my father is?"

"I don't care if your old man owns all of the southern states combined," Caleb snapped. "All I care about is finding the child that was stolen from Madelyn Andrews."

Madelyn inched forward. "How could you and Dr. Emery allow me to believe that my little girl died? You all let me have a memorial service for her, watch that tiny casket be buried."

"I'm sorry for your loss," Mansfield said, desperately striving to turn on the charm. "But just because Nina Nash's baby was kidnapped—a kidnapping I swear I had no knowledge of—that doesn't mean your baby was, too."

"Mr. Mansfield, Dr. Emery delivered Mrs. Andrews's twins five years ago, and as she said, told her one of them died. But we just exhumed that casket and there is no baby inside."

Shock flared across Mansfield's face. "Even if he deceived her, you have no evidence that I had any part in it."

"You can check your files to see if you handled the baby's adoption," Caleb said.

"I don't have to check my files," Mansfield blurted. "I remember names and I did not arrange an adoption for any baby named Andrews."

"Her first name was Cissy," Madelyn said.

"As I said, I wasn't involved."

Caleb felt like choking the man. "You're lying and we're going to prove it."

Brenda tottered back in with a faint knock at the open door. "Excuse me. Mr. Mansfield, your father and lawyer are on their way."

"Thanks, Brenda." Mansfield swung his head toward Madelyn, slightly calmer now he knew the cavalry was near.

"Please," Madelyn said in a pained voice. "I think my little girl is in danger. You can help us save her."

"I told you I don't know what you're talking about. All I did was handle paperwork for a few adoptions, but they were all legitimate."

"The Nash baby's wasn't," Caleb pointed out.

Mansfield's eyes bulged. "I was a victim the same as that mother! Now Emery killed himself, everyone wants to use me as a scapegoat!"

Caleb grunted sarcastically. "You are anything but a victim, Mansfield. You got paid well for your silence and now you're lying to cover your ass."

Anger reddened Mansfield's face. "You have no right to talk to me like that."

"Then prove you're telling the truth by showing me your records," Caleb pushed.

A vein throbbed in Mansfield's neck. "Even if I wanted to let you see them, I couldn't. There are confidentiality laws. I could lose my license as well as trust from clients and future clients."

"When I get through with you, you won't have any clients," Caleb growled.

A tense second passed as Mansfield fidgeted and glanced at the door, obviously searching for help.

"Please," Madelyn said softly. "I'm begging you. Cissy is in danger. Who adopted her?"

His face twisted with unease. "Any adoptions I arranged were between willing parties. Trust me, the adoptive parents were desperate for babies."

"So desperate they didn't care where the child came from or if he or she was stolen," Caleb said bitterly. "Or how much money they had to pay to get the baby."

Mansfield's long-winded sigh punctuated the air. Footsteps clattered behind them, a door slammed, and another man's voice boomed as the man cleared the front office and stepped into the doorway.

"I'm Mansfield's lawyer, Leo Holbrook," a young man in an expensive, black suit said with authority. "What's going on here?"

"These people are harassing me," Mansfield said, his look flying to his father, an astute, gray-haired man with ice cubes for eyes, who appeared beside Holbrook.

"Mrs. Andrews just discovered that the baby she thought died five years ago may be alive," Caleb explained. "We thought Mr. Mansfield would do the right thing and help us determine what happened to her child."

"Mr. Mansfield knows nothing of this," Mansfield, Sr., said with a snarl. "Now get out before I sue you both for harassment."

Madelyn lifted her chin. "You don't frighten me, Mr. Mansfield. My daughter is alive, and she may be in danger. And I will do anything to find her." She stabbed a finger in his chest punctuating her point. "And nothing you or any of your lawyers do or say will stop me."

A small grin tugged at Caleb's face, admiration stirring in his gut as Madelyn squared her shoulders and brushed past the men leaving them stunned by her boldness.

MADELYN STORMED OUT to Caleb's Jeep, furious and frustrated. "Well, that was a bust."

"Maybe. Maybe not."

"How can you say that? His lawyer and father are hovering around him like guard dogs. We'll never convince him to talk."

Caleb coaxed her into the Jeep, then settled inside the driver's seat. "Shh, Madelyn. There are other ways of finding out what someone is up to."

She crossed her arms. "How? He's not about to admit anything. He's too worried about his precious career and money."

"True," Caleb said gruffly. "But trust me, Madelyn. I will do everything I can to discover the truth, to find Cissy." He took her hand in his and stroked it, and Madelyn felt like whimpering.

How long had it been since anyone except her mother had soothed her? She was the one who always comforted Sara.

But completely trust him?

She didn't know if she was capable of giving her complete trust to anyone. Not after the twins' father, the man who had vowed to love, honor and cherish her, the man she'd believed would love his children no matter what, had walked out on them.

She eased her hand from Caleb's, but her gaze remained fixed on his dark brown eyes. Eyes that could swallow a woman. Seduce her. Make her want to believe anything he said.

Dangerous eyes. Sexy eyes.

Eyes laden with promises.

Ones she didn't intend to fall prey to.

She wrestled her emotions into control. "What do we do now?"

Caleb drummed his fingers in thought. "Who assisted Dr. Emery in your delivery?"

Madelyn massaged her temple. She had relived that night so many times. Had berated herself for driving. Had blamed herself. If only she'd waited on Tim to go to the store, if she'd stayed home, if she hadn't been so hysterical when Dr. Emery had relayed the devastating news about Cissy...

The list of recriminations was endless.

"Madelyn?" Caleb asked.

"I'm sorry." She banished the guilt to that faraway corner in her mind in order to survive. After all, she had Sara, and Sara needed her. "I was unconscious," she said. "But there had to be some hospital staff on duty. Nurses. Assistants."

"Do you remember anyone specifically who talked to you about Cissy afterward? Anyone else who saw Cissy?"

Chills skated along Madelyn's spine. If Cissy had been born normal, if Dr. Emery had whisked her away to sell her, then someone else had to know. "My God. Dr. Emery had to have a helper."

Caleb arched a brow. "I'm going to ask Gage to track down the doctor who signed off on your baby's release to the funeral home. Which funeral home did you use?"

Madelyn frowned. "The one in Sanctuary. You think the director at the funeral home knew?"

"It's possible," Caleb said. "Think about the staff that night, the nurses. Anyone stand out?"

A shudder coursed through her. "I was so trauma-tized, it's a blur," she whispered. Images of faces, white coats, a man with glasses...a woman, heavy, short, curly brown hair, a gap between her front teeth...spun in and out of her head. "Come to think of it, there was a nurse, an older, heavyset woman who tried to console me the next day. Her name was Nadine."

Caleb sped up. "Let's find Nadine and stop by the hos-pital. Maybe another employee remembers something."

Madelyn nodded, hope desperately budding to life in her chest. But if Nadine knew something, why hadn't she come forward sooner?

CALEB PUNCHED IN Ben's number. "It's Caleb. Have you found anything on those files?"

"Still working on it, but I'm getting close."

"How about Mansfield?"

"When you left, he and his father had words. His old man is irate that he's scandalizing the family name."

Caleb grunted his distaste. "Not that he was involved in the phony adoptions, just that he got caught."

"Right." Ben made a sound of disgust. "Old Man Mansfield wants the case tied up and fast."

"Did Mansfield admit that he knew Emery kidnapped the Nash baby without the mother's permission?"

"No outright confession. His lawyer shut him up fast the moment he mentioned Emery."

Damn. "How about financials?"

"That gets interesting. Mansfield made sizeable de-posits over the past few years in both his personal and business accounts, some corresponding with the Nash baby's disappearance and Madelyn's daughter's, as well as a boatload more. According to the D.A., Mansfield admitted to professionally handling adoptions, but he insists he thought they were legit." Ben heaved a sigh. "I suppose it's possible that Emery passed on forged papers to Mansfield without his knowledge."

"Possible but unlikely," Caleb muttered.

"All the defense needs is to create reasonable doubt," Ben said darkly.

True. "But we're going to nail him." Caleb glanced at Madelyn, his chest clenching. "Will you have Amanda find out who signed the baby's release to the funeral home, and see if the same people are still running the business? If the director or one of his employees knew the coffin was empty, maybe we can force them to talk."

"Copy that," Ben said. "Maybe Mansfield will make a mistake, too, and we can catch him."

Caleb had started driving toward the hospital but had a second thought. "Listen, Ben, can you access Sanctuary's hospital records and find out if a nurse named Nadine currently works there? She was on duty the night Madelyn gave birth." He gave him the date and year. "I'd like a list of any staff working the E.R. or delivery as well, especially if they have a record."

"You don't ask much, do you?" Ben said sarcastically.

Caleb chuckled. "I have a feeling you can handle it, Camp."

This time Ben laughed. "I'll try to work my magic. Hang on and I'll search for the nurse."

"We should talk to the hospital director," Caleb said, thinking out loud.

"Doubt that will do you any good," Ben muttered. "He's denied any involvement in Emery's wrongdoings, and his lawyer has hired personal guards to protect him. The hospital is facing multiple charges in both criminal and civil court, and he's received threats and hate mail from anonymous sources."

Damn. Caleb heard the sound of keys clicking on the computer.

"Okay, I found Nadine. Last name is Cotter. She left the hospital and works for a private home health care service." Ben paused. "Looks like she resigned a couple of months after the Andrews's twins were delivered."

Suspicious. "Do you have a home address?"

"One second." More keys clicked, then Ben came back. "Cotter lives at Widow's Peak just north of here." He recited the address. "And Caleb, I found something else."

"What?"

"Her bank records." Ben whistled. "Looks like Nadine came into some money about five years ago."

"How much?"

"Ten thousand," Ben said. "Could have been a pay-off."

Caleb grunted. Ten thousand for her silence. For a baby's life.

Disgusting.

But that bribe had allowed Emery to go free so he could rob more women of their children and profit from it.

"We're on our way to Nadine's house," Caleb said. "With Emery dead, maybe the threat of jail will convince her to talk."

THE SUN WAS starting to set as Caleb and Madelyn drove up to Widow's Peak. Nadine Cotter lived at the top of a ridge surrounded by the Blue Ridge Mountains, miles from town or neighbors. Had Nadine turned into some kind of hermit, or was she hiding out from someone?

Madelyn studied the scenery. She liked her privacy, but she couldn't imagine living so far out that she wouldn't have contact with friends or neighbors. It was dangerous, too—black bears, coyotes and foxes roamed these mountains.

"What did your friend at GAI say?" Madelyn asked.

"Ben's still investigating."

"Did he have information about Nadine?"

A muscle ticked in Caleb's jaw.

"Tell me," Madelyn insisted. "I hired you for the truth, not to protect me from it."

His eyes darkened with concern and she realized the truth must be ugly.

"Caleb, please," she said, then touched his hand, immediately feeling a jolt connecting them.

His fingers tightened around the steering wheel. "Nadine deposited ten thousand dollars a few days after you gave birth."

Madelyn gritted her teeth, blinking back tears as she turned to stare out the window. Ten thousand lousy dollars? Was that what her baby had been worth to the woman?

The winter chill suffused her, the brittle bare branches and brown leaves mirroring how empty and dead she felt inside. "I don't understand how a woman could do that to another woman," she said, haunted by the memory of crying in Nadine's arms. "For God's sake. She consoled me, she saw how grief-stricken I was."

"You'd be surprised at what people will do for money. Especially if they're desperate." He lowered his voice to a soothing pitch. "Maybe she had a good reason, Madelyn."

Bitterness shot through Madelyn. "There is no reason good enough to lie to a mother about her child or to steal her baby from her arms."

"I agree," Caleb said gently.

His compassion made her throat close, and she fought against breaking down. She had to remain strong, see this through, for her and for Sara.

And for Cissy. Especially for Cissy.

Gravel spewed from Caleb's Jeep as he sped up the drive. A faded yellow house with white shutters sat at the top of the hill surrounded by oaks and hickory trees. A cheap, metal carport had been erected beside the house to shelter the car, a rusted dark green sedan that looked as if it needed painting. A bird feeder that had seen better days was littered with dry leaves and twigs, its base tilting as if the ground was sucking it into the earth.

Caleb cut the engine and turned to her. "Do you want to wait here while I see if she's home?"

"No way," Madelyn said as she reached for the door handle. "I'm going to make her look me in the eye and tell me the truth."

Caleb clenched his jaw. "All right. But follow my lead."

Anxious to confront Nadine, Madelyn strode up the driveway to the porch, Caleb on her heels. Adrenaline surged through her as she knocked on the door. This woman might know where her other daughter was.

Then she could find her and bring her home. Sara's nightmares would end, and the twins would be together as they should have been all along.

There was no answer, so she knocked again while Caleb scanned the front yard. Several long seconds passed, her heart beating like a drum while she waited. But again silence.

Caleb frowned, then reached for the doorknob and turned it. Instead of being locked, the door screeched open. Surprised, Madelyn started to step inside, but Caleb caught her arm.

"Wait, let me go first."

An acrid odor permeated the air as she entered the foyer. The ticktock of an ancient grandfather clock punctuated the eerie silence. Caleb paused again, listening. "Something's wrong."

Madelyn's heart beat faster.

"Go back to the Jeep," he murmured.

"No, I'm staying with you." Madelyn latched onto his arm and trailed him as he peered into the connecting living room and kitchen. The room was dusty, filled with magazines and outdated furniture, and dirty dishes were stacked in the sink, flies swarming.

Desk drawers stood open as if they'd been ransacked, the contents spilling out.

Had someone broken in? If so, what were they looking for? And where was Nadine?

A rumbling sounded from the furnace, old pipes groaning, and wind whistled through the eaves as Caleb moved to the staircase. He placed a palm on the rail, and his big body went still.

The sound of water pinging onto the floor echoed from above, and the screech of a cat followed, shrill and nerve-racking.

Caleb inched up the stairs, and Madelyn stayed tucked close behind him until they reached the landing. A master bedroom sat to the right, the source of the water coming from somewhere beyond. A connecting bathroom?

Caleb halted, throwing out a hand to stop her, and she noticed the disarray in the bedroom. Clothes tossed from the dresser drawers, underwear dangling, cotton panties and bras dumped on a flowered chair in the corner. A jewelry cabinet plundered through, costume jewelry scattered across the carpet as if the intruder had been searching for something valuable, then had been furious when he hadn't found a treasure chest.

Judging from the outside of the house and the furniture, why would a burglar have thought Nadine had valuables?

The metallic scent of blood suddenly assaulted Madelyn, the foul odors of death swirling around her in a rush. Water dripped and pinged against the floor, then she spotted blood, a river of it streaking the worn, white linoleum in the bathroom.

"Dear God." Caleb spun around, gripped her arms and tried to shield her from the sight with his body.

But Madelyn was frozen in horror, her gaze riveted to the floor where Nadine lay, her eyes staring blankly into space, her neck slashed, naked except for the towel wrapped around her.

A towel drenched in blood.

CHAPTER SIX

CALEB SILENTLY MURMURED a Cherokee prayer at the sight of the dead woman. She'd been brutally assaulted and left naked lying in her own blood. Whoever had killed her was not only a cold-blooded killer, but he had no respect for women...or human life itself.

Madelyn gasped in horror, and he instinctively yanked her into his arms and backed her away from the bedroom into the hallway. He'd known something was wrong when he'd entered, had felt the violence in the house.

"Oh, my God," Madelyn whispered. "Nadine...she's been murdered."

"Don't touch anything, Madelyn."

Madelyn nodded, trembling. "I can't believe this. The poor woman. Who would do such a horrible thing?"

Caleb stilled, listening, his mind already ticking away possibilities. Judging from the signs of rigor and the bloodstains, Nadine had probably been dead for hours, maybe even a day or two.

"Why would someone come all the way out here to rob Nadine?" Madelyn frowned at the mess. "What were they looking for?"

Caleb's thoughts fast-tracked into detective mode. If the perp was a drug addict or homeless person, they might be looking for cash or anything to sell.

But the pervading presence of evil simmered in the tension-laden air. "This doesn't look like a burglary gone bad," Caleb said. "The degree of violence, the lack of hesitation wounds, the force and depth of the slice on the woman's throat indicates intent." And the timing definitely added to his suspicions. If Nadine had information about Cissy's abduction, someone could have killed her to keep her quiet.

Madelyn's pallor turned a dismal gray as the implications sank in. "You think it has to do with me? With us looking for her?" Hysteria tinged her voice. "How would anyone know we were coming here?"

"I don't know," Caleb said, ushering her down the stairs. Unless the killer learned Madelyn had hired a detective. It was a small town, and word had probably spread that they'd been asking questions. And if the exhumation itself had been leaked, the killer/abductor would realize they knew the grave was empty.

"Mansfield knew we were working together. He might have guessed our intentions and warned whoever else was involved," Caleb finally answered.

"So either Mansfield or another accomplice is trying to shut people up," Madelyn said, her tone tinged with disbelief.

"Right." The thought made fury rail through him. The conniving, lying bastard.

And even if Mansfield hadn't killed the woman himself, he could have hired cronies. A man like him—or his father—wouldn't bloody his own hands.

However, he might murder to protect himself from prison.

He coaxed Madelyn into the living room, scanning the outside of the house through the windows as he punched in Ben's number.

"GAI. Camp speaking."

"It's Walker. We're at Nadine Cotter's. She's dead."

Caleb paced by the window, checking outside again as Madelyn sank into a chair. He could see the wheels turning in her head. She was probably thinking about Nadine, that she'd lost her chance to find out whatever information the woman possessed.

"What happened?" Ben asked.

"Someone slashed her throat. I need you to call the local sheriff and get him out here with a crime unit. But give me a few minutes. I'd like to look around first." Although if whoever had broken in was hunting for evidence Nadine had hidden about the adoptions, they might have already found it.

Still, he had to search himself.

"You got it," Ben said.

"And keep an ear out for Mansfield," Caleb added. "If he was behind this woman's murder, maybe he'll spill his guts and we can catch him."

THE IMAGE OF NADINE's dead body was imprinted in Madelyn's brain. She had seen news reports of murders before but never anyone close and personal. All that blood…

And with Nadine gone, how would Madelyn know if she'd been involved in her daughter's disappearance?

What if she never found Cissy?

Accepting Cissy's death had been difficult enough, but she couldn't rest now, not knowing she was alive and possibly in danger.

Caleb disconnected the call, then shifted. "I'm going to my car for gloves, then I'll search the house before the police arrive."

Madelyn shifted. "What are you looking for?"

Caleb shrugged. "Evidence that Nadine knew about the adoptions. Maybe someone sent her a threatening note. Or she could have kept a journal or date book."

Madelyn's gaze swung across the kitchen to the adjoining living room. The killer might have ransacked the house to cover his tracks.

Which meant that the killer was aware that Nadine knew about Emery's illicit dealings. But who?

The back door from the kitchen stood slightly ajar, and Caleb walked over and studied it. "The lock's been jimmied," Caleb said. "This is how the killer got in."

Madelyn pulled herself together and removed her own gloves from her jacket pocket. Nadine's body needed to be tended to. Her family notified.

Guilt assaulted her for searching her private space.

But if Nadine had known about Cissy and kept silent all these years, then Madelyn shouldn't feel guilty.

Caleb clenched her arms. "Madelyn, let me do this. I don't want you involved."

Hysterical laughter bubbled in her throat. "I am involved, Caleb. If we both search, we can finish faster, then the police can come."

He stared at her for a heartbeat, then nodded in concession. "All right. But let me get some latex gloves for both of us. I'll take the upstairs and you check the kitchen and living room."

Madelyn's heart raced as he hurried outside to the Jeep. Seconds later, he returned and they both donned the gloves. "Put everything back like you found it," Caleb added. "We don't want to interfere with the investigation, just see if there's anything that can help us nail Mansfield or lead us to Cissy."

Madelyn agreed, then started with the kitchen desk and drawers while Caleb disappeared up the stairs. She found shopping receipts, coupons, thank-you notes from several patients' families, paycheck stubs from the medical service where Nadine was employed and insurance statements along with bills that hadn't been paid.

Frustrated when the kitchen turned up nothing, she moved to the den and examined the coffee table, the drawers in the end tables and the coat closet. Nothing there, either.

Footsteps sounded, and Caleb descended the steps, his expression solemn. "Did you find anything?"

"No. How about you?"

He shook his head. "If she had a journal or received threats, the killer must have taken the evidence." His gaze fell to the fireplace, and he strode over and squatted down.

Using the fire poker, he dug through the ashes, unearthing the charred remains of a leather-bound book.

Madelyn's pulse pounded. "Is it salvageable?"

Caleb lifted it to study the contents, but the pages disintegrated into ashes, scattering onto the hearth. A siren wailed in the distance, and Madelyn wanted to scream.

They had been too late for the evidence and too late for Nadine.

What were they going to do now?

CALEB POCKETED HIS and Madelyn's gloves, then he and Madelyn stepped onto the front porch to meet the sheriff.

Sheriff Gray stepped from the squad car; a deputy emerged from the passenger side.

Sheriff Gray crooked his head toward the deputy. "This is Deputy Stone Alexander."

Caleb extended his hand. "Caleb Walker, GAI. This is Madelyn Andrews, my client."

"The sheriff filled me in about the exhumation," Deputy Stone said.

"What are you doing here?" Gray asked. "You found a body?"

Caleb nodded. "Mrs. Andrews and I drove out to talk to Nadine Cotter, the woman who lives here, about Mrs. Andrews's missing child."

"I remembered her from the hospital," Madelyn said. "She was on duty the night I delivered the twins."

"I see." Sheriff Gray made a sound in his throat. "Go upstairs, Alexander. Check out the scene. I'll be right up."

Deputy Alexander nodded and climbed the stairs, then Gray turned back to them. "So you broke into the house and found her dead?"

Madelyn started to speak, but Caleb cleared his throat, piping up first. The last thing he wanted was for Madelyn to implicate herself with a motive. "No. We knocked several times but when there was no answer, I tried the door. It swung open, and I noticed that the place was in disarray then smelled blood, so I came in to see if Nadine was all right."

Sheriff Gray gave them both a long, assessing stare.

"It looks like she might have been dead for a while," Caleb said before the sheriff could ask more questions. "Someone slashed her throat."

"Did either of you touch anything?"

Caleb shook his head. "No. But Madelyn was in shock, so I brought her downstairs to sit down."

The sheriff gave them another curious look as if he was trying to decide whether or not to believe them, then moved toward the front door. "Wait outside until the crime van arrives." He glared at Caleb. "You will wait, won't you?"

"Of course," Caleb said. "I'm a professional, Sheriff. All we want are answers."

The next two hours dragged by as the medical examiner arrived, and the sheriff and crime unit examined the scene.

"You were right," Dr. Rollo said after he'd completed his initial exam. "I'd put time of death sometime during the night or early this morning. Rigor's already setting in."

"My bet is on Mansfield," Caleb said. "He was pretty upset when we questioned him."

The sheriff cocked his head sideways. "You think he killed Miss Cotter to cover himself."

Caleb shrugged. "What better way to silence her than murder?"

MADELYN WRESTLED WITH GUILT as Caleb drove her to pick up her car at GAI.

"I'm going to phone Ben and see if he's made any headway hacking into that list."

"It's late. I need to pick up Sara." Madelyn jiggled her keys. "My mom adores her, but she needs her rest."

Caleb nodded. "I'll let you know if Ben finds anything."

The weight of the day washed over Madelyn. Cissy was alive.

But Nadine, her only lead, was dead. Murdered.

Perhaps because someone didn't want her to find Cissy.

Caleb squeezed her shoulder, and Madelyn had the insane urge to lean into him. To ask him to hold her and make her forget the image of Nadine's blood splattered all over the bathroom floor.

"Madelyn, it's not your fault, you know," Caleb said gruffly.

She jerked her gaze to his. "Isn't it?"

"No," Caleb said matter-of-factly. "If Nadine was killed because of her involvement in Cissy's disappearance, she was guilty of conspiracy and should have come forward."

"Maybe." Madelyn ached inside. "But what if Emery or Mansfield, or whoever else was involved, coerced her into cooperating? Maybe they threatened her family or her. Then she was a victim, too."

"That's possible. But she could have turned to the police or someone else for help," Caleb suggested.

Madelyn's mind worked. "Maybe she'd decided to come forward."

"That's possible," Caleb agreed.

But they might never know. The secrets Nadine had hidden would be buried with her in her grave.

And what about Cissy? Did her adopted parents know she'd been stolen from her real mother? Was she in danger?

Would she ever find her now?

Her shoulders sagging from the stress of the day, she climbed in her minivan and started for her mom's. Caleb watched as she backed from the drive, and once again, she had the crazy urge to stop and ask him to go home with her. To hold her hand tonight.

To stay with her and help her forget.

But Madelyn had a daughter to think of. She had no time to think about herself.

One man had hurt her terribly and abandoned her and their child. She wouldn't give another man the chance to break her heart.

Swinging the van around, she sped toward Sanctuary's seniors home, pushing thoughts of Caleb from her mind. He was a detective. A man she'd hired to help her.

That was all he would ever be.

The quiet of the small town reminded her that Sanctuary was supposed to be safe, but Madelyn felt the darkness smothering her like a storm cloud ready to unleash more misery on her soul.

The ten-minute drive passed in a blur, and she parked and rushed in to get Sara.

"We've had a great day." Her mother patted Sara where she lay curled on the sofa with her blanket asleep.

Madelyn hugged her mother. "Thanks for letting her stay so long."

"You don't have to thank me, honey. We're family." The corners of her eyes crinkled with worry. "Poor child was so exhausted she conked out about a half hour ago."

"She didn't sleep well last night," Madelyn admitted.

Madelyn's mother clutched her hand. "Did you make any progress?"

Madelyn flinched. "The lawyer who handled the adoptions won't talk. And we went to see one of the nurses who was on staff the night I delivered, but she had been murdered."

"Oh, my God, that's horrible." Madelyn's mother squared her shoulders. "But you can't give up, honey. You will find Cissy and bring her home where she belongs."

The tears were threatening, but Madelyn blinked them back. "You're always so strong, Mom, so positive." She hugged her hard. "Thank you for giving me courage."

Her mother held her for a long moment, massaging her back like she had when Madelyn was little, and emotions nearly overwhelmed her. Three generations—her mother, her, Sara and Cissy—were all bound together in love and loyalty.

They all needed answers and closure to move on.

"I love you, Madelyn," her mother whispered. "But I

won't be around forever. I want you to find someone, a good man for you, a father for the girls."

"Mom, hush, don't even talk like that." In spite of her best efforts, a tear slipped down Madelyn's cheek. "Sara and I love you with all our hearts. *You* are all we need. And one day soon I'll bring Sara and Cissy here to see you, and you're going to take a walk with us and everything will be all right again."

Her mother laughed softly. "Yes, darling, that is the picture I see, too."

Madelyn clung to her for a moment, then realized she needed to let her mother rest. So she blinked back her tears, kissed her mother on the cheek, then released her and scooped a sleepy Sara into her arms and carried her to the car.

Sara roused for a moment. "Mommy?"

"Yes, precious, I'm here." Madelyn kissed Sara's cheek then buckled her in and drove them home.

Her house seemed unusually quiet and lonely, she thought, as she carried Sara up the stairs and tucked her into the white twin bed.

Then haunted by the memory of Nadine's blood and too anxious to sleep, she descended the steps to make a cup of tea. Or maybe she'd break down and have a glass of wine.

But the phone trilled as she hit the bottom step. Thinking it might be her mother or her nurse, or Caleb, she rushed over and yanked up the handset. "Hello."

"Stop nosing around," a low, coarse voice growled. "Or you'll lose Daughter Number Two this time."

CHAPTER SEVEN

CALEB RAPPED HIS KNUCKLES on the glass windows of Camp's office door, mentally stewing over the fact that Nadine, their closest lead, had been murdered.

The bastard who'd slashed her throat had wanted to keep her quiet. Which meant he was scared.

Ben motioned him in, then leaned back in his chair. Caleb sensed he was wired and wondered what he'd discovered. "Sheriff met you at the Cotter house," Ben said.

Caleb nodded. "Forensics is processing the place now. I doubt they find anything though. Killer ransacked the house to make it look like a robbery. I found a journal that had been burned in the fireplace."

Ben chewed the inside of his cheek. "You must be on the right track."

Yeah, but not fast enough. "Can you examine Nadine Cotter's phone records?" Caleb asked. "Maybe the killer has had contact with her the past few weeks…or months."

Ben began digging through computer printouts on his desk. He was like a mad scientist, scattered, but brilliant at his job. Even better, he covered his tracks so the cops and feds couldn't trace him.

"Madelyn said there were late bills in Nadine's kitchen," Caleb continued. "Maybe she went back for more blackmail money."

"And the killer got nervous and ended it."

Caleb's cell phone vibrated on his hip, and he reached for it to check the number just as Ben pushed the papers toward him.

"Here's a preliminary list of people who used Mansfield's services for adoptions."

"There were ten names I've found so far. Six babies were boys, so I ruled those out. Three couples lived in North Carolina. The fourth couple moved to Tennessee, although they've fallen off the radar. I'll keep searching for an address."

Caleb's phone vibrated again, and he punched the connect key. "Madelyn?"

"Caleb, I… A man just called and threatened me."

Caleb rushed down the stairs and outside. "What did he say?"

Madelyn's shaky breath echoed back.

"Madelyn? Is someone there?"

"No… At least not now." She sighed shakily. "But I'm scared, Caleb. He said if I didn't stop nosing around, that I'd lose D…Daughter Number Two."

Son of a bitch!

Caleb jumped in his Jeep. "Lock all the doors, Madelyn. I'll be right there."

You'll lose Daughter Number Two this time. Daughter Number Two…Daughter Number Two…

The taunting voice echoed over and over in Madelyn's head.

No! She ran to the kitchen and checked the lock on the back door, then raced from room to room checking the windows. Her heart pounded as she slipped into Sara's room and stood by her bed watching her sleep, soaking in the fact that for now she was safe and alive and in her own bed.

She clenched and unclenched her fists. No one would hurt Sara. They would have to kill her first.

She needed a gun. Some way to defend them. She'd ask Caleb to suggest the best place for her to buy one in the morning. There was no way she'd let anyone hurt Sara.

You'll lose Daughter Number Two this time...

Whoever this man was, he knew what had happened to Cissy.

Did he know where she was now?

Frantic, she raced back down the steps, grabbed the phone and checked the caller log for a number, but the display screen showed *Unknown.*

Coward. He was a coward who stole children and threatened mothers and didn't even leave his name.

She'd kill him if she ever found him. Kill him if he hurt Cissy....

A car engine sounded, rumbling as it beat a path up her drive. The wind howled off the mountain, whipping at the roof of the wooden house. Clenching the phone in one hand, she dashed to the window, flipped on the porch light and peered out.

Car lights fanned the front porch, then a Jeep screeched to a stop. Her breath puffed out in relief, and she started to run to the door but caution made her wait until she saw Caleb emerge from the SUV. His big body looked ominous in the moonlight, his long hair falling loose and brushing his collar, his expression dark as he scanned the yard and perimeter in search of a predator.

The threatening call taunted her again, and she flew to the door and swung it open. Caleb climbed the porch steps in three quick strides, his strong jaw snapped taut as he met her gaze.

"Are you all right?"

She shook her head no, then fell into his arms.

CALEB WRAPPED HIS ARMS around Madelyn and held her tight. His heart had nearly pounded out of his chest on the way over. He kept imagining that someone had been outside Madelyn's house, lurking in the bushes, waiting to attack.

Waiting to slash her throat just as he had Nadine Cotter's.

And then little Sara… Was this killer so evil that he would hurt a child?

Madelyn clung to him, and he stroked her back, rocking her gently. She felt so tiny in his arms, so fragile, and she had been through so much today already that he had to make her feel safe. "It's all right, Madelyn. I won't let him hurt you or Sara."

Even as he made the promise, recriminations screamed in his head. He'd vowed to protect Mara, too, but he had lost her and his unborn son.

He couldn't fail this woman and her child, too.

"I can't believe this is happening," Madelyn said, then stared up at him, her big eyes swimming in shock. "I want a gun, Caleb," she said, that fierceness back in her tone. "I need protection for me and Sara."

Mixed feelings warred in Caleb's head. "Madelyn, I know you're scared, but I'm not sure a gun is the answer. Not with a child in the house."

"But you carry a weapon," she argued. "And I can't leave us vulnerable. I have to take action."

"You took action," he said in a soothing tone. "You hired me, and I promise to protect you and Sara and find the person who kidnapped Cissy."

"But you won't always be around," Madelyn said.

"One day we'll be alone, and I need to know that I can keep my girls safe. They need to know it, too. They shouldn't have to grow up afraid all the time."

That picture disturbed Caleb, as well. He wanted to promise Madelyn he would be around forever, but that would be a lie. When the case ended, she'd move on with her life. Find some man worthy to be her husband and a father to her girls.

He admired Madeline's gutsy attitude. But considering shooting someone and actually following through were two different things. Too many times an intruder managed to wrestle the person's gun away and turn it against him.

Tormented by the desperation in her voice though, he spoke softly. "Listen, when there's time to teach you how to use a weapon safely, I'll teach you myself. It would probably be a good idea for you to take some self-defense classes, too. But for now, trust me."

He hoped to hell he wasn't asking for blind trust that he couldn't deliver.

Fear darkened her eyes, but he sensed he was getting through. "I guess I'm just panicking," she said in a hoarse whisper. "That man…the threat… His voice sounded so ominous."

"Which means we're on the right track and he's scared," Caleb said. A strand of hair fell across her cheek and he brushed it back. "It means Nadine's death must be related to our investigation, that she was hiding something."

"But she died and now we'll never find out what she knew," Madelyn said, her voice warbling.

"Not necessarily," Caleb said. "Ben is examining her phone records, so if the killer has been communicating with her, we can track him down. He's also cross-checking her calls with yours to see if there's a common number." He paused, arching a brow. "And if you'll agree, I'll have him place a trace on your phone so if this bastard calls back, we might be able to track his location."

Hope flickered in her eyes. "Of course you can trace my calls," she said. "Anything to protect Sara."

"Good." Caleb forced himself to release her. He liked the feel of her close to him too damn much. This was a case, and that was all it could be. He couldn't become attached to her or her child.

"Ben gave me a list of couples who used Mansfield to handle their adoptions," Caleb said. "There are four names we need to check out. They may not have Cissy, but it's a place to start."

Excitement lit her face. "Oh, my God, Mansfield disclosed his list?"

"Not exactly." Caleb shot her a warning look not to probe, then led her to the kitchen table and handed her the printout. "Study these names and see if any of them sound familiar."

She frowned as she read the names. "No one rings a bell. You think the person who adopted Cissy was someone I knew?" she asked in an incredulous tone.

"I don't know," Caleb said honestly. "The adoptive parents could have been innocent, unaware that Cissy was kidnapped."

Anxiety replaced the hope in her expression. "That's true, but Cissy is my little girl. And if Sara says she's in trouble, I believe her." She jutted up her chin. "If you don't, Caleb, I need to find someone who does."

Caleb wanted to deny that he believed Sara's gift, but how could he when he was cursed with his own sixth sense? When he knew gifts like theirs couldn't be trusted, but they sure as hell couldn't be ignored, either?

Because if Sara was right about a man threatening Cissy and her mother, and this killer was panicked enough to kill Nadine to silence her, he might kill Cissy and her mother to cover his tracks.

"SHOULD I CALL someone else?" Madelyn asked.

Caleb shook his head. "No. I promised I'd find out what happened to your daughter, and I will. But there is something I need to ask you."

Madelyn stared at him warily. "What?"

"Is there anyone you can think of who would have wanted to hurt you years ago?"

Madelyn frowned. "No. Not that I know of."

"Did your family support the pregnancy and your marriage?"

"Yes."

"Tell me about them."

"My father walked out on us before I was born," Madelyn said matter-of-factly. "So my mother was hesitant about me marrying Tim, but she supported my decision and was ecstatic about the twins."

"How about Tim? Did he want children?"

"We hadn't exactly planned on children so soon, but he acted happy about the pregnancy."

"What does he do for a living?"

"I'm not sure what he's doing now. When we were married, Tim was a salesman for a hardware store."

"He traveled a lot?"

"All the time." Despair threatened again. "He felt horrible for not being home the night I had the accident."

"Where was he?"

"Raleigh, on business, but he rushed to the hospital as soon as he received word."

"How did he react over losing the baby?"

Madelyn massaged her temple, remembering those first shocked, grief-stricken days.

"Madelyn?"

"He was understandably upset," she said shakily. "Riddled with guilt. I think that's what eventually caused the rift between us. He couldn't get past the guilt." Her voice dropped. "Neither could I."

"It wasn't your fault," Caleb said gruffly.

Other people had assured Madelyn of the same thing, but guilt wasn't rational. She was the mother; she was supposed to protect her child at all costs.

"Tim abandoned you and Sara when you needed him most." Caleb's tone reeked of disgust.

Madelyn had long ago tried to let go of the anger. If she'd allowed it to fester, it would have clouded every moment of her day and affected Sara. And she'd vowed to be a good mother to the little baby who'd survived.

"We were no good to each other back then," Madelyn said. "I suppose it was my fault, too. I was so obsessed with being a mother and grieving that I had no time for him."

Caleb muttered a curse. "Don't blame yourself or defend the creep. Any man who leaves his wife and child is not worthy of having a family."

His words soothed the ache building in her chest from the troubling memories.

"I'm going to phone Ben in the morning to start that trace and check your phone records. You'd better get some sleep."

Their fingers brushed as she handed him the printout, and a tingle shot through her, the warmth of knowing that he'd come to her rescue tonight creating an intimacy in the small kitchen.

An intimacy she hadn't shared with anyone in ages. One she didn't dare dwell on now.

"Thank you for staying," she said quietly. "I'll leave a pillow and blanket on the sofa."

"Thanks," Caleb said. "We'll start fresh in the morning."

His gaze locked with hers, emotions flickering in its depth. The air felt charged, electric. Sensual. Filled with the kind of tension that made her pulse pound and her breasts feel heavy.

But she stifled her feelings. If Cissy was in danger, they had to hurry.

CISSY HEARD HER mommy's scream, jumped out of bed and ran down the hall. The kitchen door was open, the big man hovering over her mommy.

No...

Her mommy had told the big man to leave them alone, but he'd come back.

Now he had her by the throat. Something shiny glinted in the dim light. Cissy stared at it, terrified. It was big and sharp and jagged...

A knife!

No, no, no! She wanted to scream, but the sound died in her throat. She had to do something. Help her mommy.

Think, Cissy, think.

Help, Sara, help!

The man jerked her mother around like a rag doll and flung her against the kitchen sink. Her mother pushed against him, but he slapped her in the face so hard her mother's legs buckled.

She hated the meanie. Her mommy said he was her uncle, but he'd never been nice to her. And he was always yelling at her mommy.

She had to stop him!

Cissy ran to her room to get the bat she'd gotten for her birthday. But she stumbled and tripped in the hall. Her knees hit the cold wood, her hands clawing for something to hold on to.

A cry pierced the air behind her, and she choked on a scream herself. The man was hurting her mama. She had to get help.

But it was dark and spooky and tears burned her eyes as she crawled to her room. She swept her hand along the floor behind the doorway searching for it, but the bat was gone.

No, no, no! Where was it?

Choking back another sob, she slid on her belly and felt beneath the bed. Her fingers closed around the bat's end, and she grabbed it and ran toward the kitchen.

But another loud scream pierced the air just as she made it to the door.

"Run, Cissy!" her mother shouted.

The shiny metal thing flickered in the light. The monster swung it up and jabbed it straight into her mommy's throat.

Her mommy screamed again. Her throat gurgled. Her head fell back.

Then all Cissy saw was red....

CHAPTER EIGHT

SARA'S TERRIFIED SCREAM cut through Madelyn like a knife, and she jerked from sleep, jumped from bed and raced across the hall. Another nightmare?

Or could the man who'd threatened her have sneaked in?

Caleb's boots pounded up the steps, and he reached out his arm to push her behind him, then scanned the dark room.

A ribbon of sunlight peeked through the blinds, and Madelyn searched the room, as well. Nothing.

Except Sara was thrashing in the sheets again, sobs racking her body.

"It's clear," he said, then stepped aside for her to enter.

Her heart in her throat, Madelyn rushed toward her daughter.

"No, no, no…" Sara cried. "Run, Cissy, run!" Sara twisted back and forth, tangling the sheets around her. Tears flowed down her little face. "Go the other way. Hurry! He's gonna get you!"

Madelyn gently shook Sara. "Honey, wake up. You're dreaming again."

Another scream pierced the air, and Sara's body convulsed with fear. "Run, Cissy!"

"Sara," Madelyn said more firmly. "Please wake up. You're safe, honey."

But Sara beat her fists at Madelyn's chest, lost in the

throes of the nightmare. Madelyn hugged her daughter, swaying her back and forth. "Shh, honey, Mommy's here. I won't let anyone hurt you."

The lamp flickered on, casting a faint glow across the room, and she glanced at Caleb, tears blurring her eyes. Her little girl was in agony and Madelyn felt helpless.

Caleb inched toward her, his big body filling the room with his presence as he placed a comforting hand on her shoulder.

"Cissy, hide..." Sara whimpered. "No, mister, please, don't hurt her!"

Madelyn's throat ached. She wanted to scream that it wasn't fair for Sara to be plagued with these nightmares. Why hadn't God given her this second sight instead of little Sara? "Honey, wake up and talk to Mommy."

Slowly Sara stirred from the dream, her body trembling. A terrified, glazed look clouded her eyes.

"Sara, look, it's Mommy. And Caleb is here, too." Madelyn cradled Sara, rocking her again. "You're safe in your room and no one is going to hurt you."

Shock and fear etched itself on Sara's small face. "But Mommy... He killed Cissy's mama... He had a knife... then it was red...so red...red everywhere..." Sara's voice cracked. "And now he's got Cissy, and he's gonna kill her, too."

CALEB CLENCHED HIS JAW at the fear in the child's voice.

Madelyn's teary-eyed look sent a wave of unexpected feelings over him. More than anything, he wanted to help her and Sara.

Maybe somehow it would make up for failing his own family.

He knelt by the bed and pulled one of Sara's tiny hands in his. Suddenly the images from Sara's mind filled his own. A dark crimson stain bled across the floor. The knife glinted in the dark, the jagged blade carving a hole in the woman's throat. Then splatters of red spurted from her neck and dripped down her body.

Blood. It was everywhere.

His heart thrummed. He squeezed Sara's hand, hoping to deepen the connection. "Tell me what you see, Sara."

Sara made a strangled sound and clutched his hand tighter. Once again the images in her mind appeared in his as if a camera was showing him live feed. The red grew brighter, stronger, filling up the space in her mind. Then sounds and scents flooded him as if she was reliving the gruesome murder.

A loud scream pierced the air. A woman's. The sound of a struggle. A glass breaking. A man's grunt. Another scream from the woman, shrill with pain. The metallic scent of blood assaulted him along with the other acrid odors of death.

A little girl's gasp followed, low, scared. Shocked.

What else?

He tried to hone in on everything in the room, but he could only see through Sara's eyes. And at the moment, Sara was in shock over the sight of the blood.

"Sara, I know it's dark and it's red. Really red." He lowered his voice to a soothing pitch. "But try to drag your eyes away from the red. Look around the room, at the man and tell us what else you saw."

Madelyn's fingernails dug into his arm, disapproving, desperate. "Caleb stop. She needs to forget about it, not remember."

Caleb met Madelyn's agonized gaze. "If what she's seeing is real, the only way to make the nightmares end is to find Cissy and save her."

Surprise flickered in Madelyn's eyes as if she'd just

realized that he believed Sara when no one else did. Then turmoil, because if Sara was right, her sister was in terrible danger.

That meant they had to encourage her to talk.

"Sara, baby," Madelyn said softly. "It's important. Where is Cissy? Is she with her mommy?"

Sara shook her head. "I don't know. I can't see her anymore."

"What happened when she saw the red?" Caleb asked. "Where was she?"

"In the hall by the kitchen."

"Now look up past the red, past the floor. Do you see the man?"

Sara nodded, a tremor making her body shake. "His hand?"

"His hand? What else?"

"A knife," she whispered. "It's shiny and sharp and the red… It's dripping from the end…."

Caleb silently cursed. So the image he'd seen in his mind was the same as Sara's visions. She'd witnessed the poor woman's murder.

Sucking in a calming breath, he rubbed Sara's hand. Her skin was clammy, her hand jittery. "Look past the knife, Sara. Do you see the man's face?"

Suddenly Sara released a wail, buried her head in her mommy's chest and the connection between her and Caleb was lost. "No," Sara cried. "I don't wants to see him. He's a monster."

"I know, Sara, but you're safe here, and I know you want to help Cissy, don't you?" Caleb said gently.

She gulped. "Yes."

Caleb wiped a tear from her cheek with his thumb. "If we know what this man looks like, we can catch him, honey."

Sara hiccupped on another sob. "He's mean and ugly and gots big hands."

Caleb gave Madelyn a sympathetic look as she soothed her little girl. He hated pushing the child, but any detail she offered might help.

"Sara," he said quietly. "Why don't you rest with your mommy for a while. Then when you feel better, maybe you can draw some pictures of the man. Okay?"

Sara nodded, and clung to her mother, obviously terrified the man might come and hurt them, as well.

If Sara was right and the killer had murdered Cissy's adopted mother, he must be getting rid of everyone who could nail him for the kidnapping.

Which meant he might come after Sara and Madelyn.

Caleb stepped into the hallway then removed his cell phone from the clip on his belt and punched in the number for GAI. They needed to find out if any women with five-year-old daughters had been reported murdered.

Every second counted.

MADELYN'S STOMACH KNOTTED with fear. Cissy might be running from a crazed killer this very second.

She wanted to scream and cry and rail against the injustice. What if they weren't doing enough? What if they didn't find Cissy in time?

Guilt mingled with terror. If only she'd trusted Sara earlier and insisted on exhuming that coffin herself. Then maybe she could have discovered the truth and found Cissy before…

Don't give up. If Sara had a connection with Cissy, Sara would know if it was too late….

Sara sniffled, her breath choppy. Poor baby.

Madelyn tucked a strand of hair behind Sara's ear. "You are such a courageous little girl, Sara," Madelyn said softly. "I know you're scared and what you saw was awful. But you're brave to tell Caleb and me about it."

Sara clung to her. "I wants to find her, Mommy. To saves her."

"Oh, baby…" Madelyn almost choked herself. "We will find her." God, she prayed she was right. How would Sara survive if they didn't?

How would she?

Feeling helpless, she sagged against the chair. Then Sara reached up and kissed her cheek. "I loves you, Mommy. I don't wants to ever lose you."

Anger suffused Madelyn. Her five-year-old should be contemplating what game to play next, planning tea parties with her friends, thinking about learning to ride her bike without training wheels, and sledding down the big hill during the next snowfall, not about death and murder and monster men attacking her.

"Don't you worry, precious." She kissed away her daughter's tears. "Mommy will always be here with you."

Sara studied her for a long moment, then took a deep breath, pushed away and straightened as if she'd gotten a bolt of courage. "I'm ready to draw that picture now."

Madelyn cradled her daughter's face in her hands. She was so beautiful that her heart ached. "Are you sure? You don't have to do anything you don't want to do."

Sara pursed her lips in a stubborn gesture that Madelyn recognized well.

"Yes, Mommy. I need my crayons and paper."

"All right. Go get them."

Sara scooted off the bed and raced over to her craft table with a determined gleam in her eyes.

"Mommy's going to make coffee while you get started," Madelyn said. "Is that all right?"

Sara nodded, and studied the paper as if trying to decide where to begin. Madelyn didn't want to leave her alone for long, but she hadn't slept well either and needed some caffeine so she hurried down the steps.

Caleb stood at the kitchen window looking out, yet he must have heard her footsteps because he turned around, his phone pressed to his ear. His gaze met hers, his eyes stormy.

Then his gaze raked down her body, over the flannel shirt to her bare legs, and she suddenly felt naked.

As if he was literally touching her with his eyes.

Shivering at the mere thought of his hands on her bare skin, Madelyn crossed her arms, wishing she'd donned a robe.

Self-recriminations quickly followed. Good heavens, what Caleb thought of her should be the last thing on her mind. Cissy's life depended on them.

Caleb's jaw snapped tight, and he glanced away, speaking low into the phone, and she quickly set the coffee to brew and retrieved a couple of hand-painted mugs from the cabinet.

"Thanks, Gage," Caleb said. "I'll discuss it with Madelyn."

He ended the call, then turned back to her, his professional look tacked into place as if they hadn't shared an intimate moment earlier. "Coffee smells good."

She tapped her fingers on the counter. "Did you sleep?"

"Some. I hope you don't mind," he said, "but I keep a duffel bag with clean clothes in my car. I grabbed a shower down here to clean up."

"That's fine." Lord help her. He looked fresh and sexy with his damp hair brushing his collar.

"Sara all right?"

"She's terrified. But she's drawing that picture now."

Caleb eyes flickered with admiration. "She's a brave little girl, Madelyn."

"I know." Madelyn's throat thickened. "But I don't want her to have to be brave. I want her to be a child, to have fun...."

Caleb moved toward her to comfort her, but Madelyn threw up a warning hand. If he touched her now, if he held her, she might completely fall apart.

Either that or beg him to never leave her.

Neither one would help them find Cissy. And finding her was all that mattered.

She gestured to his phone as he tucked it into his belt. "What are you supposed to discuss with me?"

He sighed. "I'm going to track down those couples on the list today. If you want to go, Gage suggested we drop Sara at his house to play with his little girl, Ruby. His wife Leah loves kids, and it might do Sara good to distract her for a while."

His sensitivity touched her. "That sounds like a good idea." She jerked her head toward the doorway. "I should get back. I hate for her to be alone."

He nodded, then surprised her by brushing her hair back with his hand. "I understand this is difficult, Madelyn, but she's a tough little girl." His gaze darkened, fastening so intently on her face that Madelyn squirmed.

"She's just like her mother," he finished. "She'll be okay."

Madelyn's throat thickened at his praise. If only her husband had seen Sara that way. Instead he'd bought into her psychosis and deserted them.

Unable to reply for fear she'd reveal how much his comment meant to her, she simply nodded, then reached for the coffee mug. But she felt his gaze on her as she poured herself some coffee, added sweetener and turned to go back upstairs.

He filled the other mug, then followed her, making her body tingle with awareness. She should have gotten her robe, shouldn't have looked into his eyes and seen that spark of heat.

But as she walked into Sara's room and spotted the crimson splatters her daughter had drawn, her breath hitched. The dead woman lay on the floor in the middle of the blood, the crude drawing of the killer erasing all thoughts of heat and Caleb's eyes.

Sara's description of the man as being a monster was mirrored in the sketch. Madelyn studied the details—his face was round, and Sara had added stray marks that gave him a wooly look suggesting he had a beard. A long, jagged line ran across the upper right side of his forehead. A scar?

Her heart pounded. For a brief second, the man looked familiar.

Clenching the coffee mug with a white-knuckled grip, she tried to remember if she'd seen him before, but the brief image in her mind faded, and she couldn't put her finger on anything specific.

Then again, Sara's crude drawing might not be accurate at all. Certainly not enough for an ID.

Still, what if she had seen the man? What if he lived around Sanctuary or had been lurking around town? Maybe he'd shopped in her own store?

No… She would have remembered customers…

Her nerves pinged. Dear God. He could have been at the grocery store or the park or even the library.

And if he was watching, he'd know she hadn't called off her search.

THEY HAD EXHUMED the coffin. And now they knew it was empty.

Damn Madelyn. She should have heeded his warning. But he'd watched her house all night, and he had planted a bug on her phone, and the bitch wasn't giving up. She'd called that private investigator the minute he'd hung up.

He balled his hands into fists. She would be sorry for making that call.

Hell, he didn't want to hurt the kid.

But he had to protect himself and his family.

That meant he had to tie up all loose ends.

Dammit, it was her fault the others had to die. Her fault if she lost her little girl this time.

Hunching in his coat, he slunk back to his car and headed toward the funeral home. Five years ago, Howard Zimmerman had needed money just like him. And he'd done his part and kept quiet.

But now?

If the police linked that wimpy funeral director to the kidnapping, he might spill his guts.

Laughter bubbled in his throat. The wimpy moron wouldn't get the chance.

CHAPTER NINE

CALEB WAS ANXIOUS to start tracking down the couples on the list Ben had given him, so he rustled up some eggs and toast while he waited on Madelyn and Sara. He figured they needed time alone, and he hoped Sara could offer some clue through her sketches as to Cissy's location and the identity of the killer.

He had just poured some orange juice for the three of them when they entered the kitchen. Madelyn's look of surprise made his pulse jump.

"You cooked?" she asked.

He shrugged. "Thought we could use something to eat before we get started today."

Sara plopped into a chair, then dug the spoon into the jelly jar and spread a glob on her toast while Madelyn showed him Sara's drawings. He glanced at them but refrained from asking questions until Sara had a chance to eat. Madelyn even managed a few bites herself, although anxiety riddled her every movement.

"Brush your teeth and get dressed, Sara," Madelyn said after handing Sara a napkin. "We're going to drop you off to play with a little girl named Ruby. She's the daughter of one of Caleb's friends."

Sara looked wary. "But I wants to go with you to find Cissy."

Madelyn folded her napkin into a tiny square. "Honey, Caleb and I need to do this alone today."

Caleb wiped jelly off his mouth. "You'll like Ruby, Sara. And I promise to bring your mother back safe and sound."

Reluctantly Sara agreed and lumbered up the steps to dress. Caleb studied the drawings. "Did Sara relay any more details about this man or where her sister might be?"

"Not really." Madelyn sighed, then gestured at the sketch of the man's face. "Just that he had a beard. And the line on his forehead is a scar."

"That's helpful," Caleb said. "Did Cissy ever call the man by name?"

"No. And when I asked her to draw a picture of Cissy's mommy and daddy, she said she'd never seen Cissy's daddy."

Hmm. The sketch indicated the woman had short reddish hair. Brown eyes. And she was slightly plump. Other than that, there was nothing distinctive.

"How about her name?" Caleb asked.

"No." Frustration lined Madelyn's face. "Cissy just calls her Mommy."

Of course.

"Madelyn, when I first talked to Sara, she mentioned that she and Cissy shared secrets. Can you try to find out what those secrets are?"

Madelyn scraped the scraps into the trash, then began loading the dishwasher. "You think there might have been abuse?"

Caleb shrugged, hating the fear and horror he'd planted in Madelyn's mind. But Sara's comment about secrets had needled him. "I don't know. The girls might have been discussing which boy they liked at preschool. On the other hand, it might be a lead. Maybe there's a special place they visit, or the name of that preschool or a family member that might lead us to their location."

"Right, I hadn't thought of that. I'll talk to Sara."

Caleb's cell phone buzzed. The caller ID showed it was Amanda Peterson, so he excused himself and answered the call while Madelyn went to help Sara dress.

"Caleb, I spoke with the hospital. Dr. Emery claimed Madelyn refused an autopsy. But get this. The medical examiner didn't sign off on the death certificate—Dr. Emery did."

"What about the funeral director?"

"His name is Howard Zimmerman. He's still with the local funeral home," Amanda said. "Do you want me to pay him a visit?"

"No, I'll stop by there then track down the couples on the list Ben gave me." He paused. "Thanks, Amanda. Maybe you could check with Derek's wife and see if her contacts with the adoption agency have a lead. Also, check with the Department of Children and Family Services. Perhaps they've had reports of abuse regarding a little girl named Cissy."

"I'm on it. Oh, and by the way, Caleb, forensics didn't find anything in that coffin. No skin cells, DNA, no sign at all that a body had ever been placed inside."

Good news, Caleb thought.

But the images from Sara's nightmare taunted him. Cissy had survived five years ago.

But her time might be running out now.

MADELYN STUDIED LEAH AND Gage's home; the sense that they were a happy, trustworthy family was evident in the way the couple exchanged loving looks between themselves and their daughter, Ruby. On the ride over, Caleb had explained that Gage had adopted Ruby, but Madelyn would never have guessed that the little girl wasn't his own daughter.

"We can play dress up in my room." Ruby's eyes sparkled with excitement as she offered her hand to Sara. "Mommy gave me a trunk full of prom dresses and high heels. There's even a princess's tiara!"

Sara smiled, obviously torn between what sounded like a fun adventure and the search for her sister, but Madelyn gave her an encouraging pat, and Sara followed Ruby to her room.

"She's adorable," Leah said with a sincere smile. "Gage explained about her twin. I'm so sorry, Madelyn. We went through a terrible scare with Ruby a while back. I still wake up in a cold sweat just thinking about it."

"Thank you." Madelyn fidgeted, picking at an invisible piece of lint on her jacket. "I appreciate you watching Sara today."

"No problem." Leah rubbed her swollen abdomen. "Ruby loves playmates. And Sara needs a friend right now, too."

Madelyn sighed. "I've tried to do everything I can to protect her, but what if I fail?"

"You won't," Leah assured her. "Gage and Caleb are on your side now. They'll find your other daughter."

But what if she was too late? If Cissy's adopted mother was dead, who was protecting Cissy now?

Madelyn forced the negative thoughts aside. She could not think like that. "When are you due?"

Leah grinned. "Six weeks. We're having a boy this time."

Gage pulled Leah up against him with a proud grin. "Little girls are special, but I have to admit I can't wait to have a son and take him fishing."

Leah poked him. "Hey, Ruby and I like to fish, too."

They laughed and Madelyn's heart clenched. They obviously loved each other dearly and were a happy family. She wanted that for Sara and Cissy.

And for the first time in her life, she wanted it for herself.

Her gaze shot to Caleb, and an image of him holding her, kissing her, looking at her and the twins with love filled her head.

Oblivious, Caleb cleared his throat. "Thanks, Leah. We really need to go. We have several leads to check out."

Madelyn wrung her hands. "I'm not sure what time we'll be back."

"Don't worry. If it's late, Sara can sleep over. Tonight's movie night anyway. We usually make popcorn and spread sleeping bags out on the floor."

Exactly what she'd like to be doing with her daughter.

Madelyn glanced anxiously at Ruby's room. "I hope Sara won't be a problem. She's been having terrible nightmares."

Leah squeezed her hands. "All the more reason for you to skedaddle and find her sister so those nightmares will end."

Madelyn nodded. That was the best thing she could do for Sara.

Gage walked them out to the car. "I talked to the sheriff," Gage said. "He agreed to inform us about any reported female murders in the state that fit our profile."

Caleb jangled his keys. "Thanks. Although he should expand that to include neighboring states. We have no idea if the couple who adopted Cissy stayed in North Carolina or moved."

"True. I'll talk to him and ask him to widen the search. Ben is also checking."

The details in Sara's sketches nagged at Madelyn. "I don't know if this means anything, but Cissy has been drawing sunflowers. Once, she depicted her sister hiding in a building with sunflowers growing inside."

Caleb quirked his mouth in thought. "Like a hothouse."

Gage's interest perked up. "I'll ask Slade to check on that angle. A specific type of greenhouse might help narrow down the location where the mother lives or works."

Madelyn climbed in the car, knotting her hands in her lap as Caleb drove them to the funeral home. The brick building with its adjoining chapel stirred painful memories of the memorial service she'd held for Cissy. She'd been in shock, grief stricken, and recovering from the C-section.

Yet now she knew her daughter hadn't been dead.

"I can't believe Dr. Emery lied to me and that he persuaded other people to cover for him."

Caleb's strong jaw twitched as he parked. "If Zimmerman was involved, he'll pay."

But justice would not replace the years she'd lost with her child.

She pushed aside the thought and squared her shoulders. She had to be strong. Focus on the future.

Together she and Caleb walked up to the front door of the funeral parlor. The bare flowerbeds mocked her. Ironically it had been the first day of spring when she'd held Cissy's memorial service. The azaleas had glowed with color, the air fragrant with spring. She'd stood in this very spot and wondered how she could possibly bury a child on such a beautiful day.

But she hadn't buried her. She'd buried an empty casket.

Renewed anger fortified her, and she shoved her way through the door. Inside, the scent of cleaning chemicals mingled with the sickening-sweet aroma of roses. The same soft elevator music echoed through the intercom, grating on her nerves.

A quick inventory of the interior, and she noted that the decor hadn't changed, either. Seating areas in grays and burgundy offered conversation areas to mourners, an office to the right served as the headquarters for the director and four viewing rooms flanked the hallway. Though usually at least one of them held a casket and was overflowing with visitors, this morning all four were empty, giving the place an eerie, morbid feel.

Caleb veered toward the office where a young blond man in his early twenties sat doing paperwork. Caleb knocked. "Excuse me, we need to speak to Howard Zimmerman."

The young man stood, fastening his dark suit jacket. "I'm his son, Roy. Maybe I can help you? Are you here for a consultation about a lost loved one?"

Caleb's gaze cut across the sterile surroundings. "No, we really must speak with Howard. Is he here?"

Roy shifted, obviously curious now. "He's downstairs. I can get him for you if you'll just tell me what this is about."

Madelyn tried lamely to wrestle her emotions under control. But the cloying scents of the roses and memories of grief-filled faces and voices haunted her.

"It's regarding a missing child case." Caleb flashed his GAI identification. "Now lead the way, and we'll follow."

Roy looked uncertain, but Caleb's voice had been commanding, and his size obviously intimidated the young man, so he motioned for them to follow him down a flight of stairs, then a dark hall. The scent of formaldehyde, alcohol, bleach and other chemicals reeked from the end room, obviously meant to mask the stench of death, but failing.

Roy cracked the door and glanced inside, then shook his head. "Not in there. He must be inventorying the coffins."

Nerves gathered along Madelyn's spine, a chilling bleakness filling the air. Then Roy veered to the left and opened a set of double doors. Inside, caskets in various shades of gray, bronze and silver lined the room. Roy flicked on the overhead light making Madelyn blink against the sudden brightness.

Then Roy gasped and staggered backward.

Madelyn peered around him, and bile rose to her throat.

Howard Zimmerman was sprawled inside a pewter casket, his limbs askew, his chest torn open by a bullet wound, blood soaking the white satin bedding and pillow.

CALEB SHOVED MADELYN behind him and out the door.

"Dad?" Roy's face turned a pasty white, and he stumbled forward toward the body, but Caleb blocked him.

"No, Roy, don't touch anything. This is a crime scene."

"My father…" Roy doubled over with shock and grief, then started to shake.

Madelyn pulled herself together faster than he would have imagined and gently gripped Roy's arm. "Come on, Roy. Step into the hall and take a deep breath."

Not that the hallway was any less of a reminder of death. The scents of chemicals permeated the floors and walls. The overwhelming feeling of grief and death and lost spirits lingered, their whispers taunting him. Angry spirits. Lost souls. Ones hanging in limbo and desperate for redemption. Others determined to exact revenge for a life cut short.

Then others who simply weren't ready to accept their fate and let go of loved ones.

Was that the reason Mara's spirit hovered by her grave? Was she angry with him? Or was she ready to move on but needed some kind of closure with him?

For a moment, he wondered if that could be the case between Sara and Cissy, if Cissy had already passed. Was her spirit hanging on, needing Sara to find her murderer so she could rest in peace?

No. He had to remain positive.

Sara's images had been reflected in his own mind. He'd heard Cissy's screams and felt her terror as if she was very much alive.

A low, keening sound erupted from Roy, jerking Caleb from his thoughts.

Madelyn helped the undertaker into a chair, and Roy leaned over, his elbows on his knees, gasping for air as if he might faint.

Caleb glanced back at Howard and silently cursed. Dammit, another lead gone.

How had the killer known they were going to question Nadine and Howard? Was there anyone else on his hit list?

Caleb punched the sheriff's number. "Sheriff Gray, this is Caleb Walker. I'm at the funeral home. Howard Zimmerman is dead."

"I'll be right there." Sheriff Gray's breath quickened as if he was hurrying outside. "What happened?"

Caleb explained his suspicions about the exhumation and funeral home. "Howard's son Roy brought us downstairs to speak to his father, but we found his body in one of the caskets."

"Damn," Sheriff Gray muttered. "Seems like everyone connected to Emery and the adoptions is being killed off."

"Yeah, someone is determined not to leave any witnesses behind." Caleb remembered the threat to Madelyn and Sara.

But the bastard would not hurt either one of them. Not unless he killed Caleb first.

HE CURSED AS HE watched little Sara Andrews playing with Gage McDermont's kid. The damn P.I. was watching them like a freaking hawk.

He'd never get the kid without getting caught.

Hell. He dropped his head into his hands and groaned. What was he going to do?

Nadine was dead and now Zimmerman was, too.

Two off his list.

And Cissy's mother. Number three. Stupid bitch shouldn't have started asking questions. He'd warned her, but just like Madelyn, she hadn't listened.

What to do with Cissy though... That was the big question.

He studied the P.I. and the kids again, then considered his options. Madelyn loved family more than anything. The fool woman would throw herself in front of a bus to protect her babies.

She had another family member that she worshipped, too.

Her mother.

He'd already researched her. Knew her phone number. Her address. Where she shopped. Who administered her meds at that senior home.

And when the woman was alone.

A grin curled his lips. He knew exactly how to force Madelyn to do as he ordered.

She'd learn the hard way.

He didn't like it, but it had to be.

Bye-bye Mama...

CHAPTER TEN

ALTHOUGH ROY ZIMMERMAN was visibly distraught over his father's murder, Caleb approached him as a suspect. Being upset or even in shock didn't negate the fact that he might have information.

"Roy." Caleb crossed his arms and faced the young man. "We need to talk about your father."

Roy squinted through the bright morning sunlight. Around them trees swayed in the wind and a flock of birds flew above, heading farther south.

"He's dead," Roy said in a high-pitched voice. "Why would someone kill Daddy?"

"That's what I'd like to know," Caleb said. "Maybe we should go into your office."

Roy's brows furrowed in confusion, and he led them back to his office like a kid who needed to be told what to do.

"Are you sure we should question him now?" Madelyn asked in a low voice. "He's in shock."

"If he's hiding something, it's better to catch him before he has time to think about it." And plan a cover-up.

Madelyn's eyes flickered with understanding, and they stepped inside Zimmerman's office. Roy filled a paper cup with water from the dispenser in the corner and slumped down in the desk chair, his hand shaking as he drank.

Madelyn claimed one of the chairs and Caleb settled

his bulk in the other one, facing Roy. "Roy, we're investigating a possible kidnapping from five years ago with Mrs. Andrews." Caleb gestured toward Madelyn. "We suspect your father had information that could help us."

Clearly confused, Roy glanced back and forth between them. "Do we have to do this now?"

Caleb sensed the man's rising panic. "The sheriff is on his way, Roy. But this case might be related to your father's murder."

Roy crunched the paper cup and tossed it into the trash. "What are you talking about?"

Caleb forced himself to tread slowly. He didn't want to spook Roy; he wanted to reel him in. "Did you work here with your father five years ago?"

Roy shook his head. "No. I was away at school." Suspicion filled his eyes. "Why? What is this about?"

"Does your dad have financial problems?" Caleb asked instead of answering.

"No." Roy indicated the funeral parlor with a sweep of one narrow hand. "The business has done well."

"How about five years ago? Any problems back then?"

Roy's complexion paled slightly. "No," he stammered, although this time his response had a false ring to it. "Why do you want to know?"

Caleb explained about the twins' birth and the exhumation. "So you see, Roy, someone here, your father probably, buried that empty casket, and we want to know who put him up to it."

Roy shot up from his seat, his eyes twitching. "My father would never do something like that. He was an upstanding citizen. In the Rotary Club. A friend of the mayor."

"We believe he did," Caleb said, standing as well, and bracing himself in case the man turned violent. "It's possible someone paid him to cover up the fact that there was no body."

"No…" Roy shook his head vehemently. "How dare you bad-mouth my father. For God's sake, his body isn't even cold and you're accusing him of a crime!"

"Think about it, Roy," Caleb said sharply. "Your father's murder wasn't random. Someone had a reason, a motive, to murder him. Do you know what it was?"

"I have no idea," Roy's voice cracked with disbelief. "My father is a good man. He wouldn't do anything illegal."

Caleb sighed. "Roy, maybe you are innocent. But we believe your father was murdered to keep him from talking to us."

Roy shook his head in denial. "No, you're wrong."

"Please," Madelyn cut in. "Somebody stole my baby, Roy. And I think she's in danger now. Help us find her."

Roy swallowed hard as his gaze veered toward Madelyn. "I'm sorry but I can't." He swung his hand toward Caleb. "Now, this conversation is over."

"It's not over." Caleb jammed his face into Roy's. "And it won't be until we find Madelyn's missing child. So if you know anything about it, then step up. Because if you're covering for your father, I'll make sure you're charged with accessory, and your butt will go to jail."

SIRENS SCREECHED OUTSIDE. Roy shouted at Caleb and Madelyn to leave again, so they went outside to meet the sheriff.

Needing some fresh air, Madelyn waited on the park bench as Caleb relayed their conversation with Roy and how they'd discovered Howard's corpse. Then he accompanied the sheriff inside to the crime scene.

She shivered as the cool breeze rustled trees and tossed drying leaves to the ground.

Poor Roy. He was devastated.

And Howard... She had mixed feelings about his death. On a basic human level, it disgusted her that he'd been shot in cold blood. But his murder suggested he had been involved in Cissy's disappearance.

Damn him.

She balled her hands into fists. How could all these people have lied to her? How could they have stolen her child and allowed her to believe her baby was dead? That was beyond cruel....

Caleb strode outside, the sight of him automatically filling her with relief. He looked so big and strong and formidable, that she wanted to melt in his arms and let him make the horrid memory of all that blood fade.

He gave her a concerned look, then slid down beside her and spread his hands on his knees. "They're searching for forensics, but the medical examiner puts Zimmerman's death at around 11:00 p.m."

A shudder coursed through Madelyn. "Then he's been lying there all night?"

"Yes." Caleb wrapped an arm around her. Immediately his warmth seeped through her, warding off the chill from the wind and the memory of seeing Howard's bulging eyes staring up at them in death.

"I can't believe this is happening. Two people murdered," Madelyn whispered.

Caleb cupped her face in his hands. "It must mean that we're on to something, Madelyn. Try to hold on to that fact."

She nodded, then looked into his dark eyes. Compassion, worry and determination flickered in the depths, along with a sensitivity that made her pulse pound.

A sliver of desire sparked, heating her blood and making her yearn to lean into him even more. To place her lips on his and taste his sexy mouth.

But noises intruded, reminding her that a dead man lay inside, quickly obliterating any fantasies of kissing Caleb and having him return that kiss.

"The sheriff sent his deputy to Zimmerman's house with another forensics team. Maybe they'll find a lead for us." Caleb glanced into the woods surrounding the funeral home. "I also called Ben, and he's checking Zimmerman's financials."

"Even if you find something, what good will it do now?" Madelyn asked. "He's dead. He can't tell us where Cissy is."

Caleb rubbed her arms. "A paper trail could lead us to the killer or whoever hired him," Caleb said. "And we want concrete evidence to be able to nail him in court."

"Right." Madelyn wasn't thinking about court. Only finding Cissy. "I should check on Sara."

"Done. Gage is staying with the girls and Leah to make sure Sara is safe."

Madelyn sighed in relief. It had been so long since anyone had taken care of her and Sara that it felt oddly unsettling. Uncomfortable in one regard and blissful in another. But she couldn't allow herself to grow accustomed to it. Still, for now, it was nice. "Thank you, Caleb."

His gaze softened. "I told you I'd protect you and find the truth and I keep my promises."

"I guess I'm not accustomed to men I can count on," she said, then wished she hadn't revealed so much.

He rubbed the back of her neck with his thumb, and a frisson of something sweet and sensual rippled between them. "Not every man is your ex, Madelyn. Some of us care about family and honor, about protecting women and children."

Madelyn desperately wanted to believe him. All the agents at GAI must care about families or they wouldn't have dedicated their careers to finding missing children. "But you don't have a family of your own?"

Intense pain flashed in his eyes so quickly that it sucked the air from Madelyn's lungs. Then a shuttered look fell across his face, and he pulled away as if she'd crossed some invisible line.

"Since the police have the crime scene covered, we should get moving," he said, back to business.

"I'm sorry if I said something wrong, Caleb." Madelyn touched his arm, needing to apologize, to make up for whatever she'd said to upset him, but he launched himself to his feet and slanted her a look that warned her that the conversation was over.

"The first couple on Ben's list lives about an hour from here." He headed to his Jeep and she raced to catch up with him.

"Their names are Bill and Ava Butterworth." His keys jangled in his hands. "He's an accountant. She's a pharmacist but gave up her job to stay home with the kids."

Madelyn missed the intimacy she'd felt between them. But he was right to keep their relationship focused on the case.

Still, the anguish in his eyes haunted her. Caleb had his own secrets. Secrets he obviously didn't want to share. Secrets that had hurt him deeply.

And for once, instead of thinking about her own pain, she wanted to alleviate his.

CALEB REALIZED HE'D BEEN rude by cutting Madelyn off, but he wasn't prepared to discuss the loss of his wife and child, not with her.

Not with anyone.

Guilt plagued him for the momentary spark of attraction he'd felt for her. He could not allow himself to fantasize about holding her or having her. And he sure as hell didn't deserve for her to look at him as if he was a savior when he hadn't been able to save his own family.

But he'd do his best to save hers.

She lapsed into silence as he drove from town onto the highway leading to Hopewell, the small town where Ava and Bill Butterworth lived. Mountains fanned out, the rolling hills and valleys picturesque, although those same ridges and cliffs offered hiding places for those who didn't want to be found.

It was nearly noon by the time they crawled into the town. Signs for winter sales filled shops while people hunched in their coats and hurried from their cars to their destinations, too rushed and cold to stop and chat.

He followed the GPS directions down a small side street that led to an older subdivision, the houses a mixture of wood cottages and brick ranches. Children's bicycles, outdoor play equipment and remnants of a snowman painted it as a family neighborhood.

Caleb parked in front of a gray, well-kept, one-story house with white shutters and sprawling oaks that swept the ground with yards of Spanish moss.

Madelyn twisted her hands. "God, Caleb. What if this couple has Cissy? What do we do?"

His hands tightened around the steering wheel. If Sara was right, they might walk in and find another dead body.

"We'll cross that bridge when we come to it," he replied.

Madelyn gritted her teeth, then opened her car door. He slid from the driver's side, circled the front of the car to her and placed his hand at the small of her back for reassurance as they made their way up the pebbled path to the front door. Caleb's mind ticked over the details of the history Ben had printed out on the couple. From the looks of the Butterworths' financials, their house and the van parked in the drive, the couple appeared to be a normal, middle-class family.

One who wouldn't welcome his questions, even if they hadn't adopted Cissy. Of course, no adopted parent wanted their histories dug up or exposed.

He didn't blame them, especially if they were legitimate and innocent and had been deceived themselves.

But he approached with caution. Who knew what secrets lay behind closed doors?

Madelyn ran her fingers through her hair. "Do we tell them who we are?"

Caleb contemplated that question. Being honest might work in their favor or send people running. Either way, Sara and Cissy were identical twins, so Madelyn would recognize her child if she was here.

"Let's just feel them out," he said. He rang the doorbell and they waited several seconds. The sound of voices echoed from behind the door, then the door opened and a brunette stood in the doorway with a baby on her hip. Behind her, two more children appeared, somewhere between the ages of two and four, then a tow-headed child about five joined them, jelly streaking her mouth.

"Can I help you?" The woman ushered the kids behind her in a protective gesture.

But they tugged and shouted at her. "Mommy, we want cookies."

"When are we going to Nana's?"

"Jamie looked at me."

"I did not."

"He did, too."

Ava rolled her eyes. "Enough, Jacob and Jamie. Hang on a minute."

Caleb cleared his throat and glanced at Madelyn who was intently studying the oldest child.

"My name is Caleb Walker." He presented his identification. "I'm with a private investigative firm called GAI."

She spun around and directed her comment to the oldest child. "Esme, take the others into the kitchen. Hand out the sandwiches. I'll be there in a minute."

Esme gave her mother an obedient smile, then gathered the bickering brood and shooed them toward the kitchen. "Come on, cookies for dessert!"

After they skedaddled away, Ava turned back to them. "I don't know how I can help you."

"I hired him," Madelyn softly cut him off. "Five years ago, I gave birth to twins at Sanctuary Hospital, but Dr. Emery told me one of them died. Recently I learned that wasn't true. I believe he sold my baby to a couple who adopted her, and I'm trying to locate them now."

Panic stretched across Ava's face. "I heard about Dr. Emery's death and the accusations against him, but Esme is not your child." Her throat worked as she swallowed. "We met the young woman who gave birth to her. Her name was Penelope, and we paid her expenses during childbirth. She was only fifteen and was grateful to find us."

"How about your other children?" Caleb asked. "Did you adopt them through Dr. Emery?"

"No." The woman gave a humorless laugh. "A month after we adopted, I learned I was pregnant. Since then, I've been a hotbed of fertility."

Madelyn chewed her bottom lip. "Did you know any of the other couples who adopted?"

"No." Ava clenched the door edge. The sound of the kids escalated. "You really believe this doctor stole your baby?"

Madelyn removed a photo of Sara from her purse. "Yes. This is my little girl Sara. She has a twin named Cissy, the baby Dr. Emery told me had died. But I buried an empty casket."

Ava's shocked gasp rattled in the silence.

"Please, if there's any way you can help us, I'd appreciate it. I think Cissy and her adopted mother are in danger." Madelyn drew a labored breath. "I want to save them both if I can."

A seed of doubt flickered in Ava's eyes. "I'm sorry," she said, her tone sincere. "But I don't know anything about your baby or where she is now."

Then she closed the door in their faces.

"What do you think?" Caleb asked.

"Esme is not Cissy," Madelyn said wearily.

"No, but we scared Ava," Caleb said. "I say we head to the others on the list before Ava has a chance to contact anyone."

Madelyn had a stricken look. "You think she knows where Cissy is?"

"Not necessarily," Caleb said. "But I don't want to take the chance just in case she's hiding something."

MADELYN CONTEMPLATED CALEB'S comment as they drove the forty-five minutes to the next house on the list. This place was much more ritzy, a private estate in the mountains that belonged to a couple named Stacy and James Ingles. Judging from their property and the Mercedes and BMW parked in the three-car garage, they definitely had the money to pay for a child.

And more.

When Stacy Ingles opened the door and greeted them, Caleb quickly explained who they were and Madelyn filled in the rest.

"I'm sorry to hear your story," Stacy said. "But you have a lot of nerve invading our privacy."

"I'm not here to make trouble for you," Madelyn said.

"Mrs. Ingles," Caleb cut in. "Whoever adopted Cissy needs to know that she was kidnapped, not given up willingly."

"So you're going to tear her family's lives apart," Stacy said. "And that child's. If she's with a loving family, think what that will do to her."

Madelyn's lungs tightened. "If that's the case, we'll work together for whatever is best for Cissy," Madelyn said through gritted teeth.

Her child belonged with her. She had not given her up and she wanted her back. Sara deserved to have her sister.

"However," Caleb said sharply. "We don't think that's the case. We have reason to believe that Cissy and her adopted mother are in danger." He explained about Nadine Cotter's and Howard Zimmerman's murders. "We're trying to save their lives."

Stacy's fingers tightened to a white-knuckled grip around the door edge as she stared at them, obviously struggling for a response. Finally she drew a deep breath. "I don't have your child, Mrs. Andrews." She walked to the table in the foyer, picked up a family photo and brought it back. The moment Madelyn saw it she knew the Ingles hadn't adopted Cissy.

Their child was Asian. "We didn't adopt through Dr.

Emery," Stacy said quietly. "He referred us to an international adoption agency when our fertility treatments failed. Sue Li is from China."

Desperation tore at Madelyn's insides. "I'm sorry we bothered you."

Caleb removed a business card and pushed it into Stacy's hand. "If you think of anything that can help, a name, maybe, someone who might have a lead for us, please call me."

Stacy chewed her bottom lip but accepted the business card with a nod.

Frustration filled Madelyn as they headed back to Caleb's Jeep.

"We're not giving up, Madelyn," Caleb said.

But a thick silence fell between them as they drove away. Madelyn stared out the window at the desolate mountains, the sharp cliffs and ridges, the winter wind biting through her bones.

What if Cissy was out there now, running from that madman, lost?

The late afternoon sun was waning as they stopped at a small barbecue restaurant, and Caleb ordered a late lunch for them both. He wolfed down two barbecue sandwiches, but she could barely force herself to eat a bite. Instead the images from Sara's drawings, the images of Nadine and Howard both lying in their own blood, taunted her.

What if Sara was right, and Cissy's adopted mother was dead, too? Would they find Cissy in time?

Nausea flooded her, and she had to force herself not to think as they walked to the car, and Caleb drove into the mountains near Boone.

"Third couple—the Peddersons," Caleb said. "Rayland Pedderson bought a mountain lodge six years ago. Wife helps him run it."

Madelyn glanced around the log cabin resort. It had obviously been designed for hunters, people who wanted to escape to a rustic, more primitive life.

Remembering Sara's sketch of the greenhouse, she glanced to the side in search of another building, but the outbuildings were individual dining halls and clubhouses for guests and special functions.

Caleb climbed out, and Madelyn followed, her legs weak as she mounted the stairs. Rocking chairs lined the front porch with checkerboards arranged strategically throughout, and the sound of the river rushing over rocks echoed from behind the lodge, slivers of sunlight slanting through the pines.

Caleb escorted her inside, the mountain theme continuing with deer, elk heads and fish mounted on the rustic walls. A gun cabinet behind the registration desk was filled with rifles and shotguns and a second cabinet in the corner held various knives.

A grunt indicated someone was behind the counter. Caleb rang the bell, and a mountain of a man suddenly stood.

"Rayland Pedderson?" Caleb called out as they approached.

"That's me." The big, burly man leaned across the registration desk, clawing beefy fingers through his thick beard.

Madelyn's heart pounded. The image Sara had drawn of the monster flashed in her head.

Rayland Pedderson could be their man.

CHAPTER ELEVEN

"WOULD YOU TWO like a room?" Pedderson's gaze skated over Madelyn insinuating he thought their visit was a clandestine love affair.

Caleb flashed his ID. "No, thanks. We're here for information."

All friendliness fled from the man's beefy face. "Oh, hell. You're that damn P.I. and the chick asking questions about Dr. Emery."

"You were expecting us?" Caleb asked, senses alert. "Who told we were coming?"

"Don't matter," Pedderson muttered. "I can't help you."

"Can't or won't?" Caleb asked.

"Can't." Pedderson retrieved a photo from the mantle and showed them a framed five-by-seven of him, a dyed-blonde woman and a chubby, brown-haired girl with dimples. "This is me and Beatrice and little Bea."

"You adopted little Bea," Caleb said. "Through Dr. Emery?"

Pedderson yanked a rifle from below the desk. "Don't you go spreadin' rumors like that. Little Bea is *ours*." He braced the rifle on his shoulder and aimed at Caleb. "Ours, you hear me? And no one is sayin' any different and takin' her away." He gestured toward the door with the moose's head mounted above it. "Now git."

Beside Caleb, Madelyn's breath hitched. "Mr. Pedderson, please help us…"

"*Please* git," Pedderson said with a snarl that showcased tobacco-stained teeth. "And don't come back or meddle in our lives or you'll be sorry."

Caleb held up his hands to indicate they were not a threat, then led Madelyn toward the exit. Outside, she sighed against him.

"He's a nasty man and he does have a beard, but he didn't adopt Cissy."

"No," Caleb agreed. "But he may be hiding something. I'll ask Ben to keep these names on file. GAI is receiving other calls from people who claim to have been duped by Emery. If Pedderson is on the list and illegally adopted Bea, someone needs to know."

Madelyn shivered as they rushed to Caleb's SUV and headed back toward town. "It's getting late. I should pick up Sara."

"We have one more stop," Caleb said. "Don't worry. Leah and Gage are taking care of Sara. I know it's difficult, Madelyn. But trust us to help you."

He didn't know why it was important to him that she did, but he wanted her trust. And he wanted to deliver for her more than anything he'd wanted in a long time.

"All right," she said softly. "At least now I feel like I'm finally doing something, taking action. Hopefully Sara will understand."

"She will, she's a tough little girl." Caleb squeezed her hand. "Cissy must be strong, too, Madelyn. She's reaching out to Sara. We'll find her because of that connection."

Hope filled Madelyn's haunted eyes. Damn her sorry ex-husband. Obviously she wasn't accustomed to accepting help or to people believing Sara, and he was going to do both.

Madelyn licked her lips. "Tell me about this last couple on the list."

He mentally ticked away the few details on the printout. They were, by far, the couple with the least background information, which raised suspicions in itself. "The Smiths. Husband was in the service. Wife was an admin assistant at a lawyer's office."

"Could that lawyer have handled the adoption?"

Caleb shrugged. "It's possible. But there's not much here to go on. The file is slim, which makes me wonder if Smith is an alias." Caleb followed that logic. "Hell, now that I think about it, your accident could have been a set-up. Maybe the driver sideswiped you hoping you'd go into labor, then followed you to the hospital and set the adoption in place with Emery."

Madelyn grew silent as if she'd collapsed within herself, making him desperately want to erase her pain. But they'd both known digging for answers might lead to painful truths. And there was no turning back now.

"If someone orchestrated that attack and took Cissy, he deserves to rot in jail," Madelyn said, her voice strained.

"He will pay," Caleb assured her. Although, hell, he'd like to kill the bastard himself.

Finally Madelyn closed her eyes and dozed while he wound around the mountain and crossed into Tennessee. But even in her sleep, Madelyn didn't relax. She twitched and moaned and a tear trickled down her cheek.

Caleb gently wiped it away with the pad of his thumb, then covered her hand with his. "It's going to be okay, Madelyn. You're not alone now."

Slowly she opened her eyes and looked at him. Her

lost look twisted him inside out. Made him want to step up and be the man she needed.

To hold her, forget his own problems and assuage her pain.

The thought terrified him. Yet at the same time, he ached to do it, anyway. To jump in without caution.

"Are we almost there?" she asked in a low voice.

Thank God she was oblivious to his thoughts. Dangerous ones for a man who'd failed one family and didn't deserve to dream about another one.

"Yeah." He swung the SUV up the graveled road, and they bounced over the ruts, spitting dust and rocks as they barreled up the drive to the remote cabin at the top of the ridge. The wind hurled leaves and broken branches from a recent storm across the patchwork drive as he pulled to a stop. Storm clouds gathered above, rumbling and threatening sleet, and the sun disappeared, night descending.

He scanned the property, the clapboard house, the woods beyond. A stray dog barked from the woods somewhere, but there were no cars in sight.

Madelyn leaned forward, surveying the property. "This is where the Smiths live?"

"It's the latest address Ben found." But Caleb sensed Madelyn's train of thought. Any family who'd bought a child would have money. They wouldn't live in a broken-down shack like this.

Unless they were on the run. Maybe they hadn't adopted Cissy at all. Maybe they had stolen her from the hospital, and Emery had covered it up.

And if Pedderson had been warned, someone might have tipped off this couple and they'd disappeared.

Checking his gun to make sure it was still tucked into his pants, he climbed out. But his sixth sense hinted that something was wrong. So far, the body count had been piling up. He hoped to hell he wasn't about to stumble on another corpse.

Especially a woman's. Or worse, a child's. Madelyn's child.

"Caleb?" Madelyn reached for the door handle.

"Wait here, Madelyn."

She dropped her hand to her lap and looked warily around. He locked the car doors and inched forward, senses honed as he scanned left and right.

His pulse pounded as he made his way up to the cabin. The steps to the front stoop squeaked, brittle wood sagging beneath the weight of his boots, and he paused on each step, scanning all directions, braced for an attack.

But when he reached the front, a sense of desolation overwhelmed him. An emptiness. The scent of dust and mold and decay.

Wielding his gun, he peered inside the window to the right and saw no movement inside. Jaw clenched, he pushed open the door and inched inside just to make sure. Cissy had supposedly seen the mother killed in the kitchen.

The wood floor creaked as he crossed the foyer. The living area was small, a faded green sofa and plaid chair left behind, but no other furniture or signs of life. To the right he spotted a small hallway which led to the bedrooms but the kitchen adjoined the living area, separated by swinging doors. He elbowed through them and scanned the room. Worn, yellowed linoleum. Beat up cabinets. The scent of cigarette smoke and stale beer.

Empty otherwise.

Removing a penlight from his pocket, he shined it across the floor in search of blood, but detected none. Just mud stains, dust and spilled beer. Obviously Mrs.

Smith wasn't a housekeeper. And there was no sign or hint of bleach used to remove blood.

Instincts sharpened, he strode to the bedrooms, expecting the worst.

But he found no body there, either.

Determined to know if they'd been here, he searched for clues as to the couple's whereabouts—mail, a note left behind, an address of a friend—but barring the metal beds in the rooms, the space had been cleaned out completely.

The Smiths had left without a trace.

THE ISOLATED LOCATION of this place made Madelyn's skin crawl. Were the couple simply outdoors people, hermits, or were they hiding from someone?

She scanned the deep, dark pockets of the forests. If Cissy lived here and had run from this madman, she could be anywhere, lost in those woods. Alone. Scared.

Maybe hurt.

Wild animals, bears, coyotes, snakes, the elements... Any one of them could be lethal to a small child. And if she hadn't escaped...

No, she couldn't allow herself to think the worst. Couldn't let herself believe that her precious little girl was in the hands of a killer.

But she might be. Sara had seen the man murder Cissy's adopted mother.

Caleb stalked down the front steps of the porch, and she released a pained breath. His chiseled jaw was set firmly as if he had bad news, making her stomach pitch.

He flung open the car door and settled inside, reaching for his cell phone.

"What did you find?" she asked, anxiety knotting her shoulders.

He sighed warily. "Good and bad news. No one was there. No body. But no Cissy, either."

She clung to hope. "Did you see anything? Photos maybe?"

"No. There was no sign of them, nothing personal. No clothes, dishes, toys, food." He clasped her hand. "No blood, either. So if this couple is the one who adopted Cissy, they moved on."

"And if the mother was killed?"

"It didn't happen in this house," Caleb said. "There was no evidence of blood or indication that someone had cleaned up after a crime. In fact, the house was dusty, as though no one has lived here for a while."

Her optimism deflated. She hadn't wanted to find a dead woman, but she needed to know they were making progress, that they were on the right track.

"Let me phone GAI and check in." Caleb started the engine and headed down the mountain. "Maybe Ben will have some information."

She looked out the window again, the forest growing more ominous as night swallowed the horizon. She tried to wrangle her thoughts out of despair while she listened to Caleb confer with his colleague.

"Looks like this couple left a while back. Smith could be an alias, so see what else you can dig up." He paused. "Any word on Nadine's or Mansfield's phones, or a murder victim fitting our profile?" He made a low sound in his throat. "Okay, we're headed back to Sanctuary. Keep us posted."

"Any news?" Madelyn asked as soon as he ended the call.

"Nadine's phone records indicate she called this address last month shortly after Emery was arrested. Mansfield also made phone calls around the same time."

Madelyn twined her fingers in her lap. "Meaning Nadine and Mansfield both covered for Emery?"

"It looks that way."

Madelyn glanced back at the deserted house. "Where is this couple now?" And did they have Cissy?

Caleb covered her hand with his again. "We're working on it, Madelyn. Hang in there, okay?"

Her throat closed. "I will. I just hope Cissy can."

Madelyn felt herself shutting down, physically and mentally. Caleb lapsed into silence, as well, and seemed to focus on driving. She studied his face wondering about his Native American roots.

Anything to take her mind off the fact that they might not find Cissy in time.

CALEB STEWED OVER the last few hours, trying to piece together the truth.

"What tribe are you from?" Madelyn asked, interrupting his thoughts. "Cherokee? Apache?"

Caleb whipped his head toward her, surprised at the question. He'd thought prejudices would die with time but still occasionally encountered them. "Does it matter?"

"No, not at all," Madelyn said. "I was just curious. Trying to distract myself from worrying."

At the quiver in her voice, Caleb relaxed his steely grip on the steering wheel. So she was just making conversation. Madelyn didn't have a mean bone in her body.

But she had no idea she'd hit one of his hot buttons. "My mother was white, my father Cherokee," he said, battling bitterness. "But my mother's parents never accepted my father."

"What happened?"

Did he really want to revisit his past? "It's not important," Caleb said.

"You know everything about me, Caleb," Madelyn said softly. "I'd really like to know more about you. I think of you as a friend."

A bead of perspiration trickled down his temple. He itched to touch her but tightened his fingers around the steering wheel instead. A friend? Unfortunately he was starting to want more than that.

Starting to want Madelyn in his arms, in his life.

But friendship was all they could have.

Besides, better the subject of his cultural heritage than Mara. "My mother's parents accused my father of taking advantage of my mother. Eventually they pressured her into giving me up. My red skin embarrassed them."

"That's awful," Madelyn said. "How could your mother have given in to that pressure, though? How could she give up her child?"

Caleb glanced at her, moved that she was incensed over his mother's abandonment. "Her family was prestigious, she was young." Excuses, excuses, excuses. "I don't think she really wanted to be saddled with a child anyway."

"I can't imagine ever feeling like that," Madelyn said. "Children are a blessing and should be treasured."

He chuckled at her vehement tone. She was a barracuda when it came to kids. A trait that stirred his admiration.

He wished his own mother had been as nurturing and protective as Madelyn.

But not all women were as unselfish.

"Where's your father?" Madelyn asked.

"He died about ten years ago. A couple of bikers jumped him in an alley and beat him to death. That's when I decided to be a cop." And the reason he'd decided to marry a Native American. He didn't want his own family to endure the prejudice he'd encountered. Prejudices that had no place in modern times, but nonetheless seeped through like poison.

"He must have been very special for you to honor him that way," Madelyn said.

He simply gave a clipped nod. Let her think what she wanted. Truth was, his old man had been bitter after the way Caleb's mother had treated him, and he'd carried a chip on his shoulder that had attracted trouble.

But he'd said enough. Talking about his family and past wasn't something he intended to dwell on.

His cell phone buzzed, thankfully ending Madelyn's questions. He grabbed the phone from his belt and punched Connect. "Walker here."

"Caleb, it's Gage. I just talked to Ben. Mansfield has disappeared."

"What?"

"Don't worry, I'm with Leah and the girls and they're safe. But Ben said he heard him talking about needing a new passport."

"Under a different name?"

"That's right. Ben tried to trace the call but it was a throwaway cell. I sent Colt Mason over but Mansfield was gone. Looks like he packed up and skipped town."

"Does the sheriff know?"

"Yes. He's already issued an APB on Mansfield, but I wanted to give you a heads-up."

Caleb sighed. Dammit. Mansfield knew they were closing in on him, linking him to Cissy's kidnapping and the sketchy adoptions. And he was probably afraid whoever killed Nadine would come after him, too.

Unless he was more involved than they'd thought.

Maybe he was the mastermind behind the adoption ring and he had ordered the hit on Nadine.

Either way, they had to track him down and make him talk.

THE LIGHTS WERE turned off at Sanctuary Seniors at ten. Just like little kids, the old folks had a bedtime. The nurses checked in. Made sure the residents took their blood pressure medicines and countless other pills. Helped them to the bathroom if they needed it. Changed their diapers if that was the case. Then tucked them in for the night.

Madelyn's mother, Cora Barker—the old bag—was probably sleeping. Snoring away like some pampered princess in her little garden suite.

Well, her peaceful sleep was about to come to an end.

Pulling the janitor's hat low on his forehead, he leaned the broom against the concrete wall, careful to keep his face averted from the security cameras as he ducked behind the red-tips flanking the back windows of Cora's unit. Using his handy tool kit, he jiggled open a window in seconds and slipped inside.

Just as he'd expected, the place was dark. Silent. It didn't smell of old people like he expected, not like that nursing home where his grandpa had been shoved for the last ten years of his sorry life.

Instead, the kitchen smelled like chocolate chip cookies as if the old broad had been baking. He thought she was in a wheelchair now, half crippled in her body and mind.

Inching past the oven, sure enough, he spotted the batch of cookies and snagged one, then wolfed it down, and grabbed another one and jammed it in his pocket.

Then moving slowly, he scanned the tiny apartment

and tiptoed into the living room. The single bedroom was to the right. Inhaling a deep breath, he darted through the doorway as quiet as a mouse.

Cora was curled in bed, her white hair fanned across the pillow like Snow White. He stared at her for a moment, his Grandma Giselle's face flashing in his mind.

Dammit, he couldn't go soft now. The old biddy's own daughter had brought this on herself.

Gritting his teeth, he removed his phone from his pocket and texted Madelyn.

"I warned you to back off."

Then he slowly eased a pillow from the rocking chair beside Cora's bed and pressed it over her face.

CHAPTER TWELVE

MADELYN'S CELL PHONE DINGED, indicating she had a text. But the message on the screen made her pulse spike with fear.

I warned you to back off.

"Oh, my God…"

Caleb had just turned onto the main street of Sanctuary. "What's wrong?"

Panic rose in Madelyn's throat as she showed him the text. "What if he has Sara? Oh, God, oh, God, he warned me…" Tears blurred her vision.

"Don't panic. I just talked to Gage." Caleb grabbed his cell phone and punched Gage's number again. "It's Caleb. Is Sara all right?" A pause, then Caleb breathed out. "Good. Madelyn just received another text from the guy who threatened her before."

"Is Sara awake? If she is, let me speak to her," Madelyn pleaded. "Please. I need to hear her voice."

Caleb nodded. "Gage, if Sara is awake, put her on the phone. And watch out in case this guy tries something."

He handed the phone to Madelyn, and she gripped it with a shaky hand, unable to breathe for the few seconds it took for Gage to retrieve her daughter.

"Mommy," Sara said in a sleepy voice.

Relief nearly overwhelmed her. "Sara, baby, are you okay?"

"Yes. We're watching the movie—and Ruby likes to

play dress up and paint, and we made Rudolph sandwiches with peanut butter and pretzels and raisins and a cherry for his nose."

Madelyn choked on a sob. Her daughter sounded so happy.

Caleb gently massaged her shoulder, and she took a deep breath.

"Mommy, what's wrong?" Sara asked as if she suddenly sensed Madelyn was upset. "Did you find Cissy?"

Oh, Lord, how was she going to answer Sara?

With the truth. That's all she could do. "Not yet, honey, but we're not giving up. Caleb and I are on our way to pick you up. We'll be there soon."

"'Kay. But Mommy, I likes Ruby so you don't gots to hurry."

Madelyn smiled, her heart finally calming as she heard the joy in her daughter's voice. Sara deserved to have friends and be normal, not plagued with worry or visions of murder.

Her cell phone jangled in her lap, and she checked the Caller ID. Sanctuary Seniors. "Grandma's calling, baby, let me talk to her and I'll see you in a bit."

"'Kay, Mommy. Love you."

"Love you, too." Madelyn clicked on the incoming one.

"Mrs. Andrews, this is security from Sanctuary Seniors. I'm sorry to have to call you this late, but there's been an incident."

Madelyn's blood ran cold. "What do you mean, an incident?"

"It's your mother," he said gruffly. "You should come over here."

"What happened?" Madelyn cried.

Instead of replying though, the phone went dead in

her hand. Shuddering with fear, Madelyn gave Caleb a panicked look. The warning, the text…

Sara was safe. But the threat?

This maniac had gone after her mother.…

MADELYN CLUTCHED CALEB'S ARM. "Caleb, go to my mom's complex. Hurry!"

Caleb's stomach roiled at the fear in her eyes. "Madelyn, what's wrong?"

"That was security at Sanctuary Seniors. Something's happened to Mom."

Caleb sped down the street leading to the seniors' community. He remembered the text message, and cold fear clenched his gut. The killer must have been watching. He knew Sara was being guarded, so he'd targeted the only other person in the world Madelyn cared about—her mother.

Frustration burned his gut. Dammit, who was this bastard? How could he be all over the place at once?

Because he wasn't working alone. First Nadine, then Howard and now Madelyn's mother… Someone was cleaning up the past and determined to keep them from finding Cissy.

Headlights glared from an oncoming vehicle, and he blinked his lights as a signal, but the car nearly skimmed his side and raced on.

Cursing, he spun the SUV into the parking lot of the seniors' home and screeched to a halt. But his mind remained on the car that had nearly run them off the road.

That driver could have been the killer leaving the scene.

Madelyn wrenched open the door and vaulted out at a dead run toward her mother's unit. Bright lights from the outside shot across the lawn like golden spikes. Afraid she might be walking into a trap, he dashed after her. If the killer had called instead of security and hadn't been in that car, he might be hiding out, waiting to ambush Madelyn.

"Madelyn, wait." He grabbed her arm. "Let me check first. If your mother was attacked, her attacker might still be here."

"But I have to go to her," she protested, yanking at his arm.

"Stop and think for a second." He massaged her shoulder. "Are you sure the caller was security? Did he give you his name?"

"No...he hung up before I could get it." Her gaze filled with terror as she realized his train of thought. "Oh, God, Caleb, what if he's hurt her?"

His pulse accelerated. He hoped to hell that wasn't the case. "Stay behind me."

Madelyn nodded and trailed him as they slowly walked up the sidewalk. If security had called, they would have phoned the police. But the police were nowhere in sight.

Caleb jiggled the front door and found it locked.

Madelyn dug in her purse. "I have a key." She handed it to him, and he unlocked the door, then threw up a warning hand urging her to pause for a moment.

A thump echoed from the bedroom, then a scream.

Caleb pulled a gun from inside his jacket, then scanned the dark interior, alert and posed in defense mode.

A low cry erupted from the bedroom this time, and Madelyn lunged toward the sound. But he pushed her behind him, and inched through the small living room. The window was open, cold air blowing in, chilling the room. The bedroom sat to the right of the hallway. Slowly they closed the distance to it.

But a board squeaked, and a gunshot zinged toward them. Madelyn screamed, and he shoved her down. "Stay low. I'm going after him."

Cocking his gun, he edged close to the wall and inched to the bedroom doorway. The man was leaning over Madelyn's mother, one hand shoving a pillow over her face while he aimed the gun at him.

Her mother was kicking and fighting, desperately trying to shove him off of her.

Caleb pointed his Glock at the attacker. "Let her go."

The man spun around, the mask over his face hiding his features.

"It's over," Caleb said. "Let her go and drop it."

They stared at each other for a long, tense moment, then suddenly the man released the pillow and vaulted through the window. Madelyn's mother wheezed and coughed, struggling for air.

He raced to her. "Are you all right?"

A sob erupted from her, but she gestured for him to go after the intruder. Madelyn raced to them.

"Call 911," Caleb shouted as he climbed through the window. He visually scanned the shadows for the culprit. Behind him, he heard Madelyn and her mother crying.

"Maddie?"

"I'm here, Mom," Madelyn whispered.

A shot zipped by Caleb's head, and he crouched to his knees taking cover by the corner of the building.

The back of the building was wooded, trees jutting up to the property with the units lined in a row, small yards and gardens separating them. Lights began flickering on in various homes, the residents obviously disturbed by the gunshots. Footsteps pounded to the left, and he headed in that direction.

A large courtyard sat to the left with walkways that wound through a garden and to a small man-made lake nestled by woods.

He spotted a shadow slinking through the maze and jogged toward it. Did the perp have a getaway vehicle stashed on a side road nearby?

A siren wailed in the distance, but Caleb saw the figure move again and followed him toward the wooded area. Then the man suddenly fled into the dense forest.

Squinting in the darkness, Caleb tried to see which direction he went, but the sound of a gun firing forced him to duck behind a tree. The bullet grazed his arm, and he cursed.

A second later, a car engine revved up. He ran after it and fired, but the son of a bitch had disappeared out of sight.

MADELYN'S PULSE THRUMMED with fear. Her mother was hysterical and breathing so hard she thought she might be having a heart attack.

"Mom, you're safe now." Madelyn gripped her mother's arms and forced her mother to look at her. The terror in her eyes was so stark it robbed Madelyn's breath.

"He... Someone was here," she cried. "He shoved a pillow over my face...."

Madelyn hugged her mother close. If they'd been a few minutes later, her mother might not be here.

"I know, Mom. Caleb ran after him." They clung together, both crying for a moment, hanging on to each other for dear life.

Finally when her mother calmed, Madelyn pulled back to examine her. "Does your chest hurt, Mom?"

"No...no, I just couldn't breathe for a minute." She raised a shaky hand to her throat. "Why would some man try to kill me? I'm an old woman, I don't have anything valuable...."

Guilt and anger suffused Madelyn. "I know, Mom. He attacked you to get at me." She swallowed hard and forced out the words. "I received a phone call warning me he'd hurt Sara if I didn't stop nosing around, but we left her with Caleb's friend, so he came after you instead."

Her mother's nails dug into Madelyn's arms. "What? Who threatened Sara?"

"I don't know his name," Madelyn said, shaking with fury. "But he knows I'm looking for Cissy and warned me to stop."

"You are not going to stop," her mother declared emphatically. "You're going to find Cissy and this maniac and put him in jail where he belongs."

"Mrs. Barker!" A loud pounding on the front door followed the shout, and Madelyn ran to the door. A security guard from the complex stood on the threshold, the sheriff on his heels along with an ambulance. "You called 911," the guard said. "What happened?"

Madelyn raked her hair back. "My mother was attacked tonight. The man escaped through the window, but Caleb ran after him."

"Where's your mother?" one of the medics asked.

She gestured toward the bedroom and the medics rushed to check on her. Madelyn crossed her arms in an attempt to hold her emotions at bay.

"Did you see your mother's attacker?" Sheriff Gray asked.

Madelyn shook her head. "Just his shadow, then he fired at me and Caleb."

"He had a gun?"

Madelyn nodded.

"Then we'll get a crime unit here. I also need to question your mother."

"Of course. She's shaken up, but I'm sure she'll talk to you." Madelyn led him to the bedroom but stopped before they entered. "I think this may be the same man who killed Nadine Cotter and Howard Zimmerman. He called me and told me to stop investigating. Caleb and I left Sara with Gage McDermont. Then I got a call from some man claiming to be security saying that someone attacked my mother."

Sheriff Gray muttered something under his breath. "We should have your phone analyzed."

"Caleb already has one of his agents working on it."

Her mother was propped against the pillows now, her pallor slowly returning to normal, a stubborn gleam in her eyes. "I told these gentlemen that I'm fine."

"Her vitals are steady," one of the medics said. "But we can transport her to the hospital for observation overnight if you want."

"That's not necessary," Madelyn's mother said. But she absentmindedly rubbed at her neck, a sign that the ordeal had terrified her. "I'm just angry that that madman escaped."

Madelyn smiled at her mother. She might be partially paralyzed but she had spunk. "Mom, Sheriff Gray needs to ask you about the attack. Are you up to it?"

Her mother nodded. "Yes, of course."

The sheriff crossed the room and took the chair across from Madelyn's mother. "Mrs. Barker, tell me exactly what happened tonight."

Madelyn's mother cleared her throat, her look haunted. But anger flushed her cheeks, as well. A good sign. If she and Sara and Cissy had fight in them, Cora Barker was their inspiration.

"I was sleeping," she began. "Then suddenly the floor squeaked. That sound woke me. When I looked up, a big man was hovering over me. Then he shoved a pillow over my face and tried to smother me."

Sheriff Gray propped his hands on his knees. "Did you see the man's face?"

She fiddled with the sheet edge. "No, he wore a ski mask. One of those that cover your face."

"Did he say anything to you?" Sheriff Gray asked.

Madelyn's mother shook her head no.

"How about anything else distinctive? Did you notice an odor or hear another sound?"

Madelyn's mother closed her eyes for a moment and massaged her temple. When she opened her eyes, a frown marred her face. "Come to think of it, there was a smell. Some kind of oil, maybe cleaning oil or machine oil."

"Gun oil?" Sheriff Gray suggested.

Madelyn stiffened. Rayland Pedderson was a hunter. He had a shotgun that he'd aimed at them. And dozens of trophies on the walls of his lodge.

Had Pedderson attacked her mother?

CALEB CURSED AS HE jogged back to Cora Barker's apartment. Several neighbors peeped from behind curtains, curious about the commotion, but obviously too frightened to step outside. Had one of them witnessed something?

Thankfully the sheriff and a crime unit had arrived. He stowed his weapon as he met Madelyn on the porch steps. She looked as if she was barely holding herself together. "Caleb, did you catch him?"

The sheriff appeared behind her, eyebrows raised.

"Afraid not." He scrubbed a hand through his hair. "He had a car waiting on the street."

"Did you get a look at him or the vehicle?" the sheriff asked.

Caleb shook his head. "No, it was too dark and far away to see the car. The perp was dressed in all black and wore a ski mask." He turned to Madelyn. "How's your mother?"

"Hanging in there," Madelyn said. "She smelled some kind of oil on her attacker. It made me think of Rayland Pedderson. Could it be gun oil?"

Caleb frowned. "It's possible."

"Who is Pedderson?" Sheriff Gray asked.

Caleb filled him in. "He wasn't very happy to see us," Caleb said. "I'm sure he's hiding something."

"Adopted parents can become defensive when their adoptions are questioned," Sheriff Gray said. "I'm adopted myself so I can't say as I blame them."

"But we're not trying to tear their lives apart," Madelyn said. "We just want to find my daughter."

"You think Pedderson kidnapped your baby?" Sheriff Gray asked.

Madelyn shifted, jamming her hands in her jacket. "No, at least not from the photo of his family. But he might have information about the person who did."

"There's another couple we're looking for," Caleb admitted. "They go by the name Smith. When we tracked down their latest address, the place had been cleaned out. There were no signs indicating where they'd moved, either."

"I guess word has spread about Emery's adoptions

being questionable and people are panicking. The adopted parents are afraid they'll lose their children," Sheriff Gray said. "Just raising that question could cause legal problems for the couples, as well as upset their families."

"It is a conundrum," Caleb agreed. "But Madelyn didn't give her daughter away, and if she's in danger, she needs us to save her."

"I'll check out Pedderson," Sheriff Gray agreed. "And this Smith couple. But first a crime unit needs to process your mother's room. Maybe the bullet casings will lead to something." He descended the steps to make the call, leaving the two of them alone on the porch.

Madelyn's gaze fell to Caleb's arm, then a horror-stricken expression crossed her face. "Caleb, you're hurt."

He glanced down at the rip in his shirt. A few drops of blood had seeped through the denim fabric. "It's just a flesh wound," he said shrugging it off.

Madelyn lifted his arm to examine it. Her adrenaline was waning, the worry in her eyes nagging at him. He wanted to wipe away that worry. Find her daughter and place her in Madelyn's arms.

Hell, he wanted to hold her so bad he ached.

She traced her fingers over his injury, leaning close to make sure he hadn't lied, that the bullet wasn't embedded in his arm. Her simple touch sent shards of sensations rippling through him.

He pressed his hand over hers. "It's nothing, I promise," he said, heat thrumming through him. When he'd chased after the shooter, he'd been terrified that the guy might have had an accomplice. That while he was distracted chasing one guy, another one would hurt Madelyn.

"Caleb," Madelyn whispered. "You should have the medics tend to this."

"I told you it's just a scratch. I'll clean it later." Her gaze locked with his, and need and desire heated his blood, hardening his body.

Desperate to touch her, to hold her, he feathered a strand of hair behind her ear. The temptation to kiss her seized him. He wanted to feel her against him, to know she was safe in his arms.

But voices inside interceded, jerking him back to reality, and he stepped away.

"I'm going to call Gage and have him post one of our agents with your mother."

Fear flashed in Madelyn's eyes for a moment, then gratitude. "Yes, please. Then I need to pick up Sara."

"Gage offered for her to spend the night."

"No," Madelyn said. "I need to see her. To have her home with me."

Caleb nodded. He understood that need. He felt the same way about being with her.

And that was crazy.

Madelyn was just a case to him.

But even as he phoned Gage and set up the guard, he knew he was lying to himself. Madelyn was not just a case.

He cared about her, dammit.

And that was dangerous.

CHAPTER THIRTEEN

LEAVING HER MOTHER was difficult for Madelyn. But her mom assured Madelyn she was fine, then insisted that Madelyn be with Sara and continue the investigation.

Gage had sent Colt Mason over to guard her mother. He and Slade Blackburn planned to take shifts. Knowing they were guarding her mother helped alleviate the anxiety knotting Madelyn's shoulders as she and Caleb drove to Gage's.

But too many unanswered questions remained. The attacker was still free. People were dead. Cissy was missing.

Ben Camp had tried to trace the source of that text, but it turned out to be a dead lead. The message had come from a throwaway cell.

The sheriff had canvassed the neighbors to see if anyone had seen or heard anything, but with hearing impairments, poor vision, and the late hour, most of the seniors had only been aware something had happened when the sheriff and ambulance arrived.

Caleb was quiet on the drive, as well. In fact, he'd acted distant ever since she'd touched his arm and examined his wound. The big guy was definitely the silent type. Intense. Focused. Angry.

But she'd sensed his anger was triggered by the brute who had attacked her mother and escaped, not at her.

That some part of him wanted her, at least on a primal level.

The same part of her that craved him.

The lights were still on at Gage's house when they arrived, and they hurried to the door together. Gage met them, his expression concerned.

"Are you all right, Madelyn?" Gage asked.

Madelyn nodded. "Thanks for assigning a guard to protect my mother. I don't know what I'd do if I lost her."

"We'll make sure that doesn't happen," Gage assured her.

Madelyn glanced over his shoulder. "Where are the girls?"

"They fell asleep watching a movie." They followed Gage through the foyer, and Madelyn spotted Ruby and Sara sprawled on a big, pink sleeping bag in front of the TV.

Leah looked up from the sofa with a smile. "Sara's an angel," she said softly. "The girls had a great time today."

"Thank you, I'm so grateful to you," Madelyn said, her emotions beginning to unfurl. "I'd be glad to return the favor sometime."

Leah stood, rubbing her lower back, then squeezed Madelyn's hands between hers. "Of course. I think we're all going to be good friends."

Madelyn nearly choked with gratitude. She hadn't realized how much she'd isolated herself since Tim had abandoned her. She'd been afraid of getting close to anyone, including another woman. But she was tired of being afraid. She and Sara both needed friends, a support group, as well as family.

Madelyn knelt to get Sara, but Caleb swooped her into his big arms instead. Sara stirred slightly, then curled against his broad chest, and Madelyn couldn't help but remember the connection her daughter shared with this man. She'd trusted him immediately.

Madelyn was so moved she couldn't speak. Caleb was tough and strong, protective and kind, and looked like an ancient Indian warrior. Yet he held her precious child more gently and with more care than Sara's father ever had.

The thought stayed with her while they drove back to her house.

"Let me check the house before you go inside," Caleb insisted as he pulled into the drive.

Reality made fear return, and she nodded, waiting in the Jeep until Caleb cleared the house. Thankfully, he returned and said it was safe. Then he carried Sara up to bed.

Sara stirred and looked up at her as Madelyn tucked her in bed. "Today was fun, Mommy. I like Ruby. Cissy will, too."

Madelyn dropped a kiss on Sara's cheek. "I love you, baby."

"I love you, too." Then Sara closed her eyes again and drifted back to sleep. Today had been harrowing. She'd nearly lost her mother.

And she couldn't lose her or Sara. Then she would be all alone.

She said a small prayer that Sara would rest tonight and be spared the nightmares.

But Sara's nightmares were the only real connection they had to her sister. And if Sara didn't dream of Cissy or see her in her sleep, she was terrified of what that meant.

That they were too late. That they'd never find her other daughter.

CALEB COULDN'T STOP THINKING about the fear on Madelyn's face when they'd heard her mother scream.

Or the way his body had tingled when Madelyn had touched him.

And then when he'd carried her daughter up the stairs, he'd seen the longing in Madelyn's eyes. She'd shut herself off from friends, from love, from relationships because she'd unselfishly been taking care of her daughter and her mother.

But who had taken care of Madelyn?

No one.

Her husband had deserted her. So had her father.

He would not desert her now.

Desperately trying to distract himself from wanting Madelyn, he studied her house. Homey, cozy furnishings. Comfortable, big club chairs draped with afghans that looked homemade. The fact that she owned a craft and hobby shop showed in the hand-painted folk art, stenciled walls and quilts in the room.

Her footsteps echoed as she descended the steps, and he jammed his hands in the pockets of his jacket, vying for control when he wanted to pull her into his arms and feel her up against him.

"Is she asleep?"

Madelyn nodded, then went to the corner cabinet and removed a wooden plaque. When she turned back, he saw that it was a nameplate with Cissy's name on it, one similar to the nameplate he'd seen hanging above Sara's bed. Both were painted with flowers in pinks and greens, their names decorated with swirls of color.

"You saved that all these years?" Caleb asked.

She nodded and hugged it to her chest. "I know we need to ask Sara about the secrets, but I couldn't bear to wake her."

"It's been a long day for all of us. We'll talk to her in the morning."

A relieved sigh escaped her, then she glanced at the nameplate again and a tear trickled down her cheek. "Thanks. I'm not sure how much more I could take today."

Her admission did it. He couldn't help himself.

He closed the distance between them in one stride, set the nameplate on the desk and pulled her up against him. "You're not alone, Madelyn," he whispered as she collapsed into his arms. "I'm here. Tonight you and Sara are safe."

"But what about Cissy?" she choked out.

Caleb closed his eyes, praying that Cissy was safe, too. "Remember, she's strong. We'll find her. I promise."

God, take him from this earth if he broke that promise. Madelyn deserved to find her daughter. Sara deserved to have her twin.

And him… He didn't deserve to be holding her or to even entertain ideas of being a family with them, but he'd punished himself for so long that he sent up a second prayer. A prayer that Mara would understand. That she would want him to help Madelyn and her daughters.

That somehow God would give him the strength to perform a miracle and reunite the twins and their mother and catch the man who'd tried to kill Cora.

Madelyn's small body trembled against him, and he forgot about prayers and simply gave in to the need to comfort her. He stroked her back, rubbing circles between her shoulder blades, at the same time breathing in her sweet scent.

She made a soft sound of pleasure, and he savored the sound, nuzzling her hair with his face.

"Caleb, thank you for being here," she whispered.

He didn't want her thanks. He wanted her to want him. To crave him as much as he craved her.

"You don't need to thank me," he said gruffly. "I'm just doing my job."

She suddenly pulled away and dropped her hands, confusion and hurt mingling with the desire darkening her eyes. "I'm sorry, Caleb. You're right. You're just doing your job, and I'm being foolish, falling all over you."

Guilt hit him swift and hard. Desire and something primal and hot, something out of control, snapped inside him. Too many people had hurt Madelyn.

He couldn't allow her to think that he was rejecting her.

"It's not just my job," he said between gritted teeth because admitting his own needs cost him. "I want you, Madelyn. I want to help you, to protect you, to…hold you."

The truth of his words registered in her eyes and made them sparkle with desire and a hunger that mirrored the aching hole clawing at his gut.

Emboldened by that look, he yanked her up against him, angled his head and closed his mouth over hers.

She seemed stunned at first, and he ordered himself to move slowly, not to frighten her with his raging need for her. But it had been so long since he'd held a woman, desired a woman, that emotions and lust and hunger made him run his tongue along her lips, pushing, probing, begging to venture inside.

A low, throaty moan escaped her, and she leaned into him and tunneled her fingers through his hair and parted her lips. Then she whispered his name on a moan and sucked his tongue into her mouth.

The feel of her lips closing around his tongue sent white-hot heat blazing through his body. His bloodstream flooded with sensations, his sex going rock-hard.

She shifted her body against him as if she felt his thick length and ached for it, and he backed her against the wall, running his hands down the sides of her body until one hand cupped her breast and the other pressed her hips forward, planting her sex into the V of his thighs.

"Caleb…" She moaned again, dragged her mouth from his and sucked and nibbled at his neck.

"Madelyn," he whispered against her hair. His body ached for her.

He kneaded her breast, heaving for a breath as she slowly unbuttoned his shirt and dropped kisses along his chest and torso. When her head dipped lower, he cupped her face between his hands, lifted her face and stared into her eyes. "You have to slow down or I'm not going to make it," he said with a wicked grin.

The sensuous look she returned nearly undid him. "I can't help it," Madelyn whispered. "I want you, Caleb. Like I've never wanted a man."

"I want you, too," he admitted. But dammit, he didn't have a condom. It had been so damn long that he had stopped carrying protection.

And he'd never take the chance of impregnating another woman. Not unless they were married and he knew she wanted his child.

His child…her child.

Guilt slammed into him. He couldn't screw up this case because of his own needs for Madelyn.

She deserved better.

"You changed your mind?" Madelyn said, hurt flashing in her eyes.

"No, I want you," he said, his voice gruff with desire. "But I want to do right by you even more."

MADELYN'S PULSE CLAMORED. Caleb wanted to do right by her.

But right now all she wanted was to have him kiss her again. To have him take her upstairs, strip her clothes and make love to her.

And she was going to have it.

"Please, Caleb," she whispered. "I need you tonight."

Questions filled his eyes. Then a flash of raw, primal need that took her breath away. She didn't know his story, but knew enough to realize that he didn't do this lightly. He was honorable, decent. He kept his promises.

And he was all man. She felt it in the thick, hard length between her thighs. In the control he maintained. In the heat flaring in his expression.

"Are you sure?" he asked gruffly.

She nodded.

"I don't have protection," he said with a frown.

Madelyn smiled. "I do." She blushed at the surprised look on his face. One of the times her mother had tried to fix her up, she'd given her a gift basket.

His mouth closed over hers again, gentle, then probing, then demanding, and she parted her lips and welcomed him inside. His tongue danced and teased her lips, played a game of tag with her own, then he suddenly swept her in his arms and carried her to her bedroom.

A sliver of moonlight flickered through the sheers illuminating his broad body, and her heart raced as he allowed her to remove his shirt. She ran her hands over his slick, smooth, bronzed chest, then flicked the leather thong from his hair and threaded her fingers through the decadent strands.

His gruff moan spurned her on and she nibbled and kissed and licked his neck and chest, until he grabbed her hands and pushed her back onto the bed. "My turn," he murmured as he began to strip her clothes.

"Condom?"

She gestured toward the decorative basket on her nightstand, and he chuckled. "You were prepared?"

"My mother," she said with a smile.

A sensual almost possessive look flared in his eyes, and he buried his head in her hair for a moment, as if savoring the way she felt in his arms. Madelyn felt a tenderness for him wash over her.

Then he lifted his head and a wicked gleam replaced that look, the raw, primal need in his eyes sending a buzz of euphoric anticipation through her as he began to peel off her clothes.

Madelyn hadn't been naked for anyone except her ex, and now she had a scar from the C-section. For a moment, she threw her hands down to cover it, but Caleb shook his head and flung her hands by her sides, holding them down as he ravaged her mouth again.

"You're beautiful," he growled. "I want to taste all of you."

Erotic sensations rippled through her as he swept his tongue down her neck, then he teased and nibbled and sucked her nipples into his mouth until she arched and cried out for more. She parted her legs, silently begging for him to fill her, but his tongue found its way down her belly and into her heat, and pure pleasure shot through her.

A million butterflies danced in her stomach as he kissed the insides of her thighs then tilted her hips to taste her.

"Caleb…"

Then she could speak no more. Her body became a minefield of sensations, exploding with each touch and caress, each kiss and lap of his tongue, and when she shouted his name as her orgasm claimed her, he rose above her, kissed her again, then plunged his huge length inside her.

CALEB SHIFTED, ALLOWING Madelyn to adjust to his size. She was so damn small and tight that he was afraid he would hurt her. But stopping now was out of the question. Her pleas for him to take her echoed in his head, the heat in his blood roaring.

Her body quivered around his sex, hugging him, holding him, then she wrapped her legs around him, and any rational thoughts fled. On some basic, male level, he had wanted her from the moment he'd seen her.

And it was destiny that he have her.

Her pain, her sweetness, her strength, her love for her family all made her sexy. And her body... She had the body of a vixen.

Tempting. Delicious. Sensual.

She clawed at his back, and his muscles rippled. She raked her feet down his calves and his sex hardened even more. She suckled his neck, and he rocked inside her, plunging to her core.

Need and desire and emotions he didn't want to name drove him faster, and he built a tempo that had his own climax teetering to the surface. Then she lowered her hands to grip his hips, and pleasure overcame him.

He stroked her inside and out, lifted her legs and sank deeper, so deep he felt another orgasm shivering through her. So deep his own came so swift and hard that he lost all thought and shouted her name as his body unloaded inside her.

MADELYN QUIVERED FROM the delicious sensations buzzing through her body. She had never been made love to like that, not with such force and need and...emotion.

She stroked his hair back from his forehead as he rolled them to their sides and cradled her against his chest.

She was falling in love with Caleb.

How stupid was she?

For a man, sex was sex. And she had practically begged Caleb for it. She couldn't become emotional and declare her feelings. She needed him to finish the investigation.

A sound from Sara's room startled her, then Sara's cry rent the air. She was having another nightmare.

Caleb heard it, too, and instantly released her. "You'd better check on her."

Madelyn nodded, her skin still tingling from his touch, her breasts heavy and aching. But she put aside her desires, grabbed a nightshirt from her dresser, yanked it on and rushed to her daughter.

Lost in the throes of another nightmare, Sara thrashed beneath the covers, a low sob ripping from her. "No, don't put me in there. It's dark...."

Madelyn sank down on the bed beside her and shook her gently. "Wake up, sweetie. You're having another bad dream."

Sara cried out again, then opened her eyes. The glazed fear in her expression made Madelyn's stomach knot. "Sara, what did you see, baby?"

Sara stared at her for a heartbeat, the air vibrating with her terror. Behind her, Madelyn heard Caleb step to the door and realized he was watching. Listening. Waiting.

"What did you see?" Madelyn asked gently.

"Cissy," Sara said in a strained voice. "She's scared."

"Why is she scared, honey?"

"The mean man, he gots her and he dragged her away from the sunflowers."

Madelyn's gaze flew to Caleb's, and he slowly walked over to join them. He'd put on his jeans and shirt, although the shirt was half buttoned, reminding her of what they'd been doing. Making her want him again.

Making her feel guilty for indulging in pleasure when her daughters both needed her.

"Where are they now?" Caleb asked.

Sara tightened her fingers around the edge of her comforter. "He put her in the back of his car. But it's dark. She can't see anything."

"The back? You mean the backseat?" Caleb asked.

Sara shook her head. "No, the back where you puts stuff."

"You mean the trunk?" Madelyn said unable to keep the horror from her voice.

Sara bobbed her head up and down. "He slammed the top and closed Cissy in, and it's really dark and she's scared, and she's crying."

Madelyn shook with anger.

"What kind of car is he driving?" Caleb asked. "Can you see what color it is?"

Sara pressed her fist to her mouth. "Black."

"Does it have two doors or are there doors in the back?" Caleb asked.

Sara shrugged. "I don't know. Cissy can't see the doors. It's too dark in the trunk."

Madelyn ached for both of her girls. Apparently Sara saw everything through Cissy's eyes. And she felt her emotions. Her fear.

"Did the man say where he was taking Cissy?" Caleb asked.

Sara shook her head. "No, but the man killed her mama, and now he's taking her away."

Madelyn exchanged a worried look with Caleb. He knelt by Sara's bed. "Sara, you said once that Cissy shared her secrets with you. Can you tell us about those secrets?"

Sara's traumatized gaze flew to Caleb. "You're not supposed to tell each other's secrets."

Madelyn chewed her bottom lip, then gathered Sara's hand in hers. "You're right, honey. But Cissy's in trouble. And if there's something about her secrets that can help us find her, I don't think she'd mind if you told us."

"Your mom is right," Caleb said in a soothing tone.

Sara studied them both for a moment, indecision in her eyes. She was loyal to her twin, but she was terrified for Cissy's life. She clutched her teddy bear under one arm and clung to Madelyn's hand, squeezing it for dear life. "Cissy said no one's supposed to know."

"Know what, Sara?" Caleb asked.

Sara heaved a weary sigh. "That we gots the same daddy."

CISSY ROLLED INTO a ball, hugging her blanket to her chest. Tears leaked from her eyes and dripped down her face. Her breath hitched. She'd screamed so much already that her throat hurt and her voice sounded like a frog.

But nobody had heard.

Unless Sara had....

The car bounced over the rough road, tossing her back and forth. It was so dark she couldn't see anything. It smelled awful, too. Dirty and greasy, and she felt a spider crawling up her leg.

She swiped at the spider with her hand and felt along

the inside of the trunk for something to help her get out. But her hand hit something sharp. A shovel.

She jerked her hand back.

Her mommy's face flashed in her mind. Her mommy lying on the floor in all that red. The red was blood. Her mommy's blood cause the mean monster man had cut her throat.

The monster man had killed her. And now he'd left her mommy behind.

Where was he taking her now? To her daddy? Back to Sara?

No... He was going to kill her, too. That's why he had that shovel. He was going to kill her, then he would bury her in the ground and no one would ever find her.

And she would never get to be with Sara.

CHAPTER FOURTEEN

MADELYN'S MIND RACED as Sara's words sank in.

Cissy knew that she shared a daddy with Sara. Had she actually met her father?

If that was the case, then her ex-husband knew that Cissy had survived. He might have even seen her. He might even know where she was.

Pain knifed through her. No... Tim would not have betrayed her like that. He couldn't be involved in Cissy's disappearance, in her adoption.

He wouldn't have given away one of his own children....

Would he?

"Thank you for sharing with us." Caleb patted Sara's shoulder. "You're a brave little girl and a big help, Sara."

Panic mushroomed inside Madelyn. "Sara, is the mean man who hurt Cissy's mother—is that man Cissy's daddy?"

Sara scrunched her nose. "No... Her mama says it's her uncle. But he don't like Cissy. And he and Cissy's mama was yelling at each other and then...the knife..."

A horror-stricken look filled Sara's eyes again, and Madelyn pulled her into her arms. "It's okay, honey. It's over. We'll find Cissy. I promise."

Caleb stood, indicating his phone, then left the room as if he was on a mission. She laid down beside Sara and comforted her until she finally drifted back to sleep.

Madelyn closed her eyes, too, sleep pulling at her.

They had to find Tim.

And if he'd had any part in Cissy's adoption, she would kill him.

CALEB COULD BARELY contain his rage. Had Madelyn's husband sold their daughter?

And what was this about an uncle killing the mother?

He strode to Madelyn's kitchen table, the scent of her still lingering on his skin and tormenting him. Making love with her had been a mistake. He'd thought it would sate him, but now that he'd tasted her, touched her, felt her body join with his, he couldn't shake the need for her.

He checked his watch—too late to call Ben. So he stretched out on the couch and closed his eyes. He dozed for a few hours, but woke with a start, adrenaline pumping through him. He retrieved his duffel bag from his car and hurriedly showered in the downstairs bath, not wanting to disturb Madelyn and Sara.

His mind spinning, he grabbed a pad and began to jot down the leads they had so far as he punched Ben's number.

"Hello. Camp here."

Caleb winced. Ben sounded half asleep.

"Ben, I'm sorry. I know it's early, but I think Madelyn's ex may have had something to do with her daughter's disappearance. Do you have a current address on him?"

"Hang on and let me pull up his file."

Caleb heard computer keys clicking, and continued to make his list, trying to pinpoint a connection. Emery had sold babies. Mansfield had helped arrange the adoptions.

Madelyn had a car accident—or had it been an accident?

Out of the couples who'd adopted through Emery, Pedderson was the most suspicious, and his beard matched Sara's description.

The last couple, the Smiths—probably a phony name—had disappeared, making them jump to the top of his suspect list.

Also, the two people who might have known that Cissy hadn't died had been murdered.

The killer was still at large. He'd sent Madelyn a threatening text and attacked her mother.

And he might not be working alone....

"Last address for Tim Andrews is a small town in the mountains of Tennessee," Ben said, interrupting his thoughts. "555 Trinity Lane, Bear's Landing."

Caleb jotted down the address, then Tim's name and drew a big question mark beside his name. "Anything else?"

Ben cleared his throat. "I ran his financials. Guy's in debt up to his eyeballs. He seems to have a pattern of big deposits, then equally large withdrawals. I'd say investments, but there's no evidence of a portfolio."

Son of a bitch. "Gambling," Caleb suggested.

"Sounds like it to me, too," Ben said.

Caleb glanced at the stairs, grateful Madelyn was still with Sara. "If the guy was in trouble five years ago, maybe he was desperate enough to sell his daughter to pay off his debt."

Ben whistled.

"Sara said something else disturbing. She said the man who killed her mother is her uncle." He paused. "See if any of the mothers or fathers on our list have brothers, then dig up everything you can on them. Maybe one of them has a police record or we'll find another connection."

"That'll take time, but I'm on it."

Caleb spotted one of Sara's sketches on the refrigerator. "Oh, and see if there are any greenhouses that specialize in sunflowers near Bear's Landing."

"Okay, hang on."

"I don't see any commercial greenhouses," Ben said a moment later. "That doesn't mean someone might not own a private one, but there are no wholesale ones in the area."

"It was a long shot," Caleb said, although he wanted to curse.

"Do you want me to ask Gage to send another agent to Andrews's place?"

"No," Caleb said. "I'm heading up there myself." He had a feeling Madelyn would insist on going, as well.

As much as he hated to put her through such an ordeal, they both needed to see her ex's face when they confronted him.

Sunlight shimmered through the blinds in Sara's room, but Madelyn had barely closed her eyes. Each time she did, images of her husband trading their baby for money taunted her.

She had to be wrong. Surely Tim wouldn't do something so horrible....

Madelyn slipped from bed and tiptoed to her room, then showered, closing her eyes and willing the images to fade, but they refused to go away.

She shampooed her hair, rinsed and dried off, then blew it dry and dressed in jeans and a loose sweater. She headed downstairs for coffee, wondering where Caleb was, if he'd slept on her sofa.

Their heated lovemaking the night before flashed back, and she inwardly groaned. That had been wonderful. Then Sara's cry had reminded her of the reason Caleb was there, that he'd be leaving as soon as they found her daughter.

The scent of coffee permeated the air, and Madelyn found Caleb in the kitchen with a mug, his face stony. No remnants of desire. No heated looks.

No good morning kiss or embrace or a hint that they would repeat it.

"Did you sleep?" he asked.

"Some." She poured herself a mug, aching to touch him again, but knowing she shouldn't. She had to put distance between them, couldn't let herself fantasize about a life with Caleb when she was certain the night before had only been sex for him. "You?"

He gave a nod. "I talked to Ben. I have an address for your ex. I'm heading to his place to talk to him."

Madelyn's stomach pitched, but she steeled herself. "Where is he?"

"A small town in the Smokies called Bear's Landing."

"I'm going with you."

Caleb didn't argue. He simply nodded. "I already talked to Gage. Leah and Ruby are expecting Sara."

Madelyn stared down into her coffee, tears threatening. "I'm going to owe her again."

"Leah and Gage are friends who want to help, Madelyn." Caleb placed both hands on her shoulders and massaged them. "So you don't owe anyone anything."

"I owed it to my daughters to protect them." She whirled around, anguish nearly suffocating her. "What if Tim did this, Caleb? What kind of mother am I if I didn't see what their father was capable of?"

"You are a wonderful mother," Caleb said gruffly. "And you trusted your husband. There's no crime in that."

Madelyn choked back a sob. "There is if he sold one of my children."

"We don't know that for sure," Caleb said. "But we are going to find out. Do you want me to get Sara?"

She sucked in a breath. "No, I need to get her dressed. While she has breakfast, I'll fill us some to-go mugs and we can take our coffee with us."

"Good idea. It's a long drive."

A half hour later, they drove to Leah's. "Did you have more bad dreams last night, Sara?" Caleb asked as he parked at Gage's.

She shook her head. "I think Cissy's sleeping."

He prayed the child was right, that her silence didn't mean something worse.

Madelyn walked Sara to the door, and Sara hugged her so tightly, Madelyn feared she wouldn't let her go. As much as she hated leaving Sara, she had to spare her the trauma ahead. Sara hadn't seen Tim in years; she wouldn't even recognize him. She certainly didn't need to watch her mother confront him with her suspicions.

"Come on, Sara," Ruby squealed. "Mommy made playdough for us!"

Sara smiled at Ruby and clasped her hand, then followed her to the kitchen.

Storm clouds gathered as Madelyn and Caleb left Sanctuary and headed toward Tennessee. Caleb concentrated on the road, and she concentrated on not falling apart.

Because with every mile that passed, her sense that Tim had lied to her and done the unspeakable mounted.

Four hours later, Caleb steered the Jeep up the winding road toward Bear's Landing. The sun had battled to make its way through the ominous clouds, the temperature dropping. Wind rattled trees, shaking leaves and sending them skittering to the ground, the shrill whistle of it roaring off the mountain like a siren screeching.

The small town of Bear's Landing was barely a blip on the map, a quaint little place with two stoplights, a couple of tourist shops, a diner and a gas station. A Native American reservation bordered the town with signs offering handmade crafts. Signs for a fishing lodge, waterfalls and camping pointed to a dirt road; another sign indicated a group of log homes built along the creek running along the mountain.

Madelyn gazed out the window, but he sensed she wasn't looking at the scenery, that she was contemplating what her husband might have done.

He spotted a sign for a place called Hog's Valley, then Trinity Lane, and turned left, then followed it along the creek. The graveled road ended at a split-level log house surrounded by natural woods. A deer grazed in the field to the side, the creek rippling behind the property.

Caleb scanned the drive and surrounding property in search of Andrews, his vehicle, even toys indicating that Tim might have actually taken custody of Cissy himself.

A shiny black pickup sat adjacent to the house. But he saw no sign of the man or any evidence of a child.

"This is where Tim lives?" Madelyn asked surprised.

"It's the address Ben gave me."

"Odd. Tim never seemed like the outdoors type." She reached for the door handle. "Then again, I obviously didn't know my husband at all, did I?"

"Some people are masters of deception," he said, hating the self-recriminations in her tone.

Instincts kicking in, Caleb checked his weapon as he exited the Jeep, then took Madelyn's arm. "We have to be careful. If he's on to us, he might be armed and dangerous."

"I wish I had that gun we talked about," Madelyn said. "I'd show him dangerous."

A tiny smile quirked at the corners of Caleb's mouth. He didn't blame her.

They slowly made their way up to the door, the wind beating at the porch rocking chair and sending it swinging back and forth as if a ghost was sitting in it. Dead ferns hung from the rail as if long forgotten, an empty beer can was tipped on its side by a hammock, a newspaper rattled in the breeze.

The paper was an old issue—the front-page story featuring the arrest of Dr. Emery. That event had obviously triggered panic among those involved in the illegal adoptions. Everyone had been scrambling to cover their butts.

And Nadine and Zimmerman were dead because of it.

Madelyn exhaled beside him, and he squeezed her arm, silently offering encouragement. He opened the screen door, then rapped the bear-paw door knocker.

Shadows from the storm clouds darkened the porch, the wind pounding the roof.

Caleb knocked again, then wielded his gun at the ready as he turned the knob. The door was locked so he removed a clip from his pocket and picked the lock.

The door swung open with a screech. He threw up a hand, silently commanding Madelyn to stay behind him.

Slowly he inched inside the house. The rooms were dark, the sound of a clock ticking in the silence. He scanned the foyer, then moved toward the open room spanning the back of the house, a large den with a stone fireplace that adjoined the kitchen. All rustic decor. A plain, beige rug. Brown sofa. Cheap paintings of deer and wildlife. A barrel-shaped lamp had been knocked on the floor, magazines scattered, another wooden chair overturned as if there had been some kind of trouble.

Caleb eased through the room, careful not to touch anything, then spotted a dark reddish-brown stain on the braided rug beneath the oak table.

A stain that looked like blood.

Dammit.

"Stay here, Madelyn. I'm going to check upstairs."

He hoped to hell he found Andrews alive so they could get some answers. Then he could have the pleasure of killing him.

But that blood wasn't a good sign. Tim Andrews might already be dead.

If he was, then who in the hell was behind all the murders?

MADELYN SHUDDERED AS SHE glanced across the room. Something bad had happened here. A fight.

Where was Tim?

Her gaze swept across the overturned chair, the broken lamp, then the bare furnishings, the lack of personal touches, the lack of warmth, and she realized Tim hadn't made a home here.

The cheap watercolors on the walls were probably from a discount store. There were no videos or CD's, no comfortable throw pillows, no sign of the man she'd known.

Except for the one framed photo on the mantle. Sara.

Had he been watching them?

She picked up the photograph, zeroing in on the details. Sara wore a red bathing suit, and she was standing in front of a kiddie pool in the backyard, her hair in pigtails.

Her breath caught.

Except Sara didn't have a red bathing suit. And that yard was not Madelyn's.

Her throat flooded with nausea and happiness and shock.

It wasn't Sara.

This was a picture of Cissy. The little girl she'd lost. The baby her husband had told her had died.

The extent of Tim's betrayal hit her like a fist in the gut. She doubled over, the pain and grief so intense her legs buckled and she collapsed on the floor, hugging the picture to her.

Tim had known where Cissy was all this time and hadn't told her....

CHAPTER FIFTEEN

CALEB RECOGNIZED THE SIGNS of a bachelor living in the house. No personal items. No warmth of a woman's touch. Basic black comforter and lack of pictures on the walls upstairs. There was also a desolate, lonely feel to the place as if it had been a self-imposed prison of sorts.

You should have been locked in a damn cell for what you've done, Andrews.

He quickly surveyed the two bedrooms and found them empty, the master bed unmade. But there was no blood or signs of a struggle upstairs.

He glanced around for a computer, hoping to glean information from it, but didn't find one. He dug in the man's dresser drawers searching for notes, a secret file, but came up empty, as well.

Suddenly a heart-wrenching sob echoed from downstairs, then another, and Caleb's heart constricted.

Madelyn.

Forgetting all else but her, he stormed down the steps. When he saw her kneeling on the floor, her anguish seeped into his soul.

Dear God, had she found something? Evidence that Cissy was dead?

Fear clawed at him as he slowly approached her. He stooped down to her level, terrified what that photo might reveal. Gently he stroked her arms, then pulled her to him, rocking her back and forth and rubbing slow circles around her back while she sobbed.

Several tense minutes passed while she purged her emotions, but he waited until her crying subsided before he spoke.

"Madelyn, honey, I'm so sorry," he said gruffly. "Talk to me. Tell me what's wrong."

Dragging in a cleansing breath, she lifted her face and showed him the photo. "It's Cissy," she whispered raggedly. "Not Sara. This is Cissy and it was taken recently."

Which meant that her damn husband had not only known her daughter had survived, but he'd known where she was all along.

His gaze flew toward the blood on the floor. So where was the bastard now?

Madelyn suddenly raced over to the built-in bookcases, flung open the doors and began to search inside.

"What are you doing?" Caleb asked.

"Looking for more pictures, a scrapbook, an address. Something that will give us a clue as to where Cissy and her adopted mother live." She heaved a breath. "Did you find anything upstairs?"

"No. No computer. Nothing about Cissy."

Caleb's phone jangled, so he connected the call.

"Caleb, it's Gage. Have you made it to Andrews's place?"

"Yeah. But he's not here, and I found blood." Caleb released a frustrated sigh, then lowered his voice. "Madelyn also found a photo of Cissy."

"She's alive?"

He angled his body away from Madelyn. "She was in the picture, and it looks as if it was taken recently."

Gage emitted a long-winded sigh. "He deserves to rot for this."

"I agree. Can you have the sheriff issue an APB for Andrews? And send word to the Tennessee authorities, too."

"I'll do it as soon as we hang up."

"Is Sara all right?"

"Yes, but I'm here with Ben, and we're on speakerphone. We may have a lead."

"Thank God. We need one. Did Brianna find something on the adoptions or through DFAS?"

"No, but Ben accessed incoming police reports and there's been a murder not too far from Bear's Landing. Woman with her throat slashed."

Caleb's adrenaline kicked in. "Did she have a child?"

"Yes, a daughter. Police report said they identified the woman as Danielle Smith."

"We were hunting for the Smiths." Caleb clicked his teeth. "What about the child?"

"No sign of her at the house. But I figured you'd want to check it out."

"Definitely." Caleb reached in his pocket for a pen and a notepad, then scribbled down the address. "Now see if you can find out the Smiths' real name. I think the woman's brother may be responsible for her death."

"I'm on it," Ben said. "Let us know what you find at the Smith house."

"Right." Caleb disconnected the call. "Madelyn," he said in a quiet tone.

She whirled around, then flung out her hands. "There's nothing else here. No photo albums. No letters or signs of where she is." She gestured toward the framed photo. "Why would he have that photo and nothing more?"

"I don't know," Caleb said honestly. "There's a lot I don't understand about your ex. Why he left you. How he could have abandoned his children."

Hurt flickered in her eyes. "I can't believe he knew where Cissy was all these years and let me believe she was dead."

Caleb moved toward her, wanting to comfort her, yet they didn't have time. He had a lead and they needed to act upon it. "He'll pay. I promise, Madelyn." He gently took her face and cupped it between his hands. "I know you're hurting, but Gage phoned. There's been a murder, a woman killed, not too far from here. We need to go."

"Oh, God, you think it's Cissy's adopted mother?"

"It's possible." He coaxed her toward the door. "Police said her name is Danielle Smith."

"Did they find a child?"

He shook his head. "No. The woman had a little girl, but she wasn't at the house."

Still there might be evidence confirming that this Smith woman had adopted Cissy. And some lead as to where the killer had taken her.

Fear and shock settled over Madelyn but she forced her mind to turn itself off. The horrible scenarios bombarding her were too painful to bear.

Caleb raced around the mountain, cutting through side roads and speeding around curves. The short drive felt like hours.

Ten minutes. Tim had lived *ten* damn minutes from their daughter and never told her. He'd watched Cissy grow up.

Had he shared birthdays with her and this woman? Had she called him Daddy?

And what had they told Cissy about her? Did Cissy think she had given her away?

She balled her hands into fists in her lap as they turned up a drive and climbed a hill which leveled off to an acre at the top offering a majestic view of the mountain. Two police cars were parked in front of the house, an ambulance and a black sedan beside them.

A white two-story house sat on the edge of the ridge, but to the left Madelyn spotted a greenhouse.

Her breath quickened. The sunflower greenhouse Sara had seen through Cissy. "This is it, Caleb. This is where Cissy has been living."

Caleb reached for his door handle. "Wait here. I'll talk to the sheriff."

"No way." Madelyn leaped from the Jeep and jogged up the hill to the house, but Caleb caught up with her.

"Remember, Madelyn, this woman has been murdered. The police are going to be suspicious of everyone until they catch the killer, so watch what you say."

Madelyn froze and stared at him, her lungs tightening. "You mean they'll think I killed her?"

"You have motive," he said in a low voice. "But thankfully, I can alibi you. Still, be careful."

Madelyn nodded, swallowing back a protest, then walked with Caleb to the front door. The uniformed officer guarding the entrance narrowed his eyes at them. "Deputy Holbrook," the man said. "Who are you and what are you doing here?"

Caleb flashed his ID. "I'm an investigator with GAI in Sanctuary, North Carolina, and we're looking into a missing child case," he explained. "Sheriff Gray is aware of our investigation and notified us there was a murder here. We believe the victim may be related to our case."

"Did you know the victim?" Deputy Holbrook asked.

"Not personally," Caleb said. "We think she may have adopted Mrs. Andrews's daughter."

The deputy spoke into his mike. "Sheriff, there's a couple here demanding to speak to you."

Voices from the back indicated the police, crime scene techs and probably a medical examiner were consulting, then footsteps sounded and a short, stocky man with wavy, brown hair appeared.

"Sheriff Dwight Haynes," the man said, looking back and forth between the two of them.

"Caleb Walker from GAI in Sanctuary, North Carolina, and this is Madelyn Andrews."

"What are you doing in Tennessee?"

Caleb explained about Cissy's disappearance. "I'm sure you're aware that a doctor at Sanctuary Hospital was arrested for kidnapping and arranging illegal adoptions?"

Sheriff Haynes nodded. "Yeah, I heard about the case."

"Mrs. Andrews was told that her baby died at birth," Caleb continued. "But recently we've uncovered evidence indicating she's alive, and we think your victim adopted her. She also might have been an accomplice in the baby's kidnapping."

The sheriff narrowed his eyes. "What led you to believe that?"

Caleb explained about Nadine Cotter's and Howard Zimmerman's deaths, the connection between phone calls, then the link with Madelyn's ex-husband.

Madelyn stood on tiptoe, struggling to see past the deputy and sheriff to the inside of the foyer. She wanted pictures, proof, anything to confirm that Cissy had actually lived in this house. She was starved to know what her life had been like, if she had friends, if she was...loved.

"Interesting story," the sheriff said. "We'll let you know what we find here."

Caleb refused to be dismissed so easily. "The victim's name was Danielle Smith, correct?"

Sheriff Haynes nodded.

"Smith was the name of one of the adopted couples on the list we're investigating."

"If you'd just let us look around," Madelyn cut in. "Maybe there are pictures of this woman and my daughter that will prove our theory."

"If you lost her when she was born, how would you even know what she looked like?" Haynes asked.

"She was an identical twin," Madelyn said, irritated. "Please, I think she may be in danger. I need to know if she was here."

"This is a crime scene," the sheriff said. "I'm sorry, but I can't allow you inside."

"Listen to me," Madelyn said, desperation tingeing her voice. "My other daughter Sara has a connection with her sister. She saw this woman being murdered."

"You're telling me that your child witnessed Ms. Smith's murder?" Sheriff Haynes asked sharply. "If so, where is she? We need to question her."

Perspiration beaded on Madelyn's neck. "She wasn't here at the time. I told you they have a connection, a psychic, twin connection," Madelyn said, then quickly realized by the skeptical expression on his face that he didn't believe her.

Instead he gave her a dismissive look, then addressed Caleb. "Mr. Walker, I suggest you take your client and leave. I'm investigating a murder, and I don't have time for these games." With that curt statement, he turned around and walked away.

"He has to let us in," Madelyn said, ready to plow her way through.

But Caleb pulled her back from the doorway. She pushed at him, but he gently grabbed her hands and urged her down the stairs. "We'll come back when they're gone, Madelyn. Then we'll search the inside. I promise."

Still Madelyn's heart ached and panic clawed at her as he escorted her to the Jeep. If Sara was right and the killer had put Cissy in the trunk of his car, there was no telling where he was now or what he intended to do with her.

Every second counted.

Sara plunged her paintbrush into the brown paint. Ruby was painting a beautiful sunset in red and yellow and orange.

But Sara's vision blurred, and suddenly she saw Cissy crying.

"Sara, I don't like it here."

"Where are you, Cissy?"

"I don't know. It's dark," she whispered.

Sara gripped the paintbrush tighter. "Tell me, so I can find you."

"He dragged me from the trunk into this old cabin," Cissy whispered. "But I can't move 'cause he tied me in the closet." She sniffled. "But I saw an old well house outside."

Sara's hand began to move, drawing a picture of the old wooden house. She closed her eyes for a minute, then she was in Cissy's mind. She saw the house, the dirty floor, the woods, the old well house.

There were long buildings on the hill beside the house, too. Long and narrow. Three of them. And they smelled like…poop.

Her hand shook as she opened her eyes and began to give them shape on the canvas.

Ruby walked over and looked at her painting. "That's good, Sara. Those must be chicken houses."

Sara added a wooden sign with a rooster etched on it. "It's where the mean man has my sister." She turned and ran to the kitchen. "Miss Leah, Miss Leah."

Leah stooped down and patted her shoulder. "What is it, honey?"

"I gots to call Mommy and Mr. Firewalker and tell them where Cissy is."

CHAPTER SIXTEEN

CALEB DROVE TO the small diner in town and ordered a late lunch, hoping the crime unit would finish with the house by the time they were done. Although truthfully it might take hours before they finished processing the place.

He scarfed down two burgers, but Madelyn barely touched her turkey sandwich. Her gaunt face disturbed him. "You should try to eat something to keep up your strength."

"I can't think about food." She traced a drop of water from her tea glass then glanced out the window at the snow that had started to fall. "Just look at the weather. It's getting colder, and the weatherman is predicting a blizzard."

Caleb covered her hand with his, searching for words to console her, but his cell phone buzzed. He checked the caller ID. Gage's home phone.

He quickly punched Connect. "Caleb speaking."

"Caleb, it's Leah. Sara needs to speak to her mother."

"Is everything okay?"

Madelyn tensed across from him, and he squeezed her hand.

"Yes, but she saw Cissy again and she needs to tell you where she is."

A sliver of alarm ran up Caleb's spine. "Put her on the phone."

A second later, Sara's tiny voice echoed over the line. "Mr. Firewalker?"

"Yes, Sara. Miss Leah said that you know where Cissy is."

Madelyn's eyes widened, and she gestured for him to hand her the phone, but he held up a finger silently asking her to wait.

"She's in an old cabin, but he tied her in the closet." Tears laced Sara's voice.

Damn. He forced himself not to react so as not to frighten Madelyn.

"Can you tell me more about the cabin?"

"There's a well house outside." Sara sniffled loudly. "And three chicken houses that smell like poop and a wood sign."

"That's good, Sara," Caleb said. "Anything else?"

"The sign has a picture of a rooster on it."

He frowned. Maybe it was an old chicken farm. Probably an abandoned one.

"Anything else, honey?"

Sara's shaky breath echoed back. "No. Does that help, Mr. Firewalker? Can you find Cissy now?"

"That is a huge help," Caleb assured her. "If you think of anything more, ask Miss Leah to call back."

"'Kay."

"Let me speak to her," Madelyn insisted.

"Sara, I'm going to have your mommy call back on her phone. I need to use mine to call my friends so we can track down those chicken houses."

He said goodbye, then looked up at Madelyn. "Sara described an old house with a well and chicken houses. Maybe Ben can search maps of the area and we can pinpoint a location."

He tossed some cash on the table to pay the bill,

punching Ben's number as he strode toward the door. Madelyn hurried after him, dialing Sara.

"I'll start searching now," Ben said after Caleb had caught him up-to-date.

Caleb opened the door and let Madelyn go through, then they rushed through the snow to his Jeep. "Thanks. We're going back to the Smith woman's house to see if we can get inside this time. Maybe we'll find a lead there."

The snow began to thicken as he cranked the Jeep and drove from the diner, the wind howling. Madelyn was talking to Sara in a low voice, praising her for her help.

Unease settled in his gut. With the blizzard threatening and visibility poor, tracking anyone through the mountains was going to be nearly impossible.

But there was a little girl out there missing, a terrified little girl tied in a dark closet somewhere who needed him.

And nothing was going to stop him from finding her.

MADELYN STARED AT THE snowstorm outside as the Jeep ate the miles to the Smith house, her heart thundering. What if this madman left Cissy out there in this cold?

No, she couldn't think like that. They'd come this far. They were going to find her.

Thankfully, the police and crime units had dispersed by the time they reached the house. She assumed the woman's body had been transported to the morgue for an autopsy.

"Where was Danielle Smith's husband?"

Caleb shrugged. "Good question. Maybe we'll find that answer as well as a clue to the killer's identity inside."

Caleb removed latex gloves again and shoved a pair in Madelyn's hands. "We're not supposed to be here, so wear these."

Nerves knotted her stomach as she stared at the yellow crime scene tape and signs warning them not to enter. Caleb motioned for her to follow him around back, and he found a window that wasn't locked. He climbed through it, then rushed and opened the back door for her.

Bile flooded her throat when she spotted the dark crimson stain on the white tile floor. There were also blood splatters on the sink and wall, the smell nauseating.

"Don't think about it," Caleb said matter-of-factly. "We need to hurry, Madelyn. Just look for notes, addresses, something that might tie the Smith woman to the adoptions."

But Madelyn barely heard him. Her gaze was fixed to the refrigerator where a crude child's drawing hung by a magnet. A drawing of twin blonde girls holding hands dancing in the midst of a sea of sunflowers.

A strangled sob caught in her throat, and she raced over and snatched it. "God, Caleb, look. This is just like Sara's drawing."

Caleb's eyes widened, the realization that Cissy had lived here, that her connection with Sara was real, was undeniable.

Spurred by the sketch, Madelyn's adrenaline kicked in. She needed more, to see pictures of her lost child. To see what she'd been doing, what her life was like.

To see if Tim had been part of it.

Caleb began searching the kitchen desk and she took the drawers, racing from one to the other, hastily pushing through bills and grocery lists and random items. She found other drawings Cissy had made, some depicting herself alone, at the park, some with a woman who must have been Danielle Smith.

But none with her father.

Frantic for more, she rushed into the living area

and scanned the room. Photos of Cissy chronicling her growth from infancy to present-day filled the wall. Tears burned Madelyn's throat as she saw the years of her missing daughter's life laid out in front of her. Cissy cradled in a pink blanket shortly after birth. Cissy learning to crawl. Her first step. Playing in the laundry basket. Splashing in a baby pool. Blowing bubbles in the bathtub. Learning to ride a tricycle.

Christmases and birthdays and other holidays—all photographed and honored, all ones she had missed.

The pain threatened to bring her to her knees. But she found something in those photos to hang on to, something to stop her from collapsing with utter grief. The young woman who had adopted Cissy looked at her with such love and adoration that Madelyn's heart swelled with gratitude.

Gratitude and anger.

That should have been her holding Cissy, feeding her, teaching her to ride a trike. Sharing birthdays and holidays and watching her play and grow with her twin.

Had Danielle Smith known she had robbed Cissy's birth mother of those treasured moments? Or had she been innocent? Simply a woman wanting a child and getting caught up in an adoption scheme she knew nothing about?

Caleb's voice jerked her from her emotional tirade. "Did you find anything?"

She gestured toward the photographs unable to speak.

A muscle ticked in Caleb's jaw as he scanned the wall of memories.

"Danielle's husband was killed in Iraq while they were waiting to adopt." Caleb showed her a photo he'd found in the kitchen desk. "Apparently he received an award. Died a hero."

And Danielle—had she died protecting Cissy?

"Madelyn, come on. I found a crude map I think the killer might have dropped. It could lead us to where he took Cissy."

Madelyn choked back the tears and took a deep breath. "Then let's go. Danielle Smith may have loved Cissy, but we're all my little girl has now."

CALEB WAS ON the phone the moment they stepped out the door. "Ben, Gage, I found a map at the Smiths' house." He described the details to them and waited while Ben cross-checked it with the topographical maps online.

"There is an abandoned chicken farm near where you're describing," Ben said, then gave him the coordinates. "Used to be called Rooster's."

"We're heading there now," Caleb said as he and Madelyn jogged to the Jeep and jumped in.

Caleb ended the call, then tore away from the house, gravel and snow spewing behind his wheels as he careened down the driveway.

"Do you know where this place is?" Madelyn asked.

"I know the general area," Caleb said. "We may have to park and hike in on foot."

Although the storm was growing thicker, the windchill dangerous. And the killer was armed.

Visibility was poor, slowing him down on the road, and tension thrummed in the car as he maneuvered along the mountain road. A half hour later, he found the turnoff. He veered left, then cursed as he spotted a fallen tree blocking the road.

"Dammit. We'll have to go on foot from here."

Madelyn buttoned her coat and yanked on a hat and gloves she retrieved from her pocket. "Then let's go."

Caleb tugged on gloves himself, then climbed out, checked to make sure he had an extra clip for his gun, then took Madelyn's hand and they began to hike. The storm swirled snow and leaves and twigs around them, branches breaking off as the blizzard gained momentum.

Trees swayed with the downfall, the snow so thick that their boots sank in the slush, but they continued to trudge, Caleb using his instincts to follow the road. Madelyn shivered, and he pulled her against him, helping her over stumps and through the thick slush. Animal life scurried for cover and to seek protection while the sun disappeared into the haze of white.

"What if she's out here?" Madelyn shouted over the roar of the wind.

"Sara said she was inside the house." He purposefully omitted the part about her being tied up in the closet fearing that would send Madelyn over the edge. And he needed her to be strong now.

Three miles in, and the storm intensified. Ahead, he spotted a cave and guided Madelyn to it. Maybe she could wait inside.

But a gunshot suddenly rent the air, skating near their heads. Madelyn screamed, and he grabbed her hand and ran toward the cave. Another bullet zinged toward them and Caleb shoved Madelyn down, crouching low as he tried to usher her to safety.

Just as they reached the cave and Madelyn ducked inside, someone jumped Caleb from behind. He felt a hard whack on his head, then struggled with the man, but his attacker slammed the butt of the gun against his head and stars spun in front of Caleb's eyes.

He must have blacked out because when he roused a moment later, he was lying in the snow, blood dripping in his eyes.

And a bearded man was holding a gun to Madelyn's head.

CHAPTER SEVENTEEN

SHEER TERROR SEIZED Madelyn as Rayland Pedderson jammed the barrel of his gun into her temple. His fingers tightened around her neck, his grip steely and locking her body against his. The urge to kick and bite and fight him shot through her.

But one wrong move, and she would be dead.

Then her girls would be alone, with no one to love and care for them.

Forcing herself to remain calm took every ounce of restraint she possessed.

When she'd noticed the blood running down Caleb's head, she was terrified he was dead.

And she'd realized she really did love him. Heart-pounding, soul-deep love that could last a lifetime. What if she never got to tell him?

"You bitch, you couldn't leave it alone, could you?" Pedderson growled near her ear.

"No," Madelyn said between gritted teeth. "Cissy is my little girl. Why did you take her?"

"My sister wanted a child and you had two," he hissed. "Your husband thought you'd get over it and be happy with the baby you had."

The pain of Tim's betrayal knifed through her again. "But why did Tim sell our little girl?"

His fingers dug into her throat as he tried to drag her toward the woods. Snow pelted them, the brittle wind biting at her face. "Because the damn fool owed me money for some property he bought. Thought he'd develop it into some condos and make a fortune. But he spent that money gambling and owed me and his bookie. Hell, it was your damn husband who thought up the idea of side-swiping you to make you go into labor."

Madelyn had thought she couldn't be shocked anymore, but the realization that Tim had purposely been a part of her accident made her head reel.

At least Danielle's husband had died with honor. But Tim... "He sold our little girl for cash to pay off gambling debts?" Madelyn cried. "I'm going to kill him."

"Don't worry, I took care of him myself. He panicked in the end and wanted to call you. He even tried to get the girl back."

Tim was dead? She should be relieved, but she felt robbed of the chance to vent her anger and bitterness toward him.

"But Danielle was your sister. How could you kill her?" Madelyn asked, putting the pieces together in her mind.

"Damn idiot woman found out how we got Cissy and wanted to contact you. Said that little girl was psychic or something, that she kept talking about her twin. I warned her if she called you, she'd lose her kid."

Tears blurred Madelyn's eyes, trickling down and freezing on her cheeks. Poor Danielle. She'd obviously loved Cissy, but she'd still planned to do the right thing. Sara and Cissy were right. This man was a monster.

"Where's Cissy?" Madelyn asked. "Please let me have her back, and you can disappear. I don't care. I just want my daughter back."

"You hired a damn P.I.," Pedderson growled. "It's too late to make a deal."

"Please don't hurt Cissy," Madelyn pleaded. "She's just a child."

"I warned you," he mumbled, then a click sounded as he cocked the trigger. He was going to shoot her in cold blood.

A second later, a gunshot echoed, and she felt herself falling.

Falling, falling, falling...

Pedderson collapsed on her, blood soaking her shirt, his weight trapping her.

It took her a moment to realize she hadn't been shot. Pedderson had.

Sobbing with relief, she shoved at his chest, desperate to move him off her.

"Madelyn!" Then suddenly Caleb was there, yanking at Pedderson's beefy body.

"Madelyn, are you hit?"

He dragged the heavy man off her, then shoved his body to the side. Blood pooled from his chest, his eyes were open stark wide, his body limp.

She should feel pity, but she felt nothing for the man except a cold rage. Caleb had shot him straight in the heart.

"Are you hurt?" Caleb raked his hands over her arms and legs and body, searching for injuries.

She shook her head, still in shock, then he hugged her against his chest.

"Dammit. I thought I'd lost you." His voice was hoarse with emotion, his hands soothing. She didn't realize she was crying until he pulled back and wiped her cheeks with his thumbs.

"Tim sold Cissy to him for money," she said, choking on the words. "He sold our baby to pay off gambling debts."

He cradled her face between his hands. "I heard everything. I'm so sorry, Madelyn."

Tears streamed down her face. Snow pelted them. Blood was clotting in Caleb's hair, and she reached up to feel his wound, but he pushed her hand away.

"I'm fine. We have to find Cissy."

Panic threatened to immobilize her. "If she's out here alone, she'll never survive."

Determination hardened Caleb's face. "Sara said she's in a cabin," he said. "We'll follow Pedderson's tracks."

A surge of adrenaline shot through Madelyn, and she pushed to her feet. "Then let's go. We can't waste a minute."

CALEB LED MADELYN through the woods, tracking Pedderson, although the snow was making it almost impossible to move quickly or spot his footfalls. But he had the GPS coordinates and an innate sense of direction that guided him along the way.

"Look over there!" Madelyn tugged away from him and ran toward a tree stump. He jogged after her and caught up with her just as she lifted a pink blanket from the ground.

"This is Cissy's," Madelyn cried. "She was holding it in one of the pictures."

"Let me hold the blanket for a moment." Caleb reached for the blanket. "Maybe I can get a vision from it." Madelyn shoved it in his hands, and he closed his eyes and concentrated, but nothing came. Cissy's connection was with her sister, not with him. He needed Sara here, but bringing her out in this storm would be crazy. Choppers would never make it.

They were on their own.

He grabbed Madelyn's hand. "Come on, I think the cabin's close to here." Caleb pointed to the right.

Madelyn tucked the blanket beneath her arm, and they slogged through the snow, running as fast as they could. Wind and snow pummeled them, but they climbed over tree stumps and wove through the woods following the stream until they spotted a small, brown structure nestled on the hill.

"There it is!" Caleb shouted over the howling wind.

Together they ran toward the cabin, heaving for breath as they stumbled to the entrance. Caleb shoved at the door and entered first, still on guard in case Pedderson had had an accomplice.

Madelyn froze, her body going rigid. "Tim, you rotten, lying bastard."

Caleb clenched his jaw at the sight of the man slumped on the floor. Blood soaked his shirt and his body lay at an odd angle.

Caleb kicked at the man's feet to see if he was still alive. Not that he cared. Except he might know where his daughter was.

Andrews groaned and opened his eyes, although they were half-slitted and dull as if he was struggling for air.

"You jerk, how could you sell my baby?" Madelyn dropped to her knees and shook him. "Where's Cissy?"

Caleb scanned the room, found the closet and flung the door open, but Cissy wasn't inside. Dammit!

"Where is she?" Madelyn jerked Tim so hard his head flopped back. "What did you do with our little girl?"

"So sorry," Tim muttered on another groan. "Never meant for this to happen."

"What? You didn't intend to get caught?" Caleb barked.

"Not for Cissy to get hurt," he said in a hoarse whisper. "Tried to get her, stop Pedderson, save her."

Madelyn slapped his jaw. "Did he hurt her? Where is she now?"

Tears choked the man, and he coughed, pressing his hand over his bloody chest. "She ran outside... Thought he was coming back for her... Find her...find her, Mad..."

His voice trailed off and he coughed again.

Caleb removed his gun and crammed it against Tim's temple. "Who else was in on this besides Pedderson and Emery?"

Tim's eyes widened, but he blinked as if he wasn't fazed by the gun. He knew he was going to die anyway.

"Mansfield," Tim croaked. "He handled everything...." He angled his head toward Madelyn. "He hit you with his car, Madelyn. He wanted the money...."

"That picture in your house," Madelyn said. "Have you been seeing Cissy all along?"

Tim shook his head. "No, I followed Danielle one day and saw Cissy. She never knew I took the picture...." Tim wheezed for a breath, his eyes bulged then rolled in his head, and his body went slack.

Caleb knelt and felt his pulse, but Tim had just drawn his last breath. But at least he'd given them enough to hang Mansfield.

Madelyn was shaking violently, but she pushed to her feet and kicked his leg. "I hope you rot in hell."

Then she whirled around, eyes panicked. "Caleb, Cissy's out there somewhere. We have to find her."

Caleb's phone buzzed, and he connected the call.

"Caleb, I'm with Leah and the girls. Sara is upset. She said Cissy is crying and calling to her."

Sweat beaded on Caleb's neck. "Ask her where Cissy is."

He heard Sara crying in the background, Leah consoling her, Gage talking to her. Then Gage came back. "The chicken house," Gage said. "Cissy thought it was a greenhouse. She was looking for sunflowers, but it's empty and dark and she's hiding there."

"Thanks, Gage. Tell Sara she did great." He snapped the phone closed.

"What?" Madelyn clawed at his arms.

"The chicken house," Caleb said. "Cissy thought it was a greenhouse."

"The sunflowers," Madelyn whispered hoarsely. Then she took off running.

MADELYN DASHED OUTSIDE, her heart racing.

Caleb followed on her heels. Three rotting buildings sat to the right on the hill, the storm swirling snow in a blinding fog as they hurried toward them.

She held her breath as Caleb wrenched open the door to the first one, then stepped inside. It was dark and reeked of chicken feces, but it was empty. They hurried to the second one, the snow pulling at her boots as she waded through the downfall.

Frantic, she shoved tree limbs out of the way to make a path. The rusty door screeched open, the building dark, the stench of chickens lingering in the air. Dirt and straw snapped as Caleb stepped inside, scanning the interior.

Old tools had been stored inside, a wheelbarrow filled with junk, a lawnmower, bags of feed and gardening supplies.

"Cissy," Madelyn called. "Cissy, we're here to save you, honey."

"Sara sent us," Caleb said. "She wants us to bring you home."

Madelyn inched forward, searching behind supplies while Caleb checked the wheelbarrow.

"Cissy," Madelyn said softly. "I'm Sara's mommy. She told me about the sunflowers. She draws them just like you do."

"I know you're scared, Cissy," Caleb said, walking toward the far end. "But the bad man is gone now. We took care of him and he can't hurt you anymore."

Madelyn thought she detected a movement behind the bags of feed to the right and slowly crept toward it. "Sara wants to play with you, Cissy. She heard you ask her for help, and she wants us to bring you there to see her."

A muffled sound reverberated from the corner behind the feed, and Madelyn's heart raced. But she forced herself to tread slowly, determined not to scare her daughter. Then she rounded the corner and spotted Cissy huddled on the floor with her arms around her knees, her little body trembling.

Tears thickened her throat. Cissy was terrified. She'd witnessed Danielle's murder. Danielle was the only mother she'd known.

And Pedderson had threatened her, stuffed her in his trunk and dragged her away from her home.

"Cissy," Madelyn whispered. "Look at me, sweetheart. I'm Sara's mommy and your birth mommy, too." There would be years to help her understand the truth.

Cissy slowly lifted her little head, her big eyes wide with the horrors of what had happened to her. "You're Sara's mommy?" she asked in a tinny voice.

Madelyn nodded, tears burning her eyes. "Yes. And yours, too. Sara and I got lost from you but that was a mistake. We've been looking for you for a long time, and we want you to come home with us."

Cissy scrunched her button nose, her eyes wary, her lower lip quivering. "I'm scared of the mean man."

Madelyn heard Caleb walk up behind her, his presence offering strength. But he kept his distance, giving them space.

"He's gone now, gone forever. He can't ever hurt you again," Madelyn said in a strained voice. Her heart swelled with love and longing, and she knelt beside Cissy and held out her arms. "Come on, sweetheart. Let's go meet your sister."

Cissy nodded slowly, then lifted her arms, and Madelyn pulled her up against her and hugged her little girl.

She finally had her missing daughter back.

And no one would ever separate them again.

CHAPTER EIGHTEEN

THE NEXT FEW hours passed in a blur as Caleb contacted the authorities. Tim Andrews's and Rayland Pedderson's bodies were both transported to the morgue. Caleb and Madelyn had given statements to the local sheriff, then Caleb drove Madelyn and Cissy back to Madelyn's.

Gage, Leah and Ruby met them there with Sara.

Caleb's heart clenched as he watched Sara vault from the car. "Cissy!"

Cissy clung to her blanket like a lifeline, but when she spotted Sara, her eyes lit up with a smile and she raced toward her. The girls flew into each other's arms, twirling and swinging each other around as if they'd been waiting for this moment for years.

And they had.

Ecstatic to have both girls safe and reunited, Madelyn's tears flowed freely. She even managed to laugh as she wiped them from her face.

"So Sara was right all along?" Gage asked.

Caleb nodded. "She and her twin have a special connection that saved Cissy's life."

"You saved them," Madelyn said, a look of gratitude warming her face.

He didn't want her gratitude. He wanted her love.

"The authorities caught Mansfield," Gage told them. "Judge revoked his bail, and he'll be going away for a long time."

Caleb sighed. But he'd caused so much damage to so many lives.

Gage and Leah said good-night, then Gage scooped up Ruby and carried her to their car. Caleb watched the happy family, the way Gage protected his pregnant wife, the way he adored his adopted daughter and realized that family was the one thing missing in his life.

The drive back to Sanctuary had been bittersweet. He was happy he'd reunited Madelyn with her daughter, but now the case was over, she no longer needed him.

He needed her though. When he'd seen that man holding the gun to her head, his life had flashed in vivid clarity. He had intended to build a life with Mara and his son.

But that was not to be.

He had been faithful, even loved Mara. Did that mean he couldn't love again?

He did love Madelyn, he realized. He loved her and her girls and he wanted a life with them.

But now was not the time to confess his feelings. Maybe it would never be time. Madelyn needed to be with her daughters, and he didn't have the right to intrude on the family reunion she'd been waiting a lifetime to have.

Besides, he had some things to think through now.

Afraid he would break down and ruin her homecoming with her children by admitting his feelings, he turned and headed back to his car.

Ten minutes later, he found himself standing in front of Mara's grave. Snow littered the grass and tombstone, adding an ethereal touch to the scene as Mara's spirit appeared in front of him, a golden glow shimmering amidst the pristine white.

"I saved them, Mara," he said. "I wish I could have saved you and our son, too."

Suddenly she moved toward him, and he felt a gentle brush of her lips against his cheek. Her image was fading even more, though there was something peaceful and beautiful about her now. "Be happy," she whispered against his ear. "Love the new woman you have found and build a family with them."

He shook himself, certain he had imagined her words, but when he glanced up she was floating away, her hand lifted in a wave, a smile on her face.

She knew he had fallen in love with Madelyn, and she was at peace, moving on into the light.

For a moment, he stood and watched, aching for her and their lost son, aching for Madelyn and her daughters and the life he wanted.

The one he wasn't sure he could have. Or that Madelyn wanted with him.

MADELYN WAS SO EXCITED about having her daughters together and Cissy home that she had barely slept. The only thing that would have made it more perfect was to have Caleb with her. To have him as a part of her family.

But he had his own life.

She woke to the sound of the girls giggling, then they rushed into her room and hopped on her bed. "Good morning, girls," Madelyn said with a beaming smile.

"Morning, Mommy," Sara sang.

Cissy looked a little more hesitant but crawled up and gave her a hug. "Morning."

Madelyn blinked back tears. She had assured Cissy the night before that it was okay that she'd loved her adopted mother, that she could talk about Danielle anytime. She'd also promised they'd take sunflowers to her grave and keep them there year-round.

Then Cissy had told her something disturbing, something she needed to share with Caleb. But first they had to see her mother.

Madelyn winked at the girls. "You know what we need to do today?"

Sara's eyes sparkled. "What?"

"Go see Gran." Madelyn glanced at Cissy, soaking in her features and trying not to let the bitterness over all she'd missed seep into her voice. Cissy was alive and here now. She had to cherish the future, not dwell on the past.

"We gots to get sunflowers for her," Sara said.

Cissy looped her arm through Sara's. "Yep, 'cause sunflowers are the bestest."

An hour later, Madelyn knocked on the door to her mother's unit and found her standing at the door waiting. Her heart overflowed with joy to see her mother standing, then she took a step and more tears flowed.

"Gran, this is Cissy," Sara said proudly.

Madelyn's mother beamed at Cissy and wiped at her own tears as she took the twins by the hands. "We need some girl time," she said and gave Madelyn a pointed look, then gestured toward the kitchen door.

When she glanced up, Caleb was standing in the doorway looking sheepish and wary and more handsome than any man had a right to be.

"Leave the girls with me for a bit, Madelyn. Caleb needs to talk to you."

Madelyn frowned. "I need to talk to him, too."

Her mother grinned. "Go on, then. Sara and I need to show Cissy how we decorate cookies."

"I can help?" Cissy asked.

"Of course." Madelyn's mother pulled her into a hug, and Caleb took Madelyn's hand and led her outside.

He was quiet as he drove, seemingly lost in thought,

and her nerves skittered out of control. Then he parked at her house, and remained stony as they went inside.

"Now, what's going on with you, Caleb?" She tossed her jacket on a chair.

He shifted. "You first."

She took a deep breath. "Last night, Cissy talked some about what happened. She said she heard her mommy say something about other missing kids. That's when he killed her."

Caleb frowned. "You mean other phony adoptions?"

"I don't know." Madelyn sighed. "But it makes me wonder if something bigger was going on."

"We'll look into it," Caleb said.

"Is there some problem with my assuming custody of Cissy?"

He closed the distance between them, then gathered her hands in his. "God...no. I'm sorry. I didn't mean to frighten you."

She exhaled in relief. "Then what is it? Why were you at my mother's?"

"I needed to ask her something."

Madelyn frowned in confusion. "I don't understand."

He stroked her arms with his hands. "Just sit down and listen, please."

Madelyn allowed him to guide her to the sofa, then settled on the seat. He joined her, but anxiety lined his face.

"Come on, Caleb. What's going on?"

He sighed wearily, then looked at her, wrestling with his emotions. "You asked me about my family once and I clammed up."

Oh, God, he was married. That was the reason he'd acted so strange. The reason he'd never mentioned the night they'd made love.

She swallowed back the hurt and humiliation. She'd wanted him so badly. "You have a wife?"

He gripped her hands in his. "I had a wife," he said in a gruff voice. "And we were going to have a child, a son, but my wife died."

"Oh, Caleb." Madelyn heard the sorrow and guilt in his voice. "What happened?"

"She was shot by a man who was after me." He paused, gut wrenching. "I should have died instead of them."

No wonder he'd been so tormented when she'd probed into his past. "I'm so sorry."

He shrugged. "It was over three years ago, but I never got over their deaths. I blamed myself."

And he still loved his wife. How could he love Madelyn?

"It wasn't your fault," she said simply. "I'm sure she knows that. That she'd want you to move on, to have a happy life."

He looked at her with such torment in his expression that she wanted to cradle him to her chest.

"I didn't believe that I deserved to have a family again," he said brokenly. "To have someone love me. To move on."

Anguish for him rippled through her. "But that's not true, Caleb. You're a wonderful man. Strong. Protective. Kind. Loving."

His gaze shot to hers and she smiled. "You are. I saw you with my girls." A blush slowly crept onto her face. "You're also the sexiest, most wonderful man I've ever known. The only man I've desperately wanted in my bed."

Heat flared in his eyes. "I love you, Madelyn. I think I fell in love with you the moment I saw you at GAI that first day."

Shock mingled with joy in her heart. "You did?"

He nodded. "I wanted you then, and I want you now. That's the reason I had to talk to your mother."

She struggled to follow his logic. "I don't understand."

"Since your father is not around, I needed to ask her permission to do this." He lowered himself to one knee, then pulled her hands in his.

Madelyn gaped at him, stunned. "Caleb?"

"Do you love me, Madelyn?"

Good Lord, did she? "Yes. Last night I thought my life was perfect. I had my girls together again, and we were safe. But then you weren't there, and it felt like a piece was missing, that you should have been with us, too."

A slow smile spread on his face, and he reached in his pocket and removed a diamond ring, the simple diamond surrounded by tiny, glittering stones. "Will you marry me, Madelyn, and let me be your husband and the father to your girls?"

Her heart burst with love. "Yes, Caleb. Of course, I'll marry you. I love you with all my heart." She leaned forward, then kissed him tenderly. "And I'd be proud for you to be a father to my girls and to any other little people that come along."

He threw his head back and chuckled, then picked her up and spun her around as he carried her to the bedroom. A second later, they'd stripped and lay curled in each other's arms. His hands and mouth and body loved her in only the way a true friend and lover could do. And when he joined his body with hers, she knew that their union would last forever.

* * * * *

We hope you enjoyed reading this
special collection from Harlequin® books.

If you liked reading these stories,
then you will love
Harlequin Intrigue® books!

You crave excitement!
Harlequin Intrigue stories deal in serious
romantic suspense, keeping you on the edge
of your seat as resourceful, true-to-life women
and strong, fearless men fight for survival.

Enjoy six *new* stories from
Harlequin Intrigue every month!

Available wherever books and
ebooks are sold.

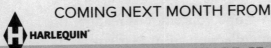

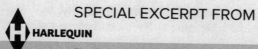
"So, your turn. Tell me what you've been doing for the last
two years," Claire asked. "Have you made yourself a new,
happy life? Found a new love? I heard through the grapevine
that you're living in Jackson now."

Bo nodded at the same time the sound of rain splattered
against the window. "I opened a little bar and grill, Bo's
Place, although it's nothing like the original." His dark
brows tugged together in a frown, as if remembering the
highly successful business he'd had here in town before he
was ostracized.

He took another big drink and then continued, "There's
no new woman in my life. I don't even have friends. Hell,
I'm not even sure what I'm doing here with you."

"You're here because I'm a bossy woman," she replied.
She got up to refill his glass. "And I thought you could use
an extra friend while you're here."

She handed him the fresh drink and then curled back up

in the corner of the sofa. The rain fell steadily now. She turned on the end table lamp as the room darkened with the storm.

For a few minutes they remained silent. She could tell by his distant stare toward the opposite wall that he was lost inside his head.

Despite his somber expression, she couldn't help but feel a physical attraction to him that she'd never felt before. Still, that wasn't what had driven her to seek contact with him, to invite him into her home. She had an ulterior motive.

A low rumble of thunder seemed to pull him out of his head. He focused on her and offered a small smile of apology. "Sorry about that. I got lost in thoughts of everything I need to get done before I leave town."

"I wanted to talk to you about that," she said.

He raised a dark brow. "About all the things I need to take care of?"

"No, about you leaving town."

"What about it?"

She drew a deep breath, knowing she was putting her nose in business that wasn't her own, and yet unable to stop herself. "Doesn't it bother you knowing that Shelly's murderer is still walking these streets, free as a bird?"

His eyes narrowed slightly. "Why are you so sure I'm innocent?" he asked.

Don't miss
SCENE OF THE CRIME: KILLER COVE
by New York Times *bestselling author Carla Cassidy,*
available May 2015 wherever
Harlequin® Intrigue books and ebooks are sold.

www.Harlequin.com